Rachael Lucas

The Telephone Box Library

PAN BOOKS

First published 2020 by Pan Books
an imprint of Pan Macmillan
The Smithson, 6 Briset Street, London EC1M 5NR
Associated companies throughout the world
www.panmacmillan.com

ISBN 978-1-5098-8277-9

1 3 5 7 9 8 6 4 2

A CIP catalogue record for this book is available from the British Library.

Typeset by Palimpsest Book Production Ltd, Falkirk, Stirlingshire
Printed and bound by CPI Group (UK) Ltd, Croydon, CR0 4YY

Rachael Lucas writes novels for adults and teenagers, including the Carnegie-nominated *The State of Grace*, which was selected as an Outstanding Book for Children with Disabilities by IBBY. She lives by the seaside with her husband, their five teenagers and three dogs. Unsurprisingly, she is very grateful to the inventor of noise-cancelling headphones.

Rachael loves to hear from her readers. You can get in touch via her website at rachaellucas.com, or say hello on Instagram @rachaellucas or on Twitter @karamina.

To my brave, wise and beautiful Aunty June

Chapter One

If you were going to find yourself stranded in a village, Lucy tried to console herself, Little Maudley had to be one of the nicest ones there was.

The houses – glowing, honey-coloured terraces – curved down the narrow hill towards the main street, interspersed with the occasional chocolate-box white thatched cottage. A signpost, hung with an overflowing basket of geraniums, indicated the local shop and post office was somewhere beyond the village green, which sloped gently down towards the churchyard. A huge, solid church of blonde stone stood majestic in the midsummer sunlight, set against a cerulean blue sky where tiny clouds scudded past in a slight breeze.

A faded red telephone box stood at the edge of the green, its once cherry-red livery now a dull, washed-out pink. One of the panes of glass had a spider's web of cracks, and several others were missing altogether. Lucy peered inside and grimaced – it smelled utterly disgusting. Even the weeds that had grown through the broken glass looked as if they were trying to escape.

It was the only neglected-looking thing she could see in the village. Flowers poured in a rainbow of tasteful colour from window boxes, and lavender hedges edged neatly trimmed lawns. The doors were almost all a uniform shade of pale greyish-green, as if they'd been painted to order. Wisteria climbed over the windows, the last few blossoms still hanging on to their tendrils of twisted wood. Each house had a neat sign outside declaring its name: Bell Cottage, Lavender House, The Old Mill . . . it was so perfect that it was almost ridiculous. Where was all the mess and the stacked-up rubbish bins? Even in the pretty Brighton street where she lived, not every house was immaculate – some of them stuffed full of students, some flats. This place was like stepping into an episode of *Midsomer Murders*. In fact, come to think of it, there wasn't a single person to be seen. Maybe they'd all been done in already, and she was the last woman standing.

Hamish barked sharply from across the road.

'Coming.' Lucy stood up. Hamish panted in a slightly over-dramatic fashion (both windows were open, and the car was sitting in the shade) and she opened the door, letting him jump out. He pootled around, sniffing his way along the road, and then cocked his leg on a neatly trimmed fuchsia bush. Lucy scanned for approaching gardeners, and seeing none, let out a breath of relief. He had a terrible habit of peeing wherever he felt like it – he'd done it in her brother's girlfriend's handbag not long ago. She hadn't seen the funny side. Lucy and Tom, on the other hand, had been doubled over with laughter. The new girlfriend became an ex quite quickly after that.

Lucy opened the Corsa and slid back into the driver's seat, feeling deflated. Hamish jumped back in too before settling down to sleep. She'd driven over the brow of the hill and into the village, and for a second she'd felt her spirits soar. It was exactly what she'd imagined.

As she sat and waited, she sighed. It had all started so well.

An hour earlier, she'd pulled the car up to a halt on Church Lane. The journey up from Brighton had been easier than expected – the traffic was on her side, the sun shining as she sped up the motorway with her sunglasses on, singing along to Taylor Swift with Hamish sitting on the back seat, occasionally barking. She'd parked the little car between two whopping great black 4x4s, feeling quite smug that all her Brighton parking experience meant she could reverse in on a sixpence. After a wander up and down, taking in the sights of the village while Hamish left his mark on virtually every lamp-post he could find, she'd popped him back into the car. And then she'd taken one final look at her phone, scrolling through her emails until she found the one she needed. It never hurt to have it there as backup – not that she needed it, because everything was organized, of course . . .

A magpie hopped onto the fence beside her and cocked his head, looking at her thoughtfully. Lucy saluted him for luck, and he flew off with a chattering call.

She hesitated for a moment, took a deep breath and headed for the white-painted wooden gate of Wisteria Cottage. Pausing, she felt the roughness of the flaking paint on her palm and then moved forward, peering through the window into the gloom. It definitely looked a bit less – well, a lot less – well cared for than the others. Where all the other cottages in the village seemed to be spick and span, this one looked like it could do with a visit from Marie Kondo and a serious declutter. On the window-ledge there were stacks of old plastic plant pots, and two rolls of string. A grey cat looked out at her and blinked sleepily. Several huge, blowsy pink geraniums pressed up against the glass as if soaking up the sunshine. And – she stood on tiptoe for a better angle – she could just about make out what looked like a stack of old boxes filled with newspapers next to the kitchen sink. It was definitely a bit – well, chaotic would be a reasonable description.

'Are you going to stand there all day?'

Lucy jumped.

A tiny, bird-like woman, with steely grey hair pulled back in an untidy bun, stood in the doorway. She wore a men's checked shirt over a pair of green polyester trousers, and a thick woollen cardigan that hung from her shoulders like a blanket. She was glaring at Lucy through rheumy, narrowed eyes.

'No, I – I'm here about the cottage. I'm Lucy Evans. I'm looking for a woman called Margaret?' She held out her phone.

The woman recoiled slightly. 'Why are you thrusting that thing at me?'

'The details are here, look.' Lucy held it out, tentatively.

The woman took the glasses which were on a string

around her neck and put them on, peering down at the screen.

'Can't see a thing. That's far too small for me to read.'

'It says,' said Lucy, aiming for a tone that sounded authoritative but not patronizing, 'Beautiful cottage in Cotswold village available. Reduced rent in exchange for keeping an eye on elderly neighbour. Duties to include shopping, light tidying and daily company. Contact Margaret Nicolson for further details.'

The woman looked at her, and for a second Lucy saw a glimpse of determination in her eyes. She must have been quite formidable in her younger days.

'Margaret Nicolson? There's nobody of that name here. I'm afraid you've come to the wrong place. Terribly sorry, but you've had a wasted journey.'

The door closed.

Lucy stood on the doorstep for a moment, blinking. The woman hadn't looked the least bit sorry.

After a second, the door opened again and Lucy stepped forward, smiling in what she hoped was a warm and encouraging manner. Oh, thank goodness.

'Are you still here?'

The woman bent down and put a glass milk bottle on the step, straightened up, glared at Lucy, and then closed the door again.

Well. *That* hadn't exactly gone to plan. She opened her phone and dialled the number in the advert, pulling a face at the sight of the words in the email. She hadn't thought anything of the sentence, 'If you have any trouble, please give me a call and I'll smooth things over.' Looking at it now as she waited for Margaret Nicolson to pick up, she realized that she should have read between the lines. This woman was clearly expecting trouble. *Don't look a gift horse in the mouth*, wasn't that the old saying? Her mum liked that one. *You don't get anything for nothing* was more like it. A gorgeous cottage for a tiny rent, in a village like this? Of course it was too good to be true.

Half an hour later, Lucy was sitting in the car, wondering what on earth to do next. Margaret still wasn't answering the phone. Hamish had woken up and was scratching at the gap in the car window; he whined queru- lously and then yapped in frustration. In the silence it seemed incredibly loud, and having been rejected, Lucy felt like she'd very much prefer to stay unnoticed. This was not on the list of things she'd expected to happen. When she'd told everyone at work that she was taking a sabbatical to go and do some research in the countryside, it had sounded romantic and free-spirited; now she was stranded, with no idea what to do. Not to mention a car full of bags and boxes, an extremely unimpressed West Highland terrier, and nowhere to live.

'You wait there,' she said to Hamish, getting out of the car again. She sat down on a bench beside the faded telephone box and began tapping out an email. Hamish stuck his nose through the gap in the window and snuf- fled hopefully. 'I'll take you out in a second. Hang on.'

The phone rang while she was still typing.

'Hello?'

'Gosh, that was quick. It didn't even ring. Lucy. I'm so sorry. Margaret Nicolson here. Have you arrived? Is everything under control?'

Lucy bit her lip. 'Not – exactly.'

There was a groan from the other end of the line. 'Oh, for goodness' sake. Honestly.'

'I'm sorry,' said Lucy, automatically. Why on earth was she apologizing when she was the one stranded?

'Not at all. It's me who should be apologizing. I'll be with you shortly. If you want to pop up to the village shop you can get a cup of coffee, and I'll meet you there in about half an hour?'

'It's fine – I have to walk the dog in any case. Shall I meet you by the cottage?'

She squared her shoulders. She hadn't come all this way and given up a perfectly good (all right, extremely stressful and ridiculously high-pressure) teaching job to be knocked down at the first hurdle. Whatever was going on with the cottage would just have to be sorted out. She took a deep breath. She'd spent her entire working life dealing with obstreperous teenagers. She wasn't going to let this minor hiccup get in the way. She gave a decided sort of nod, as if to reassure herself. It would be fine, somehow. It *had* to be.

Checking the time, she took another wander around the village with Hamish. He sniffed lamp-posts while she read the signs on them: village cinema night, 1950s theme night, PTA summer party. There seemed to be an awful lot on for such a tiny place. A gang of children ran past, laughing and playing music from a Bluetooth speaker. Hamish barked at them crossly, and she tugged his lead and pulled him in the opposite direction.

There was a huge house at the edge of the village, set back from the road with high laurel hedging. She peeked through the gates to see a sweep of pebbled driveway and a beautiful Queen Anne building with two neat bay trees flanking the heavy wooden front door. A solid-looking woman wearing a striped Breton top, her streaky blonde hair cut in a neat bob, was standing on a ladder, watering the hanging baskets. Sensing Lucy's presence, she turned and waved.

'Hello there! Lovely afternoon!'

'Mmm,' said Lucy. 'Beautiful.' She felt her cheeks going pink. She'd been staring. It was just all so posh, and so tidy – everything looked like a set for a Richard Curtis film. She half-expected a young Hugh Grant to rush onto the scene, hair tousled, apologizing with a sheepish grin.

'Are you lost?' The woman's face appeared through a gap in the hedge. She raised her eyebrows slightly, a pleasant smile on her face.

'No,' Lucy shook her head. 'Just having a little stroll.'

'Wonderful day for it,' said the woman, cheerfully.

There was a crunch of gravel as she headed back across the driveway. Lucy got the distinct impression that she'd been sized up. Perhaps this woman was the local Neighbourhood Watch. She turned down a lane and Hamish shot off, his extending lead pulling out to full length as he chased after a black-and-white cat that had been sitting cleaning its paws on a low wall.

'Don't start that again,' Lucy said, calling him back. He'd disappeared on a wild goose – or cat – chase on her last morning at work in Brighton. She'd eventually found him wedged in a hawthorn hedge, barking furiously, and had arrived fifteen minutes late, missing the surprise mini-celebration her colleagues had put on in the staffroom. Leaving her job for a six-month sabbatical had felt significant, even though it was being kept open for her; it was the first time in her life that she'd taken a real risk, made a rash decision. And now here she was – only things weren't turning out exactly as she'd imagined.

She took a left turn and found herself back on Main Street. Crossing the road, trying to look inconspicuous, she stood by the telephone box. She could see the woman, a small silhouette, moving about in her kitchen window. Despite its shabby state, the cottage really was beautiful – long and low, with upstairs windows peeking through the thatch like mournful eyes on a shaggy dog. There were pale pink roses round the door, and a low wall held back a border of candy-coloured mixed flowers. Tiny blue flowers spilled over the edges of the wall, the colour setting off the gold of the Cotswold stone perfectly. The gate opened onto a narrow flagstone path which meandered through spires of almost-grown foxgloves. Clematis climbed up the wall and twined through a trellis. It was – from the outside, at least – the English village dream.

She popped Hamish back in the car and sat down in the driver's seat, waiting. A couple of minutes later, a sleek black BMW pulled up opposite and a woman climbed out of the driver's seat, unfolding herself grace-fully, knees together, as if she'd been trained like one of the royals.

'I am terribly sorry about this,' she began, extending a hand. Lucy shook it, and then stepped back, curling her fingers into her palms. Margaret Nicolson had ash-blonde hair that curled to her collar in neatly blow-dried layers. She was wearing a blue-and-white striped blouse with the collar turned up, spotless pale beige trousers and neat, dark blue deck shoes. Lucy, who had got up and pulled on the jeans she'd worn the day before and a grey vest top (because the car had no air condi-tioning, and she couldn't have the windows open on the motorway or the wind howled so loudly it drowned out Taylor Swift) under a slightly crumpled linen jacket, felt scruffy and unfinished by comparison.

'I'm afraid my mother-in-law can be rather – well, very – difficult.'

'It's fine,' Lucy's mouth said. Her head said *Funnily enough, you didn't mention that in the advert.*

'She's . . . well, she's getting on. She's ninety-six. She's really very independent-minded and is utterly convinced she can manage perfectly well without any help at all. I've managed to persuade her to have a cleaner come in three times a week, but we really want someone on hand who can pop in, get what she needs from the supermarket

– I mean, the village shop is very good, of course, but you can't get everything there – and that sort of thing. Probably only an hour a day, I should think.'

That *was* what the advert had said. And in exchange, a tiny little cottage with bills included, for a rent which was half the going rate for a room in Brighton. And best of all, it was in a village that skirted Oxfordshire and Buckinghamshire, was close to Milton Keynes and Oxford and – most importantly for a history teacher with a fascination for the Home Front during World War Two – Bletchley Park. Lucy had planned to gather as much information as she could, and maybe even to apply for that master's degree she'd been dreaming of for years.

'Come on.' Margaret blipped her car locked. 'I'll take you in and we'll get things sorted. Will your little dog be okay out here for a moment, or –' she cast a doubtful eye towards the cottage – 'do you want to bring him in?'

'He'll be fine.'

'Mother?' Margaret knocked briefly at the door of the pretty little thatched cottage before turning the handle firmly and walking inside.

Lucy, following behind, opened her mouth to say something but found that no words were coming out.

'Hello-oo?' Margaret called. Then she turned to Lucy. 'I'm sorry. It's a bit of a state, as you can see.' She gestured to the piles of old wellington boots and squashed dog beds on the flagstone floor of the hall. 'Ideally the cleaner would be sorting this too, but I think she's having a bit of a battle over what's needed and what's—'

'That's because I've already told you, I don't need any help.' A cross voice was approaching from behind a glass door at the end of the hallway. 'I don't need you or Gordon coming round here, tidying up my things, winding me up before I'm ready to be finished off. You're like damned vultures, the two of you.'

The door opened. Standing there was the elderly woman, a jar of honey in one hand and a sticky-looking knife in the other. She avoided Lucy's eye.

'I believe you've met my mother-in-law. Bunty, this is Lucy.' Margaret spoke through gritted teeth.

'Yes, we've met,' Bunty said, turning away and heading into the kitchen. With a glance at each other, Margaret and Lucy followed.

'Hello again,' said Lucy, bracing herself for another blast of disapproval.

Bunty ignored her. 'I've told you already, Margaret,' she said crossly, 'I don't need a nursemaid. Or a carer. Or a home help. I am perfectly happy here *on my own*.'

'Nobody is suggesting you need a nursemaid,' said Margaret, picking up a tea towel from the table and folding it before putting it back on top of a pile of faded, sepia-toned photographs in an old wooden box. Bunty beetled across the room and picked up the tea towel, shaking it out and then hanging it on the shiny metal rail of the range cooker that stood in the mouth of a huge stone fireplace.

'No Gordon today?' She lifted her chin slightly and regarded Lucy through beady eyes. Lucy shifted from one foot to the other, feeling uncomfortable.

'No,' said Margaret. 'He's playing golf. Sends his love.'

'Knows when to stay out of the way, if you ask me. This is a conspiracy,' Bunty chuntered. She shook her head and pursed her lips. 'I don't need a babysitter.' She glared again at Lucy, as if to make the point. 'I'm perfectly fine as I am.'

'I'm sure you are,' Margaret said, in what she clearly thought were soothing tones. 'But you're not getting any younger, and . . .'

'And I'm not going anywhere. So there.' Bunty sounded as petulant as a child, but twice as stubborn.

'Nobody is asking you to move anywhere.'

'You want me shipped off to an old folks' home, so you can sell this place and make a fortune.'

'I do not. Honestly. I don't know where you get these ideas from.'

'I saw it in the newspaper the other day. It's happening all the time. And you know what happens as soon as people get shifted off to places like that – God's waiting rooms, I call them. I'm having none of it.'

In spite of her discomfort, Lucy's mouth twitched with amusement.

'Nobody is moving you anywhere.' Margaret slid a sideways glance at Lucy.

It was becoming increasingly clear that there was no such thing as a free lunch – or a cheap cottage, for that matter – and Lucy's idyllic Cotswolds escape wasn't going to be quite as anticipated. She'd imagined sharing cups of tea and cosy chats with an apple-cheeked, benevolent old lady, with a cat on her lap and a tray of scones in the oven. Bunty Nicolson was as far from that description as it was possible to be.

'I'm really very busy,' Bunty said, somehow managing to shoo both Lucy and Margaret back into the hallway.

'We need to make arrangements,' protested Margaret.

'You can make them without me,' said Bunty with asperity. 'You seem to have done quite a good job of that already.'

'I'm very sorry that—' began Lucy, hoping to smooth things over a little.

'Not your fault,' said Bunty.

There was an awkward silence. Lucy's gaze shifted round the room, taking in the smooth, age-worn flag-stones on the floor and the paintings of horses and dogs that lined the walls. The coat rack was overflowing with battered waxed jackets of varying ages; below them, rows of wellingtons and walking boots toppled sideways. A faded tartan dog bed that had seen better days was askew in the doorway.

'If you don't get this place sorted,' Margaret began again in conciliatory tones, 'you're going to fall and break a hip or something like that, and then you'll end up in hospital.'

'I'm not going to hospital.' Bunty looked mutinous.

'No. I think you would absolutely hate that. In which

case,' Margaret said, raising an eyebrow slightly, 'perhaps you'd better let us stay a little while, and then you can get to know Lucy. Maybe we could offer her a cup of tea. She's driven all the way from Brighton, you know.'

'She could have come all the way from Timbuktu and I wouldn't care.'

But Bunty moved out of the way, grumbling under her breath, and allowed Margaret to lead them back to the kitchen. Lucy tried to look unobtrusive.

With Bunty installed on a battered pine chair, her back against the window, Lucy was able to have a better look around. There was stuff *everywhere*. There was a geranium in the kitchen sink, and two pairs of shoes were upturned on the worktop on a pile of newspapers. Beside them was a wooden box, a tin of old-fashioned polish and a set of wooden brushes. The grey cat Lucy had seen in the window sat on top of a pile of folded tea towels on the Aga. Lucy could see why Margaret thought it was chaos, but it was really quite nice chaos. Comforting, even. As she tried to slip off her linen jacket, it slid out of her hands. Before she could react, Margaret had swooped down and picked it up.

'Pop your things down there,' she said, moving a newspaper, some more string and an old shoebox full of seed packets so there was a clear space on the big oak table. 'And let's pop your jacket – ' she scanned around, looking for somewhere safe to put it. 'Over there on the dresser.'

'Not there,' said Bunty, sitting up slightly. She looked

towards the big wooden Welsh dresser with narrowed eyes.

'There is fine,' Margaret said, taking the jacket and plonking it on the dresser. It slid slightly, as if it was about to fall onto the floor, then appeared to rise up of its own accord. Lucy recoiled.

'I said –' Bunty pushed her chair back with a screech of wood on tiled floor – 'not there.' She tutted loudly. Lucy looked on as her jacket continued to rise up, as if slowly lifted by a ghostly arm. The hairs on the back of her neck stood up. She was in an apparently deserted village in the middle of nowhere, alone, with two strangers. And now her jacket was possessed. This wasn't going to plan at all.

'I'm terribly sorry, Stanley,' Bunty said, lifting the jacket up and dumping it over the back of a chair. 'Some people have absolutely appalling manners.'

Stanley blinked slowly and thoughtfully, and his tongue slid in and out of his mouth. Lucy stepped backwards rapidly and sat down hard on a chair, before her legs gave way underneath her.

'I don't suppose Margaret thought to mention Stanley, did she?' Bunty tipped her head to one side. There was the faintest hint of a smile playing at the corners of her mouth.

Lucy shook her head. Her lips were pressed together. Snakes were fine. Snakes were *absolutely* fine. Unexpected, but fine. Lots of people had snakes as pets.

Margaret looked slightly shamefaced. 'I didn't *deliberately* not mention it—'

'Him,' Bunty interrupted.

Lucy stole a glance across the room at Stanley, who had curled up again – or was it *coiled*? – on her jacket.

'Mention *him*,' Margaret corrected herself. 'I – well, it might have slipped my mind.'

Bloody big thing to slip anyone's mind, Lucy thought. He must be six feet long and he wasn't one of those nice, skinny, easy-going sort of snakes, either. He looked like the kind that sizes you up while getting ready to swallow you whole in bed one night.

Margaret bustled about, boiling the kettle on the Aga and gathering mismatched china cups and a teapot. Bunty sat with her hands clasped together, a slightly amused expression on her face.

'Tea?' Margaret lifted the pot and her eyebrows.

'I – I'm not sure,' Lucy said, making to stand up. Her legs really were very wobbly, so she sat down again.

'I think perhaps you ought to,' Bunty said, not unkindly. 'You do seem to have had rather a shock. Have you never seen a snake before?'

'In zoos,' Lucy nodded. 'I didn't think I had a problem with snakes.'

'People often don't, when they're behind glass. It's when they're out and about, minding their own business, that people tend to overreact.' Bunty looked at her with mild disapproval.

'Not many people of your age own a boa constrictor, Mother. It's ridiculous, really,' Margaret said, putting the teapot down on the table and glaring at Bunty. She pushed a pile of yellowing newspapers over to the far side, making space for three cups.

'Where is your milk jug?'

'Haven't a clue.' There was the ghost of a chuckle. Bunty, Lucy realized, was rather enjoying this. Margaret rummaged in the fridge.

'Watch out for the chicks. They're defrosting on the bottom shelf. Stanley's lunch,' she explained to Lucy.

Lucy nodded faintly.

Holding a bottle of milk, Margaret closed the fridge door. She looked slightly green. 'So sorry, we'll have to pour it from the bottle,' she said, looking genuinely distressed by this. Lucy, still recovering from the trauma of having used an actual live snake as a coat rack, couldn't have cared less. She took the cup gratefully and sipped a reviving, if too-hot mouthful.

'So let's get down to business,' said Margaret, steepling her fingers and looking across the table towards Lucy. 'Mother, we've been through this already. Bluebell Cottage is sitting there empty, and you really need some help.'

'I don't need any help,' Bunty said, firmly, taking a sip of tea. 'Ugh. You do make dreadful tea, Margaret. I don't know how Gordon puts up with it.'

'He makes his own.' Margaret widened her eyes and turned to Lucy for backup.

'Just as well,' said Bunty. She looked at Lucy as well. Lucy wasn't quite sure how to react to either of the looks, so she gazed into the depths of her teacup and then, as the pause stretched into another awkward silence, looked up and around the room. It was cluttered, yes, but full of memories of a life well lived. Faded photographs in dusty frames showed a small boy on a pony festooned with rosettes. Dusty, faded rosettes – the same ones, perhaps? – hung over the lintel above the Aga. The bookshelf groaned with a double layer of cookbooks and folders, and the rack that hung from the ceiling was swathed with bunches of herbs and battered, heavy cast-iron pots and pans. It felt like a house full of history. She could see why Margaret would see it as a project to be tidied up and organized, but in Lucy's eyes it was really quite magical.

'I don't want you fussing,' said Bunty suddenly.

Margaret leaned forward slightly, and she and Lucy waited for what was coming next.

'I'm perfectly capable of living here alone. I don't need someone looking after me, and I don't want to be nurse-maided, or fussed over, or tidied up, or any of that nonsense.'

'Of course not,' said Margaret.

'I can see you have lots of special memories here,' Lucy began carefully. 'I wouldn't be coming in here to do anything other than check if you needed something from the supermarket, see if there was anything you needed me to do . . . that sort of thing.'

'Hmm.' Bunty looked at her thoughtfully.

'Well, that sounds all right, doesn't it?' Margaret brightened.

'Fine.' Bunty put her teacup down on her saucer and rubbed her hands briefly. 'Now, if you can recover from your shell shock, we'll get you on your way and I can get on with cleaning out the guinea pigs. I've got Freya from across the road popping round this afternoon, and I have things to do.'

And with that, they were dismissed. Somehow Margaret managed to manoeuvre Lucy's jacket from underneath Stanley's coils. They left Bunty sitting in the kitchen, clearly feeling pleased that she'd been the one to make the final decision.

'You see,' Margaret smiled, as they pulled the door closed behind them, 'her bark really is worse than her bite.'

'Not sure the same could be said for Stanley.'

'He doesn't bark,' said Margaret, with a wry smile. 'Sorry I forgot to mention him. I admit it's an unusual sort of pet for a woman of Bunty's age to keep, but she's always been mad about animals. She had three dogs until recently – sisters – but sadly, they all passed away within the space of a year.'

'That must have been awful.'

Margaret nodded briefly. 'Yes, she was really quite distraught.'

'Perhaps she'll enjoy spending time with Hamish when I pop in.'

'How is he with snakes?' Margaret raised an eyebrow.

'I have no idea, funnily enough.' They both laughed.

'This way,' Margaret said.

Beside Bunty's house there was a little row of terraced cottages, topped with steeply sloping slate-tiled roofs. The end cottage was as pretty as it had looked in the photograph Margaret had sent. She turned the key in the door, and stepped back to allow Lucy to look inside.

It was gorgeous, and absolutely dinky. Standing in the doorway, which opened into the sitting room, Lucy took it all in. To her left were twisting, narrow stairs that could be hidden by a heavy curtain, which was tied back with a thick cord. Beside that was an arch that framed a narrow galley kitchen and the back door, with sunshine spilling in through its glass panes. The walls were cool stone. There was a proper old-fashioned butler's sink, and a Welsh dresser stacked with cups and plates. The walls were hung with shelves and plate racks crammed with blue-and-white china. In contrast to the clutter of Bunty's house, it was dust-free and felt oddly empty. Lucy ran a hand along the wooden worktop, feeling the smoothness of the oak.

'We rented it out for a while to a couple who worked in London – they used to commute back and forth, so they were hardly ever here. They redecorated so it's all very neutral, as you can see, and there's a new cooker and we've replaced the fridge.'

It was perfect. Unbidden, a thought popped into Lucy's head. Back home, the exams were getting under way and her pupils would be working hard, the department humming with stress and the head pressurizing them to offer extra revision classes to try and get the grade averages up. The momentary fear that Bunty was going to put a stop to this chance of freedom had been like the first domino in a chain, and Lucy had started worrying again – which was precisely what coming here was supposed to prevent.

That's why I'm here, she reminded herself firmly. I have six months to unwind, not think the world is going to end if I don't get everything done yesterday, and to focus on life. She put a hand to her chest, steadying herself, and turned to smile at Margaret.

'It looks lovely.'

In the tiny sitting room a little two-seater sofa, covered with a soft grey woollen blanket, faced a small, squat log-burning stove. Beside the fireplace, a cosy-looking armchair sat beside a little round table dressed with an embroidered cloth, and the kind of old-fashioned library light that Lucy had always wanted. There was another big – too big, really, for the room – wooden dresser stacked with books, and a tiny window on the back wall. On the rug there was a patch of sunlight which she already knew Hamish was going to declare his own.

It was so small and so perfect that she instantly forgot about the capricious Bunty and the fact that she'd almost been rejected before she even saw the place. She turned to look at Margaret, who was waiting on the front step.

'I love it.'

'You can see why pictures didn't really do it justice.'

Lucy had decided that she would love it based on the wonky and fuzzy phone photos Margaret had sent – but it was a million times prettier in real life. She ran her hand along the stone wall.

'Can I get Hamish? He's been waiting very patiently in the car.'

'Of course!' Margaret stepped out of the way.

Hamish galloped in, sniffed everything, and curled up as predicted on the rug.

'I'll show you how the shower works – there's a bit of a knack to it.' Margaret beckoned Lucy to follow her upstairs.

There was a sweet little bathroom with a half-sized bath, a slightly temperamental shower ('it's fine as long as you make sure you turn this tap on first') and a frosted window looking out over the garden. The bedroom had an old-fashioned iron bedstead, and a patchwork quilt covered the plain white bed linen.

'We replaced the mattress for you. I hope it's comfortable.'

'I'm sure it'll be perfect.'

'And there's a little spare room too, in case you have anyone to stay.' She opened the door to a tiny box room, big enough for a single bed and a tall chest of drawers, with a lamp balanced on top.

Lucy looked down at her feet. How do you explain to someone that you've been so wrapped up in your job – and in making it your life – that you've somehow managed to have plenty of work acquaintances, but nobody who'd actually want to visit? It sounded pretty tragic. She'd always been an introverted sort of person, who spent most of her time at university in the library – and yes, she'd kept in touch with Anna and Dawn, the friends she'd shared a flat with, but now one of them was married and living in Inverness, and the other was teaching art at a college in Sydney. Neither would be popping round. She lifted her head and smiled as bravely as she could. 'Thanks.'

'I think it's rather courageous of you to take the plunge and do something like this. I wish I'd done it when I was your age.'

'Thanks.' Lucy bit the inside of her cheek. She must look a lot more convincing than she felt. Right now she was having a very quiet internal wobble about what on earth she'd done.

'You said you'll be planning to spend time at Bletchley Park?'

'Yes, I'm going to enjoy having time to do some research into the women of Bletchley, and the work they did – and the Home Front.'

'Well, you're in the right place. Plenty of women here in the village who'll have something to say about that, I should think. If you catch Bunty in the right mood, she's got a few stories to tell.'

'Really?'

'Oh yes. Worth a try, anyway. She's very buttoned up about it – it's her generation, I think. Don't mention the war, and all that. But she's lived here since she was in her teens, I think.'

'She's not from the village originally?'

'Gosh no. London.'

Lucy made a mental note to work – carefully – on Bunty and find out what she could. If she was as sharp as she seemed, she must have a mine of memories to share.

'Anyway, I think that's everything. If you're happy –'

Margaret glanced at her watch – 'I really ought to get on. I'll pop back later in the week and make sure you're settling in, but I'm sure you'll be fine.'

If she scuttled off with haste, Lucy thought, it was probably because she felt relieved at being slightly less responsible – in her own mind, at least – for Bunty. She would be quite a mother-in-law to have.

Closing the door behind Margaret, she slid the bolt and turned to look at Hamish.

'We did it!'

She pulled off her shoes and stood for a moment with her feet flat on the cold flagstones of the kitchen floor. They'd done it. This was home – for the next six months, anyway.

She hauled in the boxes from the car and plonked them on the sofa, and then – mindful of what her doctor had said about balancing work and taking it easy – sat down with a large glass of water. Relaxing wasn't something she did naturally. She still felt guilty about leaving everyone in the lurch, but there were teachers left, right and centre being signed off with stress-related illnesses. Somehow – pushing herself as hard as she could to do the best job she could, under increasingly trying circumstances – it hadn't ever occurred to her that she'd be one of the casualties. She closed her eyes for a moment, and it all came back to her.

'No.'

The word – so unusual for Lucy – had popped out before she even realized what she'd said.

'Come on, Luce. There'll be more money in it, of course, and it'll look great on your appraisal.' His voice was smooth and charming. Nick was used to getting his own way, and he knew *no* wasn't in Lucy's vocabulary. *No* is what she should have said when he asked if she – as head of the history department – would mind collating a report over half term. And yet, somehow, *no* was what she found herself repeating.

'I can't.'

'Luce,' he said, his voice softening. 'Come on. You are an absolute star. I can always rely on you.'

'Not this time, you can't.'

There was a click as the hand on the clock moved to indicate eight thirty, and a buzzer on Nick's desk rang. He reached out a hand and switched it off, looking irritated. Outside there was a rising feeling of energy as the day started to take shape – the first, early pupils making their way past the window of his office, the last – late – members of staff sneaking in, glancing gratefully through his window to see he was there and not standing in the car park, an eye on the clock. Nick had been shipped in as a superhead, designated the saviour of their rundown secondary school. He ran the school like a business, and on paper he was getting results. In reality, though, he was breaking the long-standing, most dedicated members of staff. Lucy had been teaching for almost a decade, and now, at thirty-three, she knew what was about to happen.

'I'm only asking you to take it on for this term. I

promise we'll get you some non-contact time, give you some extra TA support.'

She knew that was rubbish – half their teaching assistants had been sacked at the end of the last school year, when the school had lost loads of money in budget cuts. Lucy twisted her grandma's wedding ring, which she wore on the pinky of her right hand. It comforted her when she was stressed, which was pretty much all the time at the moment. She rubbed the back of her neck and gazed out of the window, only vaguely aware Nick was still talking. Her head was aching as usual, and she was so tired that she could have curled up under his desk and gone to sleep. In fact, he probably wouldn't even notice if she did.

' . . . I know it's not ideal,' Nick was saying. He was going on and on, wearing her down. She still had a load of NQT lesson plans to check over.

'Oh God. Fine.' Anything to get him to shut up. She couldn't believe she was saying it. It wasn't fine at all. Lucy had a class of rowdy year eights first lesson, and three missed calls from a number she didn't recognize. Nick had already sent through a barrage of emails about head of department meetings. At break, she stayed in her room and checked her voicemail.

Hello, Lucy? It's Amal, from the flat downstairs. I don't want to worry you, but there seems to be a leak coming through our ceiling, and I wondered if I—

Oh *hell*.

Lucy shoved the phone back in her bag. The pretty

Victorian house she shared with her brother Tom – a parting gift from their mother before she left for Australia – was divided into two flats. She lived in the top half with Tom and the bottom half was let out to tenants. The only trouble was, it seemed to have one thing wrong after another, and Tom was never around to solve the problems. She sighed, and then quietly laid her head down on the cool surface of her desk. Perhaps if she just lay here for a moment, nobody would notice . . .

'Miss!'

She shot upright in a split second.

'Tyler. Hello. What can I do for you?'

'Was you sleeping?'

'No.' Had she been? God. No, she'd been resting her eyes. And why was her head hurting so much? Those painkillers were hopeless. She reached down to her bag to see if she had any ibuprofen to take alongside them.

'I wanted to know if you had any of that revision stuff from the session last week. I couldn't come because I was looking after my little sister, but . . .'

'Two seconds.' She rifled in her bag and pulled out a packet, popping out another two pills and swigging them back with the bottle of water on her desk. 'Yes. I've got some of the notes in my car, I'll get them for you at lunch if you can nip back later?'

Tyler beamed. He was one of the kids that reminded her why she loved teaching. He had a difficult home life, no parental support, forgot his homework nine times out of ten, but genuinely loved the subject. His love for history made perfect sense to her, and he'd explained it recently in a way that summed it up.

'Fing is, Miss, that history doesn't change. Everything –' he'd motioned with a massive arm in the direction of the window, where everyone else could be seen leaving for lunch '– it's all kind of – unpredictable, y'know? And history stuff's – like – it stays the same.'

Lucy had smiled and waved him off, sighing as she watched him stride out of the classroom. God, she knew exactly what he meant. Her love of history had stemmed from a childhood spent poring over old books at her grandpa's house on the seafront. He'd been an inveterate collector of World War Two memorabilia, which had triggered her own fascination with the subject. She'd studied social history at university in Brighton, and spent hours trawling through the National Archives. When she'd gone into teaching, it had been with a desire to share her passion for the subject with her pupils, and because she loved working with teenagers. What she'd completely disregarded was the ever-increasing amount of stress, paperwork and admin that came with the job. And then when the well-meaning but inefficient head had been ousted after the school was put in special measures, and the new superhead bussed in, she'd found herself working twelve-hour days and falling asleep in front of the television every night. It wasn't a life. And now she was dropping off in the middle of break. And her nose was running.

She reached across to the side of her desk and pulled out a tissue, wiping her nose and tossing it into the bin.

It was only because she missed, and the tissue fell onto the floor, that she realized that it was scarlet with blood, and her nose was still dripping. She grabbed another tissue, holding it to her nostrils and tipping her head back. Or was it forward? God, she couldn't remember which one you were supposed to do. The tissue leaked wetly all over her fingers.

When Lucy woke up again, a kind-faced paramedic was strapping belts around her waist. She was lying on a trolley in an ambulance, with wads of blue paper towel stuff tucked into her chin like a bib. She made to sit up, but the belts, and a wave of blinding headache and nausea, stopped her in her tracks.

'No you don't, young lady,' said the paramedic. 'Let's keep you nice and still, and don't you worry about anything. We've got everything under control.' She looked at a monitor fastened to the side of the trolley and gave a nod. 'Right, Dave, we're in. Wagons roll.'

With a clonk, the doors closed at her feet.

'What? Where are we going?'

'Don't you worry. Just lie still there, and we're going to get you sorted.'

It all seemed a bit of a fuss for a nosebleed. She'd had a nosebleed and now somehow she was in an ambulance. And she was so, so tired. And her head felt like it was going to explode. The last thing Lucy remembered, before she slipped back to sleep, was that she'd left the test papers for Year 8 in the boot of the car.

*

'Bloody hell, Luce.'

The lights were dim and she was vaguely aware of rustling behind the curtain. Her brother Tom was perched on the edge of a plastic chair and shot up, knocking it sideways with a screech of metal on hard tiled floor.

'You okay?'

'Mmph,' Lucy heard herself saying. She lifted her arm, realized there was a tube in it and looked away, grimacing.

'Thought you didn't like all those *Real Life A&E* programmes?' Tom grinned and rolled his eyes. 'Don't want to sound like a cliché, but you gave me a bloody fright.'

Vague images of the kind woman in the ambulance filtered through her mind, and the sound of sirens.

'What happened?'

'You work too hard is what happened.' Tom bit his thumbnail, his brows knitted together. He looked unusually serious. 'Your blood pressure went up, probably because you're constantly mega-stressed. Apparently nosebleeds are a side effect of that.'

Oh God, Lucy thought, remembering the tissue and the drips all over the desk and the spreading pool of crimson and . . .

'How did I get to the ambulance?'

'One of the pupils found you, apparently. He'd left something on your desk and went back to find you there, passed out in a pool of blood. I imagine you'll be the talk of the school for all eternity.'

She could feel her eyes drifting closed again. 'Really . . . tired.'

'Not surprised.' Tom reached out and gave her arm a squeeze. 'I've only got you, sis. You need to look after yourself a bit better.'

She tried to nod, but she was so sleepy that it was more of an intention than an actual movement.

And that was how it had all begun. Then, idly surfing the internet – she couldn't ever remember how it had happened – she'd come across Margaret's advert. Before, she'd always convinced herself that keeping hold of the money she'd inherited from her grandpa had been a sensible option – a decent little nest egg for a rainy day. It was Tom – who'd spent his on a round-the-world trip and a snazzy convertible BMW – who pointed out to her that this *was* a rainy day, and that this was the wake-up call she needed.

Before she knew it, Tom was standing on the doorstep of their shared flat, her bags were packed, the little Corsa loaded up with books and boxes and an eager Hamish, and she had a whole six months ahead of her, right on the doorstep of the very area that was so full of history and the secrets of the women of Bletchley Park. For the first time in what felt like forever, Lucy had been excited – she was doing something for herself. Not to please the head, or to smooth the way for other people – and even though she'd felt a ripple of guilt, the idea that she could read all the books she'd piled up beside her bed and visit interesting places was exhilarating. She could completely absorb herself in her love of history and have time to actually *relax.* Maybe she'd even make some friends.

So now here she was. All she had to do was keep a daily eye on Bunty, and the rest of her time was her own. She could stay in bed all day if she wanted to, or wander round antique shops and visit farmers' markets. A whole six months of nothingness stretched out ahead of her. She rolled herself off the sofa and went to poke around in the dresser, pulling out a few local maps.

It wasn't all that easy, doing nothing. She'd chosen a pile of interesting-looking local history books and stacked them neatly on the little table by the armchair, and pored over the maps. There were a few lovely-looking circular walks around the village – Hamish would enjoy them. Maybe she'd unpack first.

She took a bag upstairs and sorted out her clothes, putting them in the little wooden drawers beside the bed. Then she hung her things in the wardrobe and carefully arranged her toiletries in the bathroom. The bath was tiny – as if someone had taken a normal one and shrunk it. She caught a glimpse of herself in the mirror. Still pale, still not quite back to – well, what was normal? She'd been stressed and exhausted for so long that she couldn't remember what she looked like. She splashed some cold water on her face and rubbed it with a towel, loosened her hair from the scruffy bun she'd tied it up in whilst bringing in all the bags from the car, and shook it out. There. At least with it down, she didn't look quite so frazzled. A bit of country air and she'd be fine, hopefully.

Downstairs, Hamish had woken from his power nap and was gnawing happily on a corner of the rug. He looked up, wagging his tail and grinning toothily. Oh God, he'd actually chewed the entire corner off.

'That's probably an antique,' wailed Lucy. Hamish ducked his head, ready for another chew at it. 'Leave it. In fact, come on. You've been stuck in the car for ages. Let's go exploring.'

Outside, a small and very cross-looking teenage girl was sitting on the same bench Lucy had been perched on an hour before. She didn't look up as Lucy approached but carried on scrolling through her phone, her hair hanging in two smooth curtains of black and obscuring her face. Lucy walked past. It was a relief not to have to deal with teenage angst for a while. All she had to do was shut herself away in her little cottage with no complications. Nothing but rest, relaxation, peace and quiet. A daily check in on Bunty next door was a pretty good exchange for all of that. For the first time in ages, Lucy felt a little bit like her old self again.

Chapter Two

At the end of a long day, groaning with exhaustion and desperate to put his feet up with a coffee and the TV remote, Sam Travis secured the roofing felt he'd need for tomorrow to the back of his flatbed truck. Pulling the straps tightly, he jumped down from the back, landing lightly on the cobblestoned driveway of Bell Cottage, and fastened up the truck catches. He had to admit to himself, there was something quite satisfying about getting everything sorted for the next day as soon as he got home after dropping off the lads who worked alongside him – it meant the mornings, which were stressful enough with lost homework and trying to prise a reluctant teenager out of bed, were a little bit easier to cope with. At least with school breaking up next week, he wouldn't have to extract Freya from under the covers with fifteen minutes to spare for a whole six weeks.

There. That was tomorrow sorted, at least. He gave the truck an absent-minded pat, as if it were a horse.

'Freya?' he shouted across the top of the truck, in through the window of the kitchen. It was propped open, as always, to allow the cats to hop in and out. Trevor, chair of the village Neighbourhood Watch committee, had rapped on the door earlier that week to inform him that not only was he putting his own belongings at risk, but he was enticing burglars into the village. Sam, who suspected it was unlikely that the tiny, out-of-the-way village of Little Maudley was going to become overrun by organized crime, had reassured Trevor that yes, he'd consider putting in a cat flap instead. When he was supposed to do that, between running a business, acting as taxi for a fourteen-year-old with a non-stop social life, and managing as a single parent running a house, he wasn't quite sure. Like most people who ran their own business, his own place was the domestic version of the shoemaker's children going barefoot. There were outstanding jobs that harked back years. He looked at the back of the cottage, where heaps of reclaimed bricks for the conservatory he'd been planning years ago were still sitting untouched. Grass was growing over a heap of topsoil he'd dumped with the best intentions of sorting out the garden, so it looked as if a miniature hill had landed out of nowhere on the cobblestoned driveway. God, he really needed to get his act together. And – he rubbed the bristles of stubble on his chin – he really needed to shave, which required razor blades, which he wasn't going to get unless they made it to the shop . . .

'Freya!' he called again, but louder this time.

'Just a minute.'

In teenager speak, that could mean anything from thirty seconds to half an hour. He climbed back into the truck and shifted slightly, and the two spaniels waiting inside shot to attention. Amber caught his eye and craned her neck upwards hopefully, her full tail whirling like a flag. Amber's mum, Bee, scrambled over her daughter, barking loudly. They pressed their wet noses against the already filthy window.

'She said just a minute,' Sam said to the dogs, laughing. He shook his head and leaned back against the truck, pulling out his phone from the back of a pair of battered, mud-splattered Levis. Four messages from Annabel Bevan, his current – and very demanding – client. He'd only left Green Acres half an hour ago. He scrolled through them absent-mindedly.

15.01: Sam if you haven't left, I wonder if you'd like to nip in for a cup of tea and a little bite before you do? xxx

15.08: Popped down the garden, think you must have gone already x

15.20: I'll put some brownies in the oven for tomorrow – come and have one before you get to work first thing! Xx

15.21: Wonder if you could give me a ring. Have emailed! Xxx

Annabel was persistent, he had to give her that. Unfortunately there was something that came along with the job that made women – a certain type of woman, anyway – think that his practical services came with an option of . . . extras. The best way to handle it, he'd worked out, was to pretend he hadn't noticed. He thumbed his phone closed and pulled open the car door, shoving a folder of plans and a thermos of coffee from this morning off the passenger seat to make space for Freya.

Ten minutes later, Freya appeared, wearing a heavy

layer of some sort of face make-up and her perfectly nice eyebrows pencilled in so they were thick and dark. The whole make-up thing was a mystery to Sam in any case – he'd worked out that the answer was to buy whatever Freya said she needed – but why she needed to apply an entire coating of war-paint to go the library and the 24-hour supermarket was beyond him.

'Ready?' She gave him a grin.

'Are you having a laugh?'

'I needed to find the notes for history so I could work out what it was I needed for the test.'

'And after all that fuss about the wi-fi, you can't find this stuff online?'

Freya shook her head as they made their way through the little village, up the hill towards town. 'I need to look at old photos and stuff and photocopy some. Our printer's still dead, because *you* haven't fixed it yet.'

'All right, all right. I'll get the ink when we're in Tesco if you remind me. Then you can always print it off at home.'

'There's leaflets and stuff in the library I want to see too. Archive stuff from the war.'

'Fair enough.'

They drove out of the village, down narrow lanes that frothed with cow parsley and the bright acid green of summer. Turning the corner, he slowed the Land Rover to a stop behind a row of cars which were waiting patiently for a herd of brown-and-white cows to cross from one field to another. A couple of minutes passed, and with the gate secured, the farmhand raised an arm in thanks.

They pulled into the car park beside the little library that hid down an alley behind Bletchingham's picture-postcard high street. Willows drooped over the narrow canal, and beyond that the park sloped gently towards the red bricks of the housing estate that had sprung up on the old common where they'd hung out as teenagers. He watched two teenage boys cycle past on BMX bikes, hopping off the kerb and laughing, and wondered if he'd still be able to do any tricks. He'd spent years hanging out at the skate park, which was where the boys were headed.

'Dad? You coming?' Freya paused, her hand on the door. Sam shook his head.

'I'll wait here. Got a couple of calls to make.'

'Okay.'

'Freya?' He called her and she spun round, hair flying. 'Do you need money for the photocopier?'

She shook her head and patted her jeans pocket. 'I've got change.'

He watched her striding off. Once she'd disappeared out of view, Sam pulled out the rough plans he'd drawn for Annabel's treehouse. He'd fallen into the job as a treehouse designer by accident, somehow. After school, he'd trained as a joiner and spent a few years creating luxury kitchens for a bespoke company. Then when the company he worked for went bust, he'd decided to fill in time and keep money ticking over with odds and sods locally. He'd built the first treehouse for the local park after a conversation in the pub one evening, and – after a long and detailed battle over health and safety elements, which had taught him exactly what was and wasn't safe – the build had ended with a celebration barbecue opening, a horde of delighted children from the village, and three commissions that evening alone. Word had spread – money was plentiful in the Cotswold/Buckinghamshire borders, where they lived – and somehow TreeTops Treehouse Design had blossomed into a business that made a decent living. If he could deal with the fact that the clients could be a little bit demanding, which he could, and he could cope with the nagging concern that he was doing something that wasn't really making a difference, he'd be fine. Making treehouses for children who lived a privileged, well-off life at least meant they'd be outside, instead of glued to their phones or Xboxes all weekend long. He couldn't help thinking, though, about how much he would have loved something like that for himself when he was growing up. And there were so many children out there who equally deserved somewhere special to play and didn't even have a garden, let alone one with a bespoke treehouse.

He rang a supplier, hoping he might catch someone before they left the office. No luck. He tapped at the steering wheel, staring out of the window, not really focusing. A couple walked by with a toddler girl, swinging her by the arms as they headed towards the canal. The woman was carrying a bag of bread for the ducks. If

Freya was there, she'd be chuntering crossly about the dangers of feeding them unsuitable food. Instead, though, she was taking ages in the library. The dogs sighed heavily from the back seat – really he should have left them behind, but they were so nosy they liked to be with the rest of their pack. And then Bee shot to attention, aware of Freya before Sam could even see her.

She marched towards the car, huge clumpy trainers at the end of skinny matchstick legs clad in tight black leggings. She had braces on her teeth, and her hair was tied back with a band to keep it off her face. She looked, as ever, as if she had the cares of the world on her shoulders. She was a worrier, the absolute opposite of her mum, and he wanted to scoop every one of those imaginary worries off her narrow shoulders and make life as easy for her as possible. It was the least he could do. Growing up without a mum was hard. He'd grown up without a dad – he knew. Back then, the whole village had seemed to be stuffed full of nuclear families, and he'd felt like he was missing out. His mother had muttered darkly on more than one occasion that he definitely wasn't, and that if he'd known his dad he'd know what she was on about. But he didn't, so he felt, if not his absence, then the absence of something he'd never had.

When Stella, Freya's mum, had left, scandalizing the villagers, he'd reeled with guilt that somehow here he was in the exact same situation with his daughter. He'd resolved to be careful never to say a bad word against Stella, and to try and do everything by the book. But he still felt consumed with guilt that he wasn't doing the best he could, or trying his hardest to make their family unit of two feel complete. The one thing he'd resolved – and stuck to – was that he wasn't going to bring anyone else into her life. His mum had introduced a series of boyfriends, but none of them had ever stuck around. He didn't want that for Freya. And if that meant staying single until she was safely off to university – well, that's what he would do.

'Get everything you need?'

'They're closing the library.' Freya carefully placed the bag of books at her feet and looked up. She had a smudge of mascara under one eye, and he wanted to reach out and brush it away. He lifted a hand, but she flopped back against the window.

'Closing it for what? Renovations?'

'No, permanently. If you need a library service, there's one in Bletchley, or Aylesbury, it says.' Freya held a flyer in her hand and waggled it so it made a crackling sound. Sam saw the letters swimming around but couldn't make out what it said.

Freya strapped herself in. 'Which is handy,' she continued, sounding cross, 'because I'm hardly about to get on the bus and travel half an hour to Bletchley just to go to the library.'

He looked at her and raised his eyebrows.

'Yeah, all right. Maybe I will.'

'I can always give you a lift.'

'Thanks. But that doesn't help with school stuff. How

am I supposed to get anything done? I'm trying to get good grades and now we don't have a bloody printer, the library's closing, we live half an hour from school in the back end of beyond, and . . . ' She tailed off as Sam reversed and headed out of the car park. God, she was persistent. She'd make a good politician.

'You need to stop worrying so much about this stuff,' he said, flicking a glance at her as he waited to pull out and head to the supermarket.

'I'm not stressing. I just want to get decent grades.'

'I know, sweetheart.'

'Really?' She looked at him, eyebrows raised. Her tone was crisp. Ever since she was tiny, she'd had a way of making him laugh by sounding like she was the adult.

'Yes. Of course. I want you to do the best you can.' He indicated and pulled off the roundabout and into the supermarket car park. 'Just because I didn't do well at school doesn't mean I don't want you to.'

'Why'd you keep going on about there being more to life than school and grades, then?'

'Oh God,' he groaned, laughing. 'Can I buy your silence with some ice cream?'

'Only if it's posh stuff. Not just Tesco own-brand.'

They stopped and he turned off the engine. Freya jumped out before he'd even unfastened his seatbelt, and grabbed a trolley. He followed behind, locking the car and heading to the entrance, where Freya was saying hello to a Labrador puppy in the arms of a rather frazzled-looking woman.

'Isn't she gorgeous? Can we get another dog?'

He rolled his eyes at the woman. 'We've already got two waiting in the car.'

'Another one wouldn't hurt,' wheedled Freya.

'That's exactly what my boys said to me,' the woman told her. 'Now they're in there buying pizza, and I'm the one staying up all night potty-training a puppy.'

'Exactly,' Sam said, taking Freya's arm and prising her away. He pushed the trolley and she headed towards the fruit and vegetable section.

'What d'you want for dinner?' His stomach growled. He was ravenous, and there was nothing in the fridge.

'Sausages?'

'And mash?' He grinned at her.

'And peas,' they said, in unison. It was their favourite dinner. They headed for the fridges and gathered what they needed. Somehow he found himself being conned into buying three tubs of Ben & Jerry's because it was on special offer (even though they both knew she'd devour it with her friend Cammie in the space of twenty-four hours). Purchases made, they headed home.

It wasn't until he was turning the sausages under the grill later that evening that he remembered he'd forgotten razor blades again.

Chapter Three

Sam had woken up feeling out of sorts after a night where he couldn't sleep. At half past two, he'd given up and gone downstairs. He'd curled up on the sofa with some toast and one of Freya's fleecy blankets. He'd sat for ages, finally falling asleep in front of the television, only to be woken up at six when the dogs had trodden on him on hearing his alarm go off upstairs. It was going to be a long, long day. And then Freya – who'd been a lark all of her childhood, springing out of bed, but who over the last year or so as puberty had hit had become typically bed-hogging – had groaned and pulled the covers over her head when he'd gone in to wake her up. So the day had begun with the tension that only a teenager reluctant to get ready brought to the morning. He'd tried to stay calm, ignoring the minutes as they ticked by, but as the time for the school bus edged closer and closer he strode to the bottom of the stairs and yelled one last time.

'You don't need to stress,' she'd said, appearing with her tie hanging loosely round her neck. 'Have I ever missed the bus?'

'No,' he said, teeth gritted, but still amused at her insouciance. 'But I have better things to do in the morning than spend my time standing at the bottom of the stairs giving you a countdown.'

'Do you, though?' She'd winked and grinned at him, ducking under his arm.

'Watch it, madam,' he'd said, laughing. She'd texted him a couple of moments later with a photograph of herself – cross-eyed and tongue poking out – next to her best friend Cammie.

Very funny, he'd replied. He'd snapped a picture and sent it back to her. He looked down at it. His stubble was crossing over towards beard territory, and his hair really needed a trim. And God, the eye bags under his brown eyes were almost grey. He really needed a decent night's sleep tonight – and meanwhile, a bucket of coffee. Several of them.

'I thought I'd bring you coffee down, as you didn't reply to my invite for breakfast,' purred Annabel, flicking away her long blonde hair as she carefully deposited a tray on the wide stump where the old oak tree had stood in their garden for years.

'Careful with that, it's got treatment on it,' Sam said, scooping the tray up quickly and placing it on the ground.

'Coffee, cream, sugar – although I'm sure you're sweet enough,' Annabel said, with a giggle.

'Three, please,' said Sam, firmly.

'And can I tempt you to one of these lovely brownies I made? I got the recipe when I was in Oslo with girl-friends the other week. They're glorious.'

'I'm fine, thanks.' Sam, who wanted to swill back a mouthful of coffee and get on, shook his head.

'This is looking quite lovely!' Annabel motioned to the framework of wide wooden boards that would make the platform on which the treehouse stood. There was a gap where the staircase would lead, and a space underneath for a picnic table. 'I wanted to talk to you about the picnic table idea.' She looked at him over her coffee mug. Her honey-coloured hair was tied back in a pony-tail, and there was a pair of sunglasses perched on her head. The weather forecast suggested they had another four days of grey, dull weather before the rain set in, and he was determined to get on as much as possible. Or he would be, if Annabel would stop interrupting him.

'I've been thinking it would be fun to have a hot tub under the treehouse. There's *just* the right amount of space, and it wouldn't be too tricky to pop some pipes and stuff like that along here, would it?'

God, this job was a nightmare. He'd known it was going to be from the moment he'd turned up at Annabel's house to discover she'd set out a little lunch for them to *brainstorm some ideas, darling*. But self-employment meant he had to go where the work was, even if that meant gritting his teeth and putting up with entitled, bored, rich housewives. Normally he'd have his two apprentices with him, but this was their day at college, so he was on his own.

'I'll need to have a word with a couple of subcontractors about that. Might hold everything up a bit.'

Annabel's mouth curved into a catlike smile. 'Oh, what a shame that would be. Do you think you can put up with me for a bit longer?'

'Of course,' said Sam, politely. His jaw was rigid, but Annabel seemed to be oblivious. 'But if you don't mind, I really ought to get on. I'm racing the weather.' He looked at the sky, where a couple of clouds were looming.

'Absolutely.' Annabel bent over to pick up the tray, angling herself carefully to show off her bottom, clad in a pair of clinging blue jodhpurs. She stood up and turned around, giving a little laugh. 'I don't want to be distracting you, now, do I?'

Sam closed his eyes and took a breath. He might be businesslike, but he was still human. 'Definitely not.' He picked up a tape measure and clicked it onto the edge of one of the bars. 'Thanks so much for the coffee. I'll measure up the hot tub space and get back to you, okay?'

'Fab.' Annabel gave a little wave of her fingers. 'I'm off for a riding lesson now. Back soon!'

Sam turned back to the trunk of the beech tree and banged his forehead gently against the bark. Bloody *hell*. He'd better ring Jack, the plumber. Not only was he a dab hand with this sort of thing, but he had no scruples whatsoever about shagging the clients. If Annabel realized he was up for it, Sam would be able to get on with work without temptation. He had enough on his plate being mum and dad to Freya without getting caught up in some messy work romance, let alone one with Annabel Bevan, wife of the head of MI6 or whatever it was

Malcolm did. If Jack wanted to risk being offed by an anonymous man in a suit for the sake of getting his end away, that was his business. All Sam wanted to do was do the job, get the money and get out. With a sigh, he picked up his saw and got back to work.

'I was thinking,' an elderly voice said later, from beyond the hedge in the garden, 'that you could perhaps check those hedgehog houses in the garden, if you have a moment.'

Sam, home from work and rifling through a pile of junk mail on the doorstep, jumped. He'd finally got rid of Annabel, and had made good progress – which was a relief, because that was one job he'd be glad to see the back of.

'You mean at your place?'

'And the cottage, if you don't mind. I want to know if we've got any new residents.'

Bunty, who lived in the cottage opposite, had a habit of surprising him, which even after all these years he'd still not learned to predict. She would also continue conversations that they'd begun days, if not weeks before. It was, he supposed, something to do with being as old as she was. Perhaps time ceased to have the same meaning when you were ninety-six. Whatever it was, Sam wished she'd clear her throat or even try something radical like saying *hello* before she launched into a conversation. She emerged from behind the hedge and stood with one gnarled hand holding onto the gatepost.

'Course I will. I'll pop in tomorrow, if it's okay with you? Am I checking for hedgehogs, or . . . ?'

'Rats.'

He looked up. Bunty looked back at him, her face seemingly untroubled.

'Rats?'

'Just something I read. I don't want any little visitors moving in. And don't forget to check the cottage garden next door too. I don't want any of them scampering into the garden, or worse.'

'Right.'

Well, that was something to look forward to. It was never dull with Bunty, he'd give her that. It wasn't being ninety-six that made her irascible and prone to eccentricity – he'd grown up with her, and she'd always been the same. She was just what people called *a bit of a character*.

Despite all of that, Sam would do anything for his neighbour. She was obstinate, apparently planned to live forever, and stubborn as an old mountain goat. Despite the best efforts of her daughter-in-law, Margaret, she remained at home with only a twice-weekly cleaning company popping by to help out. Or – as Bunty put it – interfere.

'Where's Freya?'

'Lurking inside somewhere, I should think.'

'She should be out enjoying the fresh air.' Bunty tutted, and adjusted the thick cardigan she was wearing despite the warm weather.

'I know. I can't physically drag her out. And she claims she's doing homework, so who am I to stop her?'

'It's the end of term, isn't it?'

'Next week.'

'If she wants to do something useful, I've got a few odd jobs she could do. She can earn herself a bit of pocket money. How old is she now?'

'Fourteen. Not old enough for a holiday job, so she'd love that. Might stop her tapping me for money constantly.'

'Hrmm.' Bunty nodded shrewdly. 'I remember being that age. I was always after money for trips to the cinema, and nice things to eat, and – oh, it was a lovely age. Old enough to have a bit of freedom, not old enough to be worrying about boys and all that sort of thing.'

Luckily, Freya hadn't shown any interest in boys – or girls – or relationships of any kind, for that matter. He looked at Bunty and found himself counting backwards: eighty years ago. He tried to imagine her as a teenager, full of life and arguing with her parents.

'You'd be surprised what I remember – I'm not senile yet.' She cackled with amusement. 'Oh, I was desperate to get out of Walthamstow and do something with my life. All I could see ahead of me was ending up married to a nice boy and getting trapped in a two-up, two-down like my big sister, Ethel.'

'How did you escape?'

'I got on a train out here. Just as well I did, given what happened to Ethel and Jack.'

Sam raised his eyebrows enquiringly.

'Blown up. A bomb dropped, and the whole house was gone. The whole terrace, in fact.'

'I'm sorry.'

'Don't be,' Bunty was brisk. 'It was years ago. A lifetime, in fact. Anyway, about these hedgehogs. You will pop in? I can't bend down that far. Or if I did, I can't be sure I'd ever get back up.' She laughed again.

'Of course I will.'

'And how's *your* love life? Any young ladies on the scene?'

'I've told you before, I've got enough on my plate with Freya.'

'Hrmm.'

'Don't you *hrmm* me. I've got that one –' he motioned towards the house with a nod – 'on a mission to prove herself. I've got enough hassle keeping the lads at work on the straight and narrow. I don't need any complications in my life.'

'I'm not talking about complications, I'm talking about sex.'

Sam felt himself redden. He was almost certain Bunty did it just to get a rise out of him.

'Gosh, you young things are such prudes.' Cackling once again, Bunty turned around and headed back to her cottage. One hand on the gate, she turned around. 'There's a matchmaking programme on the television tonight. You should go on it. Might meet a nice girl.'

'I'm fine, honestly.'

'You should watch it anyway. It's splendid viewing. Makes me laugh, anyway.'

When Sam finally finished preparing for the next day, he went inside. Noting the time, he pinched the remote control from Freya, who was parked in front of the television in a heap of dogs and cushions with a sea of crisp packets on the floor at her feet.

'Bunty says there's a programme on I should watch. God knows what she's doing watching dating programmes at her age.'

They both burst out laughing when they realized the show was *Naked Attraction*. The idea of Bunty sitting with her feet up watching a naked dating show was hysterical. Freya was still sniggering about it after dinner – they had cheese on toast in front of the television – when they nipped up to the shop just before it closed.

'Imagine Bunty sitting there with a cup of tea, watching all those people with no clothes on.'

'Shush, you.'

He left Freya outside the shop holding the dogs, promising to get her a Magnum, and headed inside.

'Evening, Sam.'

'Beth.' Could he get out without the ten-minute rundown on everything that had been going on in the village? He grabbed milk, cereal and cheese – almost forgetting Freya's ice cream in the process – and plonked them down on the counter.

'There's a meeting at the village hall tomorrow night, don't forget.'

He glanced at the A4 sheet taped to the wall beside her till.

'I'll try and make it.'

'We need all the help we can get,' she began. 'The thing is—'

'I'll see you at seven.'

He pulled the door open. It was easier to just agree than to get a lecture on the need for community spirit and village improvement and God knows what else. Beth had been in his class at school and she'd been in charge of every committee she could find there, too. Now she held court from her position behind the counter, keeping an eye on everyone and everything that was happening. There wasn't a thing that happened in Little Maudley that Beth didn't note down.

'How's Bunty doing?'

He paused with his hand on the half-open door. 'She's good.' Bunty would never forgive him if he let anything slip that could be misconstrued. She was convinced that her daughter-in-law was on a mission to get her shipped off to a home, and just looking for an excuse.

'Poor thing. You are kind, keeping an eye out.'

'She doesn't need looking after. She's tough as old boots. Made it through the war in one piece, and she's seen off most of the old folks in this village.'

'She's getting on, though.' Beth gave a little *moue* of sympathy. 'I hear you've got a new neighbour?'

'I have?'

Beth tipped her head, a knowing smile on her face.

There was *nothing* she liked more than being the first to impart gossip.

'I hear someone's taken the cottage next to Bunty's place – you'll be able to wave to her from across the road.'

'Why would I want to do that?'

'Dunno,' Beth shrugged. 'Anyway, keep me posted. I haven't seen her yet. Wonder what she's like?'

'What are you looking cross about?' Freya unwrapped the ice cream and shoved the wrapper in the bin.

He tutted. 'Just Beth. You know what she's like. Giving me the third degree about Bunty. Something about a new person across the road in the empty cottage.'

'Why would Beth care about that?' Freya hauled one of the dogs back from a gate. They really needed a decent walk, and he'd been flat out with work all week.

'Beth? She wouldn't. She's just naturally nosy. She's been the same since primary school.'

Freya bit the top of her Magnum, deftly catching a piece as it cracked and fell off.

'Not surprised Lauren is the same, then. She gets it from her mother.'

Lauren was one of Freya's sworn enemies. They'd been best friends at nursery school, then fallen out at some point and for as long as he could remember they'd been at daggers drawn.

'Does Lauren still think she owns the place?'

'Totally.' Freya rolled her eyes.

'It's clearly genetic.'

'What you staring at?'

'Just thinking. Love you,' he said, nudging her with his elbow. She might be impossible to get out the door in the morning, and definitely getting a bit teenager-ish, but she was still his little girl. And maybe he was doing okay on his own.

'You too,' she said, tucking her arm through his. She pushed a stray hair away from her forehead in a motion that was so reminiscent of her mother that he had to look away and swallow, hard. He felt the old, familiar twinge of bitterness. If only he could brush that away as easily. Even after all this time, she still had the ability to get to him.

'I thought I'd come round and see what you might need.'

It had sounded better when Lucy had rehearsed it in her head before knocking on the door of Wisteria Cottage. She'd looked at the advert again while drinking her coffee, Hamish sitting curled up at her side on the sofa. 'Shopping, tidying and daily company,' it said. Bunty hadn't looked as if she'd been particularly keen on either the tidying or the company. Perhaps the best thing to do would be to start with the shopping.

Bunty had opened the door and looked at her for a long, uncomfortable moment before she stepped back.

'I suppose you had better come in, then.'

Lucy followed her into the kitchen. A kettle was beginning to whistle on the top of the Aga, and the grey cat was curling round Bunty's legs in a slightly alarming manner. It looked like an accident waiting to happen.

'Shoo, you menace,' said Bunty, waving an arm. The cat looked up at her, blinked slowly, parked himself in the middle of the flagstone floor and started washing his ears.

Lucy put a hand down, wondering if he'd come and say hello. He looked at her for a moment, one paw hovering in mid-air, then trotted over with a little chirp. She rubbed him behind the ears and he started purring like a jet engine, hopping up onto the bench beside her.

'Well, you've passed the first test.'

'Sorry?'

'Mr Darcy is a good judge of character.'

'Mr Darcy?' Lucy looked down at the cat and he blinked sleepily in greeting.

'His good opinion –' Bunty began, reaching down to run a gnarled hand along his back.

'– Once lost, is lost forever,' Lucy finished.

Bunty gave a chuckle. 'Well, you've passed the second test with that one. Now then, young lady. Would you like a cup of tea?'

'Yes, please.' Lucy opened her mouth again to offer to make it, but closed it rapidly.

'I've got some shortbread biscuits in the cupboard in the sitting room. Just a moment.'

Clearly Bunty was more than capable. Lucy got the distinct feeling that being patronized was the one thing most likely to rub her up the wrong way. Instead, she took another opportunity to gaze at the pictures on the walls, piecing together the history of Bunty's life here in the village. The small boy on the pony in the black-and-white photographs must be her son – Margaret's husband. There were countless framed photographs of cats and dogs, and several of the same shaggy-haired pony. And then, as her eyes travelled over the images, Lucy felt a prickle down her spine and the sensation that she was being sized up by something altogether more carnivorous.

Sitting opposite her on the dresser, his small, beady eyes fixed on her, was Stanley the snake. He was coiled in a neat circle, but he was definitely watching her. Bunty had said she'd be back in a moment, but she'd already been gone for what felt like ages. Time seemed to pass very slowly when there was a boa constrictor giving you the eye. Lucy looked at the paperwork on the kitchen table – she'd been reading up before she came on the signs that an elderly person wasn't coping whilst living alone, and chaotic piles of unanswered correspondence and unpaid bills was one of them. Not that she was supposed to be acting as a carer; but she'd always been the sort of person to make sure she knew what she was getting into. Walking out of one life and into another on a whim (albeit a temporary one, with a guaranteed return to reality at the end of it) was the most spontaneous thing she'd ever done.

So she eyed the envelopes discreetly, looking for signs of disorder and disorganization, but she quickly realized they'd been sorted into stacks. There was a pile of old newspapers, and a stack of brochures. The utility bills were opened, and PAID was scrawled across the top in a spidery copperplate. Bunty seemed pretty organized by anyone's standards.

'I knew I had a tin of the nice ones left.' Bunty returned with a colourful box under her arm. 'Now, tea.'

A movement in the corner of Lucy's eye made goose-bumps prickle on her arm. Stanley had lifted his head and was looking in their direction.

'I – I think Stanley's woken up,' she said, trying to sound casual. She edged along the bench surreptitiously, hoping Bunty wouldn't notice.

'Ah, yes. It's time for his breakfast. They should be defrosted by now.' Bunty went over to the sink and opened a battered-looking Tupperware tub.

Realizing that Stanley's lunch was two very dead yellow chicks, Lucy looked the other way, peering out of the window as if she'd just seen something absolutely fascinating. Her stomach lurched.

'I have to remember to defrost them. He doesn't like it one bit if they arrive still iced.'

Bunty brought over the pot of tea and sat down at the table, drying her freshly washed hands on a towel.

'I'll be mother, shall I?'

They sipped the tea in a slightly uncomfortable silence for a few moments. Lucy rather wished that Margaret was there. It was strange to go from the world of school – where she was in control of everything and knew exactly what she was doing, and precisely how little time she had to do it – to this new life, where time seemed to stretch on in front of her. She'd been up for what felt like hours, and it was only half past ten.

'So, Margaret said that you might want some help with tidying?'

'Did she, now?' Bunty made a noise of disapproval. 'We don't all want to live in a show home. She keeps her place looking like it's in a For Sale brochure at all times. I'd far rather a house looked lived in. Anyway.' She shifted the pile of brochures out of the way. 'These can go straight in the recycling bin on the way out, so that's a spot of tidying for you.' One of them slid off the top of the pile and landed on the floor. Lucy picked it up, noticing as she handed it back the wording on the front: *Bright Meadows Elderly Care*. There was a photograph of a large Victorian house set in neat gardens, with some striped deckchairs on the lawn.

Bunty saw her looking at it. 'Margaret is trying to ship me off.'

'She didn't say anything about that to me.'

'I'm sure she didn't.' Pressing her lips together, she looked at Lucy with sharp blue eyes. 'But these have been arriving through the post at a rate of knots. I'm sure she's signed me up for some sort of geriatric mailing list. I am not ending my days in a home full of old people.'

She was so indignant that Lucy had to bite her lip to stop herself from smiling as she nodded agreement. She picked up the heap of brochures.

'I'll get rid of these for you, then.'

'That sounds like a jolly good start.' Bunty put down

her teacup and gazed out of the window, across the path. Two women were standing talking beside the faded telephone box. One of them opened the door and peered inside for a moment before closing the door with an expression of distaste.

'I feel you have been brought here under false pretences. I don't know what Margaret has told you, but it is probably a load of nonsense.' Bunty's mouth pursed as she looked down at her gnarled hands, which were dotted with age spots. The only jewellery she wore was a plain watch with a leather strap. No rings, Lucy noted. 'I am quite happy with things the way they are. I don't understand why Margaret feels it necessary to organize me when I've survived quite happily this long.'

'I think she's trying to be helpful.'

'Well, she's getting on my nerves.'

Lucy's expression must have given away how uncomfortable she felt, for Bunty surprised her by putting out a hand and touching her gently on the arm.

'Not your fault, dear. But I'm quite happy here, just getting along.'

'So what would be the most helpful thing I could do for you?' There had to be some sort of compromise.

'Well.' Bunty thought. 'Perhaps – I've been to the village shop already, and completely forgot these.' She passed Lucy some letters. 'You could pop them in the post? Save me going out again?'

'Of course. And I'll be going to the supermarket later, too – is there anything you need?'

'I'm fine, thank you,' said Bunty.

Lucy kept quiet.

A moment later, she changed tack, thinking that perhaps it might be easier to get Bunty to open up if she got to know what made her tick. And it was clear from what she could see, and what she'd heard from Margaret, that animals were Bunty's priority.

'So how long have you had Stanley?' Please don't ask me to hold him, Lucy thought, trying to look interested rather than alarmed.

'Five years.' Bunty brightened, almost instantly. She pushed herself up from the chair and made her way across towards the dresser. She was small and had a curve to her spine, but moved with a quiet, self-possessed dignity that reminded Lucy of the Queen. Her back was clearly stiff, and her step was slightly uneven – she put out a hand to steady herself on the dresser, and it took her a while to get there. But when she did, Bunty put her hand on the top of the snake's raised head and smiled at him fondly. Lucy could feel her heart thudding against her ribs in perfectly justifiable alarm.

'You're a nice old boy, aren't you?'

Stanley looked back her with narrowed eyes.

'I adopted him,' said Bunty. 'A couple who lived in the little house by the church were moving abroad and they couldn't bring him along, for obvious reasons. Gordon and Margaret were appalled, of course, but if one can't surprise people at my age, when can one?'

Lucy's heart was beginning to settle back to a normal

rate. She was going to have to get used to Stanley, one way or another. Kill or cure, she thought.

'And you've never worried that he might . . . eat you?' She wasn't exactly sure how big a snake would have to be to eat a whole person, but Stanley was alarming enough.

'Heavens, no.' Bunty chuckled at the prospect. 'No, snakes are much maligned. He's quite a comfortable sort of character to have around.'

'You've always had lots of animals?'

'Oh, yes.' Bunty got up, taking down a photograph album from the shelf. This was definitely the way forward, Lucy thought. Thankfully the rest of Bunty's animals were far easier to admire.

'Finny, the pony, he was Gordon's when he was young. We used to take him to shows, Len and I. He was always in the ribbons.'

'What does that mean?'

'Oh, sorry – winning rosettes.' She waved an arm towards the array of faded prizes that hung above the Aga. 'Finny was a sweetheart. When Gordon gave up riding, he was passed from one village child to another – kept going for donkey's years. He was thirty-four when he went.'

'He looks lovely. And are these your dogs?'

Bunty took her through pages and pages of photographs. In amongst the dogs, cats, guinea pigs and horses, Lucy caught a glimpse of the woman Bunty had been when she was younger. She could see the same direct stare and sharp cheekbones, but when Bunty had been younger she'd been very beautiful in a Forties sort of way – hair set in dark waves, and an hourglass figure which suited the nipped-in waist of the houndstooth checked coat and neat trousers she seemed to spend most of her life wearing.

'When I was growing up, I always wanted a house full of animals,' Bunty said, closing the photograph album. 'But we lived in the middle of Walthamstow, with a tiny patch of garden, and my mother didn't like mess.'

'It must have been a bit of a change moving out here, then?'

Bunty nodded briefly, but turned the tables on Lucy. 'And what brought you to the village?' She adjusted her cardigan, pulling the sleeves down and dusting off the cover of the album before pushing it out of reach.

'I'm a history teacher. Well, I was. I'm having a break from teaching.'

'Not surprised,' snorted Bunty. 'Bloody hard work, especially these days. I was friends with a teacher for years. It was tough then, but for different reasons. Nowadays it seems to be all SAT exams and worrying about school assessments, if the papers are anything to go by.'

Lucy nodded. 'And not much time to teach. That's the hard bit. We spend more time worrying about paperwork than we do with the children, or that's what it feels like. Anyway, I'm having a sabbatical – I was a bit unwell.'

'You're all right now?'

'Yes. Just have to take things a bit easy for a while. So when I saw Margaret's advert come up . . .' She paused, realizing she was treading on dodgy ground, given Bunty's antipathy to the whole idea, but Bunty didn't react. 'It seemed like serendipity.'

'Did it indeed?' said Bunty. 'Well, that all sounds very good. Now –' she stood up, and Lucy took the cue and followed suit – 'I think perhaps I'd better get on. I'm sure you've got lots to do, too.'

'I'll take these and post them just now.'

'Thank you.' Bunty picked up the cups and took them towards the sink and Lucy, skirting past a snoozing Stanley, headed out to the hall.

'Oh – Lucy,' Bunty called.

She paused, noticing that on the wall there hung a small, framed black-and-white photograph of a young, beautiful woman standing by the gates of Buckingham Palace. Again it was the glamorous, much younger Bunty – this time in a neat dark suit and a pillbox hat, standing beside a tall, handsome man in a uniform. That must be Len, her husband.

'The recycling, please. And watch out for the village shop. No doubt Beth will try and give you the third degree.' Bunty handed over the sheaf of brochures.

'Perhaps I'll see you tomorrow morning?'

'Definitely.'

That felt like a win, Lucy decided. Bunty wasn't going to be easy to get to know, but at least she hadn't had the door closed in her face. That had to be something.

She dumped the papers in the recycling box, and headed back home to collect Hamish.

'You wait there,' she said, looping Hamish's lead through the ring outside the shop door. He sniffed at the bowl of water that had been left for canine visitors, then sat down with his ears pricked, tongue out and eyes bright.

It hadn't really crossed Lucy's mind that the village shop here in the rolling green countryside on the edge of the Cotswolds would be any different from the corner shop at the end of her Brighton street. She'd expected to open the door to a rack of newspapers and bright magazines, a couple of shelves of the usual emergency tinned food and last-minute groceries, and perhaps a fridge or two with some sad-looking fruit and vegetables.

This was like a high-end deli. The bell on the door alerted everybody in the entire building to her presence, and a couple of customers looked up from their shopping. Realizing they didn't know who she was, they turned away again. But a woman with red hair turned and looked across at her from behind the counter. She was wearing a black apron with 'The Village Shop' embroidered across the front, and her hair was tied back in a low ponytail. She looked perfectly friendly, and waved a cheery hello. Lucy smiled back, politely.

She picked up a wicker basket – no bog-standard wire ones here – and paused, taking it all in. Just beside the door there was a wooden shelf lined with artisan breads. She picked up a delicious-looking loaf studded with black olives, and then peered through the window to double check that Hamish was still happily tied outside – he was cleaning his toes, and looked quite content. The shelves were definitely not the average corner-shop fare. In the freezer there were locally made ready meals that sounded absolutely amazing – they'd have to be, at that price. And there weren't just normal eggs – there were beautiful pale blue and dusty olive-green ones, packaged in a brown cardboard box, hand-stamped. They were double the price of the normal free-range ones she usually bought, but she couldn't resist them. Then she threw in some chocolate for good measure – the ordinary kind, not the £4-a-bar handmade stuff that was wrapped in waxed paper. They even had organic, freshly made dog food in its own special freezer. Little Maudley was clearly doing all right for itself.

An archway led through to a busy little cafe, which she'd have to explore later when she didn't have Hamish tied outside. The blackboard announced that local strawberries and cream were back on the menu, and her stomach growled at the thought. She shoved in a few other essentials and headed for the checkout, which doubled as the post office counter.

'Can I post these here?'

'Letterbox is just outside. I'll take them, if you like – John's just arriving to pick them up, look.' The woman pointed out to the road where a shiny red post office van had just pulled up. Hamish, predictably, was barking furiously.

'Oh God, my dog. Can I just leave this here and make sure he's okay?'

'Course. I'll ring this stuff through for you. Have you brought a bag?'

Lucy shook her head.

'I'll give you one of ours.'

'Hamish!'

Outside, bouncing on the end of his leash, his little legs stiff and his hackles rising, Hamish was defending the honour of the village shop with all his might.

'I'm so sorry,' Lucy said, as the postman paused to look at the Westie with amusement. 'He thinks he's a German Shepherd.'

'Small dog syndrome. Hello, mate,' said the postie, squatting down to Hamish's level. He extended a hand, gently. Hamish melted instantly, rolling over onto his back and waving one paw in the air.

'I thought he'd got over his barking-at-strangers stage. Maybe it starts again when we come somewhere new.'

She gave him a quick scratch behind the ears and left him there, following the postman into the shop.

'All right, John, I see you've met my new guard dog.'

'He's not much use, is he, Beth? Rolled over the second I got within three feet of him.'

'Sorry about that,' Lucy said again, rummaging in her bag for her purse. 'How much do I owe you?'

As she paid with her debit card, John the postman gathered the sacks of parcels from behind the counter and made to head off back to the car.

'Hang on, don't forget these after all that.' Beth reached across and handed over Bunty's letters. John stuffed them into one of the postbags.

'So you've moved into the cottage next to Bunty, then?'

The bell jingled again as John headed back out, with a smile and a wave.

'Only for a little while,' Lucy said, not wanting to give too much away.

'Only I saw the return address on the back of the letters and put two and two together. Otherwise I'd have thought you were a tourist.'

'No, but I will be doing a bit of exploring while I'm here,' Lucy found herself saying.

'Well, if you want any inside info on where to go or what to do, you know where to come. I'm pretty good on all that stuff. Comes with the job, y'see.' Beth gave a queenly wave of her arm.

'Thanks.' Lucy picked up the bag. 'I'll bear it in mind.'

As she left, one of the other customers who'd been pottering about headed for the till, and she could hear Beth talking to her in a low voice. Lucy was sure they were talking about her. It was a little bit like finding yourself in an episode of *The Archers*.

She headed home, dropped off the shopping and took Hamish for a run on the footpath that led up between two fields behind the cottages. The sky was threatening rain, deep purple clouds gathering above the treeline. They made it home just as the first drops splashed down on Lucy's face, and she heard what could have been a distant rumble of thunder. She closed the door and sat down on the sofa.

It was four o'clock. Hamish had been walked, Bunty had been helped, and there was nothing left to do. She unpacked everything, and – dodging the rain – put her suitcase in the little shed in the back garden, then sat down heavily. She hadn't realized how much of her life – well, all of it, if she was honest – had been taken up by work. After she'd been rushed into hospital and then signed off sick, her mum had returned home briefly for a fortnight from Australia, so she hadn't really had time on her own until now. This was exactly what the doctor had ordered – rest, peace and quiet, no stress – but until now she hadn't had a chance to realize just how *long* every day was with no work in it. She turned on the radio for company.

This is Radio 4. Recent studies have shown that lone-liness has reached new levels in rural areas. This programme will examine the causes of this . . .

Bloody hell. Making a face at herself in the mirror, Lucy switched it off and turned on the television instead.

Chapter Four

She woke up with Hamish wriggling about at the foot of the bed. Outside the sun was shining, and there was no sign of last night's rain. She looked at her watch – it was only half eight. She'd slept so well that it felt like she'd been asleep for days. It must be the country air.

'Come on, then,' she said, climbing out of bed. Hamish followed her downstairs and into the garden – she opened the back door, pausing to put on the kettle, and watched as he pottered about, sniffing. There was a strange-looking little wooden house underneath a slightly scruffy honeysuckle which grew over the side of the garden hut where she'd left her suitcase last night. Hamish sniffed it and then dismissed it. She turned back, hearing the kettle come to the boil, and headed inside to make coffee.

It was too early to go and knock on Bunty's door, and besides, she didn't want to pester her or look too eager. Maybe she'd just take Hamish for a decent walk first. Then she could leave him snoozing on the sofa, check on Bunty, and head into Bletchingham to explore the town – and the museum. Their website had been a bit out of date but had left her feeling hopeful that the curator might know the best place to start investigating the history of the area. Actually – she pulled on her trainers and whistled Hamish to heel – maybe all this free time wouldn't be that hard to fill, after all.

The village was beautiful. The golden stones of the houses and cottages glowed in the early morning sunlight, and the birds were singing in the trees, which were already laden with unripe fruit. It was everything a country village should be, Lucy thought. She strolled along the path at Hamish's pace, allowing him to sniff every single gatepost and streetlamp, and peered discreetly in the windows of the houses as she passed. They were all so *perfectly* kept. It was such a contrast to the messy, multicultural jumble that was Brighton, which she loved. Back home, you never knew what you'd find when you crossed a road or walked around a corner. A demo, or an impromptu student street party, or someone doing street art. Pop-up shops and galleries, and always noise – this place was so quiet that even her footsteps seemed loud as she walked down the lane towards the footpath. It was as if there had been a memo passed round: this was the style of woven wicker heart decoration to hang in your window. Here is the range of subtle grey planters in which to grow your lavender and tasteful white pelargoniums. No vibrant, umbrella-striped petunias pouring out of hanging baskets here.

And then she turned up the lane, following the sign that indicated a footpath. On the right was a tall stone wall, with purple flowering clematis flowing over the top and feathery ox-eye daisies growing in a wild tangle. She headed up a track with an overgrown, buttercup-strewn grass channel in the middle. The wall gave way to a chain-link fence and some gardens that looked – well, normal. Normal by the standards of the places Lucy knew, anyway. Jumbles of battered old furniture, plastic toys, overgrown grass. Kids already playing on a trampoline, throwing a football back and forth and yelling. It was a bit of a relief, actually, to see that there was a side to Little Maudley that wasn't quite as picture-perfect as the rest of it. The houses were white-painted and dilapidated, and there wasn't a bit of tasteful green-painted woodwork in sight. A small child spotted Hamish and ran to the end of one of the gardens to shout hello to him. Hamish bounced in through the long grass, his tail wagging furiously, and licked the fingers that were poking through the fence.

'Hello,' said Lucy, as she passed.

'I like your doggy,' said the little girl. She ran away then, and Hamish shot off in hot pursuit of something that smelled delicious on the path ahead. Lucy followed him, taking it slowly and cautiously. The doctor had stressed that she should carry on as normal, but take things easy. It seemed a bit of a contradictory idea – but perhaps that was just because she'd been living life at 100mph for so long that she didn't really know how to slow down.

The path wound its way up a slight hill and then opened out, displaying the countryside beautifully. To the left were neatly kept allotments dotted with pastel-painted sheds, some hung with brightly coloured bunting that flapped in the breeze. In front of her the path curled downhill and into a wood, which looked enticingly cool and interesting

– Hamish thought so, anyway. Lucy gasped at the beauty that unfolded before her. It was just like a painting – exactly what people must mean when they talked about rolling countryside. The undulating fields were dotted with cows and horses behind wooden fences. Patches of woodland covered the distant, higher hills. A bird of prey circled overhead and hovered for a moment before diving down into the woodland ahead. It was perfect. Lucy felt her face spreading into a huge smile of relief and gratitude. It was so far removed from the pressured, stressful world of teaching, attainment targets and exam results she'd left behind that it was almost unbelievable.

She leaned down and unclipped Hamish's lead. 'Off you go, boy,' she said, laughing as he bolted off immediately. 'And don't forget to come back,' she called after him, a little too late. The wood was no doubt full of exciting smells and burrows to explore, and all she had for bribery was a handful of biscuits she'd grabbed with the poo bags on the way out the door. She'd have to trust in his essential good nature. The fact that he was a terrier on a mission was a minor detail.

Walking though the soft, green wood, Hamish darted back and forth in front of her – not coming back to heel, but staying close enough that she felt reasonably sure he'd be catchable if the need arose. She ran her hand along the soft, serrated edges of ferns that had uncurled and arched over the leaf-strewn ground, just revelling in the loveliness of it all. Closing her eyes, she took a breath of the earthy, cool air.

'Is he okay with dogs?'

A voice broke through her thoughts, and she snapped her eyes open.

'Sorry, didn't mean to disturb you. Just don't want my two causing a ruckus if he's not used to other dogs.'

A tall woman of about thirty-five, with dark hair tied back in a messy bun, approached her. She was wearing a pair of filthy jeans, wellington boots that had seen better days and a stained t-shirt. She had two spaniels walking by her side, not on the lead but just obediently waiting for her instruction. They looked at her with tongue-lolling, unabashed adoration.

'Mine are perfectly friendly,' she explained, 'but you never know, particularly with terriers.'

Lucy bridled slightly. 'No, he's perfectly friendly too.'

'Good.' The woman gave a slight nod of her head. 'Go and sniff.'

With that, the two spaniels crashed through the pretty clearing, decimating the beautiful display of ferns and heading into a thicket of brambles which looked virtually impenetrable.

'Nutcases.' She smiled, then, and looked far less fierce. 'Gorgeous morning for it.'

'Beautiful,' agreed Lucy. She looked around for Hamish, aware that she was now obliged to demonstrate his slavish dedication to her and his unceasing obedience. There was no sign of him.

'Hamish?'

It was a question, rather than an instruction. A scuffling

of leaves and the sound of something moving through the undergrowth suggested that he was at least planning to answer it. Lucy gave the woman a polite sort of smile and headed up the path that forked to the left, hoping she would head off to the right. There was nothing worse than having to make polite dog-walking conversation when you'd gone out for a peaceful think. Hamish's head popped through the ferns, his nose black with mud, his bright button eyes gleaming with excitement.

'Come on, Hame, this way.'

Hamish gave a snort and shook his head, making mud fly everywhere. Then he hit reverse gear and disappeared. Lucy hoped he was going in the right direction, and decided to set off on the path that led round the outskirts of the wood in the hope he'd follow.

Five dog-free minutes later, the path turned back round to meet – oh God, the spaniel woman again. She was strolling along, not a care in the world. Lucy, meanwhile, was trying to work out where the elusive bloody Hamish had gone.

'Looking for someone?' the woman said, laughing. She pointed to the trees on her left where a brown-and-white rolling heap of dogs were barking happily and playing together. 'I think he's taken a shine to my two.'

'Oh God,' said Lucy, forgetting to act cool. 'I thought he'd buggered off. He does it a lot. It's not so much a problem in Brighton – well, it is, to be honest – but out here I'm terrified he'll leg it and I'll never see him again.'

'How old is he?' Dog people could almost always be

relied on to be friendly, Lucy had discovered. There was a camaraderie between them – out in all weathers, covered in muddy paw prints – that she'd discovered since taking on responsibility for Hamish. He'd started out as her brother Tom's puppy, bought as a last-ditch attempt to keep his relationship going – but just like sticking-plaster babies, he hadn't worked. Tom's girl-friend had moved out, and Lucy – who worked slightly less ridiculous hours than her brother – had ended up holding the baby. Well, the puppy. She'd spent a small fortune on doggy day care, which meant that he'd been trained surprisingly quickly in basic things like potty-training, but his recall could be erratic, to put it mildly. His terrier nose meant that he often got caught up in what he was doing and his ears just seemed to go out of service.

'Eighteen months,' said Lucy, holding his lead out hopefully and calling him. 'Come on, Hame.'

'I find they tend to come more easily if I keep the lead out of sight.' The scruffy woman squatted down on her haunches and gave a whistle, rummaging in her pockets. 'Call him again?'

'Hamish!'

The woman gave another whistle and her two spaniels shot towards her instantly, throwing themselves into a down position at her feet. Hamish, looking as if he didn't quite know what had come over himself, followed suit. He was delighted when she offered him a titbit of some-thing delicious, and didn't seem to object when she grasped his collar and said, 'Here you are, pop the lead on now, while he's chewing.'

'Bloody hell, you're a miracle worker.' Lucy gave Hamish a pat and looked up at the woman, who was wiping her hands down the sides of her jeans.

'Not at all,' she said, laughing. 'It's just a trick of the trade. Speak softly, and carry something irresistibly delicious in your pocket at all times.'

'Not like these,' Lucy said ruefully, holding out her handful of depressing-looking biscuits.

'Definitely not, unless you've got a dog with a perfect recall. You need something tempting. Stinky cheese is another good one.'

'Are you a dog trainer then?'

'For my sins.' She wrinkled her nose, looking much younger suddenly, and then held out her hand. Lucy went to shake it, but the other woman pulled it back to inspect it, before holding it out again. 'Sorry, just checking it wasn't all chickeny.'

'Nice to meet you.'

'I'm Mel Willis, and this is Clara and Pip.' She pointed to the two almost identical spaniels. 'And yes, I'm a dog trainer. I do classes in the village hall, and in town, and I do residential stuff for people who want me to fix their dogs for them and one-on-one classes for people who're having a problem with a particular issue.'

Lucy blushed. 'Like running away on walks?'

'Exactly like that. He's a terrier, so he's got selective deafness when it comes to going off lead. If he smells something interesting, he's going to be far more likely to head off to investigate that than to come and see if you've got a dried-up old Bonio in your pocket.'

'But I thought we weren't supposed to bribe them?'

'It's not bribery, per se,' Mel said, looking thoughtful. 'More just reminding them that we're worth listening to.'

'That's a bit like teenagers,' Lucy said.

'Oh God, yes.' Mel rolled her eyes. 'Got one of them at home. Unfortunately she can't be bribed with smelly cheese and the promise of a long walk around the corn field.'

Lucy said goodbye and they forked off in different directions – Mel over a stile and off onto a path down the side of a field tall with greenish-gold corn, and she and Hamish along the footpath that led around the wood. They came across a little pond, and she stopped for a moment to admire the way the light dappled on the water and the green leaves softly filtered the morning sunshine. Hamish admired the pond in his own way by leaping in and swimming across it, nose high in the air, looking tremendously pleased with himself.

When they reached home Lucy towelled Hamish dry as he shook grim-smelling pond water all over her clothes, then hung up his lead and went through the little archway into the galley kitchen. If she timed it right, she could shove the bacon in the oven and it would be cooked by the time she'd had a quick shower.

'Bacon sandwiches all round,' she said to Hamish, buttering two slices of bread and humming to herself.

He looked up, one eye open, then carried on snoozing on the sofa.

She hadn't factored in the slightly dodgy shower Margaret had mentioned. The bath had been fine, so she'd assumed it couldn't be that difficult. But it took an age to get a balance between icy cold needles of water and scalding hot ones, and by the time she got out and dressed, the pungent scent of burning bacon was curling its way up the little staircase.

'Ugh!' She coughed as a cloud of black smoke puffed out into her face as she opened the oven. Then 'Oh, bugger,' as the baking tray burned her hand through the tea towel. She threw the smoking tin down on the kitchen worktop and waved an arm around ineffectually as the smoke alarm started bleeping like mad. 'Shit.'

Hamish started barking.

'Oh shush, I don't need you chiming in,' she shouted, waving the tea towel in the air to try and stop the alarm going off. She hauled open the kitchen door and hurled the smoking tray with its blackened offerings onto the step and straight into the path of—

'Watch it,' said a tall, broad-shouldered man with a scruff of dark curly hair.

'Oh my God,' said Lucy. Her heart thudded and adrenalin coursed through her veins. She'd interrupted a burglar in the middle of sizing up the place. She pulled the door shut and stood for a second, trying to catch her breath. The local newsletter she'd read had said something about a spate of local break-ins that had been reported in the local paper, the culprits trying the back doors of people's houses in the hope they weren't in.

She opened the door and glared at the man's retreating back. 'Yeah, you sneak off when nobody's looking. I'm going to report you to the police. I've heard all about you,' she shouted.

He turned around at that. Lucy got a good look at his face, making a mental note for the police report. Tall – about six two – with dark untidy hair and stubble. A polo shirt with some sort of logo on it, and work trousers. He was wearing a pair of heavy tan work boots, and he had – she peered at him – dark brown eyes.

'Are you finished?'

He was mocking her.

'I'm calling the police this second before you break in to anyone else's house. And don't you go anywhere near next door – she's got a snake. It'll – it'll – *eat you.*'

'Right you are,' he said, the corners of his mouth turning down. He looked like he was trying not to laugh. 'I'll bear that in mind.'

And then he vaulted over the back gate, and crunched around the side of the cottage.

Lucy looked down at the tray and realized Hamish had ventured out. Far from being a guard dog, he had busied himself eating every one of the six burnt-to-a-crisp pieces of bacon.

'Thanks for nothing,' she said, swiping the tray away from him. 'You're supposed to be my bloody protector.'

She stood with phone in hand trying to work out if

she was supposed to call 999 (and say 'Help, someone was trying to burgle me but they've gone away') or 111, or the local police station, or . . . She googled 'what to do if someone tries to burgle your house' and was scrolling through the answers when a loud rap at the door made her jump.

'That was quick,' she said, pulling it open. 'I haven't even called you yet.'

'I don't think you have my number,' said the burglar, looking down at her with frank amusement. He paused for a second and then put out his hand. 'Sam Travis.'

Lucy took a step back and looked at him with her best teacherly frown of disapproval, honed over many years. 'You're a burglar. You're not supposed to introduce yourself.'

'On the contrary. If you knew anything about this village, you'd know that it's *de rigueur*. Along with deadheading your roses as soon as they go over, doing your bit for the village hall committee, and keeping the place looking just so.'

'I—' Lucy was aware her mouth was hanging open.

'We seem to have got off on the wrong foot. Bunty told me to pop round and check the hedgehog house I'd installed, and see if any hogs had moved in. I was supposed to do it the other day but I didn't get the chance, and when I saw her earlier she said she'd seen you going out with the dog, so I assumed the coast was clear. I didn't realize you were in, or I'd have knocked. I'm used to the cottage being empty.'

'Well, it's not,' she said.

'I can see that.' He looked at the ceiling. 'Are you going to get that?'

'Yes,' she said, crossly. She grabbed the tea towel and waved it in the direction of the smoke alarm, and after a couple of moments it stopped.

'So you're renting the cottage from Bunty? I didn't realize she'd branched out into holiday lets.'

'I'm not on holiday. Margaret – Bunty's daughter-in-law – wanted someone to keep an eye on her on a day-to-day basis.'

'Ha.' Sam gave a hollow laugh. 'Good luck with that. Bunty's pretty determined. I can't imagine she'll take kindly to having someone checking up on her.'

Lucy thought of Bunty's expression yesterday when she'd opened the door, and gave a slightly grudging smile. 'Well, no. I think it's going to be a bit of a learning curve for both of us.'

'That's one way of putting it. Good old Margaret. She tries her best – I'm sure she did it with the best of intentions.'

He rubbed his nose, looking at her with an amused expression. 'Sorry about the burglary thing. Not exactly what you need when you're trying to find your feet in a new place. Mind you, I wouldn't put it past Bunty to have done it deliberately. She's got a wicked sense of humour.'

'Has she?' Lucy made a mental note of that.

'Once she gets to know you, yes. She's got a good

heart, has Bunty. I've known her all my life. Much scarier on the outside than she is on the inside, I promise. You'll see. Anyway, I'd better let you get on with breakfast.'

He gave her a half smile and raised his eyebrows.

'I'm sure I'll be seeing you again. Hard not to, when we're living on opposite sides of the road.'

Lucy closed the door and watched through the window as he crossed Main Street in three strides.

Chapter Five

Well. That was weird, Sam thought, crossing the road and climbing back into the driver's seat of the truck.

'All right?' Freya didn't look up from her phone as she spoke.

'Absolutely fine.' Apart from being accused of burglary by a madwoman, that is. He turned the key in the ignition and headed into town to pick up the two apprentices who were working on the project with him. Hopefully between the three of them they'd get a decent chunk of work done, and get ahead before the weather changed. He shook his head in bemusement. Margaret was on a hiding to nothing if she thought finding someone to take the cottage and keep an eye on Bunty was going to work. He admired Bunty for her dogged determination to refuse to let age get in the way of her life. And she was capable of the odd wickedly naughty trick. She hadn't said a word about the cottage being occupied when she'd told him to check the hedgehog house, and it was only luck that whatever her name was hadn't called the police. He'd have a word when he got back later. Honestly.

He had enough on his plate dealing with work, and now he had someone living opposite who was probably still secretly convinced he was casing the joint. Thank

God he could rely on Mel, at least. She was coming round later to pick up some stuff he'd ordered for her from the wholesalers – he'd ask her then if she knew anything about the new neighbour. He pulled into the estate where the boys both lived and saw them sitting in the bus stop, waiting. They were wearing designer t-shirts, which were going to get wrecked, but which they insisted on wearing anyway. He must get them a couple of TreeTops Design polo shirts to wear instead.

'All right?' Will and Joe grunted a greeting as they clambered into the back seat, sliding their bums across the seat and strapping themselves in. Freya grunted back, but he noticed she'd gone a bit pink. He secretly suspected that she might have a bit of a crush on one of them, but knew better than to breathe a word about it to her.

'Well, it's just as well I've got the radio for company,' Sam said pointedly to himself as he drove off. It was amazing how they all seemed to be from another planet, wired to their phones. He struggled to get a word out of any of them on the way to work, but once they got outdoors and started doing physical stuff they became quite animated and cheerful. Freya was exactly the same. She was spending way too much time online, in his opinion. She berated him for not being academic and not understanding why she wanted to do well at school. He could appreciate why she wanted to spend all her time with her nose in a book – even if, being dyslexic, he'd struggled all the way through school and left as soon as he could – but the appeal of wasting time staring at her phone was completely beyond him.

'I really appreciate you two taking time out on a Saturday for this,' he said as they pulled up outside the gates of Greenbank House.

'Hello, Sam,' said a loud, happy voice. A moment later Freddy, the eldest boy in the family, popped his head up at his window. 'I've opened the gate for you.'

'That's really kind,' he said, smiling down at Freddy, who was twenty, and had just finished his final term at an extended education school for teenagers with learning difficulties.

'Sam.' Janet gave a wave of greeting. She wheeled her eldest daughter, Fiona, onto the grass. Fiona was – as usual – draped in a lovely set of sparkling plastic jewels, and nestling a toy baby doll in her arms. 'Thank you for coming over on a weekend.' Fiona gave a wave hello. In the distance he could hear the sounds of guitars and a drum kit – the boys who were currently placed with Janet were clearly making themselves at home. Janet smiled indulgently. She was used to chaos – thrived on it, really. Twenty-five years working as a foster parent had left her pretty much unshockable.

'I've brought the lads.'

He wound up the window, got out of the car and nodded his head to indicate to the boys they should follow. Freddy closed the gate and locked it behind them.

'Hi, Freya,' said Janet.

'Can I go and see the goats with Fiona?' Freya waved

hello to Freddy, then went across to say hello to Fiona, who was twenty-five now and had been living with the family since she'd been fostered there at the age of four. It made his heart swell with pride to see how kindly and unselfconsciously Freya admired Fiona's 'baby', picking her up and smiling, commenting on the pretty babygro she was wearing. Fiona might not be verbal, but she communicated her happiness effectively through the huge smile on her face and the waves of both arms. These were the jobs that mattered. Installing hot tubs and luxury tree-houses for people like Annabel might be the bread-and-butter work, but doing something like this felt worthwhile.

He watched as Freya checked with Janet that it was okay to go, then asked Fiona if she'd like to show her the goats. Fiona nodded vigorously and they headed off. Janet and Mick's house stood in twelve acres of land, all of it fenced securely, not for fear of people getting in, but to keep the occasional runaway safely in. She was an experienced foster carer who'd looked after more than 100 children in her time. Her husband, Mick, worked long hours doing something in computers, which meant that while he was often home, he was generally holed up in his study. But today he was waiting for them at the treehouse site, the sleeves of his checked shirt rolled up and his hair tied back in a long ponytail.

'Sam, lads – good of you to come over today. '

'No problem. I know you're flat out during the week.'

'This is what we're working on next, boys. Mick's prepared the site in his spare time—'

Janet gave a snort of laughter. 'If you could call it that.'

'Watch it, you,' said Mick, catching his wife by the waist and squeezing her.

'Anyway. We're going to be working on a special project here, like I told you. And I wanted Mick and Janet here together to talk us through it, and make sure we all know exactly what's needed.'

An hour or so later, they headed back towards the front drive. Freya and Fiona were sitting under the shade of a tree, Fiona wearing a long daisy-chain necklace and a garland of buttercups in her hair.

'Oh that's pretty, Fiona,' said Janet. 'You look lovely.'

'Aaaah,' said Fiona, waving an arm towards Freya.

'We saw the goats, too,' Freya said. 'Molly's had babies. Dad . . . '

'No, we cannot get a pet goat. Our garden's the size of a postage stamp, for one thing.'

Later that evening, having deposited the lads back home and thanked them again for going out of their way to come along on a day off, he was trying to prise Freya away from her phone and out for a walk with the dogs.

'It's not that I don't understand why you want to lie here staring at Instagram while your life passes by,' he said, for the millionth time. 'It's just – I think you really need to do something else. Something outside, preferably.'

'Like running, or hiking, or something?' She'd lifted an eyebrow and glanced up at him, then carried on scrolling, tapping in comments at great speed.

'Like walking the dogs, or volunteering to help at the lodge, or anything. Just get off the internet, and I don't want you spending all summer with your nose in a book, either. You need some fresh air.'

'I'm on it.' Freya rolled her eyes, and shifting herself off the kitchen table, ambled off (phone in hand) into the sitting room. He heard the television switching on. 'Listen,' she shouted, 'I'm doing something.'

'Netflix does not count.' Sam lifted her schoolbag off the table, hung it by the back door and turned to the fridge. He'd better find something for dinner that wasn't pizza – again.

After dinner, when they were washing the dishes that wouldn't fit in the dishwasher, Freya looked at him for a moment with an expression he couldn't quite read.

'You know my –' she began, then stopped.

'What's up?'

'I was just wondering.' She spent a long time folding the damp tea towel into squares before unfurling it and hanging it to dry on the oven door. He waited, a knot growing in his stomach.

'Cammie was talking about parents on the bus home from school the other day.'

The knot in his stomach tightened and he very carefully put down the mugs he'd been holding. He looked up at her.

'What about them?'

'You don't think it's weird that we never hear anything from – her?'

'From your mum?'

She swallowed and nodded.

'What's brought this up?' God, he wished teenagers came with a handbook. He scanned his memory, trying to think what advice Janet – who'd seen more troubled teenagers come through her doors than he'd had hot dinners – had given him in the past. He'd known Freya was going to bring it up again at some point, but it had been so long that he'd hoped maybe she'd forgotten. He shook his head imperceptibly at the ridiculousness of the idea. You don't just forget that your mother walked out when you were a toddler.

'I dunno. Just wondered.'

'I don't have any answers, sweetheart. I wish I could say something easy, but – people are complicated.' It sounded pretty lame, but it was the best he could offer.

She shrugged, and headed back to the sofa. Under the circumstances, he thought maybe he'd leave her to it, and stop trying to force her outside for a walk. And she *had* spent an hour messing around at Janet's place with Fiona. At least she'd had her daily quota of vitamin D. That was one parenting box ticked, anyway.

'I'll take these two for a run up to the woods, then.'

'Okay,' Freya replied. She didn't look up as he headed out, calling the dogs as he went.

When he got back, he found the house empty. Despite her protestations about not wanting to go out, Freya had nipped across the road to see Bunty. It was funny how well she got on with a woman of ninety-six. There were more than eighty years between them, but Bunty had been there – a surrogate great-grandma, really – since she'd been born. She'd been a calm and capable pair of hands when Stella had left, popping by with a tray of scones or a tin of biscuits. And as Freya had grown up, their bond – and their shared love of a fiendishly difficult puzzle – had grown. Crossword puzzles were a mystery to him, but Freya and Bunty loved nothing more than to sit down together and work their way through one together. It was very sweet.

He was still standing at the sitting room window looking out when she reappeared, a pile of books under her arm. She didn't spot him as she turned to wave goodbye to Bunty, and he sat down on the sofa, so that when Freya reappeared she had no idea that he'd seen her. She waved a brief hello, unplugged her phone from the charger on the sideboard, took a bag of crisps and an apple, and disappeared for the night.

Chapter Six

'Hello again!'

Mel, the woman she'd met in the woods, was standing on the pavement outside the cottage looking at her phone as Lucy opened the door. Lucy wedged it with a foot, trying to sidle out without Hamish making a bid for freedom.

'I'm not stalking you, honestly.'

'Hi – sorry – no, back!' She extricated her foot and pulled the door shut, turning around and trying to look composed.

'Hello, gorgeous.' Mel bent down and scratched Hamish under the chin. 'Are you being a little scamp and causing problems?' Hamish instantly sat and looked at her as if he wouldn't dream of misbehaving, with a butter-wouldn't-melt expression on his face.

'Something like that,' Lucy said.

'Are you staying in the cottage?' Mel took a band from around her wrist and tied her hair back in a ponytail.

How many times was she going to have the same conversation? It would be easier if she just put a little notice on the door to let everyone know. Back home in Brighton she could have been locked in the loo for a week and nobody would even have noticed – apart from at work, of course. But here in Little Maudley it seemed like everyone knew everything.

'Just for a short while.'

'That's nice. You'll have met Bunty, then?' More proof of the small-town theory. Lucy couldn't help smiling. It was – exactly as she'd already thought – just like living in some sort of gentle rural soap opera. As if to emphasize the point, a tractor rumbled past.

'Yes, I'm helping out with a bit of shopping and things for her.'

'Oh that's nice. She's lovely, isn't she?' Mel lowered her voice slightly. 'Bit stern until you get to know her, but really, she's a pussycat. So you're settling in okay?'

'Oh – um, fine.' Lucy wasn't sure if she should mention the random weirdo who had turned up in the garden, or . . . 'Well, I did have a bit of a strange experience earlier.'

'Really?' Mel's eyebrows curved upwards, as did her mouth. 'Do go on.' She leaned against a lamp-post and crossed her arms. She'd changed since earlier and was now wearing a summery, striped t-shirt dress, with bare, tanned legs and her wet hair in a ponytail. The sun was already high in the sky and the sky was bright blue. It was the beginning of a perfect English summer's day.

'Well, I got back from walking Hamish, and was in the process of burning breakfast –'

'Nice start to the morning.'

'And I opened the back door to find a man wandering around in the garden. So I tried to chase him off. Next thing, he turns up at the front door, introduces himself and says he's trying to check a hedgehog house.'

Mel snorted with laughter. 'That'll be Sam.'

'That's right! Do you know him?'

'I do. Definitely not a burglar.'

'Does he make a habit of just wandering around people's gardens?'

'Not that I know of.'

'Well, that's a relief.'

'I bet. Where are you off to?'

'I was going to pop to the shop and get something for breakfast that isn't burnt.'

'I'm going the same way, I'll walk with you.'

They headed up the lane towards the village shop. The village was humming with activity now – lawnmowers buzzing, parents and children coming and going, dressed in kit for weekend clubs. They passed two small girls in karate gear and Mel waved hello to their dad, who was locking up their cottage. A teenager in jodhpurs cycled past with a riding hat hanging from the handlebars of her bike. A group of ramblers clad in stout shoes and sensible walking clothes, led by a woman with walking poles and a loud voice, crossed the road in front of them and headed up the footpath towards the woods. Butterflies flittered around a huge buddleia bush outside the cottage by the stream.

'We're quite lucky,' Mel explained. 'We're a bit off the beaten track for the whole Cotswold tourist thing, because we're just on the very edge of it. So we get the pretty houses and the lovely village feeling, but we don't get jammed up with tourist traffic for the three months of summer.'

A solitary car drove past. 'I mean, we do get the odd one – we've got a few holiday rentals in the village – but it's not mega-touristy. There's a downside to that, though: it's a bit everyone-knows-everyone.'

Lucy thought back to last night. 'Mmm. I met the woman who runs the village shop yesterday.'

'Ah, Beth. Yeah, I was just about to warn you about her. If there's anything you don't want everyone in the village to know within about ten minutes, don't mention it to her. And if she starts trying to extract information, just get her onto the subject of emigrating to France. It's her new obsession. She'll stop giving you the third degree if you bring it up. Only trouble is, she'll go on about *that* for hours, but you can't have everything.'

'When I met her, she was . . .'

'Fishing?'

Lucy grinned. 'Something like that.'

'Basically we didn't have a village shop for years, and then when the old post office came up for sale after it'd been lying empty for ages, we decided to do a community buy-out thing. So by rights the shop sort of belongs to all of us, but Beth's in charge – and that means she thinks she's a sort of village matriarch. I mean, she's only thirty-five, but she acts about thirty years older.'

'So who runs the cafe?'

'Oh, Flo – she's a genius. Best flat white you'll get this

side of London, and bacon sandwiches to die for. I wish she stayed open all day, but she's only open from nine until two. That's where I'm going now, if you want to join me for one? I mean, only if you want to, of course. It's the perils of working with dogs all day. I end up chatting away to whoever will keep me company!'

'I'd love to,' said Lucy before she could stop herself. She was missing the bustle and camaraderie of the staffroom more than she'd expected, and Hamish wasn't much of a conversationalist.

'Morning,' said a cheerful voice as they opened the heavy wooden shop door.

'Hi, Beth.'

'Oh, hello.' Beth perked up immediately on seeing them. She gave a dazzling smile. 'Hello, Mel. And hello again.'

'This is Lucy. She's staying in Bunty's place.'

'So what are you doing there, then?'

Lucy opened her mouth without thinking. 'Oh, I'm on a sabbatical from work, so when I saw the ad Margaret had placed, it seemed like perfect timing.'

'I didn't know she'd placed an ad?'

'We're just going to have a coffee, actually. So we'll see you in a—'

'A sabbatical,' said Beth, as if Mel hadn't spoken. 'That sounds interesting. So what is it you're having a break from?'

'I'm a history teacher.'

'Oh, really? Are you going to be teaching locally?' Beth

crossed her arms and rocked back on her heels, looking at Lucy with renewed interest. She nodded towards the local paper, which had a headline about shock Ofsted school inspection results. 'The school in Bletchingham is going downhill, if you ask me. We could do with some decent new teachers.'

'I'm not teaching, no. Just having a break for a few months.'

'Very nice,' said Beth, looking impressed. 'I wouldn't mind a break myself. So is that like a holiday, then?'

'Not quite . . . I'm planning to do some research into the history of the area.'

'Oh, that sounds good. What's that for then?'

Mel stepped sideways and tapped the side of Lucy's foot with the edge of her shoe. Lucy realized what was happening and glanced at her. Mel was suppressing a smile.

'Come on,' Mel said, taking her arm. 'I'm going to take Lucy for a coffee before you give her the third degree.'

'I'm only asking,' Beth protested.

'You can grill her later,' Mel said to Beth. 'See what I mean?' She made a face.

'I didn't mean to tell her any of that stuff! She's a bit like an interviewer on television. She keeps asking questions and I'm too British and polite not to answer them.'

'*Exactly*,' said Mel, 'And of course she knew exactly who you were, too. Nothing gets past Beth.' She reached over, taking two menus and waving hello to a girl behind the counter who had a pen in her mouth and both hands occupied. 'That's Flo – who won't give you the Spanish Inquisition, incidentally.'

Mel passed her a menu and scanned her phone while Lucy read it. Having burnt breakfast, her stomach rumbled at the list of food on offer. 'Bacon roll and a flat white, please.'

'Coming up.'

Mel headed to the counter where she stood, chatting happily to Flo, fiddling with her phone as she waited for the coffees. Meanwhile Lucy looked around. They'd turned a little side room of the Victorian post office into a dinky little cafe with five tables and an assortment of old-fashioned school chairs. On the pale grey painted walls there were paintings of dogs, cats and horses, each with a tiny pink price tag on the corner. She peered a bit closer at one of them. They were incredibly lifelike and very pretty.

'They're done by Sue Cassidy. She's got a studio in her garden. She'll paint your animals from life or from photos, and she sells these ones, too. She's amazing.' Mel came back, placing the two coffees on the table, noticing Lucy admiring the paintings.

'You don't have any dog training today then?'

'Admin day,' Mel wiped a coffee moustache off her lip. 'Which means procrastinate, drink coffee and try and persuade my daughter to spend some time with me and not glued to her phone.'

'How old is she?'

'Cammie? She's fourteen.'

'Year nine? That's a nice age. I always quite liked teaching that age.' God, she'd been out of teaching for a few weeks and she'd already forgotten how many times she'd collapsed in the staffroom, swearing that her year nine group would be the death of her.

Mel pulled a face. 'Teaching's bloody brave if you ask me. Rather you than me.'

'Not at that age. The worst stage is when they've been there a year and think they know everything. Year eights are a nightmare for everyone.'

'So what is it you're wanting to investigate, then? You know we've got Bletchley Park just up the road – there's loads of historical stuff there, if it's the war you're interested in.'

'It is. I'm going this week.'

'Cammie went on a school trip last term. She said it was amazing. And that's something coming from her, because she's deeply in the *everything is SO boring* phase.'

'Oh yes, I remember that stage too. Don't worry, it does pass.'

'You'll have to grill Bunty. She'll be interesting to talk to if you're researching that sort of thing.'

Lucy's heart gave a little swoop of excitement. 'Really?'

'God, yeah. She doesn't talk about it, but she was something important in the war. Worked in a field listening to something or other – I can't remember the details, but she'll tell you all about it. Top-secret stuff. She's a dark horse. Loads of secrets, our Bunty. I reckon she was quite racy when she was young. I've seen photos

– she was really pretty. All pin curls and red lipstick and hourglass-shaped.'

Lucy thought of the glamorous photos she'd seen of Bunty when she was younger and nodded in agreement. She was fascinated with the story of Bletchley Park. It had taken years before what had been going on in all those little huts had come out, and even now there were men and women who hadn't shared their stories because they'd stuck firmly to the rule they'd been given. They'd signed the Official Secrets Act, and that was that. She'd watched countless television documentaries with the people who had talked, and they were all so matter-of-fact, all of them saying the same thing – that they'd *just been doing their bit* – when in fact they were a vital part of the war effort. It would be amazing if she could get a first-hand account of what it had been like from Bunty.

'I'll ask her.'

'Just get her in the right mood. You've probably not had a chance to spend much time with her yet.'

Lucy shook her head. 'A quick cup of tea yesterday, that's all. I get the distinct impression that I'm surplus to requirements, but I have to try and find a way to offer help, even if she doesn't really want it.'

'God, I don't envy you. She's a cantankerous old bugger.' Mel laughed and took a sip of her coffee. 'I mean, I love her to bits, but – yeah. Just time it right and she might share her secrets with you. Get it wrong and you'll be booted out the door.'

They both laughed.

'So what made you leave teaching? I've read loads of stuff about people being threatened with knives and all sorts. We don't have that round here, but I'm sure it'll be a matter of time. It's bloody scary.'

'It wasn't the pupils.' Without thinking, she rubbed a hand on her temple, thinking of the pain she'd felt that last day of school before the illness struck. 'Just the usual stuff you read about in the papers. Stress, that sort of thing.'

'Have you given it up for good?'

Lucy shook her head. 'No, but I think when I do go back it'll be part time, or I'll work somewhere that's not so stressy. So much of it depends on the management team.'

'Ugh.' Mel shuddered. 'Just the words *management team* make me feel uncomfortable. Well, you've come to the right place then. There's nothing much going on here. The biggest stress is Helen Bromsgrove worrying that we might not win Britain's Best Kept Village or feature in the *Guardian*'s most desirable country escapes.' She pulled a face.

'Who is Helen Bromsgrove?'

Flo appeared at that moment with their food. She and Mel exchanged glances.

'Oh, you'll meet her soon enough. She's like the upper-class version of Beth. Likes to think she runs the place. Chair of the village school PTA, chair of the WI committee, chair of blooming everything. She's power mad.'

'She wants the whole place to look perfect. I've seen her eyeing up the old telephone box. I reckon that'll be her new project.' Flo wiped her hands on her apron and replaced them on her hips. 'Over my dead body. She can't just wipe out bits of history.'

'It is a bit knackered,' Mel said, stirring sugar into her coffee.

'Do you mean the one on the green opposite Bunty's house?'

They both nodded.

'Nobody uses it any more, because – well, who uses phone boxes these days? Anyway, apparently BT are decommissioning it. I mean, yeah, I reckon there's been the odd after-the-pub wee in there—'

'Mmm.' Lucy nodded. 'Yeah, I opened the door to look inside the day I arrived.'

'Ugh,' Flo giggled. 'Why on earth would you do that?'

'Well, it's a phone box. The receiver was off. I think it just brought back memories.'

'God, yeah. Memories of the days before mobile phones,' Flo said.

'As it happens, I've got happy memories of snogging in that phone box as a teenager.' Mel looked misty-eyed for a moment. 'I don't want it ripped out.'

'Nor me. I reckon we should put an anti-Helen fence around it, or something. Anyway, I better get on.' Flo nodded towards the counter. 'Customers waiting.'

'I'm sure there's something we could use it for,' Mel said thoughtfully. 'Just have to work out what. But I don't want it just wiped out because people like Helen think it's making the place look untidy.'

'You know it's the topic for discussion at the village meeting tonight. You'll be going, I take it?' Flo called across the cafe.

'No bloody chance.' Mel shook her head.

A few moments later, after Flo had served her customers, she came back over to their table again, pulling up a chair and sitting down. Lucy felt caught halfway between awkwardness because she hardly knew either of the women, and an unexpected desire to be part of something. She hadn't come to Little Maudley for companionship or intrigue, and yet here she was, with both. Flo lowered her voice.

'I've been roped in to take the minutes because Judith's got a cold. You bloody well will come – I'm not going in there alone. I'll get beaten to death by Helen's opinions.'

'Oh for goodness' sake.' Mel looked at Lucy. 'You could join us?'

Lucy shook her head. 'I don't think . . .' She frowned. 'Isn't Saturday night a strange time of the week for a village meeting?'

'Yes. It's all to do with Helen's drive to bring the community together, apparently. Oh, go on,' urged Mel. 'In fact, there'll probably be people there you can talk to about war stuff. There were lots of families involved, one way or another. They sent loads of evacuees out here from London.'

What was the alternative – a quick pop in to say hello and check on Bunty, then an evening watching terrible Saturday night TV?

'Oh, go on then.'

'Excellent.' Mel gave Flo a wink. 'Another victim. I'll call for you at seven.'

Popping in to see Bunty, Lucy was momentarily surprised when the door was opened by a tall, silver-haired man in a jacket and tie.

'Oh – hello.'

'You must be Lucy.'

She smiled, hesitantly.

'Gordon. Bunty's son?'

'Oh gosh, of course, I'm so sorry.'

'Come in. She's inside. We were just about to leave, actually.'

Bunty was sitting not in the kitchen this time, but in a tall, upright armchair by the fireplace. The afternoon sun lit the room with a golden glow, making it feel as warm as if the fire was lit. Mr Darcy was sitting on the arm of Bunty's chair, his tail curled in a proprietorial manner over her hand.

'Ah, Lucy. You've met Gordon, then?'

'Just.'

He waved an arm, indicating to her to sit down on the sofa. 'Margaret's just making a cup of tea for Mother. I'll get her to make you one, too.'

Bunty gave him a sideways look. 'Are you planning to give Lucy here a list of things to do to get me organized?'

She said the word *organized* as if it was a dreadful prospect.

'No,' Gordon gave Lucy a smile as he went to open the door. 'I wouldn't dream of it.'

'I just thought I'd pop in – I'm sorry, I didn't realize you had visitors.'

'Don't worry, these two are off to dinner with friends in Oxford. Margaret was just dropping in some meals she's made for the freezer.'

'Oh that's nice,' said Lucy.

Bunty made a face and lowered her voice, leaning over towards her slightly. 'Not really. Fish pie and shepherd's pie. Nursery food. I don't really like either.'

'I love both.'

'Well, that's good news for both of us. When she's gone, you can take them and pop them in the freezer at Bluebell Cottage. She'll be none the wiser, and I can have what I want to have for my meals.' Bunty gave a quiet chuckle.

'Here we are. Hello, Lucy. You seem to be settling in well, by the looks of things?' Margaret appeared with two cups of tea on a tray.

'I am,' said Lucy, feeling quite pleased with herself that she had something to report. 'In fact, I'm going to a meeting at the village hall this evening.'

'Well, I never.' Bunty chuckled. 'Did you get roped in by Helen already?'

'No, I met a girl called Mel who trains dogs. Then we ended up going to the cafe together, and somehow the next thing I knew I was caught up in a conversation about the village phone box, and—'

'Mel's a nice girl. I'm glad you've met someone of your own age to chat to. Now, what's this about the telephone box?' Bunty looked up, her blue eyes sharp.

'Oh, something about it being taken away because it's in disrepair.'

'It is in a bit of a state, right enough.' Gordon hooked a finger round the lace curtain and peered out. 'Funny, I haven't paid it any attention in years.'

'You're not the only one,' said Margaret. 'It's an eyesore. Nobody uses it these days. They could get rid of it and put a nice bench there instead.'

Lucy caught Bunty giving Margaret a gimlet stare, but said nothing. Gordon and Magaret left soon afterwards, making their apologies and somehow taking forever to depart. Margaret kept fussing over Bunty and whether she needed anything.

'Don't worry,' Lucy pointed out, 'I'm here if she does.'

'I think she expects me to keel over at any moment. She was exactly the same when Janey was a little girl.' Bunty pointed to a photograph on the mantelpiece of a much younger Gordon and Margaret with a fair-haired girl of about twenty. 'Sometimes I wonder if that's why she disappeared off to Canada as soon as she could.'

'Is she your granddaughter?'

'Yes. Lovely girl. She's a doctor in a town outside Calgary. Three children and a very nice husband. Funny that she should end up with a Canadian, of all things.'

Surely, Lucy thought, standing up to look more closely at the picture, ending up with a Canadian was one of the more obvious side effects of moving to Canada? There was another picture beside it – this one more recent. Unmistakably the same girl, but older now, with her arm around three children in ski gear – all brown from the sun, and with the same bright blue eyes and blonde hair.

'Do you see them often?' She turned to look at Bunty, who was stroking a contentedly dozing Mr Darcy.

'No.' Bunty looked up. 'It's just the way of things, sadly. Flights are expensive, and it's a long way to come when there's so much for the children to do over there in the holidays. But we speak on the telephone.' She gave a snort of laughter. 'She calls me up sometimes to despair about her mother.'

Lucy wanted to say that Margaret seemed well-meaning, if a bit bossy; but she thought perhaps it wasn't her place. So she just smiled, sipped her tea and said nothing.

When she left shortly afterwards, Bunty – who had switched on the television and was about to watch a wildlife documentary – looked up briefly.

'Bring that little dog tomorrow when you come. I'd like to say hello. And if you hear any interesting village gossip, I want to know all about it.'

'I promise on both counts.' She raised her eyebrows knowingly, and left with an armful of frozen meals. It might be her imagination, but Bunty seemed to be thawing, slowly.

Meanwhile, at the village hall, it turned out that the gossip machine had already rolled into action.

'Hello. You're the young lady who's interested in the Second World War, aren't you?'

Lucy nodded.

'Told you, you can't keep anything to yourself round here,' Mel muttered to her. They'd only just walked in the door of the village hall; Lucy was still taking in the scent of wooden floors and school PE shoes, and wondering how all village halls seemed to smell the same. Mel was standing at the shoulder of an elderly woman who was wearing a lemon-yellow twinset and a pearl necklace, her hair blue-rinsed and neatly set.

'This is Susan.' She held out a papery hand. 'Very nice to meet you.'

'Hello.' Lucy was wondering how on earth she had already heard of her.

'My bridge partner Henry was sitting in the cafe when you were chatting this morning. He sent me a text message to tell me that he thought I'd be very excited to meet you. And I am.' She beamed at Lucy and took her arm. 'Why don't you sit down over here beside me and I'll get you a cup of tea and a biscuit. I'm sure we'll have lots to chat about. In fact, you might be just what we need.'

Sorry, mouthed Mel as Lucy looked back over her shoulder in alarm while Susan towed her away with surprising firmness.

'Little Maudley has an absolutely *fascinating* war history, as I'm sure you'll already know. I've written several articles about it for the local newspaper – you've

109

very possibly read them already – and I'm known as something of an expert in these parts.'

'I've only just arrived,' Lucy stuttered, looking across at Mel, who was helpless with laughter.

'Well, of course you're with the expert – not that she'll talk to you about it, of course – but Bunty was involved in something *TS* during the war.' Susan paused for a moment and waited for Lucy to look confused, which she did. 'Top Secret,' she continued, looking pleased, and tapping the side of her nose. 'Anyway, if you're looking for something to keep you busy, I've got just the thing that should be right up your street—'

She was interrupted by the very loud clearing of a throat, designed to catch everyone's attention.

'More in a moment,' she hissed, putting a finger to her lips. 'Better let the boss have her say.'

'Hello, everyone, terribly sorry I'm late,' said a booming, very well-spoken voice. It carried through the porch and into the room and had the effect of making everyone sit up straight. A moment later the voice was followed by a tall blonde woman in a white shirt and neatly pressed navy blue trousers, with a jaunty polka-dot scarf tied round her neck. She could have been any age between thirty and fifty. It was the woman with the Breton top who had spoken to her the day she'd arrived, Lucy realized. Chin lifted slightly, she did a sweep of the room, nodding and smiling to people as she made her way to the front where a chair sat ready beside a small oak table. She gave Lucy an extra smile of greeting, and sat down.

'Here we are.' She took a sip of water.

'That's Helen Bromsgrove,' whispered Susan. 'She's absolutely wonderful.'

That wasn't quite how Mel had described her, Lucy thought, hiding a smile. But she had to admit, Helen was pretty dynamic. Taking an iPad from her handbag, she whizzed through the first few items on the agenda (recycling bins, church roof fundraiser, don't forget to save your *plarstic* bottle tops for the preschool) and then got on to the topic *de jour*.

'And – I won't keep you too long, because I'm sure you're all desperate to get a cup of tea and some of Susan's excellent fairy cakes – just one last thing. Well, really, a rather pressing thing. We need to talk about the telephone box on the green.'

Mel caught Lucy's eye. *Here we go*, she mouthed.

'It's an eyesore, it's dilapidated, there are no plans for British Telecom – or whatever they're called these days – to sort it out, and in fact it's up for decommissioning.'

'Wouldn't take much to clear it up,' someone pointed out. Several people turned to see who had spoken, but nobody owned up.

'Wouldn't take much to knock it down,' said Helen briskly. 'And we could replace it with something far nicer, like a bench or a floral display. A floral display, of course, would tie in rather nicely to our Britain in Bloom plans.' She paused, looking rather pleased with herself.

'The phone box has always been the heart of the village.'

'Has it?' Helen looked disdainful. 'When we inspected it the other day, it smelled very strongly of – ' she grimaced and lowered her voice – 'male urine.'

'If you've got to go, you've got to go,' called a wag from the back of the room. Several people chortled for a moment. Helen looked back at them with slightly lifted eyebrows and a schoolmarmish expression.

'Anyway, I think perhaps we should have a full discussion of the benefits of removing it and replacing it with something more *in keeping* with our lovely village.'

There was a murmur. Lucy couldn't work out whether it was agreement or dissent. Helen clapped her hands together and continued, 'I think that's everything covered. And now one thing we can all agree on is – tea.'

'I met all my boyfriends at the phone box,' said Mel as they gathered round the tea table.

'The emphasis being on the *all*,' Flo said, laughing.

'Shut it, you.' Mel nudged her. Lucy stood with a cup of tea in one hand and an iced fairy cake in the other.

'I'm quite fond of the phone box, myself,' said Susan, reappearing. 'Now, about what we were discussing earlier.'

Mel widened her eyes. Susan somehow wedged herself between them and started explaining that she was trying to write a booklet for the Women's Institute that would feature some of the women in the village, and talk about their history. 'It's been eighty years since we started the WI here in Little Maudley, and we thought perhaps it would be nice to look back at some of the women who've been a part of it all along. And with you being a historian, you might find some interesting information.'

'I'd love to help.'

It was a history nerd's idea of heaven – chatting to elderly people about their memories of the past. Susan beamed at her, and then caught a glimpse of someone else in the room who she was clearly planning to commandeer.

Mel, who had vanished briefly, reappeared bearing a plate of fairy cakes. 'Susan, would you mind terribly if I borrowed Lucy for a moment?'

'Not at all. I must talk to Geoff Lewis about the line painting on the cricket green. I'll pop round one morning to the cottage, Lucy, and give you a list of people to chat to.'

'That sounds wonderful.'

Mel hooked her elbow and gently tugged her away.

'I'm so sorry, I should have known she'd commandeer you. She's got a good heart, but if you're not careful she'll tell you in incredibly boring detail about the entire history of the village going back to the Domesday Book.'

Lucy opened her mouth to say that actually the idea sounded quite interesting, but Mel nudged her again. 'Watch out, Queen Bee coming through.'

'Hello,' said a hearty voice behind Lucy. She turned. 'Helen Bromsgrove. We said hello the other day. Lovely to see you here. I hear you're a historian. How exciting!'

'I'm not, I'm just . . .' Lucy began. 'Well, sort of,' she finished, lamely.

'Awfully good of you to come along to our village

meeting, even though you're not a local. Very sweet of you. It takes a village, they say – and a village doesn't get anywhere unless everyone gets involved.'

Lucy sipped her tea and smiled.

'Anyway, very nice to see you. We have a cinema night here next Friday, and we're showing the *Mamma Mia!* sequel. Why don't you come along and join us?'

Lucy made a polite noise which she hoped passed for a yes.

'Marvellous,' said Helen. 'We'll see you then.'

'And that,' Mel intoned, as Helen made her way off to say hello and press the flesh with some other villagers, 'is how you find yourself assimilated. You're one of us now – there's no escape.'

Chapter Seven

As she'd done for donkey's years, Bunty had woken early and followed her usual routine: cup of tea in bed while listening to Radio 3 (it was often a bit much, but she couldn't bear the adverts on Classic FM) and waiting until the news at seven before rising for a quick wash. She'd never got out of the habit, despite Gordon and Margaret insisting on paying for a fancy shower. Never saw the point. In, quick scrub, and back out and downstairs, ready to face the day. She was a creature of habit. This house had been home for so long that she could scarcely imagine living anywhere else. All those brochures about sheltered accommodation – she shuddered. Even the phrase made her feel queasy. It smacked of overcooked Brussels sprouts and organized activities and everything that she couldn't bear. No, she'd lived here for as long as she could remember, and she'd prefer to die with her boots on, ideally in a peaceful manner.

Not that she had any intention of popping off just yet. The front garden was overrun with weeds, for one thing. She pulled on her gardening gloves and tied on her apron. If she did half an hour before nine, she could sit down with a cup of tea and listen to *In Our Time* on the radio.

The early morning sun was shining in a very pleasant way on her back when she heard a familiar voice calling hello.

'Hello, my darling.' She looked up with pleasure to see Freya, long hair tied in two low bunches, crossing the road. She was dressed in jeans and a white gingham shirt.

'Are you finished with school now?'

'Last day today.' She indicated her clothes. 'But it's mufti day, so we can wear what we like. And we're finishing at lunchtime. I can't wait.'

'Are they working you too hard?'

She shook her head, laughing. 'Not until next year when we start our GCSEs. But I'm so tired –' she yawned, on cue – 'and I just want to chill out and do nothing for the holidays.'

'So no big plans?'

Freya shrugged. 'Dad's working and Cammie's going to stay with her gran for a bit, so I'll just be hanging around.'

'Well, if you need anything to keep you occupied, I'm always here.'

'I'd like that.' Freya brightened. 'Oh, there's Dad.'

'Morning.'

'Freya was just telling me she's off for the summer from this afternoon.'

'Yeah, and I've got to work to keep her in books now the library is closing.'

'It is?' Bunty frowned.

'Yes, and there's no way Dad's going to be able to keep up with my reading habits.'

'You're welcome to help yourself to anything from my shelves.' Bunty had always been a voracious reader – it was nice that even in these days of computers and mobile phones, Freya was still keen.

'Oh, really?' Freya's heart-shaped face brightened as she carried on. 'Thank you. First they closed the mobile library, now they're getting rid of the one in town. And then they complain that literacy levels are dropping.'

Sam grinned and shook his head. 'I have no idea where you came from, sometimes.'

Freya shot him an odd look. 'Well, I didn't get my reading habits from you, that's for sure. Bunty, did you hear Dad's taken up a spot of light burglary on the side?'

Bunty chuckled, leaning back against the wall and folding her arms. 'No, I did not. Sam, what have you been up to?'

Sam pushed a hand through his dark curls, ducking his head and looking faintly embarrassed as he told the tale of being chased out of the garden of Bluebell Cottage by an irate Lucy.

'I'm sorry,' Bunty said, putting down her battered old secateurs. 'But that is priceless.' Sam was so earnest and sweet, his dark brows furrowed in concern.

'You didn't think to tell me someone had moved into the cottage?'

'Slipped my mind.' She chuckled, teasing him. 'I am

getting on a bit, you know. The old grey matter isn't what it once was.'

Sam shook his head.

'Dad.' Freya looked at her phone, checking the time. 'We need to go – I'm supposed to be in for half nine, remember?'

'Oh, of course. I'm all out of sorts because you're not in at the usual time. Right, let's get off.'

Bunty watched as the two of them headed back to the Land Rover and drove off towards Bletchingham. They were like two peas in a pod – both tall, with the same easy, long-legged stride and dark hair.

'Morning.'

Goodness, it was all go today. She was just pulling off her gloves, mindful of the time, when Lucy appeared with a giddy Westie on the end of his lead. The small terrier was panting and looking thoroughly overexcited. Lucy already looked noticeably less stressed, she was glad to see. She'd seemed quite pale and wan when she'd arrived with Margaret the other day.

'Hello, young chap. What's your name?'

'This is Hamish.'

'Hello, Hamish.'

Hamish wagged his tail, panting in the sunshine.

'I'm going to take him for a walk, but if there's anything you need?'

Bunty shook her head. 'I've got a parcel to send to my grandchildren in Canada, if you don't mind?'

'Not at all.'

'Come in, and I'll just find it for you.'

Lucy's little dog trotted into the cottage behind her and then stopped dead in the kitchen doorway. His hackles shot up and he growled as if he'd seen a ghost. Of course; it was Stanley, who was sitting in his glass tank, minding his own business. Not that Hamish believed that. It took a good few gravy bones as bribery before he'd cross the threshold into the kitchen, and even then he looked at Stanley's tank with a suspicious expression. Poor little chap. She gave the parcel to Lucy and saw her out.

A few moments later Bunty watched as a gaggle of children on bikes met up on the green, sitting with their backs to the phone box, drinking cartons of apple juice and laughing and chatting. Of course a bench would do just as well, but the idea of the phone box being gone made her heart squeeze with sadness. It was, in a funny way, the heart of the village. Once upon a time, before people had telephones at home, there had often been a little queue of people waiting outside to use it. And of course – well, for her it had a special significance.

Later that afternoon, having made some scones and left them to cool, Bunty carried on pottering around the garden. She had some plants which could do with repotting, and while the weather was holding she might as well get them sorted.

It was a beautiful summer day, the kind she'd always loved best. Swallows were looping back and forth in a hazy sky, and the cherry tree outside the kitchen window was heavy with fruit. It was always precious, but particularly so when one was grimly aware that it might be the last time one saw it all. Old age was a bore. And Margaret, who had been round again that afternoon with Gordon as they passed by on their way home from Oxford, still wouldn't admit that the sudden onslaught of brochures from old folks' homes was anything to do with her. She'd be measuring her up for a coffin next. It was such a strange, narrowing sort of feeling. As if her focus had shifted. It was easier to live within the confines of the village, and this street. Sometimes when she lay in bed at night she liked to run through things that had happened in the past, wondering how she'd ended up here. Such an odd sequence of events.

Of course – she tugged at a particularly stubborn geranium which had adhered itself to the terracotta pot – it had all been stirred up when the truth started to come out about what had happened at Bletchley Park during the war. She pulled – hard – and plant and pot were separated. The roots were a thick, tangled mass. Not dissimilar, she reflected, to the tissue of lies and half-truths that had kept everyone in the dark about what they did. So many years of keeping what she'd done secret. It wasn't even the half of it. She teased at the roots gently, loosening them off before placing the plant carefully into a new, slightly bigger pot of compost. So many secrets. She'd buried most of them with Len. Pushing in earth around the edges of the pot to hold the geranium firmly in place made her think fleetingly of the handfuls of soil they'd thrown down on his coffin. She looked across the green, past the telephone box, to the churchyard beyond. There he was, sleeping. She must go and put some flowers on his grave. Margaret would have been over there this weekend, of course. She never missed a birthday or an anniversary. But – Bunty shook the peat from her hands, then rubbed her arms, feeling suddenly chilly. It wasn't the weather. It was the thought of him lying in his heavy oak coffin, decomposing. Such a grim way to go. It amused her to think that Margaret, who liked to have everything in order, had no idea that Bunty had already booked and paid for her own cremation and written a careful list of what she did – and more importantly, didn't – want at the service. God knows Margaret would probably ignore most of it in any case, and it would be done as tastefully and inexpensively as her daughter-in-law could manage.

She pulled off her gardening gloves, finger by finger. Goodness, it never ceased to amaze her how *old* her hands looked. The hands of her grandmother. The knuckles swelled on bony fingers spotted with age.

She looked down the lane, casting an eye over the row of cottages beside the churchyard where Sam and Freya lived. He needed to cut back that wisteria. Ridiculous that he was so busy helping others that he didn't seem to have time to do things like that; but then, he was bringing up Freya alone. And doing a good job of it, too.

Sam was such a good, kind boy. She'd known him all his life, watched him grow up into a handsome young man. If only he'd meet a nice girl and settle down. It was a terrible waste. Wasn't like that in our day, she thought. The telephone box caught her eye once again and she smiled, remembering. If there was one thing that war taught us, it was that we should take our brief pleasures where we found them.

She put a hand on the wall and eased herself up to standing. Goodness, everything was so *slow* to move these days.

Bunty gathered up the handful of lavender she'd trimmed, intending to dry it by the Aga later. Perhaps she'd have a little doze in the armchair before cooking something for dinner.

When she woke two hours later it was chilly, and the sun had gone from the east-facing room. She'd read years ago that doing the crossword and keeping active were the keys to staying well and not losing one's marbles in old age. Well – she eased herself up from the armchair – at ninety-six she still had a reasonable complement of marbles, and she was still as healthy as a horse. That was something, she supposed. All those crosswords she'd done in the past had stood her in good stead. If she hadn't done that particular one and filled it in, she mightn't have ended up at Bletchley Park for the war, and then she wouldn't have been here, and . . . well. Life would have been very different indeed.

There was a knock at the door.

'Hello,' Lucy called. She popped her head around the door. Her face was flushed slightly pink.

Hard to think of her teaching a class of unruly teenagers. She was quite diffident – almost shy. But perhaps she put on a persona when she walked into the classroom. Bunty's friend Milly had been full of mischief, and yet one would never have guessed. She'd ruled her schoolroom with a rod of iron. Bunty looked up, realizing that Lucy was still hovering in the doorway.

'Do come in.' She shooed Mr Darcy off the chair and waved a hand to indicate Lucy could sit. Lucy sat. The little Westie looked at Mr Darcy hopefully, wagging his tail. Mr Darcy, who had seen off more dogs in his time than Hamish could count, made his way to the top of the bookcase and looked down at Hamish with narrowed eyes, tail twitching in irritation.

'Are you all right?'

'Just bumped into Helen Bromsgrove when I was out for a walk. She really does talk a lot. I had to make my excuses and run, literally.'

'Ah, that's why you're pink.'

Lucy put her hands to her cheeks. 'Yes.' She laughed. 'I couldn't think of an excuse, so I told her I'd left something in the oven.'

'And what was Helen saying?'

'She was going on about the plans she mentioned the other night – she's desperate to get rid of the old telephone box on the village green. I don't know why – I think it's lovely. Anyway, I think she's trying to get as many people as she can on side. And –' Lucy sounded breathless with excitement – 'I've been asked to help write a booklet about women in war for the WI, to celebrate their eightieth anniversary.'

'The telephone box?' Bunty sat forward and clasped her hands together, tightly. She took a careful, measured intake of breath.

'She thinks it's an eyesore. That's what the meeting was about – well, that and various other things. But apparently it's being decommissioned so they can opt to take over maintenance of it, or get rid of it.'

'And she'd rather whip out almost a century of history than give it a lick of paint.' How utterly depressing, and yet how predictable, thought Bunty. She sighed. 'I was just thinking about my friend Milly, who was a schoolteacher here during the war. We used to meet our friends at that telephone box before we went to dances in the village hall.'

'Oh, really?'

'Yes,' Bunty smiled. 'When I was washing dishes for our landlady when I first moved here, I used to look out and see couples meeting there. It looked incredibly romantic. But I don't expect Helen has much time for romance. She's more the practical sort.'

'Well, no – exactly.' Lucy grimaced.

'Such a lot of history in that one phone box; but it's not the sort of history that makes the news. It's the day-to-day stuff. I don't suppose that sort of thing matters when it comes to the history books, does it?'

'This is exactly the sort of history I love.' Lucy looked at her, clearly eager for more information. 'So you said you came here during the war?'

'I did, yes. I was seventeen. I came here to work.'

'That must have been a change from Walthamstow?'

Goodness, the girl didn't miss a trick. Bunty had only mentioned where she lived in passing.

'Yes, quite a change. Of course, the village was quite a bit smaller then – the houses up on the Rise were built in the 1960s, and the new houses were built in the gardens of Yew House.'

'I passed the Rise when I was out for a walk up to the woods the other day.'

'I suspect Helen doesn't approve of it, either. She'd like the village to be a picture postcard version, but that's not what this place is. Or was, for that matter.'

Lucy asked a few more questions, but Bunty found herself keeping the answers brief. Keeping mum had been the habit of a lifetime, and she didn't hold with what the papers called *oversharing*. Such a dreadful description, and yet all too apt. Young people these days seemed to spill out every little detail about their personal lives to anyone who'd listen. That was one thing she wouldn't miss – she gave a brief laugh. Of late, she'd noticed herself referring to the things she wouldn't miss, as if she was planning to move somewhere new and interesting, rather than her next destination being a rather more final one. It would be nice to have a good, solid faith. She'd stood in the church many times over the years and wondered how it would feel to actually *believe* all that stuff. Maybe, after all, when the time came and Anno Domini took over, she'd discover that there was in fact a friendly angel sitting on a cloud waiting to welcome her. It would be quite nice if there was. Restful.

'. . . So I just thought I'd pop in and check if there was anything you needed, as I'm off to Bletchley Park tomorrow first thing.' Lucy's voice broke through her thoughts.

'No, thank you, dear. But I'm glad you did, because I've had another chance to say hello to Hamish. Isn't he lovely?'

Hamish rolled over at her feet and waved his paws in the air. He was a merry little thing, with shiny button eyes and a wet glossy black nose. He rolled back to upright and licked her hand, nudging her for treats.

'There are some doggy chocolate drops in the tin there on the top of the bookcase.'

Lucy stood up, smiling, and took a couple out. She handed them over, saying, 'You'll be a friend for life now.'

'Well, that's good news.'

Hamish snuffled them up in an instant.

'So tell me what you've found out about Little Maudley during the war. Have you been doing lots of reading?'

'Well, yes,' Lucy said, reaching down to scratch Hamish behind the ears. 'Although I think it's much nicer when you actually hear it from the horse's mouth, so to speak. But there seem to have been so many evacuees here, not to mention the Land Girls and the Wrens who were billeted here from the air bases nearby. Did you meet lots of them?'

Bunty chuckled. 'You could say that, yes. This little

village was just stuffed full. The school was packed with little urchins from the East End, and one couldn't move for Land Girls. They were either brilliant or utterly hopeless, in my experience.'

'What do you mean?'

'Oh, well – some of them worked as hard as they could. The others – quite a few of them were a bit posh – came from nice families and wanted to do their bit. They spent more time leaning on pitchforks and mooning over the airmen than they did working on the farm. I remember the farmer's wife having a good old grumble about them every time she came to visit Mrs Brown. They were friends, you see, and they had tea together once a week. Always time for tea, even in wartime.'

'You see what I mean? You've made the stories sound more alive than a textbook ever could.'

After Lucy had left, Bunty found that the memories she usually kept well buried were now floating around in her mind, distracting her. She went to the dresser in the kitchen, pulling open the drawer with difficulty – gosh, it was stiff – and looking inside.

There it was. A black notebook with lined white pages, turned yellow with age. She opened it and looked at her own handwriting.

May 30th, 1941

Got home from King's Cross feeling wretched after a parlous train journey. Even the trains to Walthamstow are packed in like sardines now. We were absolutely crammed together – I couldn't even lift a hand to scratch my nose. But it's terribly exciting. I've been plucked from my position at Electra House and given a train warrant, and I'm being sent to Bletchley. I had to look up Bletchley on the map to find out where it was, and I'm rather puzzled as to what I can possibly do out there in the middle of the Buckinghamshire countryside.

I can hardly wait to find out what we'll be doing. Tessa has joined the Land Army because her mother didn't want her doing war work, and they don't ask for parental permission. Luckily I'm old enough that I can do what I like – luckier still, dear Mother and Dad are quite happy for me to do my bit. Gosh, it's dark this evening – darker than usual. I'm scribbling this by candlelight – Dad's such a stickler for the blackout – and I can hardly see a thing. I wonder what my digs will be like. Maybe I'll be in a big house somewhere or in billets with some nice girls. It feels rather wrong to be thrilled by the idea of doing war work, but I am . . .

She smiled at her past self. If only she'd known. Almost-eighteen-year-old Bunty had been so caught up in the glamour of it all, and the excitement of leaving Walthamstow for something as important as war work, that it hadn't even occurred to her that she might end up stuck for the duration in Little Maudley. Nor – she closed the book and slid it back into the drawer, covering it over with a pile of neatly folded napkins smelling of mothballs, dry wood and dust – that she'd still be here all these years later. And that they'd be threatening to rip out that telephone box, of all things.

She put a hand to her chest and closed her eyes for a moment. Long, long-forgotten memories flooded back. No – she pushed the drawer closed – some things were best left in the past. Lucy would have countless memories from people who wanted to tell their stories. Hers could stay where it belonged.

Chapter Eight

Bletchley Park was a revelation for Lucy. Having read about it over the years and been inspired by the story of Dr Sue Black, who drove people on social media to get involved in raising the money needed to preserve it for future generations, it gave her goosebumps to walk in the gate and see the huts for herself. It was living history, and she was in heaven. Despite arriving there as the doors opened and stopping only briefly for lunch at the cafe in hut 4, she couldn't begin to take it all in. Not only was the old manor house restored and full of atmosphere, but the huts were so authentic that they gave her chills of excitement. She paused there, taking in the old-fashioned manual typewriters and the gloomy, claustrophobic rooms where men and women had spent the whole of the war years crammed together, each working hard on a piece of a project. But there had almost never been any sense of resolution for them – just relentless, exhausting, never-ending work. In each hut there was a fat little stove that heated the room and belched out fumes; on the backs of doors, gas masks were hung up for safekeeping. It was lovely to wander about at her own pace, reading the information on the boards and listening to the spoken histories recorded by Bletchley veterans. The last time she'd been on a school trip to the Imperial War Museum in London, she'd been so busy trying to stop the two troublemakers from year nine from sneaking off to McDonald's that she'd hardly had a chance to take anything in. It was so lovely to see how excited the curators were to show her around. She'd even had a turn on the machine herself, and failed dismally at the crossword they'd used to lure the brightest minds to work at the Park on their top-secret missions.

She drifted around, soaking it all in, and then spent ages looking around the gift shop, picking up yet more books and a lovely warm Bletchley Park sweatshirt to wear on chilly evenings walking Hamish.

'And the lovely thing, dear,' said the woman on the front desk as she left, sore-footed and with a head full of stories – 'is that your ticket lasts all year, so you can come back as often as you like.'

'Oh, I will.' Lucy hugged herself as she spun round for a final look before heading reluctantly to her car and heading home.

'Hello, dear. Been somewhere exciting?' It was Susan, walking a chocolate Labrador. She paused to take in the massive pile of books Lucy was unloading from the back of her car.

'Very.' Lucy had amassed tons of notes and bought up most of the bookshop.

'Ah, Bletchley Park. Now – I must get you to come

along to the WI meeting next week. There are quite a few people I'd like you to meet.'

'Oh, really?'

'Yes, I've been telling people about our little history book idea and it's rather snowballed. It turns out that everyone wants to see their name in print, even if it is just for our little anniversary book.'

'Oh, that's lovely. I'll look forward to it.'

'See if you can bring Mel along. We need some new blood. It's so nice to have young people ready to take up the baton and keep the heart of the village beating.' Susan clapped her hands with delight. Her Labrador rootled around in the long grass, investigating a discarded ice-cream wrapper.

Lucy didn't like to remind her that she was only there temporarily, when she seemed so delighted to have some new bodies coming along. And she didn't really know Mel, so inviting her – a relative stranger – to come along to a meeting in a town where she was the incomer felt a bit awkward. She smiled politely, nonetheless.

'This is all very exciting – so nice to have someone to help with getting this booklet together. Haven't been to Bletchley for years and years. I hear it's all very exciting now. I think the last time I went, it was just some tired old huts.'

'Oh no – there was so much to do. Loads of amazing people who were full of stories, and so much information.'

*

Mel fell into step beside Sam as he walked along the lane towards the village shop. He turned to look at her. She was wearing a pair of sawn-off jeans, more practical than fashionable, a slightly grubby polo shirt and two dog leads hanging round her neck. Fairly standard Mel, he thought.

'Bloody hell. Where did you spring from?'

'Sorry.' She turned around, indicating a break in the hedge between two rows of cottages. 'I nipped down the path. I was just returning Harvey's delinquent Dalmatian after an afternoon of training.'

Harvey was an old school friend of theirs. He'd always been the one with a hare-brained scheme for making money, or making people laugh. Now he was a dad of five and ran a computer business from his scruffy, ramshackle cottage, which was a thorn in the side of the village improvement society. His latest family addition – a ten-month-old Dalmatian puppy – was as loved but as out of control as his children, who orbited the cottage on an assortment of bicycles and scooters, sticky with lollipop juice and grubby but happy.

'How did it go?' They paused for a second, waiting for a car to reverse into the driveway of one of the pretty houses on Main Street.

'I'm winning. Well, I will be.' She made a face. 'Apparently he took him on from a woman in Northampton who couldn't cope, so he's not really house-trained, and as for his recall – well . . .'

'Yeah, that'll be why I had to catch him haring down

the street the other morning. Typical Harvey. Why he couldn't just get a nice easy-going Labrador or something, I'll never know.'

'Because that would be too easy. Talking of which, how are things with Freya?'

'All right. She's glued to her phone or her laptop, and she's allergic to daylight. You don't think she's a vampire, do you?'

Mel laughed. 'Not unless Cammie is too. Honestly, I think I'm turning into my mother. If it's not *turn those lights off*, it's *were you born in a barn?* I have no idea how I've ended up sounding like an adult.'

'You are one?' Sam said.

'Never.' Mel recoiled in horror.

They walked through the village, which was buzzing with the sounds of summer holidays – children up way past their usual bedtimes were whizzing along the path on bikes, and the air was filled with the smell of barbecue smoke and sizzling sausages. Behind the wall of Helen's house they could hear the pop of a bottle being opened and the tinkle of laughter.

'Oh God, that reminds me – '

'What, champagne being opened?'

'No, Helen's place.' She dropped her voice. 'I don't want her catching us and dragging us in for drinkies, but it reminds me I wanted to ask if you'd come to this Abba night thing?' She indicated a poster tacked to the telegraph pole outside Helen's huge house.

'That'll be a no.' He shuddered. 'I can't stand Abba,

for one thing, and you know how I feel about organized fun, Helen-style.'

'Oh, come on. There'll be cakes,' Mel wheedled.

'I can get cakes any time I like. Look, here's the village shop. It's full of them.'

'That's not the point,' said Mel, shouldering the door open, 'and you know it. Anyway, Lucy's coming. Maybe you could come along and say hello, improve on your first meeting?'

'I could turn up in a stripy jumper with a bag with SWAG written on it, just to compound her image of me.' He picked up some biscuits and dropped them into the basket.

'Pleeeease? For me?'

'Oh, go on then.'

Mel beamed.

He wasn't going to admit it to Mel, because if he did he'd never hear the end of it, but there was a bit of him that had been hoping he'd bump into Lucy again after their slightly unfortunate first encounter. Maybe this way he could make it clear to her that he wasn't some sort of weirdo who made a habit of sneaking around in people's back gardens.

Chapter Nine

Over the next few days, Lucy tried several tentative attempts at getting Bunty to talk about her experience during the war, but to no avail. Every time she tried to steer the conversation round, she got nowhere. Once she bumped into Freya, the teenage girl who lived in the cottage opposite, and said a brief hello. But the days passed uneventfully. She met up with Susan for a cup of tea at the village cafe and was introduced to Henry, who had worked as an ARP warden during the war. He was the absolute opposite of Bunty – just bursting to tell her all about life in Little Maudley and his part in the war effort.

'Oh gosh, there was a lot going on here, considering it's such a sleepy little village.' Henry tore open a sachet of sugar with a gnarled, slightly shaky hand. He shook it into his mug and then carefully folded up the packet and placed it down on the tray. He was very neatly dressed in a shirt and a buttoned-up brown wool cardigan. His cuffs were fastened with monogrammed silver cufflinks. One of the things Lucy had noticed about all of the older people she'd spoken to was just how beautifully turned out they were. She smoothed down the front of her shirt, almost without thinking.

'I'd love to hear all about it. Bunty mentioned that there were lots of Land Girls here, working on the farms.'

Susan poured the tea and offered milk to Lucy. Beth, ostensibly busy refilling some village information leaflets on the rack just inside the cafe door, was craning her neck to listen in. Susan shot an old-fashioned look in her direction.

'Oh yes,' said Henry. 'Lots of those. And I was responsible for keeping everyone under control, which wasn't as easy as you might think in those days.' He gave a little chuckle of amusement, shaking his head.

Lucy nodded as Susan offered her a piece of fruit cake. She snapped it in half, popping a bit in her mouth. It was absolutely delicious.

'Len was Bunty's husband,' he said. Lucy didn't point out that she already knew that. 'He was quite a bit older than her – twenty-five to her eighteen when they met, if I remember correctly. He was the land agent for the big house back in those days, which meant he wasn't called up. I was an aircraft joiner over at the air base, so I was exempt as well. But we both felt the same way – we wanted to do our bit, so that's how we met. Right back before the beginning of the war we signed up as ARP wardens, but you might know it better as Civil Defence Service?'

Lucy nodded.

'You might think a sleepy little village like this wouldn't see much action, but you'd be surprised. We weren't that far from Bletchley Park – not that we knew

about it in those days, of course – and we had the air
base just along the road where they trained fighter pilots
to fly Blenheims. Lovely old planes, they were.'

Lucy was torn between wanting to write this all down,
asking him to stop talking so she could get out her phone
and record it, and just sitting there listening to his memories.

'He was a good old boy, Len. I miss him.' Henry tailed
off then, gazing out of the window.

'You see what I mean,' said Susan, cheerfully. 'Lots of
interesting information. And of course we have all the
women from the village who remember, as well.'

Lucy nodded. So many stories, and time was running
out to gather them before the people who'd lived
through the war years passed on. She wanted to gather
as many as she could – not the glamorous and exciting
tales of the men and women who'd been caught up on
the front line, but the everyday stories of the people
who'd lived through it all and how it had affected their
lives.

'Of course,' said Henry, beginning again, as if he'd
remembered halfway through gazing out of the window
that he was in the middle of a story, 'I'm sure you'll get
some good gen on what went on from Bunty.' He dipped
a biscuit in his tea. 'She had an interesting war.'

Susan looked at him fleetingly and shook her head.

'I've already spoken to her – not sure if you'll have
any more luck, Lucy?'

Lucy shook her head, remembering how Bunty had

begun to open up one afternoon but since then had resisted all attempts to bring the conversation round in that direction again.

'She doesn't seem keen to talk about it.'

'Oh, I know.' He lifted his cup to his mouth and then paused for a second, talking over it. 'Skeletons in cupboards, and all that. But she had – well, there's the top-secret stuff – I know she hasn't talked about that since the war – and that's not to mention that handsome chap.' He took a mouthful of tea.

'Which handsome chap?' Susan looked at him, intrigued.

'Oh, well. You know how it was in the war years. They trained Canadian and US airmen at that base I mentioned. The village hall was always busy. Dances, beetle drives, that sort of thing. We knew how to have fun. And all sorts of things used to happen in the blackout.'

'Goodness.' Susan looked surprised. 'I hope you're not casting aspersions on Bunty.'

'Not just Bunty,' Henry chuckled. 'We were all at it. Work hard, play hard. That was our motto. There's a lot more to war history than just what we did in working hours.'

Susan straightened her back and brushed some imaginary specks from the front of her blouse. She pursed her lips.

'I'm not sure we need to feature that sort of thing in our *Little Maudley Through the Years* memorial book, are you?'

Lucy hid a smile. She'd have to get Henry alone and see what he had to tell her.

Friday night – and the Abba night – came around. Lucy and Mel were parked on chairs at the back of the village hall, waiting for David, Helen's husband, to get the projector working. Tickets – £5 a time, to include tea and cake at intermission – had sold out. Mel opened her capacious bag to show a bottle of something that didn't look at all like tea.

'I've come armed. It's gin and elderflower tonic. I've brought glasses, too.'

'Gin, girls,' said Helen, noticing immediately. 'What fun!'

Mel pulled a face behind her back. 'God, sorry. It's just, she's so "head girl at St Clare's" that I can't help it. She makes me want to misbehave.'

'She is a bit terrifying.'

'D'you think David likes that?'

They looked over at David, who was taking instructions from her with a slightly fearful expression on his face, and both burst out laughing. 'Not there, David,' said Mel, in an uncanny impression of Helen. 'Unfasten my bra first!'

'Are you leading the new girl astray?'

Lucy jumped, hearing a deep, low voice behind her. She turned and saw Sam, the erstwhile burglar. He ducked his head and gave her a slightly awkward, crooked smile.

'Would I?' Mel nudged Lucy, making her laugh. 'We

were having a perfectly civilized conversation about Helen and David's sex life.'

'Right.' He made to turn away. 'Shall I come back later?'

'No,' Mel said, reaching across to the table behind them and hooking a teacup on her finger to use as an extra gin glass. 'You can join us.'

'Shhhh,' said an elderly gentleman, turning round with a finger to his lips. 'It's about to start.'

Lucy couldn't stand Abba. There had been countless awful work nights out where everyone had ended up singing karaoke, and it always seemed to end up with Abba medleys. They gave her awful flashbacks of nights when she'd drunk too much wine in an attempt to fit in and never quite managed it. And yet, oddly, here she was only a week or so into her stint of village life and she'd found two people to spend the evening with, even if they were all there under duress.

'I'm *doing my bit*,' Sam explained, still whispering. 'Thanks to you persuading me to come along, I got roped into helping out afterwards with the clearing up, and Freya –' he motioned to the other side of the room where his daughter was sitting, legs folded underneath her, beside another girl with long fair hair – 'decided she wanted in on the act.'

'Oh, I didn't see her there. That's Camille, my daughter,' Mel explained to Lucy. The girls, sensing they were being talked about, looked up and waved.

'She and Freya have been friends forever,' Mel said.

'Bit like me and whatshisname here. We've been friends since nursery school.'

Sam smiled. He had good teeth, Lucy noticed. The lights dimmed and Mel unscrewed the bottle of gin and tonic. She poured the drink into the glasses and teacup, coughing to cover up the hissing noise it made as it fizzed, and passed them round.

'Let me know when you want a top-up.'

'Shhh!' said the man again.

'Ah, lovely – are you two giving Sam a hand with the tidying up?'

After the film was over, the hall had cleared surprisingly quickly. ('Everyone knows better than to hang around,' explained Mel, 'because they know they'll get roped into helping.')

Like we have, thought Lucy; but she didn't really mind. She was helping Sam load the dishwasher. Despite getting off on the wrong foot at their first meeting, she was finding him easy company.

'Mel was telling me you were head of year in a secondary school. This must be a bit of a change of pace from teaching, then?' Sam stacked cups. Mel had been whisked off to sweep the floor.

'Well, I have to admit I didn't expect to be quite this involved in village life,' said Lucy, plunging her hands into a sink full of hot soapy water and washing the delicate china, which Helen had declared too fragile for the industrial dishwasher.

'It does tend to take over slightly,' Sam admitted, straightening up. His arms were tanned, and dusted with a smattering of freckles amongst the dark hairs. He pushed his sleeves up a bit further and unhooked a dishtowel.

'You wash, I'll dry. We might actually get out of here before midnight if we're lucky.'

There was a shriek and a giggle from the hall. Lucy and Sam both turned, looking though the kitchen hatch. Freya and Camille were waltzing in their socks across the newly swept floor, slipping and giggling, singing 'Waterloo'. Mel, leaning on the big floor sweeper, looked across at them and raised her eyes heavenward, laughing. Helen beetled into the kitchen.

'Are you two nearly done?'

'Almost.' Sam turned round and then back to the sink.

'Chop chop, then.'

'Come on, Lucy, wash those dishes a bit faster. We haven't got all night.' Sam slid Lucy a sideways glance that made her giggle. She widened her eyes in a silent response, and Sam had to turn a laugh into a cough. There was something about Helen Bromsgrove that made her feel more like a naughty schoolgirl than a fully grown adult. It was a nice change.

Outside the sky was a washed-out dark blue, with a pale moon hanging above the trees. Lucy hovered, not wanting the evening to be over.

'Well, that wasn't too bad after all,' Sam said.

'Told you,' said Mel.

'Thank you so much, chaps, for your help. Hugely appreciated! Home for a nice G and T, I think?' Helen jingled the keys to the village hall, having locked up the doors.

Freya and Camille were still dancing on the pavement beside them, singing loudly.

'Shh, you two,' said Helen, bossily. 'Time for bed, I think.'

She bustled off. Mel looked at Lucy and made a face. 'Can you imagine if she'd had children? She'd have them as well trained as her Labradors.'

'Imagine having Helen Bromsgrove as your mum.' Freya's face was a picture of horror.

'Oh my God. I'm never complaining about you again,' said Camille, lacing her arm through Mel's and looking up at her, batting her eyelashes. 'Can I sleep over at Freya's house?'

Sam shot a look at Mel, who nodded.

'Fine by me. If it's okay with you?'

Sam grimaced, but his eyes were laughing. 'Course. I didn't want any sleep anyway.'

'Result.' Mel did a fist pump of celebration, looking at Lucy. 'That means we can go to the pub for a nightcap. If you fancy one, that is?'

Tucked into a little table at the side of the pub, Lucy waited while Mel made her way to the bar. The pub was expensively furnished: all exposed beams and posh nibbles, definitely not what she'd been expecting from a village pub in the middle of nowhere. She picked up the wine menu and looked at the prices, which were eye-wateringly expensive. You only had to look around at the Range Rovers and Audi 4x4s parked in the driveways, and the well-stocked village shop, to realize that there was quite a lot of money in Little Maudley. The landlord, wearing a polo shirt monogrammed with the pub logo, looked across in her direction over Mel's shoulder and gave a wave of greeting.

'Bloody hell.' Mel slid into the chair, putting two glasses down on the table. 'It's impossible to get served round here these days. It's gone downhill since it went all posh.'

'I was wondering about that.' Lucy took a sip of her drink. She sat back, looking around at the clientele. Most of them were dressed in an expensive-looking uniform: brightly coloured open-necked shirts, neatly pressed dark jeans and brown deck shoes for the men, and taupe slim-legged trousers and nautical striped tops with scarves around the neck for the women. In contrast, she was wearing a knee-length floral dress with a denim jacket and a pair of white sneakers, and Mel was in a pair of cut-off jean shorts and a black t-shirt. Mel took a drink and pushed her untidy curls back from her face as she spoke.

'The commuters and the weekenders have taken over this place. It's just close enough to the train station for people to travel into London, at a push. Most families who grew up here can't afford to buy, and the ones who're still here are getting edged out. Especially with –' she lowered her voice – 'well, there's rumours that *royalty* might be moving nearby. And of course, the Beckhams are not far off. And then there's the whole Chipping Norton set not that far down the road. It's all terribly – *terribly*.' She made a face and put on a posh accent for the last part.

'So you and – Sam . . .' Lucy wasn't sure why, but she stumbled on his name. 'You're local, though?'

'God, yes. Cut us in half and you'll see Little Maudley stamped on us like sticks of seaside rock. Neither of us has ever moved away for long.' Mel raised her chin slightly, looking defiant.

'You weren't tempted?'

A couple squeezed past on their way out, bumping their table and apologizing.

'Oh, of course. I went to uni in Bath, swore I was going to spend the rest of my life over there. Got together with Camille's dad, bought a nice little house, got a nice little job, had a baby; then he had a nice little affair and left me for his business partner.'

Lucy swallowed. Mel didn't exactly mince her words.

'Oh, I'm sorry.'

Mel shook her head emphatically, so the curls she'd tucked behind her ears came flying loose again.

'God, don't be. It was a lucky escape. I came back here, moved in with my dad, retrained as a dog trainer, and I've been in heaven ever since. Camille still sees her dad, I get the odd weekend and some of the holidays off, and I've got the freedom to go off and get my travel fix when she's gone.' She took another drink and then put the glass down, turning to look at Lucy and dropping her chin onto folded hands. 'You didn't fancy going travelling in your time off from teaching, then?'

Lucy shook her head. 'I've done loads of travelling in my summer holidays.'

'Sounds like my friend Nic.' Mel looked suddenly bereft. 'She moved to New Zealand a few months back.' She took a large swig of her drink. 'It's stupid, but you don't think about how much you'll miss having someone to hang about with. It's like you think friends are just for when you're a kid, then your best friend buggers off to the other side of the world and . . .' She sighed.

No wonder Mel had seemed so keen to say hello when they'd first met, thought Lucy – she was dealing with her own loss, too. 'Tell me about it.' Lucy shrugged and raised her glass. 'To absent friends, who disappear to the other side of the blooming planet.'

'I'll drink to that.'

By the end of the evening, having shared another few drinks, Lucy and Mel swayed home together, both slightly merry and definitely glad they'd gone out.

'I think you've cheered me right up,' said Mel, as they reached the end of the lane that forked up to her little cottage. 'It's really weird how much I've missed having someone to hang out with. I mean, I love Sam to bits, but – it's not the same.'

Lucy smiled. 'I'm glad we met. I was a bit worried I'd be staring at the walls, with only Hamish for company.'

Mel grinned and hitched up her bra strap, which had drooped down her arm, showing below the sleeve of her top.

'No chance of that. I'll be knocking on the door demanding a coffee every five minutes now we've bonded over wine.' She blew Lucy a kiss. 'I might just pop in on Sam and the girls, check they're behaving.' She winked, and turned on her heel.

Lucy watched from the pavement opposite as Mel knocked on the door of Sam's cottage and waved, before a chink of light emerged and she slipped inside. Maybe she and Sam were a bit more friends-with-benefits than just friends, after all. She switched on the light in the darkness of the cottage to discover that Hamish had expressed his displeasure at being left alone for the evening through the medium of poo. She sighed, and went to clean it up.

Chapter Ten

'Hello-ooo! Lucy!' Margaret called across the hedge from Bunty's garden. 'I'm so glad that you seem to be settling in well.'

Bunty had pointed out on several occasions that her daughter-in-law had a habit of popping by at unexpected moments. She and Gordon only lived about half an hour away, on the Northamptonshire border – not close enough to visit every day, but 'near enough to be a menace', as Bunty had said, rolling her eyes in disapproval. Lucy privately thought that Margaret was quite nice, if a bit bossy.

Lucy was shaking the rug (almost dry and no stain, she was relieved to find) outside the front door of the cottage when Margaret reappeared. 'Problem with the rug?'

'No, no, it's fine,' lied Lucy. 'Just getting the dust off before I, er, hoover.'

Margaret gave her a slightly suspicious look. 'Good, good. Well, I must get on.'

She disappeared into Bunty's house and a moment later reappeared, carrying a battered-looking cardboard box full of yellowed old newspapers. Following her, her expression absolutely furious, was Bunty.

'Lucy, I want you here as witness.' She shook a finger at Margaret. 'Those newspapers are not for recycling. They're mine, and I don't want them thrown out.'

Margaret turned to Lucy, her expression as conciliatory as Bunty's was angry. 'Honestly, Lucy, you can back me up on this. I'm not trying to throw out your belongings, Mother. I'm simply trying to help you get the place sorted.'

'If I want help,' Bunty said, 'I'll ask for it.'

'But you don't, do you?' Margaret said, her mouth tight.

'Lucy?'

'Yes?' Please don't ask me to act as a go-between, she thought. The cottage could do with a bit of a tidy-up, but she understood why Bunty was resistant.

'I'm sure Lucy would give me a hand.' Bunty looked across, hopefully.

She nodded. 'Of course.'

Margaret's shoulders visibly dropped about two inches. 'That would be so, so helpful. Only if you're sure?'

'She might even find some of my old bits and bobs from during the war. Like –' Bunty pointed imperiously – 'that box of newspapers you're trying to recycle. Now if you don't mind, I'll have those back, thank you very much. Lucy, if you want to come over later, perhaps we can have a look.'

When Lucy was allowed to have a proper look around, she realized that the clutter in Bunty's house was nowhere near as bad as Margaret had made out. She already knew the kitchen, which was the heart of the house, was covered with detritus from years of family life. But the good sitting room was cool and immaculate, with a stiff, upright sofa made of spiky moquette. The room smelled of dust and mothballs, which hung in a bag by the curtains. The fireplace was decorated with old horse brasses, dulled with age. It was like stepping back in time to the 1940s, and Lucy felt a shiver of excitement. It was a historian's idea of heaven. Margaret must be mad – if it was up to Lucy, she'd leave the place exactly as it was. It was perfect.

'Never used this room,' Bunty said. 'It always felt like being at the dentist, or in a doctor's waiting room. When we had visitors, you could tell if they were the good kind or the bad kind by where we took them. Decent ones made themselves at home at the kitchen table with the dogs and cats.' She gave a chortle of laughter, which turned into a wheezing cough. 'Good heavens, I am falling to bits. Don't tell Margaret, she'll have me shipped off in no time.'

'I won't breathe a word.' Lucy smiled.

Clutching mugs of tea, they sat together in the kitchen and went through boxes of old newspaper clippings that Bunty had saved from the war years and beyond.

'No idea why I kept half of this old stuff.' She picked up a piece entitled 'Local News' and peered at it, pushing her glasses up her nose. 'This writing is minuscule. Can you see what it says?'

Lucy took the yellowed page out of her hand. It was

soft with age, and the writing really was tiny. She frowned and held it towards the light of the window.

'Beetle drive is a success at Little Maudley village hall, something something – sorry, it's all crumpled and the words have faded – reminder that there must be NO breach of the blackout and that torches should be carried . . .' She paused as Bunty started to laugh.

'Oh good God, yes. I remember that. Henry – I think you've met him, haven't you?'

Lucy nodded.

'Well – he was the ARP warden – and back then, he was an absolute stickler for the rules. We used to get up to all sorts of mischief when the lights went out.'

'That's funny; he said something along those lines when I met him for a cup of tea at the village shop.'

Bunty looked tickled by this. 'Did he, now? Well, let me tell you.'

Lucy put the paper down on the table and leaned forward, her chin in her hand, listening.

'One night after a lecture in the hall, Milly Fowler and I – she was the schoolteacher and terribly naughty – saw – well, heard really, it was so dark – someone cycle straight into the village pond. We roared with laughter. The blackout was dreadful, but such fun.'

'It must have been strange arriving here during the war, especially after London. Didn't you find it very quiet?' Lucy was chancing her arm, trying to get Bunty to talk. It was worth a try, at least.

'Yes. Well, I arrived in Bletchley, actually – was invited

to an interview. They used hundreds of us girls because the men were off fighting. I had to answer all sorts of peculiar questions, and then they send me a postcard telling me to report to the main house at eight thirty one sunny morning. Didn't have a clue where I was going, or what I'd be doing.'

'That's amazing. I was only there the other day. I can't believe you walked in through those gates all those years ago. Weren't you nervous?' Oh God, she was gabbling. She pressed her lips together and waited for a long moment. She had to let Bunty talk in her own time, not flatten her with her enthusiasm and a desire to know everything.

'Hmm?' Bunty had been sidetracked, picking up another piece of yellowed, faded newspaper. Her brow furrowed and she looked down at it for a moment in silence before giving a heavy sigh. Then she folded it up, putting it to one side. 'Not really. One just did what one was told in those days.'

'Oh, look. What's this?' Lucy lifted up a photograph album. The edges were battered and the leather cover scuffed and cracked with age.

'Oh, that's nothing. Just some old photographs and mementos. I'll sort that later. But I thought perhaps some of these might be interesting, seeing as you're looking into the village in wartime.' She pushed another album towards Lucy, and several curled-up black-and-white photographs slid out.

'Oh, look.' A stern-faced woman, stout in a gingham apron, was standing in the doorway of Bunty's cottage.

'That's Mrs Brown, our landlady. We were billeted here – I shared a room with Milly, and there were also four little evacuees from the East End – look, there they are, in this one.'

She passed over another photograph. Two little girls with their hair in neat plaits sat perched on the garden wall. Two older boys, their hair cropped short, stood awkwardly to the side.

'I remember that day.' Bunty chuckled. 'They'd had their heads clipped because we'd discovered that everyone in the school had nits. Mrs Brown covered the girls' hair with vinegar and plaited it up. I feel itchy just thinking about it.'

Lucy gazed at the photographs. Bunty's story made them seem so alive somehow. This was exactly why history mattered – why she wanted to record this sort of thing. It felt like a huge seal of approval; being given a window into her wartime world was a real honour. She beamed at Bunty, hoping that would suffice.

'Oh, these are amazing.' The next couple of black-and-white photographs showed a young Bunty standing, a hand shading her eyes from the sun, in a pair of knee-length shorts. She was astride a bicycle with a flower in her hair.

'I was given such a scolding when Mrs Brown saw I'd been into town in those. She was terribly fierce.' Bunty's shoulders shook as she laughed. 'We used to sneak pieces of her apple cake upstairs when she wasn't looking. She thought she had mice.'

'So how did you end up here, if you were sent to Bletchley?'

'Oh, they sent us all over the place. I thought I was in heaven when I arrived at Bletchley. All those chaps bustling around all over the place, and lots to do. You can imagine my dismay when they shunted me off to the depths of beyond. I didn't have a clue about the countryside.'

Little Maudley must have been a shock to a girl who'd been brought up in the middle of Walthamstow. Lucy looked down at the photographs of the bright-eyed young girl.

'Were lots of you sent here?'

'Gosh, no. Just me and one other – Helen, I think her name was. I used to see her when I cycled to work in the mornings. She did evenings and weekends, but she lived in Tanwick, about five miles away in the other direction. But of course, we didn't talk about what we did – one didn't, you see.'

'So you worked here all the way through the war, and never talked to anyone about what you did?'

Bunty nodded. She sifted through the photographs and picked one up, passing it over to Lucy. 'I hadn't a clue what most of the chaps were doing, you know. We just didn't mention it.'

The chaps in the photograph were in fact four young women, all standing arm in arm in stiff-looking skirts, hair set in neat waves. Bunty was at one side, her eyes closed but a huge smile on her face.

'It wasn't until all the news in the last twenty years or so, when everything came out about Bletchley, that I discovered several of us in the village had all been billeted here on similar jobs. Funny to think we were all beetling back and forth to secret listening stations and signal posts, doing our bit, and yet in the evenings all we chatted about was how to get stockings and the latest village gossip.'

'So what did you do exactly?' The question fell out of Lucy's mouth before she could stop herself. She felt her eyes widen as she realized that she'd probably pushed too far.

Bunty looked at her for a moment. 'Well.' She shifted her gaze to look out of the window. 'We had to sign the Official Secrets Act, you know.'

Lucy nodded.

'And it was hard – jolly hard – to understand when all of a sudden people started talking. I mean – well, you must appreciate, we come from a different time.'

Lucy followed her eyes, looking out across the road and to the telephone box on the green. 'There can't have been much to do in a little village like this in the war, though?'

'Gosh, tons. It wasn't like nowadays, when everyone just sits inside gawping at television. There was a bus that took us into Bletchingham twice a week for dances and lectures, and there was always something on at the village hall.'

'It sounds so much fun.'

'Oh, it was hard work as well. But we didn't have time to complain – we were either working, or dashing off to do something in the evenings. Milly used to meet me –' she looked out of the window and smiled – 'at the phone box, every night after she'd finished teaching. We'd have tea in the cafe in the next village.'

'And you did all this while the blackout was going on?'

'Oh yes. Summer was fine – we could get up to far more mischief, and it wasn't cold. But winter – we used to take hot potatoes in our pockets to keep us warm when we cycled to dances, and we'd be so wrapped up that it would take ten minutes to take off all our layers when we got there. It was worth it, though. We used to have a wonderful time, especially when the airmen came for training at the airfield in Finmere. They were good fun. Put the cat among the pigeons.'

'Were they stationed here permanently?'

'No, it was a training unit. They'd be sent over here to learn how to fly bombers, do their bit, then that would be that.'

'Did you see them in action?'

'Did I see them?' Bunty shook her head, smiling slightly. 'Goodness. The skies were full – they used to fly so low sometimes that you could wave to the pilots.'

'That sounds so romantic.' Lucy sighed happily.

'Oh, we were far too busy for that sort of thing.' Bunty picked up the photographs and stacked them neatly. Something in her face seemed to shut down. 'Anyway, that's enough nonsense from me for one day. You don't want me droning on about the past.'

And she stood up. It was clear to Lucy that the conversation was closed. It was strange – there were moments when Bunty seemed to want to let the stories from the past out, but then – there was so much that had happened in the past, and her memory wasn't what it was. Perhaps it was tiring just remembering it all.

'Hello?'

There were footsteps in the hall, and a dark head popped round the kitchen door. Bunty brightened immediately. 'Ah, hello!'

'Hi, Bunty. Oh, and hi, Lucy,' Sam added when he spotted that Bunty had a guest. 'Have you recovered from the Abba extravaganza?' He stepped into the kitchen. He was so tall that his head was close to skimming the wooden beams on the low ceiling.

'I have.' She wondered how much Mel had told him about their evening when she went back to his house after the pub. 'Did the girls enjoy their sleepover?'

He laughed, ducking his head and pushing his hair back from his face, looking at her with his dark brown eyes. She noticed a fan of lines at the corner of each eye – a nice sign, Lucy thought, of someone who doesn't take life too seriously.

'Wasn't much sleep involved, but yes. I ended up being cornered into making bacon rolls for them *and* Mel when she turned up. You should have joined us. Wouldn't have been any trouble to make an extra one.'

He rubbed the stubble on his chin and yawned widely. 'God, sorry. I've been working all hours trying to get this project finished, and it's taking forever.'

'Sam, you should show Lucy what you've been up to.' Bunty looked proud. 'He's been working on something for Janet in the village. Janet and Mick foster a number of children with disabilities – they're a lovely family.'

'What are you making for them?' Mel had explained that the hedgehog houses were something Sam did on the side, but Lucy was still in the dark about what he actually did for a living. She didn't like to pry, not least because she didn't want Mel thinking she was interested – which she definitely wasn't. But when he'd parked across the road, she'd managed to make out a painting of pine trees though the thick layer of mud that covered the side of his Land Rover. A tree surgeon, perhaps?

'I'm building a treehouse.'

'Go on – take her to see it now,' said Bunty, firmly. 'I've had enough of going over the past, and I want to get on with the crossword.'

'I – oh, what about Hamish?'

Hamish, having got over his initial (and in Lucy's view completely acceptable) fear of Stanley, was asleep on a rug beside the Aga.

'He's absolutely fine here. Off you pop, you two, and give an old woman some peace.'

'I came to ask if Freya could come over later and help with the animals.' Sam rolled his eyes at Lucy. 'She's still in bed.'

159

'She's fourteen. It's what young people do these days.'

'You're the expert,' he said, smiling at Bunty. 'I haven't a clue what I'm doing. Daughters are a lot harder work than I expected.'

'Shoo, both of you.' Bunty waved them out the door, closing it firmly behind them.

She waited until they'd walked along the lane and were well out of sight before she turned back to the kitchen table. Amongst the photograph albums, thick with dust, was her old, battered diary. She wiped it with her sleeve, looking at the familiar rough material, running a finger over it. Then she picked it up, closing her eyes, and inhaled, as if somehow she might soak up the memory of the girl she'd been back then. It was strange – it had been sitting there untouched for so many years, but talking to Lucy had brought it all back. Memories seemed to be popping into her head at the most inconvenient of times. Perhaps if she just had a look . . .

She opened the pages. The ink had faded with time, and her writing, although still familiar, was girlish and rounded. Lucy was desperate to hear all about her war, but – Bunty leafed through the pages – there were stories in there that had been locked away for more than seventy years.

Turning the pages, she looked down at an entry she'd written with a pen that had run out of ink halfway through. It started in black and ended in faded sepia. Gosh, she could remember that day as if it was yesterday

– it was the day it all began. She'd settled into life at Mrs Brown's and the routine of cycling the three miles out of the village to work each day. And then . . .

August 13th, 1941

Such a lovely night. I don't even mind one bit that I'm going to be falling asleep all day tomorrow. We went to the beetle drive at the village hall. I wore Milly's green dress and borrowed her pretty crochet cardigan, and wore my silver and blue brooch. Even though my stockings had a darn in the toe that rubbed all night I didn't notice, because there was such a handsome Canadian pilot there with his friend. They were at the table next to ours and his friend kept making little asides that had us in stitches all night. But mine (ha!) was quieter – a bit shy, I thought.

Anyway, Milly whispered that he was making eyes at me and when I went to spend a penny he turned and said hello. I smiled and said hello back but kept on walking, because Milly says 'keep them on their toes'. But when they moved the tables at the end and put some music on the gramophone, his friend came and asked me if I'd like to dance with him. I said he could ask me himself if he wanted to. I thought I might have pushed my luck then, because he didn't.

I danced right past him with Milly and she couldn't help but giggle, and he caught my eye for a moment then looked away with a little smile. Afterwards, I had to wait because Milly left her glove inside and he came up and said he didn't much like dancing, but if I wanted to go

*for a walk sometime, he'd like that. And then he and his
friend walked me and Milly home. He's called Harry –
I've always rather liked that name. Then Milly went
inside, and we stood outside on the village green by the
telephone box talking until almost midnight. He's
stationed at the aerodrome, where he's teaching chaps how
to fly Blenheims. He asked me to a dance there next Friday
evening. I can't believe it. Oh my goodness. I don't think
I could sleep tonight even if I wanted to. I'm just going
to lie here and relive it over and over again.*

Bunty closed her eyes for a moment, putting a hand
to her chest. That breathless, excited girl she'd been. It
felt like more than a lifetime ago – as if she was someone
else. She picked up the diary and held it to her face,
inhaling as if somehow she'd be able to breathe in the
freshness and excitement she'd felt back then. War had
seemed like an adventure to them – even rationing didn't
really affect them in the same way as it had back home
in Walthamstow. There were fresh eggs, and butter, and
home-baked bread for breakfast every day. She had
missed her sister and even her parents – her mother wrote
every week, telling her how they'd dug over the garden
and planted cabbages, and how Dad had made a chicken
run and next door's dog had got in and bitten the head
off one and they'd had it for the pot that evening. But
even the nights when the ARP warden's whistle went off
and they had to hide in the shelter felt exciting – especially
if she made sure she wasn't next to one of the old

fuddy-duddies from the village. They'd play cards and tell stories and sing songs and listen for the roar of the planes overhead.

The village was never hit, thankfully. There were a couple of near misses, mind you – like the time they'd overshot their mark and dropped something in a field, killing three heifers. And oh, the calamity when Mr George's greenhouses were hit by a stray bomb! He was mourning the loss of his tomatoes for months. It had been years later that one of her friends in the village had told her all about the dummy airstrip, designed to fool the Germans. She chuckled to herself. There were some parts of the war that had felt like an adventure. Perhaps she'd show Lucy, after all.

But could she really trust her with the truth about what had happened back then? She had kept it to herself for all these years. Was there any reason to share it now?

'Bunty doesn't mess about when she's had enough, does she?' Lucy observed as they walked down the garden path.

Sam gave a rueful smile. 'I think she's earned the right to have no filter. When I'm her age, I'm going to speak my mind all the time.'

'It's funny, we were having a lovely chat about her war – she was actually starting to open up – and she just decided that she'd had enough.'

'That sounds like her. She's a bit of a dark horse, our Bunty.'

The air was filled with the scent of the roses that curled round the door of Bunty's cottage. They both stepped back as a string of vintage cars appeared out of nowhere and processed slowly down the lane.

'Oh, those are beautiful.'

'There's a festival somewhere near here this weekend. They all drive through the villages en masse. Gorgeous, aren't they?'

'Amazing.'

A shining, dark green Rolls-Royce brought up the rear. Its owner doffed his cap and gave a honk of the horn as he passed them.

'Anyway, as I was saying, I'm sorry Bunty's tried to palm me off on you. Don't worry, I've got loads of work to do.'

'I'm not worried.' Sam thrust his hands into his pockets and stood facing her. He cocked his head and smiled. 'Come on, it's a gorgeous day. Too nice for work. I'll show you what I've been up to. Maybe you can give me some parenting tips.'

'Me? I don't have any children!' Lucy fell into step beside him.

'No, but you've had loads of experience teaching whole classes full of them. Freya has been dead easy until recently, but these last few weeks she's just been glued to her phone. I worry about it.'

Freya seemed pretty easy-going to Lucy. She had a good friendship with Camille, Mel's daughter, which was always a good start. Having someone to confide in made all the difference, especially when her mother didn't seem to be around.

'Adolescence hits them all in different ways. I think

thirteen/fourteen is the hardest time. They're still quite little, really, but they're under all sorts of pressure to grow up.' They stopped for a moment to let a tractor rumble past. The driver gave them a friendly wave and then turned in to a field up ahead. As they carried on walking Lucy watched him climb out of the cab and lean against the wheel, taking out his phone and making a call. It seemed strangely incongruous against the timeless background of rolling fields.

'Even farmers are permanently online. No wonder I can't get Freya off her blooming phone,' Sam laughed, following her gaze.

They turned left, down a narrow lane lined with trees. The road was a single track, banked with grassy verges and dappled with sunlight.

'It's down here. It's not far.' Sam stepped behind her so they were walking in single file on the road.

'From what I've seen, Freya seems pretty laid-back to me.'

'Yeah, she has been. Y'know, it's hard when you're doing it all yourself to know if you're doing an all right job of it. I mean, it's not like her mum's around . . .'

'You've got Mel, though,' Lucy said, without thinking. She didn't want to sound as if she was fishing for information.

'Yeah, Mel's a good mate. But it's not the same as having her mum.'

'No. Mel mentioned Freya's mum isn't really on the scene.'

The road widened, and he stepped up to walk alongside her again. His arm brushed hers and she felt a little rush of warmth that seemed to blossom and fill her chest. God, she was so out of practice at being in the company of men that her body had clearly lost all sense of perspective. She must get a grip.

Sam shook his head. 'No, she most definitely is not. Motherhood wasn't ever really on the agenda for Stella. I dunno what made me think we could make it work.'

'How does Freya feel?' This was more like it – back on familiar ground. Lucy had seen her fair share of kids who had absent parents, and knew that a lot of how they coped depended on how the parents coped.

'She's been fine. Although she did ask me a question about her mum the other night, and I didn't know what to say. I clammed up. Now I can't get near the subject because I handled it so badly. I've tried a couple of times, but she just goes silent on me – says she doesn't want to talk about it.'

He opened a heavy wooden five-barred gate. 'This is us. Sorry, I don't mean to offload all my woes on you.'

'It's fine.' Lucy smiled at him. Butterflies hovered around the lavender and rose bushes that lined the driveway. 'Won't they mind you bringing me along?'

Sam shook his head. 'No.' He opened another heavy metal gate, typing in a code. 'They've got a place down in Minehead. The whole gang of them are away for the week. Janet's amazing. She just loads them all in their minibus and off they go.'

'It's very high-security, isn't it? Like Fort Knox.'

'They get their fair share of tricky children, so they have to make sure the kids can't run away. She works wonders with them. It's why I wanted to do this – give something back.'

Lucy followed him down a neatly mown grass path that had been strimmed through a meadow seeded with long grasses and wildflowers. The air was heavy with the lazy humming of bees and the scent of flowers. It made her feel drowsy, as if she could lie down and have a rest herself. Sam's back was broad in his grey t-shirt, she noticed, and narrowed into a slim waist and a very nice bum in faded jeans – she shook her head. God. The heat was getting to her.

'Here we are.' He turned and looked at her. She felt her cheeks turn pink, as if he'd been reading her mind.

Standing at the edge of a field full of tall ox-eye daisies and blue forget-me-nots was a broad oak tree with wide branches. It supported a beautifully crafted ladder, leading up to a treehouse that looked like something from a fairy tale.

'You go first.' He stepped back, waving an arm in an old-fashioned flourish.

Lucy climbed the ladder, her heart thudding against her ribs – she hated heights. It's only a six-foot drop, she told herself. She clung onto the side of the railing. It felt secure, at least.

'You okay?' Sam's voice came from behind her.

'Yes.' Her voice sounded breathless. She climbed the

final rung onto a little platform, and stepped into the most beautiful treehouse. The walls were hung with tiny, sparkling fairy lights and a window looked out to the rolling countryside beyond the village, which looked just like something from a picture book. She felt Sam's presence just behind her and turned, crashing into the solid wall of his chest.

'God, sorry.' Her heart was still thudding.

'It's not quite finished.' He looked at her with concern. 'Are you sure you're okay?'

Lucy sat down on a wooden chair. 'Fine. Just a bit –'

'You don't like heights?' He squatted down, looking her in the eye. 'You should have said.'

'It didn't really occur to me. I mean, it's not like standing on top of the Empire State Building.'

'Yeah, that wouldn't be a great idea if you don't like heights.'

'Tell me about it.' She laughed. 'Going up that thing was the most terrifying hour of my life.'

'What? You've been up the Empire State Building?'

'Yes.' She gave a shudder of recollection. 'With my friend Anna. It was awful, I couldn't even make it out onto the viewing platform. Did you know you have to *queue* to get back on the lift to get down?'

'They don't have an emergency exit, you mean?' He was teasing.

'No.' Lucy made a face which made him laugh. 'Honestly, it was hideous.'

'This is nothing in comparison, then.' He held out a

hand, and helped her up. 'Look, I'll stand beside you and you can look through the binoculars from the peg, here. If you look to the right and focus, you'll see Helen's house.'

Lucy took a deep breath and held the binoculars to her eyes. She could feel the warmth of his arm through the loose cotton of her top.

Sam touched her hand and moved the binoculars slightly. 'Try that way – left a bit. Look closely and you might see Helen bossing David around. She's probably schooling him in the paddock.'

Lucy snorted with laughter, her fear now forgotten.

'Oh, yes, there they are –'

'And does she have a lunge whip and boots out?'

Lucy burst out laughing. They were tiny little figures, but there was no mistaking Helen. 'No, she's standing at the bottom of a ladder and he's at the top, and she's waving her arm around in a very authoritative manner.'

'Of course she is.'

She shifted her gaze, looking out over the village. If she twisted the focus she could see – there it was – the church and the horse-chestnut trees, already laden with tiny, spiked fruit that would become conkers after summer had passed. She lowered the binoculars and turned to Sam.

'I think Helen's heart is in the right place, don't you? I mean, she was really nice about asking me to join in with village stuff the moment I got here.'

'Oh, definitely. And every village needs a Helen, or nothing would get done. Has she helped with your war research stuff? Mel was saying you've gone from planning to do something on your own, to getting roped into helping with the WI guidebook or something?'

Lucy nodded. 'Yes, Susan asked me help write something for the village WI's eightieth anniversary.'

He rolled his eyes and laughed. 'And she cornered you, I bet, so you couldn't say no.'

'She did a bit. But it all ties in with the bit of history I'm interested in – the little everyday stories that don't always get written about.'

'It sounds good when you put it like that. I might have paid attention in class if I'd had a history teacher like you.'

He gave her a sideways look which made her stomach flip over.

'I'm very strict, actually.' She said it without thinking and started laughing at exactly the same time as Sam did.

'It gets more interesting by the second.'

Feeling her cheeks going pink, Lucy lifted the binoculars again and studied the landscape for a moment. She couldn't get them to focus at all – everything was hazy and blurred – but it gave her a second to gather her thoughts. She looped them over her neck and handed them back to Sam. He still had the ghost of a smile playing on his lips.

'Susan's been a help, too. I'm going to have tea with two of the women who live in the Abbeyfield retirement house, thanks to her. They're both in their nineties and have lived here in the village all their lives.'

'Sounds like you've settled in pretty well.'

In the distance, the ancient woods beyond the village marked the entrance to Lawcott Manor, the big house that had been requisitioned during the war for use as a military hospital. There was so much history here in this one little village, and every corner she turned seemed to lead to another story.

'Not a bad place to live, is it?' Sam was shading his eyes against the sun, looking out at the village.

'At first I was surprised to find how many people seem to have stayed here all their lives. But there's something about it, isn't there?'

He nodded. 'Nice to belong somewhere, I think. That's what I wanted for Freya. I think especially with – well, she's only got me. I wanted her to have roots.'

'Give them roots and wings,' she said, thoughtfully. 'That's an old saying, isn't it?'

'Think so. I didn't exactly travel far, mind you.'

'Are your parents still in the village?'

Sam shook his head. 'No. I didn't know my dad, and my mum passed away last year.'

'I'm sorry.'

'It's okay. We weren't all that close.'

'Still hard, though.'

'Yeah.' A muscle jumped in his cheek. 'It's why I want to make sure Freya's got people around her – friends, instead of family.'

'She gets on well with Bunty, doesn't she?'

'Very much so.' He laughed. 'Bunty's a real crossword

whiz. She's been training Freya up for years. She says she wants to join GCHQ when she leaves school, or HMGCC. One of the two.'

'What's HMGCC?'

'It's based near here – technological whizz kids creating all sorts of communication equipment for the government. Bunty was the one who pointed her in that direction. I half wonder if it's something to do with what she did in the war.'

Lucy looked at him thoughtfully. 'Really?'

'Mmm. She doesn't talk about it much, but I've picked up the odd thing here and there.'

'Yeah.' Lucy thought of Henry's comments when they were sharing a cup of tea. 'I'm trying to get to the bottom of it, but she's definitely taken the whole Loose Lips Sink Ships thing to heart.'

'Different generation, I think.' He turned around, leaning against the wooden frame of the treehouse so he was looking directly at her. He shaded his eyes from the sun and met her gaze. 'You wouldn't catch Bunty spilling all on social media.'

'Nor me,' Lucy wrinkled her nose. 'I mean, we were advised against it because of work – you just can't take the risk when you're a teacher – but it's not really my sort of thing.'

'Me neither.' He motioned towards the steps. 'Shall we go back down?'

She climbed down cautiously after him, and he caught her hand as she hopped off the bottom step.

'It's lovely. But I'm quite glad to be back on solid ground.'

They headed back through the gardens.

'I went to Bletchley the other day.' She grazed a hand across a huge, blowsy rose. The petals fell off and landed on the ground in a little heap. 'Oops.'

'I won't tell,' said Sam. 'I haven't been to Bletchley Park for years. If you're going again and you want company, shout. I bet Freya would love it –' He stopped himself, looking awkward, and shook his head. 'Sorry. You're probably really busy doing research stuff. You don't want us tagging along.'

'Actually, I thought I'd like to take Bunty sometime. We could make a day of it?'

'I'd love that.' Sam pulled the gate shut and locked it, checking with a shove that it was secure. 'I make tree-houses that aren't in the air, too, y'know,' he added.

'Definitely more my kind of thing. But don't you need a tree to build a treehouse?'

'Ah.' He smiled. His expression lit up when he was talking about work, she noticed. 'They're set around the trunk, sometimes. I made one from an old oak that had been struck by lightning. I'll show you one sometime, if you like.' He hesitated for a moment. 'Only if you're not too busy.'

Lucy shook her head. 'I'm busy doing nothing, really. That's the whole point of my time here.'

'Must be pretty nice to be able to just relax and take some time out.'

She nodded, remembering something Freya had said, and glanced at him as they were walking back down the lane.

'Freya was telling me at the Abba night that she reads a lot.'

'God, yes. All the time. She was obsessed from the moment she could read. I dunno where she got it from – I'm not really a reader, and her mum – well, Stella wasn't really, either. But I used to take her to baby and toddler class at the library, and we always chose a book at the end. I think that's probably where it started.'

'That's a good thing, though.'

'Of course. I'm just not – well, I wasn't ever that keen on school. I was always happier outside doing stuff than stuck in a classroom.'

'Maybe you just had the wrong teachers.' Lucy raised her eyebrows.

'Maybe.' He cocked an eyebrow.

'It's so pretty here, isn't it?'

'Gorgeous. It's funny – I take it for granted a bit, because I've grown up with it. But coming out here now, with you – well, it's making me look at it differently.'

She opened her mouth to speak, but before she could, a voice carried over from behind the hedge on the corner.

'Well, *hello*.'

It was Beth from the shop, wearing a pair of huge 1950s-style sunglasses and her red hair tied back with a polka-dot ribbon. 'Nice day for a walk,' she said. Lucy noticed her giving Sam a not-very-discreet wink.

'I was just showing Lucy the treehouse up at Janet's place. It's nearly finished,' he said. 'You could come and have a look too if you like sometime.'

'Me?' She put a hand to her chest. 'I wouldn't want to intrude.' She gave Lucy a knowing smile. 'Nice to see you *settling in*.'

'Oh God.' Sam shook his head after they'd walked out of hearing distance, then put both hands up to cover his face. 'I apologize in advance for any village gossip that might ensue as a result of that one-minute conversation.'

'Yeah, I've heard Beth likes to be on top of what's going on.'

'That's one way of putting it.' He snorted with laughter. 'She'll have us married off by the time you get back to your place. Honestly, she's a nightmare.'

'Don't worry,' Lucy said. 'She's well aware I'm only here temporarily.'

Although, for the first time, Lucy felt a pang of sadness as she imagined leaving Little Maudley. Definitely the village, not the man walking by her side, she told herself, firmly. And she had to get back to work sometime. Life for her was in Brighton, not in this sleepy little village where the biggest concern was whether or not the phone box was due to be decommissioned. Talking of which, she'd been cornered by Helen the other day, looking for her thoughts on the subject. She'd tried to tread carefully, but found herself looking up telephone boxes and their history afterwards – once a historian, always a historian. She smiled to herself at the thought. She had to admit it would be a shame to lose the iconic red box from the green – it had stood at the heart of the village for a century, seen the war and countless changes over the years. No wonder Bunty had looked so upset when she'd mentioned Helen's plans to have it whipped out and replaced with a bench and a floral display. It might not be used as a phone box these days – Lucy had tried and failed to remember the last time she'd made a call from one – but it seemed almost brutal to just wipe it out because it wasn't needed any more. It was part and parcel of village life, like the shiny red post box and the old metal pump that stood beside it on the green.

They carried on down the path, walking side by side. Lucy felt very aware of Sam's physical presence, and when their arms brushed as she swerved to avoid a low-hanging branch, she pulled hers back and moved away quickly. It was ridiculous, feeling like that. She'd spent far too much time hanging out in the company of male teaching colleagues to feel awkward about walking perfectly innocently down a country lane with a neighbour. Even if (she had to admit to herself) he was a particularly good-looking one.

Chapter Eleven

She woke up the next morning still thinking about the telephone box, and it stayed in her mind as she pottered around making tea and tidying the cottage. With his usual last-minute timing, her brother Tom had texted – waking her up – at six in the morning to say he'd be in Oxford that evening, if she fancied joining him.

I'll have to check with Mel and see if she'll take Hamish, she'd texted in reply, half-asleep. It wasn't until a couple of hours later, when she was coming home from taking Hamish for a morning walk, that she remembered Mel had mentioned something about being away for a few days.

'Don't worry at all,' Bunty said cheerfully when she explained. 'I'm more than happy to have my little chum round for the evening. Don't rush back tomorrow morning. How nice to spend some time with your brother.'

Later that evening, Lucy looked at Hamish, who was spread-eagled on the warm, pale golden stone of Bunty's garden terrace. He opened one eye briefly, and gave her a brief wag of his tail.

Bunty smiled briefly. 'As I said, he's not exactly any trouble.'

She had a copy of the local newspaper folded on the faded, silvered wood of the garden table, and a glass of water sitting beside it. Hamish looked quite at home.

'And my other little friend, Freya, said she might pop round in a while, too.'

As if she'd been summoned, Freya appeared – first her head popping over the garden gate, then an arm reaching through the honeysuckle and unfastening the catch.

'Hello.'

'How lovely to see you, my dear. Lucy's leaving us Hamish.'

'Oh, good.' Freya bent down to ruffle the hair behind his ears. 'So,' she said, cocking her head to one side and looking at Lucy with her eyebrows raised, 'I heard you were out with Dad?'

Even the teenagers here didn't miss a trick. 'Yes. He took me to see Janet's treehouse that he's been working on.'

'Cool. It's really nice, isn't it?'

'It's lovely. He's really talented.'

She caught a brief glance that was exchanged between Freya and Bunty but pretended not to notice. She wasn't going to be the victim of multi-generational matchmaking, no matter how handsome Sam might be. And Freya had enough on her mind right now, without anything else to think about.

Freya sat down on the chair next to Bunty and hooked one leg over the arm, dangling her flip-flop off the end of her big toe. Lucy was just leaning down to give Hamish a final scratch behind the ears before leaving, when Freya spoke.

'I've been thinking.'

Lucy straightened up, dusting dried-up pelargonium flowers from the knee of her jeans.

'You know how they're closing the library?'

'Yes, I read about it in the *Advertiser*.' Bunty tutted. 'It's ridiculous. This country is falling to rack and ruin. What are we without libraries? We worked hard for all these public services, and now the government is whipping them away faster than we can do anything about it.'

'Exactly.' Freya nodded emphatically. 'And you know how they're trying to get rid of the phone box?'

Bunty tightened her lips and shook her head crossly. 'Completely ridiculous. Sometimes I think I've just had enough of the people in this village.'

'Actually, Lucy, you might be able to help with this?' Freya looked up at her, pushing her long hair back from her face and winding a lock of it around her finger, thoughtfully. She pulled her phone out from the pocket of her cut-off jeans. 'I've been reading about things you can do with phone boxes . . .'

Bunty looked at Lucy – a very brief look, with her eyebrows lifted in admiration. She pushed up her cardigan sleeve and peered in at Freya's phone. 'Let me just get my specs. I can't see a thing on those tiny screens. Now where did I leave them?'

'They're round your neck,' Freya giggled. 'Okay, look.'

They all gathered round the screen of Freya's phone. Lucy shaded her eyes to stop the sun from glaring off the glass, and realized that she was looking at a telephone box just like the one in the village, only this one was decked out with flowerboxes on either side and a brightly coloured sign in one of the windows.

'Village Library,' Freya read out.

'Oh, that's gorgeous.' Lucy's heart lifted.

'Well, I never.' Bunty leaned in for a closer look. 'And who runs this library?'

'Oh, it's done by people in the village. They swap books every few months, and it's all done on goodwill.'

It was absolutely perfect. A telephone box library would give the dilapidated old phone box a new purpose, and the village a focal point that everyone would be able to appreciate. Lucy could imagine mothers and toddlers pottering along to exchange picture books, and elderly residents like Bunty would have a reason to get out and chat to people.

'You have to admit that Helen Bromsgrove would have an absolute field day with this idea, if she wasn't desperate to rip it down.' Bunty looked thoughtful.

'Precisely. I showed Dad, and he said it wouldn't be that hard to fit it out with shelves and stuff, and apparently they just sign the phone box over to the village committee.'

'That sounds like a far more sensible idea than ripping it out,' said Bunty. She gave a sigh – it sounded like one of relief to Lucy, although she still couldn't work out why Bunty had any reason to be particularly attached to the phone box. Just a strange suspicion that there was something – and she was still working, slowly and carefully, not prying or asking too many questions, to get Bunty to share her stories of wartime in Little Maudley.

'Dad said I should talk to you and see if we can make a plan, and try and persuade Helen to bin her plans to demolish it.'

'Of course, it's a great idea.' Lucy looked at her watch. 'But I must be going, or I'll be late for dinner in Oxford with my brother. Why don't we walk up to the village hall tomorrow for the meeting – I'll call for you at about half past six?'

'Deal.' Freya beamed with happiness.

She was a sweet girl, Lucy thought, waving them both goodbye and giving Hamish a brief pat. Sam had clearly done a good job of bringing her up. It was always interesting to see just how keen teenagers were to get involved in campaigns for thing like this. Despite the bad press they always seemed to be getting, in her experience most of them were passionate about something – whether it was the environment or animals. It was just a case of working out what it was that lit them up. And Freya had clearly taken a shine to this idea. It was lovely to see.

'Lucy?'

Freya popped her head out of Bunty's gate. Lucy had been just about to get in the car, and paused with one hand on its open door.

181

'Can I ask you something?'

'Of course.'

Freya stepped onto the path and faced her. She put her hands on her hips and looked indecisive for a moment.

'What is it?'

'I don't want to be rude, but – I went to the shop to get some crisps earlier and Beth was there, telling Margaret – Bunty's Margaret – that you and Dad were wandering around the lanes together and there was *definitely something going on*. I said that there was *definitely* not.'

Lucy opened her mouth to speak. Village gossip travelled even faster than she thought it would.

'There isn't, is there?' Freya narrowed her eyes, as if sizing Lucy up. She lifted her pointed little chin slightly.

'No.' Lucy shook her head, decisively.

'It's just that there are always all these women around – I mean, when he's working and stuff – and they're all, well –'

'We're just friends.' And barely that, Lucy added silently. They'd only spent the briefest of times together, but this sharp-eyed reaction from Freya was a shot across her bows. It was clear that they were a tight-knit unit, and Lucy wasn't going to get in the way of that.

She headed south towards Oxford, thinking how different Freya's close relationship with Sam was from hers with her own mother. Despite her being the youngest, somehow she'd always been dubbed the sensible one.

'You're my good girl, Luce,' her mother would say, as she heaped responsibility on her and allowed Tom to run amok. Tom was the blue-eyed boy, not expected to be anything other than charming and feckless – her mother's type, it had become apparent over the years, as one man after another moved in and then out of their colourful, busy Brighton terrace. When her mum finally decided that Roger was the one, Lucy was so exhausted by the comings and goings of her family that she was secretly quite relieved to wave her mum off at Heathrow Airport to her new life in Darwin. Thankfully Tom had settled down over the last couple of years too.

She tapped the steering wheel in irritation as the traffic snarled to a standstill. Despite finding Tom's careless charm frustrating when they were growing up, Lucy was looking forward to seeing her big brother. They'd always been close, in that way that children of slightly unconventional families often were, and looked out for each other, supporting each other through the ups and downs of their mum's love life. And he seemed to be settling down – a bit. At the very least, he'd found a demanding job that seemed to be occupying most of his attention.

Driving in Oxford was a complete nightmare. She was used to the vagaries of Brighton traffic, but the tiny, winding roads of the university town were difficult to navigate with a satnav that kept running out of battery because of a loose connection. Tourists were everywhere, and there was nowhere to park. In the end, she pulled into a loading bay and called Tom.

'Sorry, I'm just trying to find my way to you without getting trapped down a dead end somewhere.'

'No rush. I'm in the bar checking out all the hot academics,' Tom said. 'I'll keep your seat warm.'

'*Finally*,' Lucy said ten minutes later as she collapsed into a chair in the old-fashioned hotel bar. 'This place is gorgeous.'

'Perk of the job.'

She wasn't complaining – a chance of a free room in a posh hotel was something to be snapped up, no questions asked. 'What are you selling now? Coals to Newcastle?' she laughed.

'Oh God, it's far too boring to go into. But they're on the charm offensive, hence offering me a room for you as well. Some sort of hospitality package – oh, thanks, lovely,' he broke off as a very good-looking barman delivered a bottle of red. 'Never mind all of that – I want all the news. And more importantly, is Hamish behaving himself? I was hoping you might've brought him along.'

'I couldn't. Plus he was more than happy to spend the evening with Bunty.'

'You seem settled in.'

'You sound surprised.'

'Well, I honestly didn't think you'd last five minutes in the back end of beyond. How are you surviving without a Starbucks every morning?'

'There's a cafe, actually.' Lucy poured wine into both of their glasses. 'And there's quite a lot going on. I went to an Abba night the other day, I'll have you know.'

'Fancy.' Tom took a sip of wine. 'Any interesting rural gossip? How's it all going out there in the sticks?'

'Well, it's fun, actually.'

Tom raised a dubious eyebrow.

'It is. I thought everyone would be like they are back home – keeping themselves to themselves – but it's like stepping back in time. I've been roped into writing a piece for the WI celebration book—'

Tom snorted.

'Shut up. It's really interesting, actually. All about the women in wartime in Little Maudley and what they were doing.'

'Oh, you mean the Home Front type of thing? All right, I can admit that would be right up your street.'

'Not just that. Bunty had something to do with Bletchley Park, I think. *TS*, I've been told.'

He looked at her, quizzically.

'Top Secret.' Lucy gave a knowing tip of her head. 'Anyway, she's lovely, but absolutely from the Careless Talk Costs Lives generation, so trying to find anything out is like getting blood from a stone. I still don't understand how she kept a secret in that village, mind you. Everyone seems to know everyone else's business.'

'So that's what you've been up to?' he teased. 'Hanging with a load of ninety-year-olds?'

They stopped talking as the waiter came and took their order. Lucy nipped to the loo, checking her hair in the mirror. It was tangled from driving down the road with the window cracked open in the heat – the air conditioning in her beaten-up little car was non-existent. She turned her head upside down to shake her hair loose, then ran a comb through it and applied some barely there lipstick. She'd come out – without thinking – bare-faced, having got into the habit of just getting up, tying her hair up in a loose messy bun and applying some sunscreen. It seemed ridiculous putting on a full face of make-up just to hang around in the village, taking Hamish for walks and spending time with Bunty or Mel. Or Sam. A girl appeared beside her in the mirror and took out a pillar-box red lipstick. Same colour as the phone box, she found herself thinking, then shook her head. For goodness' sake. The village was getting to her.

She returned to her seat. Tom put away his phone and gave her his full attention.

'So. I want all the goss. Did you find out if Mel and that bloke are friends with benefits or not?'

Lucy shook her head. 'No, I think they're genuinely just friends. They've got daughters the same age, they're both single . . .'

'Sounds like a match made in heaven.'

'Yeah, but they've known each other since they were tiny. I think it'd be a bit –'

'So what's he like?'

Lucy felt her cheeks flushing, but hoped the dim light of the restaurant would hide it. 'He's nice. But he's a single dad.'

Tom lifted his chin slightly, sizing her up.

'Uh-huh, and?'

'Focused single dad. As in, there's history there with the mum – she's not around – and Freya is his priority.'

'Right,' said Tom. He took a mouthful of his wine and sat back in the chair, looking at her. He spread his arms out across the back, confidently, and looked her square in the eye.

'What?' Lucy looked back at him.

'What?' Tom's expression was innocent.

'Not everyone spends every second of their existence looking for a hook-up, *Tom*.'

'Right.' He grinned at her briefly. 'If you end up with him, you owe me a bottle of –' he picked up the expensive-looking bottle of red – 'A bottle of this.'

She watched as he sat back and scanned the room. He was so affable and charming that he attracted attention from both the male waiters and the women who were dotted around the room. One single woman, sitting alone with a glass of white wine and her laptop open, was quite openly giving him the eye when Lucy looked up.

'Am I cramping your style?' Lucy was used to the effect her brother had on, well, everyone.

'Nah. I'm on the straight and narrow now, anyway.'

'Really?'

'Yep. Met this girl at an event last month, and I really like her. It's early days, but –' He pulled out his phone and flicked it open, showing a photo of a girl with close-cropped dark hair. She was holding a grey-and-white cat and looking directly at the camera, her freckled nose scrunched up with laughter.

'She looks nice.'

'You mean, not like posh Hattie or weird Heather or scary Chloe?'

Tom had had a bad run of girlfriends over the last year.

'I mean, she looks relatively sane. Could you choose one who doesn't mind Hamish peeing in her handbag this time?'

'Kate wouldn't mind at all. She works at an animal sanctuary.'

'How did you meet her, then?'

'She was on a stall when we were doing hospitality for a fundraiser thing.' Lucy watched her brother looking down at the photograph for a moment before he pocketed his phone. His face softened. 'I like her a lot, Luce.'

'Oh my God.' She looked at him. 'You've actually got it bad, haven't you?'

'Shut up.'

They spent the rest of the evening catching up – Lucy telling him about her research and how she was getting on, and Tom ribbing her gently about how she'd gone native in the countryside and turned into a bumpkin.

'You couldn't even navigate through blooming Oxford,' he laughed as he picked up the bill.

'I'm just enjoying the slower pace of life.'

They went through to the luxurious hotel bar for a nightcap and she treated herself to a large brandy, cupping it in her hand and swirling it around in the wide-bottomed glass, enjoying the fact that she wasn't driving and only had to ride in the lift upstairs to her posh bedroom.

Much as she was enjoying village life, it was absolute bliss to spend the evening in a bedroom with soft white linen and a huge, full-size bath. She luxuriated, slightly hazy with wine, in bubbles that were so foamy they spilled over the edge and onto the floor, and then lay in bed in the darkness. When she fell asleep, she dreamed of the treehouse, and – disturbingly – of Sam.

Chapter Twelve

Meanwhile, back at Bunty's house, Freya was playing with the guinea pigs, lying on the grass in the evening sunshine. Swallows swooped overhead, full and replete, not even attempting to catch the insects that still buzzed around in the warm air. Bunty sat on the chair and let her eyes drift across the garden she'd loved and tended over decades. The honeysuckle climbing around the archway smelled delicious. Somewhere in the distance she could hear the low grumbling of a tractor cutting hay. So many summers sitting here in this garden, watching the plants and flowers bloom and grow and then die away – only to burst miraculously back into life again the following spring. She watched Freya rolling over, catching an escaping guinea pig with a long, graceful arm and feeding him a piece of dandelion leaf. Right then, Bunty could see the little girl who'd dashed across the road after a day at nursery school to share a painting she'd done. And then, as she rolled over, flicking her long hair back from her face and smiling, the moment was gone and once again she looked like a young woman on the cusp of growing up.

She sat up and looked at Bunty.

'Do you think Dad likes Lucy? Beth thinks he does.'

Bunty steepled her fingers and looked at Freya. She'd

picked up a piece of grass and was shredding it into thin pieces. 'Does she, now.'

'But Lucy says they're just friends. Like him and Mel.'

'Your dad and Mel have known each other since they were children.'

'Yes, but –' Freya caught her lower lip between her teeth.

'How would you feel if he did like Lucy?'

'I don't know. I – the thing is – well, I asked him –'

Bunty didn't say anything. Freya would get there in the end. She just had to find the words. She waited, patiently.

'You knew my mum, didn't you?'

There it was. Almost on cue, really. She'd wondered if it would come up as adolescence hit and Freya felt the absence of a mother she'd never known.

'I did. Not as well as I know your dad, or Mel, but I knew her a little.'

'Why do you think she left?'

Bunty thought. She'd half expected this question for a long while, and yet now that it was here she still wasn't quite sure what the answer was.

'I think . . . people are complicated. And that she was very young. And your dad – well, I think she knew you'd be safe with him.'

Freya nodded.

'And you are. He's a good man, your father. But I don't suppose that stops you wondering, does it?'

Freya got up from the grass, bent over and carefully

picked up both guinea pigs. She walked over to the hutch and put them inside. She climbed up the step and back onto the lawn where she pulled a handful of dandelion leaves and divided them carefully into two piles, then went back and placed them carefully in the food bowls of the hutch. Only then did she turn around, and her little heart-shaped face was a picture of confusion.

'It doesn't.'

Later, once Freya had gone home and Bunty's animals were safely tucked up in bed, she took a cup of tea upstairs to bed and called Hamish to follow her. Under her arm she'd tucked her old diary – just to check, she'd assured herself, that there wasn't anything in there she'd forgotten about.

Oh! I've been in such a whirl. If it's not work, it's whizzing up to the aerodrome for dances and socials. Mrs Brown does Not Approve. She's such a martinet. Luckily Harry (my Harry!) is so clever that he's come up with the perfect solution.

'I'm going to leave you a note,' he said. 'Next time I'm passing by. I'll hide it behind the shelf in the telephone box. You just have to look out for a little flash of white in the glass.'

Lo and behold, two days later when I was washing dishes at the kitchen sink I looked out of the window and I could see a flash of white against the glass. I left the soapy water in the sink and dashed across the road. It was stuffed so far down – tucked inside the window-frame

– that unless you were looking, you'd never have noticed it. But I did. I pulled it out and unfolded it and there was a little note just for me.

'Well hello, beautiful,' it said, 'I'm glad you found this. Meet me here at the telephone box at eight on Friday night, and I'll take you to the flicks.'

Well, my heart just leapt with excitement. I didn't want to risk Mrs Brown finding out, so I stuffed it inside my pocket and ran back across to the cottage just in time. When she walked into the kitchen, beetle brows gathered in disapproval, I had just plunged my hands back into the washing-up water and was scrubbing away laboriously.

Now I just have to find something nice to wear! And I must try doing some of Milly's keep-fit exercises.

Mrs Brown just came thumping up the stairs to tell me that I ought to be asleep. She's frightfully cross because Milly missed dinner because she was out for a walk with one of Harry's friends, and of course now Milly's fast asleep and I'm taking the flak.

'I'm responsible for you, young lady, in your mother's absence.'

I've told her time and time again that I'm eighteen years old and perfectly capable of making my own decisions but No, she says, I must Behave Appropriately. I might add that I haven't done a single thing wrong.

August 25th, 1941 (Friday)
It was so hot in the hut today I thought I might just melt away to nothing. The hours dragged by so slowly that I

felt I should never be free, but then when my shift was over I cycled back to the cottage at top speed, galloping up the stairs ('you sound like a herd of elephants, not a young lady') and washing as quickly as I could. I was all dressed – Milly lent me her muslin dress and I'd done my hair with the curl at the front and loose at the back – when I was summoned by Mrs B before I had a chance to put on any lipstick.

'Can you peel these potatoes for me?'

I gestured to Milly's dress and all she could say was 'very nice' and then she tossed me an apron and told me to get on with it! The cheek!

Luckily I was almost done when I looked up – and there, standing in the telephone box waving at me whilst pretending to make a call, was Harry. I threw the peelings in the pig bucket, dropped my knife and dashed across the street to see him.

'You look more beautiful every time I see you,' he said, and I thought my heart would just melt.

And then I caught a glimpse of my reflection in the window of the telephone box.

'Oh my goodness,' I said, putting a hand to my mouth. 'I've forgotten my lipstick.'

'That's good,' Harry said, with his eyes sparkling with mischief, 'because I was going to kiss it all off anyway.'

And he held me by the waist right there by the telephone box in the middle of the street and kissed me in broad daylight. Anyone could have seen us – and goodness knows what Mrs B will have to say about it if she gets word.

We went into town then – he'd borrowed a car for the night – and saw Pinocchio *at the cinema. I just love that song 'When You Wish Upon a Star'. We sang it all the way home in the car and Harry walked me to the doorstep and kissed me goodnight. And then just before he left, he turned around and put his hand in his pocket –*

'I almost forgot.' He ducked his head then, as if he was feeling shy. And then he held out his hand and turned it palm upright. 'These are for you.'

He'd brought me a roll of Canadian sweets – candy, he called them – and the most beautiful present. It was a tiny little enamelled brooch he'd bought at the jewellery shop in town. He fastened it to the bodice of my dress – his hands were shaking – and his fingers touched the skin of my chest. Oh my!

Oh, what a silly, romantic goose she'd been. Bunty closed the diary and patted the empty space beside her on the bed.

'Come on, Hamish.'

He wriggled over and rolled onto his back, demanding a tummy rub. She picked up the diary, put on her reading glasses, and sat back against the pillows with her cup of tea. How different life could have been, if only. But life was full of *if onlys*. There was no point regretting what might have been.

Chapter Thirteen

'I really appreciate this, Will.'

'No problem.' The young lad pushed back his hair for the fifteenth time that morning. Sam couldn't help thinking that if it was that much trouble, he'd be better off cutting it short instead of having it flopping in his face all the time. He grinned to himself ruefully. He sounded like a parent. An old one, at that.

They hauled the last of the bags of solidified cement mix onto the back of the truck.

'Freya, you going to be okay for half an hour while we take these to the tip?'

There was a vague grunting noise from the grass where she lay sprawled out, headphone in one ear, a hat over her face. She claimed she was sunbathing – the weather had been ridiculously warm for the last couple of weeks – and he had to admit, at least she wasn't lurking inside for a change. But she was definitely a bit – off. Secretive. He'd thought perhaps he was being paranoid after the first time she'd snapped the phone off, but he'd been observing her over the last week or so and something was definitely up. She'd stopped reading, and was on the computer all the time. And for the first time ever, she had declined to walk to the shop with him for their customary after-dinner ice cream. Perhaps he'd have a word with Mel, see if Camille had said anything? But he didn't like the idea of sneaking around behind Freya's back. They'd always had such an open relationship, and that sort of behaviour made him think of her mother.

He lifted her hat and she opened her eyes, staring up at him.

'Back in half an hour. Ring me, but Mel's in, okay?'

'I'm fourteen, Dad, not four. I'm perfectly fine here. What d'you think's going to happen to me in the village where nothing ever happens?' She pulled the hat back over her face.

He sighed. What was it Ned Stark said in *Game of Thrones*? War was easier than daughters. He wasn't bloody joking. He climbed into the front of the truck and started the engine.

As he was driving away he saw Mel walking two of her charges, a fluffy Pomeranian – which looked ridiculous on the end of the leash, like she was taking a pom-pom for a walk – and a sturdy, stumpy-legged basset hound. She gave him a wave, and out of the passenger window he saw her pausing to knock on the door of Lucy's cottage. It was nice that they'd become friends. Mel desperately missed her best friend since she'd emigrated, and Lucy was – well, Lucy was lovely.

Just before he turned the corner at the end of Main Street, he pulled up to let a delivery van out at the junction. He caught a glimpse of the two of them in his rear-view mirror. Lucy's long dark hair was tied up in a swinging ponytail and she was in a blue-and-white striped top. He could picture her freckled nose, and the way she wrinkled it when she laughed. The way she smelled of apple shampoo and touched his arm unselfconsciously when they were talking. Freya had warmed to her, too. He'd found himself thinking about her since their walk up to Susan's treehouse the other day, and trying to find opportunities to pop in. Perhaps – maybe he'd nip in later and ask her if she had any more advice on how to handle Freya. There was definitely something up. Maybe she could have a word, if it wasn't against some sort of professional code.

Will helped him unload the stuff at the tip – he'd decided that after twelve years, it was time to sort out the mess of the extension he'd been working on when Stella had left. The footings were wrecked and he'd have to start again, and the planning permission had expired. But really, he didn't need any extra space. If he put his mind to it, he could get it flattened out and a nice terrace there instead before autumn. It would be good to have the place sorted out. It was time.

When he got back, Freya was inside, sitting at her laptop at the kitchen table.

'You all right?'

'Fine.' She slammed the laptop shut and put it under her arm. 'Just going to my room.'

'Frey—'

And with that, she'd gone. It wasn't his imagination – she was withdrawing, becoming more and more silent.

Maybe she was missing Cammie, who had gone to spend a couple of weeks with her dad down in Bristol. The summer holidays were always a bit difficult, with him working and her stuck out here in the sticks. Maybe he should suggest they did something together.

'Hi,' he said later, standing at Lucy's doorway.

She looked happy to see him, at least. She stepped out with a smile, holding the door closed behind her. 'Sorry, Hamish will belt off up the road if I leave it open. D'you want to come in? I was thinking of having a beer in the garden as Dutch courage before I go to the village hall meeting later. Freya says she's coming with me.'

'Go on then.' When he'd got back from doing various errands in town after dropping Will off with a tenner for his help, Freya had disappeared inside for one of her epic, hours-long baths; so he knew he wouldn't be missed if he stayed and had a beer. In fact, she'd seemed rather pleased he was going out, which worried him slightly. Or was he just being paranoid?

'How are you?'

'Fine.' She opened a bottle and passed it to him, beckoning him to follow her through the little galley kitchen and into the tiny courtyard garden. She'd put a little pot of geraniums on top of the hedgehog house, he noticed. The wooden archway was hidden slightly by a clump of overgrown grass.

'The thing is –'

'What's –'

They both laughed.

'You go on.' Lucy tucked a strand of hair behind her ear and looked at him. She was wearing with her striped t-shirt a pair of cut-off jeans and flip-flops, with her toenails painted a shiny pink. The sun had coaxed out more freckles on her nose. She took a drink from the bottle and looked at him expectantly.

'It's Freya. I dunno, she's really – she's like a bear with a sore head. Just not herself. She's on the phone non-stop, and if I ask her a question she's a bit snappy and off.'

'Hmm.' Lucy frowned and bit her lip. 'I mean, that sounds like fairly standard teenager stuff to me.' She wrinkled her nose thoughtfully.

God, he hadn't been joking. If he'd had teachers who looked like her, he'd have been a straight-A student. Well, he'd have tried, in any case.

'I don't think it's hormones.' He ducked his head, not quite catching her eye. 'I mean, I know when she's got PMT and this doesn't seem to coincide. It's more like she's just – sullen. Can't be bothered with me.'

'She's been helping Bunty with the guinea pigs and Stanley. And she seemed okay when I saw her the other day. She was telling me about the phone box library idea. She's been quite cheery when I've been there this week.'

'Maybe it's just me.'

'Yeah, well, parents usually do tend to get the worst parts of teenagers. I've known some that behave impeccably at school, and they're nightmares at home. I'd rather that than the other way round, mind you.'

'Because they're easier to deal with?'

'No,' Lucy shook her head again and the lock of hair she'd tucked away flew loose, curling against her cheek. 'If they're misbehaving with the parents, they're comfortable. I worry most when they're placid at school *and* apparently angelic at home. Being a teenager is hard. They've got to let it out somewhere.'

'I guess.'

'Were you an angel at school?'

'God, no.' He laughed. He spread his hands on the table and looked down at them, noticing how many scrapes and bruises he had from work. 'I was a complete nightmare. Disruptive, bored, desperate to get out. But they didn't know then I was dyslexic.' He looked up at her and saw her expression change.

'Oh, that makes more sense,' she said, trailing off.

'What does?'

'Freya said you're not keen on reading. I have to confess, I just thought maybe you were one of those anti-school parents I struggle with.'

He pulled a face and laughed, feeling uncomfortable. 'Charming.'

Lucy went pink. 'Oh God, I'm so sorry. I don't mean that. I mean – well, I guess I need to watch my own prejudices. I always loved reading.'

'Whereas I struggle to read a menu when I go out for a meal. It's a nightmare.'

'I'm sorry.' She reached over and touched his arm fleetingly.

He looked down at the spot where her hand had lain

for a moment and then cleared his throat. 'It's fine.' His voice was low.

She moved her hand away and laced her fingers around the bottle, sitting back in the chair and looking at the ground for a moment.

'I'd like to help Freya. I can try talking to her, see if I can find out if there's anything that's bothering her.'

'I'd really appreciate that.'

If Lucy had thought about what a WI meeting would involve, she mightn't have been so keen to go along. But Freya was desperate to say her piece, and so they trooped into the village hall and were greeted effusively by Helen.

'Goodness, we're starting them younger and younger. Freya, you've just dropped our average age by about twenty years!'

Freya shuffled her feet and looked awkward.

'Ah, Lucy, how lovely to see you.' Susan appeared, with a tea towel in hand. 'I'm sorry, I'm on tea duty tonight. Come and chat to me while I get everything done.'

When the meeting got under way ten minutes later, Lucy heard the strains of 'Jerusalem' being sung – not particularly tunefully, but with gusto – from the main part of the hall. Freya lurked by the side of the kitchen, sitting on a table and looking at her phone, one leg swinging back and forth.

'We've been talking to the printer about how best to

do our little celebration book,' Susan was saying, 'and they're going to come up with a price.'

'I've had a lovely chat with Sarah and Joan at the Abbeyfield house. They told me all about their time here during the war, and how they ended up staying on afterwards.'

'It's lovely, isn't it? Of course, we don't have that many stories from living memory left. I don't suppose you've had any luck persuading Bunty to have a chat?'

Lucy shook her head. If she mentioned anything about writing stuff down, she knew Bunty would clam up immediately. It was more important to gain her trust than to chase her for something for the WI celebration book.

'And so,' said Helen a while later in her commanding voice, 'we come to the final issue – what to do about the telephone box. We've had some quite interesting suggestions.' She looked at Lucy and Freya. 'My idea of replacing the phone box with a commemorative bench to celebrate one hundred years of the WI here in Little Maudley has been well received.'

There was a pause while Helen looked around, pleased, as the small ripple of appreciation she expected travelled through the room.

'There's also been a suggestion that we turn it into a little museum – which I think is rather interesting, especially as we are creating our very own little piece of history with the anniversary book – but Freya here has had what I have to confess is a rather wonderful idea.'

Freya shifted in her seat, looking uncomfortable.

'Would you like to tell us what it is, Freya?'

Lucy looked sideways at her. She chewed her lip for a moment, and then tucked her hair behind her ears and stood up, bravely.

'I've been reading about a village where they turned their phone box into a library.'

Helen looked around at the faces as they registered this idea. She gave a slightly proprietorial nod, as if she was giving permission. 'Go on,' she urged.

'And the Bletchingham library is closing next month because of cuts – which I think is terrible, by the way – and a little book exchange isn't going to make up for what we're losing but it might mean we can swap books and have something to read in the meantime.'

Freya collapsed back onto the hard plastic chair and gave a gusty sigh of relief. 'That was scary,' she said, under her breath.

'I think it's actually terribly inventive,' said Helen. Murmurs of approval spread through the room.

Over tea and slices of lemon drizzle cake, Freya found herself the centre of attention.

'It's such a marvellous idea, I rather wish I'd come up with it myself.'

'Books are magical,' said a woman holding a cup of tea, with a far-off look on her face. 'I spent most of my childhood lost in stories.'

'Me too,' said Freya.

'And me,' agreed Lucy. 'It's such a wonderful way to

see the world through someone else's eyes. They teach us empathy.'

'That's what our English teacher says.'

'She's quite right,' said the older woman. 'Humour, and kindness, and so much more. What's your favourite book, Freya?'

She scrunched up her nose in thought. 'I'm not sure. I have so many. Different ones for different moods.'

'I still love *Pride and Prejudice*,' said the woman, dreamily. 'And Mr Darcy.'

'We all love him,' said Susan, appearing with an iPad in hand. 'Look, I've found an article all about a telephone box in Berkshire which has been converted into a library. It looks wonderful. Well done, Freya.'

Freya looked very pleased and slightly pink. It was agreed that they'd take the idea to the village parish council meeting the following Tuesday, and if everyone was in agreement ('which they will be,' Helen said, quietly, to Lucy, in the tones of one who was used to getting things her own way) then they'd have an extra-ordinary meeting of the WI to arrange how best to convert their battered but much-loved phone box into a tiny little village library.

Helen took Lucy by the arm as they were preparing to leave.

'Pop round to my place this week and we can have a chat about this. I'll get Susan to come along – we can have drinks in the garden.'

Susan looked up, hearing her name. Helen raised her

voice slightly, including her in the invitation. 'Drinks at mine? Tuesday?'

Lucy walked along through the summer evening to Helen's huge, imposing manor house on the edge of the village. It was the house she'd peered in at when she'd first arrived, and this was her first time through the gates. It felt like forever since she'd arrived, but it was only a matter of weeks. Already the rowan trees were laden with berries, hinting at the season to come. All around the village the fields were a hive of industry; combine harvesters were chugging from morning until well after dark, and the air was full of a dusty, wheaten smell. The hedgerows were growing heavy with fruit that was starting to ripen, and the acid brightness of the early summer leaves had been replaced with a dull, faded green.

Chapter Fourteen

Wandering through the village the next day, Lucy paused at the noticeboard by the green. Behind its glass, various flyers and bits of paper advertised everything from beekeeping classes to Zumba at the village hall.

It was funny how much longer the summer holidays felt when there wasn't the prospect of a new term at the end of them. There were a couple of rainy days where it was cold enough that Lucy had even lit the log burner, curling up on the little sofa with Hamish and scribbling notes by hand in her Moleskine notebooks. The article for Susan's WI booklet had come together nicely – there had been so many people willing to chat to her about the surrounding villages, and how women had done so much during the war to keep everything running smoothly. It was no wonder, really, that only a couple of decades later the feminist movement had taken off. Women who'd previously been stuck at home, bringing up children and expected to be silent and well behaved, had stepped out of their boxes and realized they wanted more. They were the grandmothers of today's women. She wondered how they felt, realizing that there was still such a long way to go.

'Hello.'

Sam appeared out of nowhere, making her jump. She turned around to see him standing, work polo shirt on and a bottle of water in hand. He had both spaniels at his feet, their tongues lolling.

He read one of the postcards pinned to the noticeboard. 'Cleaner wanted for large well-kept house in village – that's Helen. No chance.'

Lucy laughed. 'No, I can't imagine Helen's an easy taskmaster.'

'Not tempted to go back to teaching? It must be on your mind at this time of year.'

'A bit,' Lucy admitted. She'd been into Oxford to do some shopping that weekend, and seen all the adverts for Back to School stationery. 'I nearly bought a mountain of stickers and Post-it notes and then remembered I didn't need them.'

He looked at her with a thoughtful expression. 'That must be hard. Teaching's one of those things that's in your blood, I think.'

She smiled ruefully. 'You're not helping.'

'Sorry.' He made a face.

'No. Well, I'm supposed to be writing out some notes but I came for a walk instead, then got caught up in reading all about the parish council and their debates over the phone box library idea.'

'Right. Come with me.' He turned on his heel, the dogs instantly jumping to attention.

'How come everyone in this place has such well-trained dogs? Hamish puts me to shame.'

'Ah, having a friend who's a dog trainer puts me at a bit of an advantage.' He clicked his fingers and both spaniels dropped instantly into the down position. 'I'd like to say it was all my doing, but Mel uses them as demo dogs. They're more like demon dogs with me.' He smiled, beckoning the dogs, who got up and started trotting by their side again.

They walked down the path together until it narrowed. Lucy stepped sideways to move behind Sam, just as he stepped into her path. If only she'd met someone like this when she was teaching, and not when she was on a temporary visit to somewhere she didn't belong. She walked ahead, oddly conscious of his presence behind her. Neither of them spoke for a few minutes until the path widened again and she paused, waiting for him to fall into step beside her.

'I'd love to hear more about what Bunty did in the war,' he said. 'Will you let me in on the secret if she tells you?'

'Of course. She adores you. You'd probably have more luck getting it out of her than I have. Maybe you should come with me one day and bring some of that coffee cake from the village shop. I bet you could charm it out of her.'

He looked a bit embarrassed, pulling a face and rubbing the back of his neck. 'I'm not really known for my charm.'

'Really?' Lucy said, then blushed, realizing what she was implying.

Sam cleared his throat and said gruffly, 'Let's hope Freya hasn't climbed back into bed. It's the last day of the holidays, she's probably trying to catch up on a term's worth of sleep.'

Freya was actually lying in the back garden with headphones in, typing furiously on her phone screen. When she saw them, she jumped upright, looking slightly guilty. She shoved her phone into the back pocket of her jeans.

There's definitely something going on with her, Lucy thought. Probably a secret boyfriend – or girlfriend – or something like that.

'Hi.' Freya brushed grass off her sleeves.

'You look like you're up to something,' said Sam. Lucy shot him a look. Whatever Freya might be hiding, approaching it head-on was definitely not the way forward. It was such a typical parent thing to say. And one thing that teaching had taught her was that just at the point where teenagers started to pull away, parents tended to come down heavily in a way that made them feel claustrophobic. If she was going to get Freya to open up, she needed her dad out of the way.

'D'you know what? I am dying of thirst. Sam, can you do me a huge favour and get me a glass of water, please?'

Thankfully he took the hint. He wandered up the garden path, one hand tucked in the back pocket of his jeans.

Freya glowered after him. 'He's always giving me the third degree. He's obsessed. Where are you going, what are you doing, who are you talking to . . . '

'I think if you're not online much like your dad, it's hard to appreciate how much of life is there now.'

A large sigh. 'God, yes. If you don't reply to someone straight away, you get hassle for ignoring them.'

'You just catching up with friends before term starts? How are you feeling?'

'All right.' She looked down at the blank screen of the phone, turning it over in her hand. 'Actually, I was looking for someone.' She flicked a glance up at Lucy through the curtain of hair, then shifted, chewing her lip.

'Someone you know?' She had a suspicion she knew where this was going.

'Yeah, but—'

'Here you are. I've even put some ice in.' Sam handed her the glass with a flourish.

'Actually,' Lucy gave him a hard stare, opening her eyes wide in the hope she could communicate without speaking, 'if it's not too much trouble, you don't fancy putting the kettle on? I would love a cup of coffee.'

Sam hesitated for a moment, his forehead crinkling. She could virtually see his brain ticking over. 'Oh. Right. Yes. Coffee. Great idea.'

'Sorry,' Lucy indicated the house with her head. She knew that sometimes it was easier to talk about something with a teacher or an adult who had a bit of distance. Ten years of working with teenagers had given her an instinctive feeling for when something was bubbling away under the surface. 'So. Who is it you're looking for?' she asked Freya.

211

'My mum.' Freya picked a daisy and started pulling off the petals, one by one. 'I've found her.'

Lucy swallowed. This was good news for Freya, who must've spent years feeling like something was missing. But how would Sam feel if the mother of his child reappeared and wanted to be part of his life? She felt strangely uncomfortable at the thought of him playing happy families – but of course she was leaping miles ahead.

'She's in London. Not even that far away.'

'And you've been talking to her?'

'A bit.' Freya chewed the inside of her cheek, brows furrowed. 'I felt like I wanted to know who she was. Why she left.'

'And how do you feel?'

'I dunno. I wasn't expecting the big *running into each other's arms* thing, but – I don't feel anything.'

'Were you thinking you'd feel relieved?'

'Or happy. Or nervous.' Freya chewed on her lip. 'Maybe I am a bit nervous, actually.'

Lucy gazed across the untidy garden. The grass was in desperate need of a cut, and the flower borders were choked with tangles of bindweed and rosebay willowherb. The white seed heads were floating prettily in the hazy sunshine. Autumn was coming, and with it came all sorts of changes, and a reminder – in the form of Freya's discovery – that life here had gone on, and would go on, without her. She wasn't part of Little Maudley. She brushed a ladybird off her arm and watched it spin off into the air.

'I expect you've got a lot of mixed-up emotions about it all. I know I would.'

Freya nodded. She looked down at the pile of shredded daisies and laughed briefly. 'All the emotions,' she said, rolling her eyes.

Turning to humour was an obvious defence. She needed to talk to Sam, let him know what was going on.

'Have you told Camille?'

'Nope. I felt like she'd tell her mum, and Mel would tell Dad because they're so close. It's different telling you, because you're nothing to do with us.'

Lucy winced inwardly. Teenagers had no need of sugar-coating.

'Do you think you'll say anything to your dad?'

'Maybe?'

'Are you wondering how he'd react?'

'A bit. I don't want him to have a meltdown and tell me I'm not allowed to see her.'

'D'you want to see her?'

Freya stared off into the distance for a few moments before she spoke.

'She's my mum.'

Lucy looked at Freya. Her heart-shaped face reflected the conflicting emotions – hope, curiosity and a guarded-ness which made sense after all this time. Freya frowned slightly.

'Mums can be tricky.' Lucy pulled up a daisy, thoughtfully pulling one petal off after another. 'Mine is in Australia. It's an awful lot easier to get on with her there than it was when we were living in the same house.'

'Yeah, I know. I don't think I even want to talk to her, but at the same time . . .' She tailed off, biting her thumbnail.

'You don't need to make any decisions, though.'

'No.' Freya brightened at that.

'Maybe you should speak to your dad?'

'I don't want to upset him.'

'I don't think you're going to. I'm sure he's expected this day would come – I know I would have.'

'I don't know what to do.' Freya closed her eyes, her dark eyebrows gathering.

'Think about talking to your dad. I know you're trying to protect him, but he can cope. I'm sure of that.'

'One coffee,' Sam said, in a slightly too hearty voice. He was giving them warning that he was coming back, and Lucy was grateful for it.

'If you want to talk, I'm always here,' she told Freya quietly.

'Thanks.'

They sat in the garden, soaking up the last of the sunshine, and turned their thoughts to plans for the telephone box library.

Chapter Fifteen

Bunty watched from the window as Susan and Helen bustled up to the telephone box, dressed in overalls, and set out their painting equipment. She'd half expected a painter and decorator to be given the job, but she'd been surprised to watch as villagers came back and forth, in twos and threes – first clearing away the weeds, then someone from the telephone company came by and stripped away the entrails of the phone box. A glazier arrived and replaced the cracked and broken windows. It was quite interesting to watch how everyone was coming together. There had been a flyer posted through the letter box, too, asking if she had any books in good condition which might be suitable for the lending library. Lucy had told her all about the meeting at the parish council where they'd agreed to a schedule – which was Helen's favourite word – and now there they were, restoring it to its former bright livery. Oh, that telephone box. The stories it could tell. Bunty had stood by the window washing dishes for over seventy years, watching children meeting there, calls being made, secret meetings, drunken kisses – there wasn't much that hadn't happened in that little box. She was glad it hadn't been knocked down.

She turned away, putting the tea towel on the Aga to

dry. There was something very precious about September, Bunty thought. It was the feeling of soaking up the final days of summer, making the most of them before everything faded and went dark for the winter. She'd always hated winter – it was funny how the cold had made everything feel worse. All Lucy's questioning about the war had brought back memories of freezing in layers of clothes as she got on her bicycle in the morning and set off for the hut. That had made her think about how long it had been since she'd been there – it was funny how they'd all been so keen to whitewash over everything that happened, carry on with life as if the war was something they'd all rather forget. And here were these young things, desperate to go over it all and ask all sorts of questions. It was bringing things back in a way that was most disconcerting. She picked up her bag and opened the front door to see Lucy waiting beside her little blue car. She was looking across the lane at Bell Cottage, clearly lost in thought.

'There you are.' Lucy turned, pushing her hair back from her face and smiling. She was covered in freckles from sitting in the garden writing up notes, and looked pretty in a blue-and-white sundress and a cardigan. There wouldn't be many warm days like this left, unless there was an Indian summer.

'It's very kind of you to give me a lift,' Bunty said as she climbed into the passenger seat and pulled the seatbelt across. Goodness, these things were stiff, and her hands were so uncooperative. She tried to click it into place twice, thankful that Lucy didn't reach over to help – it was one of the things that she liked about her. Margaret was always so quick to jump in, patronizingly, treating her like she was an old woman, which was patently ridiculous. Her shoulders shook with amusement.

'Sorted?' Lucy fastened her own seatbelt and turned the ignition.

'Where's Hamish today?'

'He's being used by Mel as a demonstration dog in her training class.'

'Star pupil?'

'Probably more likely how not to behave,' Lucy giggled. 'He ate one of my sandals last night. Every time I think he's grown up a bit, he likes to remind me that he's still a puppy.'

'Mel's terribly good with them, isn't she?'

'Yes. She and –' there was a tiny beat of silence – 'and Sam are very nice. I'm glad I met them.'

'They're both good sorts. I've known them both since they were babes in arms.'

'And they're such good friends. It's nice that the girls get on so well, too.'

Interesting, Bunty thought. Lucy was definitely digging for information. She looked sideways at Lucy, taking in the soft curls and the turned-up, freckled nose. She was a very pretty girl. Clever, too. And she had a career. So nice that nowadays they weren't rushed into getting married. If Bunty herself hadn't felt the pressure not to be left on the shelf, perhaps things would have turned out very differently. She'd found herself looking at her old diary again last night. Strange how the distant past seemed more familiar in some ways than a few years ago. She could remember cycling along this road so many times – the moment when the incline started to tell on the back of her calves, burning as she'd stand on the pedals to make it to the top of the hill, breathless, before swooping down through the dappled sunshine of the tree-covered lane and left onto the –

'Can you turn left here?'

Lucy glanced at her in surprise, slowing down. 'I thought you wanted to pop to the chemist?'

'I do. But I just – oh, it doesn't matter.'

'No,' Lucy clicked on the indicator. 'I'm not in any rush. Where are we going?'

'Left again up here.' Bunty pointed a finger towards a single-track lane that curled up through overhanging trees. Sunlight and shade played on their faces as Lucy made her way along it. Steep banks lined with hedgerows, their leaves fading to olive green, towered on either side of them. They pulled into a passing place to let through a battered Land Rover, thick with dust and towing a trailer full of sheep. One of the sheep looked Bunty in the eye and bleated silently as he passed.

It had been donkey's years since she was here, and yet nothing had changed.

'Right here.'

'On this track?'

The unmade road was laid with rough hardcore, with dried-out potholes which would fill with water as soon as the weather changed. She used to get soaked to the ankles, covered in mud splashes. In summer it was hot and boring, in winter freezing cold, and the days would drag on interminably.

'Yes, go on. Might be a bit bumpy.'

The little car rattled up the rutted track until they crested a hill. She looked out at a field full of cows.

'Here.'

There was a creak as Lucy pulled the handbrake and turned, looking at her expectantly.

'Is this us?'

'Hmm,' said Bunty. She peered through the window. 'It's been such a long time. I can't believe how overgrown it is.'

Lucy frowned, following her gaze.

At the end of the path, at the top of the hill, there stood a concrete hut with a flat roof. It was overgrown with weeds, and the windows were covered with metal grilles.

'Is this something to do with your job in the war?'

'I spent almost every day in that place.'

'So you *didn't* actually work at Bletchley.'

Bunty shook her head.

'No. We were sent there, but then I was packaged off here. The work we did was top secret – I never breathed a word about it. Not even my husband knew what I did.'

It felt slightly illicit to admit it, even now. They'd

signed away their right to talk, promised king and country that they'd keep their work from everyone they knew.

'You didn't even tell Milly?'

Bunty shook her head.

'Not a word. She emigrated to Australia after the war with her husband. She died in eighty-nine, and we never talked about it once. One just didn't.'

'Didn't she wonder what you were doing?'

'Oh, everyone was doing something in those days. War work. We were far more interested in what was going on after hours. That's when the fun happened. That's what you should be looking at in that research of yours.'

'It seems as if life was incredibly full back then. When I spoke to the women in the Abbeyfield house about growing up here as evacuees, they told me the place was quite different, with lots going on. I suppose people shopped locally, and didn't drive into Bletchingham as much.'

'Oh, we caught the bus, or cycled in summer – back then we seemed to have heaps of energy. But yes, there was the post office and the shop and there was a little tea room on the corner of West Street – it's a holiday cottage now.' A breeze blew in over the hill, through the car window, making the hairs on Bunty's arms stand up. She pulled her cardigan more tightly across her chest and wound the window back up. 'We didn't have a spare moment. If we weren't working, or out dancing or going to the cinema or to talks, we were still busy. Mrs Brown had us knitting comforts for the WVS to send off to the troops. I could do a pair of gloves in no time at all back then. We used to listen to the radio and knit like the devil.'

Lucy had read all about that. Back in wartime, the Women's Voluntary Service had provided an astonishing five tons a month of knitted comforts – they included scarves, hats, balaclavas and gloves. They were doled out to servicemen and women, and constantly in demand because they were more comfortable than the standard-issue ones given out as part of their uniforms.

They both looked out of the window at the dilapidated building. Wind ruffled the trees that surrounded it and a couple of early falling leaves spun down, reminding Lucy it was September, and time was passing. She looked across at Bunty, who was lost in her thoughts.

'You don't want to get out and have a look?'

Bunty shook her head. 'No. I don't know what made me think of coming here. Just a fancy, I think. It's been so long.'

'I'd like to look.'

Bunty wavered for a second.

'Oh, go on then.'

They climbed out of the car and made their way across the shaggy grass towards the building. It was long, the roof flat and covered with cracked black bitumen, which curled in places where tangles of weeds grew in clumps.

Bunty walked ahead, and peered in through the narrow glass of the window.

'They used it after the war as a store, I think.'

'And what did you do here?'

'Oh, well,' said Bunty, and she gave a sudden shout of laughter that startled a little robin who'd been perched on a fence post, looking at them inquisitively. 'Now *that* would be telling.'

Back in the car, Bunty glanced at Lucy as she edged the vehicle carefully down the rough track towards the road. She was a sweet girl, taking her up here on a whim. Goodness knows how many times she'd driven this way in the past, and not once had she felt the urge to go and look at Signal Hill and remember. It was the diary that had triggered it, she expected. The round, excited writing of the girl who'd poured all her secrets into that little hard-backed black book, keeping it hidden from Len all the years they were married. He wouldn't ever have looked, mind you – he was such a peaceable, easy-going sort. It was peculiar that Gordon had grown up with his nature, considering.

Lucy drove them on through the countryside towards town. Tractors were already beginning their preparations for winter – fields which had been sheets of gold only a few weeks ago were now being ploughed and turned over to thick ridges of dark earth. A flock of geese flew over – early this year. That usually meant a cold winter was on the way. Another housing estate was going up in a field where she'd once walked with Harry and Milly and the evacuee children, taking them on a picnic. They'd lain on the grass, gazing up at the sky, waiting for planes to fly overhead. Bunty closed her eyes for a moment, feeling the warmth of the sun on her face as they drove, imagining the hum of the car engine was the distant noise of approaching aircraft.

Harry had been in a strange mood that afternoon. She could still remember every word of that entry. It had been prescient, somehow.

September 5th, 1941

Lovely afternoon taking the kiddies for a picnic. Milly grumbled about having to spend her day off with children, but she certainly brightened up when Harry turned up with his friend Luke. He's Australian, tall and handsome and very funny – and she definitely took a shine to him. Mrs B made us some fish paste sandwiches and some lovely lemon cake (I think she might be warming to him) and we had an apple each, as well. The kiddies dashed around trying to catch butterflies and we stretched out on the grass and looked up at the sky. Harry was in an odd sort of mood.

We lay side by side on the meadow, our fingers just touching. As always, there was the constant hum of planes passing overhead.

'You seem quiet,' I said. I turned to look at him and he gave a heavy sigh, then rolled over on his side, propping himself up on his arm.

'Bit of bad news. Three of the guys I know FTR from a flight over the Channel last night.'

'FTR?' I was puzzled by the terminology.

'Failed to return. Bought it.'

It took a moment for it to dawn on me what he meant. I sat up and took his hand in mine. 'I'm so sorry.'

He shook his head. 'Don't be. It's the nature of the beast.'

'Don't say that.' I went quite cold, just thinking about it. 'I don't want something to happen to you.'

He squeezed my hand then, and laced his fingers through mine. 'You don't need to worry. I'm on rest from operations.'

'What does that mean?' I frowned. My head knew that everyone had to do their bit – but my heart – well, it was saying something else altogether.

'I'm here for six months, training pilots. Safe as houses – well, safe as we can be.' He gestured to the sky, where three Blenheims were passing overhead.

'And once the six months are up?'

'You don't have to think about that, honey. It's a long time away.'

'Come on, you two,' Milly shouted, breaking the mood. 'The boys want to play a game of rounders.'

Harry sprang to his feet, offering me a hand to pull me upright. I dusted off my skirt and we dashed over to join them. There's no point in worrying about what might be when there's so much fun to be had right now. I've decided to make that my motto.

Fortunately the traffic into Bletchingham was quiet and, after finding a parking space down a side street, Lucy and Bunty hit the shops. Bunty headed for the chemist, and as she stood in the queue, she watched as Lucy crossed the High Street to visit the little art gallery and gift shop she loved. They met up again and spent a lovely half hour browsing in the little book shop, where Lucy bought a couple of books on World War Two to add to her collection. Bunty looked at the clock tower.

'It's almost twelve.' Her legs were beginning to tire and she fancied something nice to eat before the lunchtime rush started. 'Shall we have a bite?'

They went to the old almshouses, which had been converted into a bright, sunny cafe, and sat down by the window opposite the old castle. Lucy had thought Bunty was tiring, so it was a relief that she'd been the one to suggest lunch. She was such a strong, independent character.

'Here you are, ladies.' A cheerful woman dressed all in black appeared, holding two menus. She passed one to each of them and poured out two glasses of water.

'Do you miss teaching?' Bunty looked at her thoughtfully.

'Yes. And no. There are definitely some things I don't miss – like the headaches.' Lucy looked down at the menu for a moment. 'Or the waking up in the middle of the night worrying about Ofsted inspections.'

'There seems to be so much of that these days.' Bunty looked thoughtful. 'Of course, there was none of that when Milly was teaching. Just as well, really. She had so many children and gosh, they could be a handful. I used to go in if I had a day off during the week, and we'd take the class out for a walk so they could find wildflowers and do some sketching. All we really wanted was the chance to have a natter about what we'd been up to.'

Lucy had enjoyed a long talk with Hannah, Helen Bromsgrove's retired housekeeper, about just that. She'd been an evacuee to the village in early 1940, and had stayed on afterwards. Her mother had been widowed in the Blitz and she'd come to live in Little Maudley, taking a job working for the big house just outside the village where Len, Bunty's husband, had been the land agent. ('Lovely man, he was. Very steady,' she'd said. Lucy had felt, oddly, that there was something *un*said about Bunty in that statement.) They'd lived in a cottage provided by the landowner, and when Hannah had grown up she'd carried on in the same position. It was more common than she'd thought. Several of the evacuees had gravitated back to the village as they'd grown older, spending their later years enjoying the peace and quiet they'd remembered.

'Can I take your orders?' The woman returned with a notebook and pencil.

'Of course,' Bunty went on, after she'd left, 'we had so many evacuees at one point that they used to have to divide the school day up into halves. Poor Milly was worn out. One lot of pupils first thing in the morning, the second after lunch. And the state of some of the children . . . they were absolutely filthy when they came to us, riddled with head lice and all sorts.'

'Must have been hard for them, coming from the city and ending up in a tiny village.'

226

'I think lots of them had a ball, once they got over the homesickness. Sometimes their parents would come and visit for the weekend – the Crown was always packed with families. There were a fair few who didn't want to go back after the worst of it, as well. They stayed all the way through and never left. Old Brian Turner on the village committee was one of them. Did you talk to him yet?'

Lucy nodded. 'I've interviewed a couple of women from the WI, and collected some lovely wartime memories. It's funny how many of them mention you.' There was a long pause, during which time the waitress returned, putting down cutlery wrapped in paper napkins, and made a lot of fuss over refilling their glasses of water. Lucy shifted in her chair, and waited.

'I wondered if you'd like to be interviewed? It would be nice to have you featured in the commemorative book, too.'

Bunty looked at her through shrewd blue eyes and shook out her napkin, placing it carefully on her lap.

'I don't think so, no.'

'But you've told me so many interesting things. If we just gathered all of those memories together—'

'Here we are,' said the waitress, cheerfully. Lucy rolled her eyes behind her back. After she left she tried again.

'It wouldn't take long.'

'I don't think so, dear. I don't mind talking to you, but I don't want old memories raked up. The past is the past.'

For a few minutes they were silent as they ate. Lucy noticed Bunty looking across the window, lost in thought.

'I'm sorry I pushed you. I didn't mean to make you uncomfortable.'

Bunty shook her head. 'Not at all, Lucy. It's just that there are some parts of history that are best left there. Things were different back then. We were – well, it was a very different time.'

They ate lunch and chatted about safe subjects, like the new family who were moving into the house along the road, and talk of the big house being taken over by the youngest son of the family after some dispute over inheritance.

'Of course, Len always said that family were quite batty.'

'Your husband? Susan told me he was the land agent there during the war.'

'He was, yes. Left not long after and became an accountant when Gordon was still in short trousers.' Bunty smiled faintly. 'I think he found it easier to manage numbers than he did the unpredictable nature of a huge estate, especially after the war. It was requisitioned and used as a hospital, and it was in a terrible state afterwards. Took them years to get it back to – well, it never really went back to the way it was.'

'I'd like to go and look around. I wonder if they'd let me.'

'Goodness, yes. Tell them I sent you. They always send me a Christmas hamper, even now. Jam and cheese.' She looked out of the window. 'Very nice biscuits,' she added, as an afterthought.

'So you stayed in the village after the war? You weren't tempted to go back to London afterwards?' It slipped out before she even realized. After Bunty's reticence earlier, she was treading on dangerous ground to probe.

Bunty shook her head. 'No. Nothing to go back to. My sister was killed in the first wave of the Blitz, and my parents were killed in the second. The whole house was gone. Nothing left. '

'Oh, Bunty. I'm so sorry.' Lucy felt tears prickling at the corner of her eyes. The idea of losing everything in one fell swoop was just unimaginable.

'Long time ago now. Luckily Mrs Brown was happy to keep me on once the war work was done, and of course then there was Len.'

'And you've lived in the village ever since?'

'No. After he stopped working as a land agent, he had to give up the little cottage on the edge of the estate – that was a wrench. I loved that little house. It was my escape.'

Lucy glanced at her for a second, noticing once again that Bunty had that faraway expression. Escape – that was a curious choice of word. She was certain that there was a lot more going on than Bunty would admit to.

'And then we lived in a little house right here in Bletchingham for a long while, until Gordon was finished at the grammar school. And then Mrs Brown died, and she left me – well, us – the cottage. It was a tremendous shock. She didn't have any family to speak of – her daughter died young, and she didn't want it going into the hands of some distant relative or being sold off. Milly was gone to Australia by then, of course. So we moved back – I was delighted. Len rather less so,' she added.

'Len didn't like village life?'

'I think it always had some . . . memories he'd rather forget.'

'Oh?' Lucy tried not to look too interested.

Bunty scratched her ear, and looked down at her soup. 'I'm blethering on. Now, tell me about your plans. Are you going to return to the same school, do you think?'

Lucy's heart sank – not only because Bunty had clammed up again, but because she herself didn't want to think about what she would do in the new year when it was time to leave the village and return to Brighton.

'I'm not sure.' She chewed her lip. 'I'm going to see my old head teacher next week and have a chat with him.'

'Well, that sounds very sensible.'

'It does, doesn't it?'

What Lucy didn't want to admit was that the thought of returning to her old life in Brighton made her feel full of dread, rather than excited.

Chapter Sixteen

The gorgeous late summer weather didn't last. The heavens opened that afternoon and it poured for a week, bringing in an early, chilly autumn. And with the new term, Lucy knew her time in the village was beginning to come to a close.

She left the cottage a few days later with the weather matching her mood. Rain pelted down, trickling down her neck as she shoved her bag in the boot. Hamish was safely curled up by the Aga in Bunty's house, where she'd have quite cheerfully joined him.

'Are you off somewhere exciting?'

Helen, in a pair of expensive-looking wellies and a matching umbrella, was standing on the opposite side of the road, just outside Sam's house.

'Popping down to Brighton to speak to my boss.'

The head of her school had been in touch, saying that he knew it was early days but he wanted to have a meeting to discuss her return in January. She'd only been in the village for a couple of months and somehow she felt time was gathering up, as if a string somewhere was being tugged. The first few lazy weeks in Little Maudley had gone on forever. It wouldn't be long before the shops were full of Hallowe'en decorations and then Christmas ones, and the autumn term would be over and she'd be – she shook herself. She was overthinking things. All he'd done was ask if she'd be able to drop in for a meeting. And she couldn't carry on floating around doing nothing forever, lovely as it was. She closed the car boot and looked across at Helen, whose expression was concerned.

'Well, I don't like the sound of that. We'd like to keep you right here, thank you very much. I'm just going to see Sam about the shelves. They're coming to take away the interior fittings of the phone box this week. It's all very exciting.'

Lucy smiled, but felt wretched.

'I'll hear all about it when I get back.' She waved briefly, then climbed into the car.

The traffic wasn't on her side, either. She'd arranged to meet Tom for lunch before he set off on a trip to New York, but – she tapped irritably at the steering wheel – that wasn't going to happen. She arrived at their flat with enough time to say a quick hello before he shot out to climb into a waiting Uber, suitcase and passport in hand. His new girlfriend Kate – the one who'd finally tamed him, as Lucy teased him on the telephone – smiled apologetically and kissed hello and goodbye.

'Lovely to meet you in real life at last.' She was tall and pretty, with dark hair cut in a gamine style that emphasized huge dark brown eyes.

'Sorry it's such a flying hello. I'm sure we'll catch up properly another time soon.'

Tom beckoned to Kate. 'Got to go.'

'Have an amazing time.'

Lucy shooed him out the door and closed it, leaning back against the wall. After the cottage, it seemed huge and airy, the bright white of the hall and stairs dazzling after the muted old-fashioned shades of dull cream and the stone walls.

She opened her phone and looked at her messages. Having heard she was back in town, a couple of her teaching friends had got in touch asking if she wanted to go for a drink. She'd hardly heard from them while she'd been away – it was often the case in the holidays, when everyone retreated to their own lives away from the staffroom, but Lucy felt a bit guilty that she hadn't made much of an effort even when they had been in touch. Somehow, taking a step away had made her realize that the friendships she had were based mainly on their mutual hatred of the head teacher, and their dread of Ofsted inspections. Sipping a glass of overpriced white wine in a bar in town just brought that home to her.

'So what's the story with village life?'

Mandy, a fellow history teacher, smiled at her over the top of her glass. She looked exhausted already, as if the six-week holiday hadn't happened. Of course, Lucy thought, she'd probably spent a fair amount of it on prep work. The idea that they got thirteen weeks off a year was one of the staffroom jokes.

'Well, I've—' she began, but was cut off by Harriet, Mandy's best friend, who appeared from the bar. She gave Lucy a brief kiss hello and launched into a torrent of gossip, shouting to be heard over the pounding music. Had it always been this busy in Brighton, Lucy wondered, or had she just somehow forgotten what city life was like? She thought fondly of the pub in Little Maudley, and of sitting in the beer garden having a glass of Pimm's with Mel and Sam the other night. Mel had been regaling them with tales from her latest dog training class, which had them crying with laughter.

'Oh my God, I have to tell you what happened last night. I went out with Jamie and Sally and we went to the Arches and—'

An hour later, Lucy had heard all about the gossip from the staffroom, the latest on who was sleeping with who, and she could feel her temples beginning to pound in a way they hadn't for a long time.

'I'm just going to nip to the loo.'

Mandy nodded, looking down at her phone before she'd even turned away.

In the bathroom, Lucy ran cold water over her wrists, letting the water cool her skin. Then she put her hands to her face, pressing against her eyes. It was weird being back – like she'd stepped out of sync with Brighton life after only a few months.

She looked at herself in the mirror. Her face was freckly and looked younger – she peered forward, looking at her eyes. They definitely looked less bloodshot. The doctor in Bletchingham had been delighted with her latest blood pressure results – she was still being checked regularly

– but being back here seemed to make the blood pulse alarmingly in her ears.

'Are you going to join us in the Lion?' Mandy picked up her bag. It was only early, and they'd obviously decided to make a night of it.

The Lion was the teachers' regular haunt, just round the corner from the school. The prospect of going in there and having to make polite conversation with everyone made her stomach feel leaden. Old Lucy would have done it – old Lucy always just went along with what everyone else wanted, for the sake of a quiet life. It struck her then in a flash of clarity: all those nights out were about drinking away the stress. With that gone, the drive just wasn't there.

'I think I'll give it a miss. I feel a bit weird.'

Instead, she took a walk along the promenade, stepping down onto the pebbled beach and scrunching along towards the pier before sitting down to watch the waves. A seagull hopped past, holding the paper wrapper from a bag of chips in his mouth, before depositing it on the ground to peck the leftovers off. You never change, Brighton, Lucy thought, smiling at the gull. He eyed her beadily, picked up his wrapper and flew off.

But I've changed, she realized. She turned to look at a cackling gang of women out on a hen do, dressed in matching t-shirts with bright pink veils streaming from their hair. When she'd been teaching, the only way to let off steam after a stressful week had been to hit the pub and wake up with a hangover on a Saturday morning, before going out for breakfast and then spending the afternoon marking coursework. Since she'd moved to the village, the slower pace of life had somehow seeped into everything she did. She found herself wondering what Mel was up to, and how Freya was getting on with forging a relationship with her mum again. And how Bunty was doing. It was the nicest surprise that she'd ended up such good friends with someone old enough to be her grandmother.

She picked up a smooth stone and threw it into the water, watching it disappear in the waves. The tide was going out. Her phone pinged with a notification – Mandy, probably, trying to persuade her to come out. But no, it was a number she didn't recognize at first, but in an instant she knew who'd sent it.

Sam was working on a new treehouse – one that had been specially designed with wheelchair access for a little boy who lived in a village nearby – and he'd sent her a message with a photo.

Thought you'd like to see this.

He must've taken her number from the village group chat, which had been a hotbed of discussion as the plans for the Hallowe'en party at the village hall and the final plans for the phone box library were put into place.

It's Sam, by the way.

I guessed that, she typed, laughing.

How's the glamour of city life?

Not very glamorous at all. I think I've been brainwashed by the villagers.

Ah, it happens to us all. I mean who'd want to exchange the latest gossip at the post office for a night out in a restaurant?

Not me. I mean I'd rather the village gossip. Seriously.

Posh city friends not as much fun as us lot?

I've ducked out of a night out in favour of a bath and an early night.

Sounds good. I've got to take Freya to a party tonight, and pick her up at midnight.

Ugh.

Exactly. Speak soon? x

Smiling at her phone, Lucy put it back in her pocket. It was weird to be at home, but feeling homesick for somewhere else. She made her way back across the beach, and walked the long way back to the house.

Chapter Seventeen

Lucy pulled off the motorway, leaving Brighton and the south coast far behind her, and made her way along the now-familiar leafy lanes – now shaded in a glorious palette of russets and golds. She sang along to the radio. This was such a lovely place to live.

'Hello.' Sam appeared out of nowhere as she pulled the car into the space outside the cottage.

'Where did you spring from?' She could feel herself grinning ridiculously.

'Sixth sense. I thought you might want this –' he held up a pint of milk – 'and maybe this?' In his other hand was a freshly baked cake from the village shop.

'Oh my God, you are amazing.'

He rubbed his chin, looking pleased with himself. 'Your place or mine?'

She looked at the floor, feeling suddenly shy.

'I mean for tea. Unless you've got any other plans?' He was teasing now.

'Tea would be lovely. Coffee even better. That was a long drive.'

'In that case, come to mine. I'll ring Mel and let her know you're back – she can bring Hame over. She picked him up from Bunty earlier.'

Lucy threw her bag onto the sofa and headed back across the road.

Sam was inside his cottage, a tea towel over his shoulder. She watched as he busied himself in the kitchen, making a coffee at the expensive-looking Italian machine, steaming the milk, swirling it in the mugs and then handing it over, bringing a couple of plates from the dresser and a knife.

'Do you want to cut it? I can, but I tend to just hack off gigantic slices.'

'Gigantic slices are fine by me.'

Sam cut two pieces of cake and placed them on the plates. 'Sugar?'

'No, this is lovely, thank you.'

It was weird. They'd been chatting back and forth since he'd broken the ice sending the treehouse photograph, but somehow now they were sitting opposite each other in the little kitchen of his cottage, she found herself tongue-tied and wondering what to say. She looked at the dresser, seeing a photograph of a much younger Freya grinning toothlessly, her school tie askew. He followed her gaze.

'Found it the other day. She's cute, isn't she?'

'How's she been?'

'Well, she seemed fine yesterday. But this morning I asked her who she was emailing, and she just snapped at me and said couldn't she do anything without me bugging her all the time, and then slammed the front door on her way out.'

Lucy pulled a sympathetic face.

'So how was Brighton? Did you enjoy being back in civilization?' He put his chin in his hand and looked at her. The lines around his dark brown eyes gave the impression he found life amusing. Lucy looked down at her plate, rearranging cake crumbs with a finger.

'Well,' she began. 'It was nice to see the school, and the kids, of course.'

'They'll be looking forward to seeing you again?'

'I didn't see many of them. I was in and out of the head's office pretty quickly.'

'So you'll be back to work in January?'

'I'm not quite sure yet.'

'How come?' Sam turned in his seat slightly, so he was looking directly at her. She swallowed.

'I don't know. I just – have you ever gone back to something and realized it's just not the same?' As soon as she'd opened her mouth, she remembered that Sam had been living here in Little Maudley all his life. But he nodded, slowly.

'Yeah. Not work, but – yeah. It's weird. Like you've built it up and been absolutely convinced it's the right thing and you get there and –' He gestured, raising his palms skyward.

'Exactly.' She bit her lip. 'Just – I'm not sure where that leaves me.'

He lifted his eyebrows slightly. 'Well, I'd be happy – I mean we'd be – I mean . . .' He shook his head, laughing ruefully. 'I think you fit in here pretty well.

That's what I'm trying to say, in my own uniquely inarticulate manner.'

She loved village life. But giving up the life she'd known, to stay here? She couldn't live on her savings forever, for one thing, and – she sighed – it wasn't exactly practical. The clock chimed the hour. 'Right; well, I'd better find something to do in the meanwhile.'

'If you're stuck, I've got an idea.' Sam picked up the keys to his truck. 'D'you want to come and see the new project I've been working on?'

Lower Maudley was a tiny, even more picturesque version of their village. A tiny church stood by a village green with a phone box that was hung with baskets of autumn flowers.

'They don't have a neglected phone box, I note.'

'They don't have a neglected anything. This place makes Little Maudley look like an inner-city slum. It's the most desirable place in the area.'

'So no expense spared on the treehouse?'

'Definitely not.' He jumped out of the truck, leaving the keys in the ignition, and pushed open a heavy white-painted gate. 'You'll see in a minute.'

'And they don't mind you randomly turning up with me in the middle of the afternoon?'

'They're not here, they're in Cancun. All six of them.'

'Wow.'

He raised his eyebrows and waved an arm in the direction of the house. 'Yeah.'

Behind a huge manor house with sweeping, perfectly

manicured lawns a garden stretched out, divided by neat gravelled paths.

'Follow me, madam.'

'So have you finished work on Janet's treehouse?'

She stepped over a low lavender hedge and onto a gravelled path.

'Yes, it's all done. They're delighted with it. That sort of thing makes it all worthwhile.'

At the end of one of the paths, a hedge had been clipped into a neat archway that bore the sign 'Tim's House' in neat italics on a wooden board.

'What d'you think?'

A huge oak tree stood in front of them, with a treehouse surrounding the base. It was completely different to the first one she'd seen, but just as magical.

'It's amazing.'

'And it's at ground level. I thought you'd appreciate that.' He gave a smile that made her stomach twist disobediently.

'I love it.' She ran a hand along the smooth lines of the archway entrance. 'How do you dream these up?'

Sam looked embarrassed. He ducked his head, rubbing his forehead for a moment, then looked at her through splayed fingers.

'Honestly?'

She nodded, stepping on a fallen tree branch and wobbling sideways. He reached out with lightning reflexes and caught her by the waist, steadying her. When he moved his hand away, Lucy realized that she could

242

still feel the sensation of the warmth of his hand through the thin linen of her shirt.

'I think about what I would have wanted when I was a kid.'

Glancing up at him, Lucy caught a wistful expression on his face.

'You didn't have a treehouse when you were growing up?'

He gave a rueful laugh. 'Definitely not. My mum didn't really do the whole parenting thing. I think it's why I'm so determined to do the right thing by Freya. Come through and see the rest.'

Inside was even more beautiful. Lucy sat down on a carved wooden bench, running a hand along the smooth wooden handle. Everything had been created with such love and tenderness.

'What about you?' His voice was gruff.

'No, my mum wasn't really the treehouse type. I mean we lived in the middle of Brighton, so there wouldn't have been room, but . . .'

He nodded. 'I know what you mean. Where is she now? Still in Brighton?'

'No, Australia. She's happy, so she's low-maintenance.'

'Sounds like Freya's mum.'

They were stepping onto ground that was new, and Lucy was conscious that talking about this stuff wasn't something that came easily to him. Mel had mentioned his ex in passing several times, explaining that she was better off out of his life – and Freya's.

'Do you think she wonders what it would be like if she'd stayed?'

He shook his head. 'Definitely not. I don't think Freya fitted into her plans.'

'Well, she seems pretty happy and settled.'

'Freya?' He looked happy at that. 'D'you think? It's hard to tell. Harder still when she's been so – different – recently.'

Lucy put a hand to her mouth in a subconscious gesture. She knew Freya had been looking for her mum. It wasn't her place to break a confidence, but she couldn't help asking, 'D'you ever wonder if she'd like to get in touch with her mum?'

'God, I hope not.' Sam's hand was curved around the top of a rough-hewn wooden post, and his knuckles whitened as his fingers tightened in an involuntary movement. He cleared his throat and spoke after a moment's thought. 'I'm afraid if she came back into Freya's life she'd let her down. And if that happened, I'd be letting her down.'

She looked away, brushing a piece of wood shaving from the bench beside her. There was trouble ahead, but she wasn't the one to tell him. Perhaps she could ask Bunty's advice.

'It's funny – when I was teaching I felt like I had more of a clue about teenagers than I do now I've spent time with Freya.'

'Maybe they're easier in packs.' Sam looked thoughtful. 'No, I think maybe it's more that when you actually

THE TELEPHONE BOX LIBRARY

stop looking at the big picture, you realize there are lots of details that it's easy to miss. Getting to know her – and you – means I'm seeing it from a different perspective.'

'She's not that difficult, is she?' He laughed, holding out a hand and pulling her up. Again, she felt the imprint of his skin on hers lingering.

'No, more like – I was pretty sure that I had teenagers sussed. But seeing you with her, and Mel with Camille, I realize that the hard stuff really does happen at home. I bet Freya is an angel at school.'

'Pretty much. Not like me.'

'I always quite liked school. It was the one place that was stable.'

'D'you think that's why you went into teaching?'

'I'd never thought of that.' He opened the door for her, standing aside. He had very old-fashioned manners, which Bunty approved of, as she'd mentioned to Lucy on more than one occasion.

A moment later, he swung into the driver's seat and turned on the engine. Lucy pulled down the shade to protect her eyes from the low sunlight.

'I suppose it makes sense,' Sam went on. 'And d'you think that's why you're into history?'

Lucy remembered the final day of school: Tyler standing in the classroom, telling her he liked history because it didn't move. Her childhood, and future, had felt so uncertain, too, that there was a comfort in looking to the past.

'I think so. It's safe. I mean, there's lots to learn, always – look at Bunty.'

'Weird, isn't it. She's been through so much. She's living history.'

'That's why I want her to talk about what she experienced. She's opened up a bit, but I'm still waiting to see if she'll talk. They're recording histories at Bletchley Park and she could be part of it – and her story's so interesting. It would be good to have it preserved for the future.'

Looking at him as he drove, humming along to the radio, she felt oddly comfortable in his presence. She'd never had much luck with men back in Brighton. She'd tried online dating, with no success. Staffroom flings were unwise – there was nothing worse than having to make polite conversation in curriculum meetings with someone you'd been snogging at the end of the night in the pub twelve hours before. But she was in Little Maudley for a finite period of time. That was supposed to be the deal, anyway. It hadn't occurred to her that there was a life outside Brighton, or that she'd become attached to this little village and the people who lived there. Sam was here for life, and his sole focus was Freya. There was no getting around it. He might be ideal on paper, but life didn't work out like that.

Chapter Eighteen

Sam dropped Lucy back at her cottage and then pulled to a stop in front of his house. He watched in the rear-view mirror as she started to walk up the path to her door before swerving and heading over to Bunty's cottage instead. He smiled to himself. Bunty would miss her when she left. Locking the door of the cab, he headed into the house.

'Dad?'

He threw his keys down on the kitchen worktop and rifled through the post, tearing open envelopes and tossing them into the recycling bin one by one. All junk, except for one bill from a supplier who still did things the old-fashioned way.

'Oh, hello. How are things?'

'I need to go to Milton Keynes. Can you give me a lift?'

'Oh hi, darling, how are you? Fine, thanks, yes. Been to see the latest job and took Lucy along to show her. Got to walk the dogs in a bit, if you fancy joining me . . .'

'I wish you wouldn't do the whole imaginary conversation thing. It's so boring.' Freya rolled her eyes. 'I need some new jeans –' she plucked at the leg of the perfectly good pair she was wearing – 'and I'm going to meet the girls and have a Starbucks.'

Maybe they'd get a chance to have a chat in the truck. Sam let the dogs out into the garden, watching as they careered around, zig-zagging back and forth, following smells. Heads down, tails flagging. Thank goodness he'd gone to a breeder who didn't dock their lovely, merry tails.

'Fine, I'll give you a lift. I need to go to Jewson's anyway and pick up some bits. How long are you going to be?'

'I'll get the bus back.' She didn't catch his eye.

'I don't mind hanging around.' Maybe they could go for a pizza, or even go bowling or something like that. Lucy had suggested he try and find a laid-back way to spend some time with her and talk. No pressure. 'We could do something afterwards?'

'Nah, it's fine.' It was as if someone had flicked a switch. His funny, warm, caring little girl had been replaced by a distinctly moody teenager. 'What were you doing with Lucy?' She looked up at him briefly. She was chewing on a strand of hair, a habit she'd had since she was a little girl. It usually meant she was nervous or worried about something.

'I said.' Sometimes it felt like Freya was only listening to about half of any given conversation. 'I took her to see the treehouse I've been working on.'

'Oh,' Freya said vaguely, turning away.

She was definitely not quite on the same planet at the moment. It must be teenage hormones, or something like that. He hoped that was all it was, anyway.

Fifteen minutes later, having locked the dogs in the

kitchen, he filled a travel mug with coffee – it had been a long day, and he was flagging. As he left the house and headed for the truck, where Freya was already impatiently waiting, he was cornered by Susan and a couple of people from the parish council.

'Just wanted to check with you about fitting the shelves in our new telephone box library. You're still okay to do it?'

'Of course.' He felt like he'd had the same conversation about fifteen times already. Helen had been round the other day, complete with notepad and pen, bossily insisting he talk her through the plans. All they needed was some shelving, and some flowers for the pots that were sitting outside the door. It wasn't exactly rocket science.

'You've created a monster with this phone box library,' he told Freya as he got into the truck.

She honoured him with a brief smile.

She pleated the edge of her t-shirt and as he pulled up at a junction he could see she was chewing her lip. She was definitely anxious about something. His stomach churned with worry.

'You okay?' He turned to look at her, putting a hand on her knee.

'Fine.' She fiddled with her phone, checking it was charging from the wire plugged into the dashboard. 'I'm fine.'

She seemed anything but. They drove through the countryside, slowing to a crawl as they got stuck behind a combine harvester. It chugged along for a couple of miles. Freya changed the channel on the radio and turned it up, blasting them with Radio 1. He tapped his fingers on the steering wheel, trying to work out how best to address whatever it was that was bothering her. Every one of his parental instincts was screaming at him that something wasn't right. What if she'd got caught up in something – arranged a meeting with someone she didn't know? He felt sick at the thought.

'And you're definitely meeting someone at Starbucks?'

Freya rolled her eyes and glared at him. 'Yes. I am definitely meeting someone at Starbucks.'

'Nothing you want to talk to me about?' he said, hopefully, as he pulled over at the shopping centre.

'I just want to go to Primark and get some jeans.' She opened the door.

'I could come with you?'

She snorted. 'Hardly.' He blew her a kiss and she laughed despite herself.

'Which bus are you catching? I'm going to the timber yard, but then I can pick you up.'

'Oh my God, Dad, I don't know yet.'

'All right, all right. I'm just being paranoid. You'll phone and tell me, though?'

She nodded, jumping out of the truck without giving him her usual kiss goodbye.

Half an hour later, his phone buzzed in his pocket. He was standing in the queue at the wood merchant's with a pile of specific pieces he needed to finish off the bench for the treehouse job before the weekend.

Can you come and get me now?

'Got your membership card?' The woman at the till held out a bored hand, not even looking at him.

Of course I can. Have you got your jeans already?

Maybe his radar wasn't off after all. He'd known there was something up. Why did she want picking up so soon? His heart thudded against his ribs as he pulled his wallet out of his pocket, dropping it on the counter in his concern to keep an eye on his phone.

Yeah. Meet you at the usual place?

He handed over his membership card, paid the bill and then wheeled the flatbed trolley out to the truck, throwing the wood in the back.

I'm waiting outside M&S car park now.

A falling out with the friends, or a no-show? He should have asked who she was meeting and where exactly they were going. The tug-of-war between letting her grow up and giving her freedom, balanced with the need to keep her safe and make sure she wasn't getting into trouble or turning out like her mother – it was so bloody hard. Sam ran a hand across his jaw, feeling the tension of his muscles beneath the stubble – he really ought to shave more often. And try meditation or something. He pushed the trolley back into place and drove back to the shopping centre, feeling puzzled.

'Hi, darling.' Don't ask questions, the parenting books said. Let them open up and tell you what they're feeling. He flicked a glance at Freya, but her face was giving nothing away as she pulled open the door.

'Hi.' She got in, slumped down in her chair, and pulled her hood over her face despite the warmth of the afternoon. She slouched sideways against the window and he headed back towards home, turning on the radio to break the ominous silence.

'Bad shopping day?'

He'd waited five minutes before asking. That seemed like enough time.

'Don't.'

She looked down at her phone, scrolling endlessly.

'You'll get carsick if you do that. You know you can't look at stuff when the car is moving.'

'I'm fine.'

After a moment, he noticed, she shoved the phone back in her pocket.

They waited in a huge queue of weekend traffic. The radio burbled on a stream of mindless chatter. A red kite flew overhead, hovering for a moment over the long grass beside the hard shoulder before shooting downwards like an arrow, certain of its prey. He wished he was as certain. Right now he felt completely hopeless – out of his depth, but with a vague, gnawing worry that something was definitely not right.

Maybe he'd ask Lucy what she thought. He could pop over later, just see if she had any advice; or would she think he was being a pain? Why the hell was he agonizing over this? He'd been friends with Mel for years, and never thought for a second about spending time with her. He glanced up, seeing the golden arches of McDonald's coming into sight.

'D'you want McDinner?' That was guaranteed to put a smile on Freya's face, no matter what the cause of her grouchiness.

She shrugged her small shoulders, still gazing out of the window. 'If you like.'

He sighed and flicked on the indicator, pulling in.

Freya sat looking at her phone while she ate her burger, and couldn't be jollied into conversation. Sam watched the traffic flying past on the dual carriageway and wondered how he'd somehow managed to screw things up. He'd managed almost fourteen years of getting it right and now – God, he was catastrophizing.

When they got home, Freya slunk into her room without saying a word to him. He was slightly mollified to see that she beckoned the dogs to follow her. She hadn't gone off *them*, at least.

You about?

He fired off a text to Mel, glancing up at the clock on the kitchen wall. He looked in the fridge, realizing he should have gone shopping. There wasn't even any milk for coffee. All that was in there was half a bottle of Fanta, a dubious-looking piece of parmesan and some wilting greens. Unless he was mistaken, Freya was going to emerge in about half an hour exclaiming she was starving despite having eaten a burger and chips, and complaining that there was never anything to eat in this place. He'd have to pop to the shops.

Mel's reply came back immediately: *Kettle's on. Come round and save me from accounts.*

'I'm just going to nip over to Mel's for a coffee.' He paused for a second. The old Freya would have leapt up, hugged him, told him she was coming too, and skipped out of the front door, the dogs swirling round her feet. Now he expected, and received, silence. She didn't even look up from her phone. Sighing, Sam headed for the door, grabbing his coat off the peg and reaching for the dog leads.

'I'm coming,' a voice came from behind him as he opened the door, pulling his keys from his pocket. He spun round to see Freya, hair now tied up off her face in a complicated sort of heap. She was holding her phone, and she smiled at him as if she'd forgotten why she'd been in such a mood.

'Oh hello,' he said, teasing her. 'Nice to see you back.' For a second he wondered if he'd pushed it too far, too fast, but she grinned at him, her little heart-shaped face lighting up. She looked like her old self again. God, hormones were complicated.

'You ready, then?' Freya grabbed an apple from the fruit bowl and strode past him, leaving him open-mouthed, still holding the door.

As soon as they walked into the doggy, messy jumble of Mel's cottage Freya disappeared upstairs, thumping two steps at a time, and a moment later there were shrieks, followed by deafeningly loud music.

'It's like living with a bloody tornado.' Mel picked up

the kitchen broom and banged the handle hard on the ceiling. Cammie was clearly back from visiting her dad. A moment later the music volume dropped to a slightly less volcanic level.

'I got into this because I wanted to train dogs, not do bloody paperwork.' Mel made an open-handed gesture, indicating the kitchen table. It was covered in untidy heaps of paper, unopened envelopes and a shoe box full of receipts. A pristine file sat in a wrapper, unopened. 'I've got a delinquent Jack Russell in the utility room who's determined to make his presence felt, and I've got a one-to-one lesson at six.'

'Why don't you just hire an accountant?'

'Wouldn't that cost a fortune? I'll end up spending all my bloody profits.'

She raked a hand through her long, streaky hair, flipping it over from one side of her face to land on the other, then tucked it behind her ears.

'Honestly, use mine. All I do is gather up all the receipts and stuff and hand it over. I mean, can you imagine me doing accounts?'

Mel snorted with laughter. 'Definitely not. Dyslexia and all this –' she picked up the papers, shoving them to one side and making space for him to sit down – 'would be a nightmare.'

'How's Camille?'

'Fine. Why'd you ask?' Mel opened the fridge, pulled out a carton of milk and made two instant coffees, handing one over. The mug was chipped, and said PET

255

PROFESSIONAL PREMIUM INSURANCE on the side. Catching him looking, she grinned. 'Dishwasher's dirty. We're down to the dodgy old mugs from the dog shows. Sorry.'

He shook his head, laughing. Mel lived in a state of happy chaos. It was a constant source of amazement to him that every morning, from this place of muddle, doggy footprints and general untidiness, Camille emerged, sleek and polished with not a perfectly curled hair out of place. She was the absolute opposite of her mother in every way but in personality – in that way, the two of them were alike. Easy-going, peaceable and the sort of people you could sit with in an amicable silence without feeling the need to talk. He sipped his coffee and rubbed the head of a huge, lumbering Labradoodle.

'What's your name?'

'That's Bert. I'm dog-sitting him for a week while his mum has an op. He's adorable, isn't he?'

'Gorgeous.'

Bert looked up at Sam with huge chocolate-drop eyes and wagged his tail, hoping for more attention.

'So why are you asking about Frey? What's she up to?'

'I wasn't. I asked about Camille.'

'Yeah,' Mel raised a knowing eyebrow. 'I know. That's shorthand for "do you know anything I don't", and something's going on. What is it?'

'She's just gone – weird.'

The eyebrows raised in unison this time.

THE TELEPHONE BOX LIBRARY

'I dunno. It's like she's taken some sort of pill and transformed from lovely, easy-going Freya into this sullen, silent creature. I'm worried something's up.'

'You mean like something at school?'

'Maybe.' He bit his lip. 'I dunno. Something weird happened. She was all set for a day out shopping, then we got there and the next thing I got a "come and get me asap" message.'

'Maybe she's had a falling out with someone?' Mel frowned. 'I'll ask Cammie if she's heard anything.'

'Or maybe it's online stuff? They're never off their bloody phones.'

'I'll check with Cam. See what she says.'

'Don't make it obvious.'

Mel rolled her eyes and pulled a face. 'Duh. I'm hardly going to go in there with my big size eights and demand to know what the story is.'

'Yeah. Sorry.'

'Any other news from the village gossip machine? I have to confess, I removed myself from the village group chat because the eighteen million messages a day about the library were sending me over the edge.'

'Shush,' he laughed. 'Freya is really into the idea. Right now that's such a bloody miracle, I'm just delighted to have her take an interest in something. And she's been making plans for it with Lucy.'

Mel's smile curved around the edge of her mug and she looked at him, her eyes narrowing slightly. 'And how *is* Lucy?'

'Shut up, you.' He shook his head.

Mel raised an eyebrow and said nothing more.

'Here you are, Hame.' Lucy passed him a chew from the cupboard and watched him beetling off through the archway into the sitting room of the cottage. He gave a gruff little noise of pleasure as he hopped up onto the sofa and got to work. Lucy decided to reward herself with a glass of rosé to celebrate having done the washing and tidied the kitchen. The cottage looked particularly pretty in the slanting evening light. She poured herself a glass and set it on the worktop.

'Hang on,' she said, realizing that talking to a dog was probably the first sign of madness, 'I'm going to get my book and then I'll come back down.'

Halfway up the stairs, she heard a loud bang and some muffled swearing. A split second later, Hamish hurtled to the front door of the cottage, barking loudly. She peered out of the window and down the street. Everything was peaceful – cars parked as normal outside the houses, a couple taking an evening stroll. And then there was another crash, and a familiar voice said 'Oh, bloody *hell*.'

She hid a smile behind her fingers as she looked across to the village green, where a very large Sam was struggling with a wooden shelf in the doorway of the very small telephone box.

She went downstairs, picked up her glass, and slipped on her flip-flops. Hamish followed, barking self-righteously.

'Do you need a hand?'

'Bollocks.' Hearing her voice, Sam banged his head as he stood up.

Lucy pressed her lips together, trying not to laugh.

'Sorry. I thought I'd just take an hour to measure up these offcuts for the shelves, and then I thought seeing as I had the right sizes, I might just fit one in and see how it looked, only it's so bloody fiddly trying to get down there in that tiny space when . . .' He looked at her for a moment, sizing her up 'Actually, you could give me a hand, if you don't mind.'

'Not at all.'

'I just need you to – I'll have to hold your wine, I'm afraid,' he said, taking it from her hand. He gave a self-deprecating smile as their eyes met. 'If you could just get in the phone box and –'

He leaned close to her, his bare arm grazing across hers as he pointed to the space where the middle shelf would fit. There were two metal brackets already in place.

'I need you to bend down and screw it in from underneath. I've tried, but my hands are too big. It's really fiddly.'

'No problem.' Lucy swapped him the wine glass for the screwdriver. 'I haven't drunk from it yet – you can have it if you like.'

He pretended to mop his brow, pushing his untidy dark locks back from his forehead. 'I can't tell you how much I need this.' He took a swig from the glass. 'I'll have to owe you one.'

'Deal.' Lucy bent down into the tiny space and peered into the corner, fastening the screw in place.

'Here's the other one.' He put another screw in her hand. When she'd fastened it and stood upright, brushing concrete dust from her knees, he looked at her and smiled.

'It's going to look pretty good, isn't it?' He shifted from one foot to the other. 'I feel bad now, I've got your wine.'

'Have you much more to do?' She looked inside the empty telephone box, still holding the heavy door open with one hand.

He shook his head. 'Just wanted to get an idea of how the shelves would look – I need to get the rest of the wood sanded down and varnished and I'll put it in at the weekend. I'm glad you came over, though. I wanted to ask you a question.' He pushed up the sleeves of his shirt, rubbing a hand down his arm. She looked at him expectantly.

'It's just—'

Hamish, who had been bumbling around the village green investigating numerous exciting smells, suddenly came to life. He hurtled along the path towards a late-evening jogger, ears pricked and tail rigid.

'Hamish!' Lucy grabbed him by the collar. 'I'd better get him back. If you're not busy –' she said it in a rush, before she chickened out – 'you could come and share the wine with me?'

'I'd love that.'

He picked up his toolkit and carried it across the road

to her cottage. 'Of course if the village gossip network sees us, we'll have caused a major scandal,' he said, pretending to look both ways as if checking for spies.

'I'm game if you are,' said Lucy. She opened the cottage door and headed for the kitchen, pouring herself another glass and topping up his.

He leaned down, scratching Hamish behind the ears. Hamish rolled over, exposing his tummy, asking for a tickle.

'Hamish, you are ridiculous.' Lucy passed him the glass. 'I just always feel a bit weird about drinking on my own.'

'Well, I can help with that.'

Lucy picked up the bottle of rosé. 'D'you want to come into the garden?'

He followed her outside and they sat down on the little metal patio set, facing each other. Hamish scuttled around, sniffing things. The borders of the little cottage garden were full of huge, brightly coloured gladioli, standing tall over mounds of geraniums and delphiniums. The ox-eye daisies were past their best now, their leaves grey-green and their flowers a papery beige, curling away from autumn's arrival. Hamish pottered over to the wooden hedgehog house and lifted his leg.

'Oh God, I'm so sorry, your lovely hedgehog house.'

'Don't worry. I don't know if you've ever come into contact with a hedgehog, but they absolutely reek. They won't even notice, if you get any. They don't hibernate yet. I hope we get some, for Bunty's sake.'

'Oh, Bunty and her animals.' She smiled, cupping her glass.

'Have you seen any bats yet?' He looked up at the evening sky, which was a hazy pale pink. Summer was slipping out of reach, and autumn was creeping in.

'Bats?' She looked up at the sky. A strand of hair fell over her face and for a moment he longed to reach over and tuck it behind her ear.

He cleared his throat. 'From spring, you'll start to see them swooping round in the evenings. As soon as – ow –' he swatted at his leg as a mosquito bit. 'I was going to say, as soon as the evening light dips and the flying creatures come out to play. Or to eat, in that one's case.'

'I've never seen a bat. I think living in the city, I've missed all that stuff.'

'You get them in the city too. They're everywhere. But there are loads round here. You could come on the bat walk next week if you like, and I'll show you them?'

'The bat walk. Do we do the bat signal to get them to appear?'

'No, we just head up to the woods by the allotment at dusk. Make sure you wear some insect repellent, or you'll be bitten to pieces.'

'Not by bats?'

'No, by bugs. It's a bit of a village tradition. It started off as a fundraiser for something or other, then it just turned into one of those things we do. This place is full of them. Bunty always comes.'

'That would be lovely.' She sipped her wine and looked

at him, smiling. There was a silence. He couldn't think of what to say, and she shifted in her seat.

'Are you –'

'Did you –'

They both laughed.

'We keep doing that. You go first,' she said.

'You're the expert on teenagers. I wondered if I could ask what you thought about this. I took Freya to town this afternoon and she was all set for meeting up with friends, but half an hour later she wanted me to pick her up. Then she was sullen and grumpy all the way home. I've left her round at Mel's place, hoping she might be able to get some sense out of her.'

Lucy looked away, feeling awkward.

'She's just that age where they're realizing they're separate from you. Like toddlers, when they start having tantrums. It's the same thing all over again – at this age, they're testing the boundaries. Seeing what they can do, trying out being grown-ups.'

'You don't think there's anything going on?'

'I think . . .' Lucy frowned for a second, and then picked at the label of the wine bottle. It came away cleanly, and she rolled it up into a tiny tube and fiddled with it as she spoke. 'I think you need to have a chat with her. Make sure she knows you're there for her, whatever she's feeling.'

'She knows that.'

'I think she probably needs to hear it over and over again. It won't do any harm.'

'It's bloody hard work bringing up a daughter without her mum around. Sometimes I wonder if I'm enough – if she wishes Stella was part of her life. And then I feel sick at the thought of it.'

Lucy flattened the wine label out on the table and scrutinized it intently before she spoke.

'Maybe you need to have a chat with her about how she feels about that.'

Sam swallowed a mouthful of wine. He liked to think that he and Freya had a pretty open, honest relationship. She knew her mum wasn't around, and they muddled along happily enough without her. If he was honest with himself, he was quite happy with it like that. The prospect of Stella being anywhere near them was something he didn't know how to handle. He'd worked so hard to make up for Freya being abandoned, and he wasn't willing to take the risk of that happening again.

Lucy looked at him then. She had pulled the sleeves of her cardigan down so they covered her hands, and she chewed her lip for a moment before she spoke.

'Do you worry that if her mum did come back, you'd be edged out? Because honestly, I can't see that happening.'

He looked down at the table for a moment and didn't meet her gaze as he spoke.

'I think maybe – I don't know. I just – she left, because she said she didn't want it. Any of it.'

Lucy cleared her throat and shifted slightly in her chair, pushing it back almost imperceptibly.

'I don't want to get back together with her,' he said,

lifting both palms in a defensive gesture.

She laughed gently. 'I didn't say you did.'

'I know, I mean – it's just – God, I've had so much hassle from people about this over the years. I've tried so hard to do the right thing.'

'And you think now Freya's growing up and changing, everything you've done won't matter?'

'I sound like a complete arse when you say it like that.' She tipped more wine into their glasses and he took a large mouthful. It made him cough.

'I don't think you do. You want the best for Freya. You're just being protective.'

'*And* I'm worried she'll swoop in and take her away from me.'

'That's not going to happen. Freya adores you. Love's not a zero sum game – she can love you *and* have a relationship with her mother.'

The wind changed, bringing a coolness to the evening. Darkness was falling and moths were circling the lights that hung around the little garden hut.

'I guess I feel weird about the idea of someone else being part of our family of two.'

'I can understand that.' Lucy leaned forward, cupping her chin in her cardigan-covered hand. 'But you've got to have a life of your own, too.'

He looked at her for a moment, his eyes meeting hers, and felt a shift in the atmosphere. Was she – no. He thought of Mel teasing him earlier, and looked down at his glass of wine. It was almost finished.

'Sorry if I kept you.' He picked up the bottle. 'And led you astray.'

She looked up at him for a moment. 'I don't mind being led astray.'

His heart thudded against his ribs. For a second he wondered how it would feel to lean across and . . .

Hamish shot past them, barking furiously, breaking the spell of the moment. He skittered around the patio, making enough noise to set off the dogs in the cottages nearby.

'Hamish, will you get inside, please.' Lucy whistled him and he scuttled back into the kitchen. They stood up and followed, and she closed the door.

'I'll have a word with Freya.'

'Do.' They were standing in the narrow galley kitchen. He took the two wine glasses from her hands and put them down in the sink. 'Right, I'd better get going.'

As she opened the door and he ducked to avoid banging his head on the lintel, she laughed.

'This place isn't designed for people your height.'

'I know. Ours is exactly the same. I spend my whole time avoiding beams.'

'Let me know how you get on with Freya.' She fiddled with the heavy curtain that hung by the cottage door.

'I will. I'll give you a shout about the bat walk.'

'It's a date.' She clearly said it without thinking. He looked at her for a moment and she laughed. He was relieved she couldn't see the embarrassment on his face in the evening darkness.

'Deal.' She put out a hand, jokingly, for him to shake. And then, when he took it, she stood on tiptoe and kissed him on the cheek.

'Thanks for a lovely evening.'

When she closed the door, he stood for a moment, reeling with a million and one conflicted feelings. Most of them, he had to admit to himself, were pretty much X-rated. Whatever was going on, it was very definitely not what he had planned.

Chapter Nineteen

'Ugh, Hamish.'

Lucy woke up to the morning breath of a West Highland terrier and his shiny black nose nudging her cheek. She put a hand to her head and sat up, groaning. She'd only had half a bottle of wine, but she felt like death. The glass of water she'd taken to bed to cancel out the wine was sitting by the bed untouched. It tasted disgusting but she downed the entire glass, wincing; and then she winced even more when she remembered that she'd kissed Sam on the cheek last night as he left. Last night it had felt confident, a little bit flirty, and – oh dear God. This morning it felt like she wanted to cringe under the covers and pretend it hadn't happened.

She went downstairs, letting Hamish out into the garden and putting on the kettle. She was supposed to be here to relax and recuperate. And then somehow she'd been roped in – admittedly quite willingly – to help Susan compile memories for the WI anniversary book, which was all but complete. If only she could get Bunty's stories on record, it would be perfect. And of course she'd promised to help source books for the telephone box library. Not to mention the fact that she was there to keep an eye on Bunty. She was very definitely *not* here to flirt with an – admittedly good-looking – treehouse builder (what a bloody ridiculous thing to do as a job), or daydream about what it would be like if she stayed here permanently, didn't go back to Brighton and never returned to teaching.

She spooned in an extra half-teaspoonful of coffee and added sugar, taking her mug outside into the garden. The sky was a hazy grey, and there was a fresh nip in the air. Hamish pootled about happily and she sat on the wall watching him, listening to the silence of the village and thinking.

She showered off the wine hangover, got dressed, rubbed her hair dry with a towel and knotted it back off her face. Maybe this morning she'd try another approach.

In Bunty's cottage, one end of the huge oak table was covered with flour.

'Hello,' Bunty looked up and beamed. Such a difference from the first time they'd met, when she'd glowered at Lucy disapprovingly. Now they were friends, but even so Bunty kept pockets of her life closed off – through choice, Lucy was sure, not through forgetting. 'I'm making some scones for the WI meeting tomorrow.'

Lucy moved towards the window, realizing that Stanley was coiled in a patch of sunlight on the end of the table. She'd managed to reach an uneasy sort of truce with him – or at least, she'd worked out that the secret to living near a boa constrictor was to keep her distance. Sometimes she wondered if Stanley was quietly biding his time and that one day she'd pop in to see Bunty and find her gone, swallowed in one gulp. She shuddered involuntarily.

'Cold, dear?'

Lucy shook her head. No, I was worrying that your pet snake was going to devour you, she thought. Instead she said, 'I was speaking to Sam last night.'

'Oh yes?' Bunty raised her eyebrows slightly, looking at her through her heavily hooded lids. 'I did see him calling on you last night.' She gave a wheeze of amusement.

'He came to talk to me about Freya. Said she's been a bit – well, the thing is – I know what the problem is, but I don't know if I can break a confidence. I really don't know what to do.' Lucy chewed her lip.

Soft light illuminated the kitchen table, shining in butter-yellow squares on the wood. The guinea pigs rumbled around in their cage on the other side of the room, squeaking hopefully. Lucy bent down, checking their water bottles and filling up their food bowls. There wasn't really that much Bunty needed help with, despite Margaret's insistence. She was more than capable of living – quite fiercely – independently. And she knew her own mind.

'You can tell me, dear.' Bunty turned the disc of scone dough and floured it before rolling it out. Her movements were sure, although her hands were gnarled and spotted with age. 'As Margaret would have it, I'm so old I'll have forgotten it by this afternoon.' She chortled.

'Nonsense.' Lucy perched at the far end of the table,

watching as Bunty cut the dough into neat circles, placing them one by one on an age-blackened baking tray.

They both knew it wasn't true. Bunty might not move as fast as she used to, but she was sharp as a tack, and those faded blue eyes didn't miss a thing.

'You knew Freya's mother?' Lucy began, hesitantly.

'A little.'

'Do you think she ever regretted leaving Freya with Sam?'

Bunty shook her head. 'Not every woman has a maternal instinct. Sam's a good father to Freya, and she's got Melanie for a mother figure as well.'

Something uncomfortable shot through Lucy. She swallowed and looked away, gathering herself. 'They're not – I mean, I know they say they're not, but . . . ?'

'Sam and Mel?' Bunty laughed. 'Good God, no. Just friends, stuck together through circumstance. Both single parents, both with girls the same age.'

'You don't think they've ever thought about it?' It was like poking at a bruise to see if it hurt.

'I'm sure it's crossed their mind at one point or another.' Bunty glanced at her. 'Not that you're interested, of course.'

Lucy examined her nails. 'No!'

'Hrmm.' Bunty pursed her lips.

'I'm only trying to work out what's going on. Freya hasn't mentioned to you that anything's troubling her?'

'Well, you know what young girls are like. She's hardly about to pour out her heart to me, is she?'

Lucy thought back to her adolescence. She'd been the one holding the place together while her mother flitted about, swapping one boyfriend for another at a steady rate.

'Freya will be fine. She's a good girl.' Bunty took the tray of scones and put them in the oven.

'I'm sure she will.' Perhaps she'd try and have a word again, see what was going on. She didn't want to interfere, but at the same time, she wanted to do the right thing for Freya – and for Sam. God, why was it all so complicated?

'How's the WI book going?' Bunty asked.

'I bumped into Joan from the Abbeyfield house the other day. She keeps telling me I should ask you for your stories.' Lucy gave a hopeful smile.

'Pfft.' Bunty tossed the cloth into the sink and pulled out the chair. 'We were all in the same boat. A pretty grubby one at that. Overcrowded, too. And goodness, it was dull. And of course we didn't have a clue what we were doing at the time. But we had our fair share of adventures.'

Lucy sat still, bottom still perched on the end of the table. She was afraid to speak in case Bunty realized she was actually talking at last about her work during the war.

Bunty looked at Lucy, coming to a decision. 'Let me show you this.'

Lucy's heart was thudding against her ribcage as Bunty went over to the dresser drawer and pulled out a diary.

'Sit down,' Bunty instructed, waving towards a kitchen chair. 'You look like you're about to shoot out of the door and off somewhere more exciting.'

That couldn't have been further from the truth. Lucy shifted from the table into a chair, not even minding that Stanley was closer than she'd like, looking at her through narrow, sleepy eyes.

'Here we are,' Bunty passed over the battered black diary, rifling through the pages and then laying it out in front of Lucy. The sepia ink of the handwriting was so small that it looked like a procession of tiny ants on the page.

Lucy looked at Bunty, who nodded to the diary. 'Go ahead, read it,' she said. 'Some stories are too important not to be shared.'

July 1st, 1941

Left London with my railway warrant in a sealed envelope, clutched in my paw. I was utterly terrified that I'd misplace it and end up stranded like one of the evacuees on a platform. No such bad luck, though.

After a train journey where we were squashed together like cattle and absolutely baking hot, we arrived at Bletchley Station. It was such a relief to get out and breathe without having someone's serge sleeve in my face. As soon as the doors were open, what felt like thousands of bodies streamed out and all headed in the same direction. All my worries about not knowing where to go came to naught – it seemed like half of London was being

shipped to the same place. I whispered to a friendly-
looking Wren if she was going to Bletchley Park, and she
gave me a very cross look and furrowed her brow. Then
she looked over both shoulders before whispering that
yes, she was. So we went together, like two rather fright-
ened little lambs. There was a hut at the gates, which
were teeming with guards, where they checked our names,
and the very moment we arrived we had to sign the
Official Secrets Act.

The room in the mansion (which was very fancy – all
high plastered ceilings and carved wooden doors) was full
of girls around my age. Some of them looked like they'd
come up from the city, gas masks over their shoulder,
carrying a holdall with their worldly goods inside, but
others were clearly upper-class sorts in expensive skirts
and jackets, that sort of thing. And of course heaps and
heaps of Wrens looking very smart, who all flocked
together like their namesakes. I felt a bit of an odd one
out, but I was excited at the thought I'd be making friends
with some of them. There were posters up for dances and
plays and all sorts of jolly things, and it all seemed like
a bit of a lark. Then they divided us up, and a very
serious-faced older woman told us where we were going
and which hut we'd be in. I waited and waited, and right
at the very end, when almost everyone else had left the
room, I was still standing there. I don't mind admitting
I had a bit of a knot in my tummy. I was nervous in any
case, and there I was standing about like a spare part,
not having been assigned a role. Then a chunky young

man with a thick ginger moustache appeared, looked at a clipboard, and the next thing I knew I was following him outside.

'You're one of the Whaddon lot,' he said. Of course this didn't mean a thing to me.

'Get in,' he said. 'Shove up,' said someone else, getting in and squashing me against the window. We drove off then, and I didn't have a clue where I was going because the bus windows were painted with blackout paint. We stopped off several times. Each time people went out in twos – nobody was talking, because we were all fresh behind the ears and shy, I think. And then we stopped. The chap who was driving hopped out and opened the back door, and I waited for a second.

'All right, love, last stop.'

I peered into the darkness around me. That's when I realized I was the only one left.

'Be ready tomorrow morning at seven.'

Lucy looked up at Bunty, who was sitting very still, her hands folded in front of her on the table. She looked down at the diary, feeling torn. She desperately wanted to keep reading. Inside this book was a whole life – and Bunty's writing was so real and immediate, Lucy almost felt as if she was there, sitting beside her. In comparison, the words she'd been slaving over for the last couple of months seemed as if they were written at a remove – which of course they were. She sat back on the chair and pushed her hair behind her ears.

Bunty reached across, taking the diary back and closing it. 'Oh, that's enough of my self-indulgent nonsense.'

'It's not at all, it's amazing. I'd love to read it all. So where did you sleep? What happened the next day?'

'Oh, well, as you know – I was taken in by Mrs Brown and that's when I met Milly, the schoolteacher I was telling you about, who I was sharing a room with. I was full of dread, expecting her to be cross about sharing. But she was jolly and kind, gave me one of her blankets in case I was cold, and told me that Mrs Brown made the best breakfasts you could dream of.'

Bunty closed her eyes for a moment, and a smile curved at her lips. 'Gosh, they were lovely. The next morning she woke me up at six and we had crumpets with honey and absolutely tons of butter. You couldn't get that sort of food in London, of course, unless you were willing to get it on the black market. But Mrs Brown had a beehive, and two Jersey cows, and she made her own butter. Oh, it was delicious.'

Lucy wished she had her phone and could be recording all this. Bunty carried on.

'Of course Milly was up and off to school – she told me over breakfast that they had thirty evacuees in the village, so they'd had to extend the school day and she'd been brought in to teach. I hadn't a clue where I was going. Back to Bletchley, I supposed. But no.'

'No?'

Bunty shook her head.

'Of course I said to poor Mrs B "Is this Whaddon?"

and she looked at me as if I was slightly mad. "No, my dear," she said. "This is Little Maudley. If you're supposed to be in Whaddon you're a good ten miles off." And she laughed at her own joke, which she clearly thought was very funny.

'Anyway, I was shipped off to a field just outside the village, and reported for duty – absolutely freezing cold – to the station.'

'Train station?'

'No. Remember when I took you on a detour?'

'To that old building up on the hill?'

'Yes. That's where I spent my war. Signal Hill. I was the only girl. Thank goodness I shared a billet with Milly, or I'd have gone crackers. The boys were nice enough, of course, but they treated me as if I didn't have anything between my ears.'

'What were you doing there?'

'It's all in here,' Bunty said, tapping the faded cover of the diary with a gnarled finger. 'And lots more besides.'

'I'd love to read more.'

Bunty rifled through the pages and handed the book back to Lucy. Lucy opened a page and started to read, transported back to a summer's day many years ago.

August 2nd, 1941

It's so peculiar. Sometimes, here in the village one could almost forget there's a war on. In other ways it's not so easy. Poor Milly is having to work terribly long hours at the school, and they've decreed that the summer holiday

277

has been cancelled because the children need to be out of their mothers' hair so they can get on with important war work. Milly says it's like running a nursery school and a prison all at once.

Meanwhile I'm in the swing of things. Every morning I get on my bicycle – rain or shine – and make my way up to Signal Hill where I let myself in, and the overnighter is usually getting up and putting on a kettle of water for a cup of tea. I get the tea cups ready, and we make sure all the radio equipment is ready, and then we wait. And then the drivers arrive in a Hillman Minx saloon and deliver the boxes with the recording discs at the same time every morning, or thereabouts. They crunch up the gravel path, rain or shine, through the barbed-wire fence, and deliver us huge heavy boxes. One day last week the absolute worst almost happened – Jack, one of the drivers, was passing the box across to Bill, who is in charge of the station, and somehow they made a mistake and almost dropped the lot. The air was absolutely blue that morning, I can tell you. It wasn't until they'd mopped their brows that Bill and Jack turned to me looking horrified and apologized profusely for their language.

'It's absolutely fine,' I said, feeling more embarrassed for them than anything else.

'Terribly sorry.' Jack touched his finger to his cap, ducking his head. 'But my goodness, can you begin to imagine what would have happened if we'd broken one of these?'

He motioned to the glass recording discs that we played each day, at precise times, without fail. It sounds like gobbledegook to me – a fiercely angry military type shouting in German. But this is serious war work, and there's no time for dancing. I feel very proud that I'm doing my bit for the war effort, even if I don't really understand what it is we do.

'I don't understand either.' Lucy looked up, her brow crinkling in confusion. 'So what was the German stuff? Were you broadcasting recordings, or something?'

'Yes. That's exactly what we were doing. Have you ever heard of black propaganda? Fake German radio programmes were recorded in a studio not far from Bletchley, and then we would broadcast them from our transmitter over there on Signal Hill –' she waved an arm towards the window – 'twelve minutes to the hour, every hour. We had to watch the clock like hawks.'

This was astonishing. Lucy sat back in her chair, putting her hands flat on the table in front of her as if to steady herself. No wonder Bunty had wanted to keep her role in the war to herself.

'*Hir ist Gustav Siegfried Eins,*' said Bunty, in a perfect imitation of a German radio announcer. 'My goodness, those words still give me a chill.' She rubbed at her arms. 'I've done some reading over the years and found out what was going on. The fake radio programmes were broadcast – a mixture of news, entertainment and mis-information – and could be heard over short-wave radio across Occupied Europe.'

'And you thought you were going to be at Bletchley.

It must have been a shock. Did your parents know what you were doing?'

'Goodness, no.' Bunty looked horrified. 'I kept my diary hidden away, tucked on a shelf inside the old fireplace in my bedroom. Even writing down what went on was breaking the Official Secrets Act, you know. I was allowed to tell them I'd gone to work near Bletchley, but they didn't have a clue what that meant – and of course as it turned out I wasn't there anyway. After the first day I was taken to Whaddon Hall, not far from Bletchley, where they gave me instruction in how to operate the equipment, and a very stern warning that I mustn't breathe a word.'

'It sounds incredibly exciting.'

'I think perhaps more so in retrospect. There was a lot of waiting around, and it was jolly cold. Of course –' Bunty gave a snort of laughter – 'my parents would have been appalled if they'd realized the worst of it. The broadcasts were quite rude. Swearing, and even worse. Some of the stories that were told were quite blue, I have gathered.'

'And full of lies and misinformation.' Lucy scratched her head. 'I suppose it was their version of "fake news", wasn't it?'

'Well, quite. There's nothing new under the sun, after all.'

'And all this time, you haven't told anyone what you did?'

She shook her head. 'One was in the habit of forgetting.

It's such a strange thing – I'd spent so long *not* thinking about it. And then you came along, and all those old memories just seemed to surface. I can remember it now as clear as day.'

'Amazing.' Lucy put a hand on the diary, as if somehow she could soak up the whole experience. 'So you didn't really have anything to do with Bletchley at all?'

'Not really. We went now and again, if we could hitch a lift. I'd go to some of the dances, and they had some wonderful performances. I was green with envy for a long old time that they seemed to be having such fun and I was stuck out in the sticks.'

'I don't think it was that much fun.' Lucy thought of the people she'd heard telling their stories of life at Station X, as it had been known in wartime. They told stories of being crammed in freezing cold huts, eyes aching because they were working in dim light, the air thick with cigarette smoke.

'Perhaps not, no.'

'You must have been since they opened it up?'

Bunty shook her head. 'Old habits die hard. We were told never to breathe a word, and many of us didn't.'

'They're still looking for people to tell their stories. We could go.'

Bunty shook her head, harder this time. 'Absolutely not. My story is of no interest to anyone.'

'But would you like to go to the Park and see it? They've spent millions on renovating it.'

'Perhaps.' Bunty stood up suddenly. Her face closed

down and somehow, she managed to convey without words a feeling that Lucy that was on the verge of over-staying her welcome.

'Right.' Lucy stood up too. 'I am going to pop into Bletchingham, and then I'm going to come home and type up the last section of this booklet for Susan. And then after that, I'm going to have a look at some of the books we've been given for the telephone box.'

It was one of the privileges of age, Lucy thought, as she headed back home to take Hamish for a walk. No need for waffle or politeness – Bunty had reached a point in life where capriciousness was tolerated.

She picked up the lead from the back of the door and in a second Hamish had joined her, panting eagerly. Despite the lowering grey clouds on the far edge of the sky, she left her coat at home – it was a muggy, warm sort of day, and she couldn't stand the feeling of being baked in a waterproof. It was like being microwaved from the inside out. If it rained, she'd deal with it.

They headed off towards the allotments and up into the woods where she'd first met Mel. The trees were now a glorious palette of oranges and dark reds. Hawthorn berries weighed down branches and the blackthorn hedges were thick with dark blue sloes, misted with a white bloom. Perhaps she could try making sloe gin. She picked one and bit into it, instantly spitting it out and making a face. It was like biting into acid. They looked utterly beautiful but tasted more sour than anything she'd ever tried.

She kept coming back to Bunty and her diary. It was strange – for a moment it had seemed as if she was going to hand over the diary, which would have been amazing as – especially now – Lucy was desperate to learn more about Bunty's life during the war, and to read more about Signal Hill. But at the same time, it wasn't just history – it was Bunty's own story. And she still had a hunch that there was something more to it, some secret from the past that Bunty wasn't ready to discuss or to confront.

They wandered on through the woods. Hamish leapt through the crackling orange bracken, barking hopefully and sniffing out rabbit trails. Lucy sat on a carved wooden bench in a clearing and looked up at the sky. It was a bruised, threatening purple now. The clouds looked like they were so full of rain that they'd overflow at any second.

'Hamish!' She felt in her pocket for treats. Since Mel had been using him as a demonstration dog in some of her classes – which was a perfect opportunity to wear him out – he'd been much better at not disappearing whenever he found a scent.

But not this time. She called again. The first spots of rain landed on her hair – thick, heavy splatters. In a moment it was going to start absolutely tipping it down, and blooming Hamish had chosen this moment to go AWOL.

A rumble in the distance made the hairs on the back of her neck stand on end. She'd hated thunder and lightning since she was a child.

'Hame!'

'Lost your dog again?'

Turning around she saw Sam, his two spaniels standing obediently by his feet, a smile on his face. He was wearing a checked shirt and a khaki-coloured coat with a million pockets. He put his hand into one and pulled out a piece of hot dog.

'No "is that a sausage in your pocket" jokes,' he said, warningly.

'I wasn't going to say a word.'

'Contrary to her current super-virtuous behaviour, Bee can be a bit of a bugger if she catches a scent. Mel taught me that the secret was always to have something utterly delicious at hand.'

His brown eyes met hers and he gave a turned-down smile. Lucy thought, out of nowhere, that he was quite delicious enough. Then she shook her head, wondering where on earth that had come from.

'Hamish!' she called again, her voice slightly squeaky.

'Which way did he go?'

'I don't know,' she said, feeling guilty. 'I wasn't looking.'

'He can't have gone far.'

A crack of lightning in the distance made Lucy jump.

'He'll be okay, don't worry.' Sam reached out, putting a hand on her arm. 'Why don't we set off down here? It'll get us out of the worst of the rain, if nothing else.'

They headed down the soft path, the dogs circling and sniffing as they went. Occasional heavy drops of rain

splashed through the canopy of trees, but they were sheltered from the downpour by the branches. They walked,
regularly calling Hamish's name, not talking. Lucy bit
her lip. What if he'd been snared in a trap, or got caught
down a rabbit hole?

Sam looked over at her. 'Don't worry. I promise, we'll
find him.'

'I should have been looking.' Her head was pounding,
too. Maybe it was something to do with the atmospheric
pressure. She rubbed her temples.

'You okay?'

'Just a bit of a headache.' She needed to get a grip.
Getting stressed out was exactly what she had to avoid.
That's why she was here, in the middle of a wood, trying
to find a disappearing terrier in a thunderstorm. For a
second she found herself wondering what life would have
been like if she'd stayed in Brighton, cut down her
teaching hours, but otherwise carried on the way she
was.

'Aha!' Sam, who'd been scanning the clearing ahead
of them, put his hands on her shoulders and spun her
round. 'Look who it is.'

Hurtling towards them, his entire face black with mud
and his body not much cleaner, came Hamish. He looked
absolutely delighted. Sam's spaniels bounded towards
him and they tussled in a mad heap of excitement, rolling
over and galloping into a thicket of brambles and dried-up
rosebay willowherb. Lucy felt the weight of Sam's hands
on her shoulders and stood very still. Her head felt fine

now, but her heart was thudding irregularly. She took a sharp intake of breath, which somehow broke the spell. He took his hands away, leaving only a sensation of warmth.

They turned, heading back through the trees towards the path that led back down to the allotments and on to the village.

'He'd have been fine, you know.'

'He might have disappeared forever.'

'I bet he wouldn't. With you to come home to?' Sam cocked an eyebrow at her and smiled. His gaze held hers for a moment. She felt her cheeks turning pink and looked across at the dogs, checking they were still in sight.

Was he flirting? She couldn't tell – it had been so long, and she was so out of practice at that sort of thing. School life had left her no time for real life, and now here she was, without a clue. And of course she was only here for the short term. No, they were good friends. That was all. If anything was going to happen, surely it would have happened after she kissed his cheek last night – and it hadn't. He probably didn't look at her that way . . .

Bunty stood at the back door of her cottage, looking out at the garden. Margaret and Gordon had picked her up that morning and taken her to their place for the day, which was always a trial. She missed her own things, and Margaret's house was so painfully tidy that she always felt as if she was getting in the way, even if she just sat down in an armchair and did the crossword.

When they'd finally dropped her back at home, Gordon had crossed the road in the rain to look at the now-empty telephone box. The shelves would be going in soon. Margaret, who had thought that a nice tidy bench was a far better idea ('much more practical than all those rejected books – and who is going to police it?') had tutted from the front doorstep, waiting to get into the BMW and out of the rain.

Now the sky had cleared, but everything was still dripping. The hanging baskets needed to be taken down and put away for winter, but everything else could wait for spring. Bunty had always subscribed to the view that gardens should be left to overwinter, the dying foliage providing a home for beetles and bugs and wildlife. And in return, her garden was always full in summer of ladybirds, butterflies gathering around the buddleia and bees humming contentedly around the various species of lavender bush she had growing there. She'd learned it all from Mrs Brown. When she'd arrived at her billet here in the village, she hadn't had a clue about – well, about much at all, really. Her mother had been a bit of a stickler for doing things herself, mainly because it gave her the opportunity to grumble about how hard done by she'd been. She turned to go back inside, pausing to look at the cracked black-and-white photograph of her parents that stood in a frame on the kitchen windowsill. It was one of the only ones she had – not many people had photographs taken in those days, and everything they'd owned had been obliterated by the bombs that dropped on their street that dark night in 1941. They'd never known their grandson, Gordon, or – Bunty gave a wry laugh – known the story behind his birth. Perhaps it was as well, in a way, that she'd never had to lie to them. They would have died of shock when they'd heard, in any case.

'Hello?'

Freya's voice carried through the hall. Bunty turned to look at her.

'I had some cabbage leaves. I thought I'd bring them over for the guinea pigs.'

'Oh, that's kind of you, dear.'

Freya passed her in the hall, and slipped out into the garden. Bunty stood at the window and watched her unfastening the hutch and pausing to say hello to both of them before popping in some leaves and closing their doors.

'Thank you, Freya. Now, shall I have a look in my cake tin and see what we've got hidden in there? I seem to remember there was some ginger cake left from yesterday . . .'

'Yes please.' Freya beamed. 'I'll make some tea, shall I?'

They sat together in a peaceable silence for a while, drinking tea. Freya smoothed the leathery skin of Stanley's head and he basked in the attention, his eyes half closed.

'Lucy really doesn't understand Stanley, does she?'

'She thinks he's going to eat me in my sleep,' Bunty laughed.

'She's nice, though, Lucy.' Freya scooped up some crumbs with a finger.

'Have some more. It'll only go stale, otherwise.' She cut another slice and watched as Freya took a huge bite. The girl was as thin as a lathe; goodness knows where she put it all. She'd been the same at that age, mind you.

'I think Dad likes her, you know.'

'Lucy?' Bunty looked at her for a moment, sizing her up before she replied. 'I think you might be right.'

'But he's completely obsessed with the idea that he has to stay single to look after me. Like I'm some sort of precious object he can't let out of his sight.'

'That's because your –' Bunty stopped mid-sentence.

'Because my mother left.' Freya finished it for her. 'I know. But that doesn't mean he has to live like a monk forever. Unless he's waiting for her to come back.'

'I don't think it's that.' Bunty had a recollection of the normally even-tempered Sam arguing with Stella over the top of a motorbike. They'd always sparked, and not in a particularly good way. They were a terrible match. If it hadn't been for Stella getting pregnant with Freya, Bunty suspected she'd have been gone long since. But she'd stuck around, trying in her own way to do the right thing. It had been like trying to catch smoke. She was the direct opposite of Sam's steady easy-going nature: impetuous and careless, wild and always looking for trouble.

'I wonder if he secretly still loves her.'

'Your mother?'

Freya nodded. 'Maybe that's why he's not interested in Lucy like that.'

'I don't think so, dear. I think what he wants is for you to be happy. That's always been his priority. You come before everything, in his book.'

Chapter Twenty

Walking back along the lane, Sam barely noticed the rain that was still falling in a light, misty drizzle. He was listening to Lucy talking about her teaching job.

Her eyes lit up when she talked about the pupils, and her hands were gesturing in the air as she described what it felt like to work with a class of the most difficult pupils and feel like you were making progress.

'You must miss it like mad.'

She nodded. 'I do. But actually, being here – and going back to Brighton – made me realize I don't miss the stress, or the headaches, or being rushed into hospital for that matter.' She made a face. She'd told him and Mel a while ago about the incident that led to her coming to the village.

'Maybe if you weren't working in such a high-pressure school?'

'Possibly. I've thought about it.' Her mouth curved into a secretive smile, and she looked beautiful as she spoke – lit up from inside, confessing. 'I've looked at the local paper. They've been advertising for cover staff at Freya's school.'

'Oh, she would love that,' Sam said, laughing. 'She'd enjoy showing you off. And she'd be hoping for good grades, too.'

'She gets good grades anyway, from what I can see.'

'She does. She's a smart cookie. Not like me.'

'Dyslexia doesn't stop you being smart. Look at the gorgeous treehouses you've built. And you work with the boys, giving them a chance in life. And run a business.'

'Stop, you're going to make me big-headed.'

'I'm serious.' She stopped, lifting her chin and looking up at him.

Her hair was misted with a halo of raindrops and right then, if he could have, he would have leaned over and kissed her. She looked so passionate and so determined, and he realized it would be very easy to fall in love with someone like Lucy, if you were looking. Which – he reminded himself, firmly – he was not. Because whatever she said about cover staff, in a couple of months she was going back to Brighton. She didn't belong here, and his life and all his roots were very firmly planted in the village.

'I've spent years working with teenagers – boys, usually – who think that they can't do school, who've been written off because they have learning difficulties like dyslexia or challenges at home. And you know what? With love and support, they have all flourished. You need to stop being so hard on yourself and start realizing how amazing you are.'

His heart thudded hard against his ribs and he brushed a lock of wet hair back from his forehead, looking at her.

'Okay. I will recognize how amazing I am, if you promise me you'll at least consider going in to Freya's school to talk about your book stuff. I think it would really inspire them. I'm friends with Dave Hill, who is head of the English department – we went to school together. If I put you in touch, will you give him a shout about going in to talk about your research?'

'Deal.' She grinned at him. 'And now let's get back. I am soaked, and freezing, and I really, really want a hot bath.'

Sam tried to put the idea of Lucy in a bath out of his head, and fell into step beside her. If nothing else, he told himself firmly, he was lucky to have her as another really good friend.

A couple of weeks passed. As well as transcribing the conversations she'd had, Lucy wrote a potted history of Little Maudley during the war. She managed to weave in quite a bit of the detail Bunty had shared, even though Bunty still didn't want her story to be officially included in the booklet, and the whole thing was going to the printer's in Bletchingham shortly. Susan was delighted with how it had turned out.

Lucy had become accustomed to her routine of popping in once a day to see Bunty – it was something that they both enjoyed. Mel was busy with work, but always happy to pop round for a coffee in the afternoon, or to take an evening off to drive to the little independent cinema in Bletchingham to watch a film. Sam too was always busy working during the day, and was rushing to get the snagging done on the luxury treehouse in Lower

Maudley before the weather changed, which had caused a hold-up in the finishing of the telephone box library. Lucy's mornings with Bunty were a time for them to have a chat and for Lucy to pass on all the village news, which Bunty always loved hearing.

'Helen's on the warpath about the telephone box delay,' Lucy explained as they pottered around in the garden, planting tulip bulbs for next spring.

'Oh dear me,' chuckled Bunty. 'I hope Sam's ready for her.'

'He told me he's planning to switch his phone off and not answer the door. I don't think Helen hears "no" very often.'

'I shouldn't think she does. Well, it won't do her any harm.' Bunty put the trowel down, having patted the soil on the raised bed back into place. Lucy, who was on her hands and knees, shuffled along on the wet grass, filling in the trench she'd dug.

'Margaret asked me why I was bothering to plant these, you know.'

Lucy looked up at Bunty, who was removing her gardening gloves carefully, one finger at a time.

'Doesn't she like tulips?'

Bunty laughed. 'No, she said – I promise you, no word of a lie – that she couldn't see the point of gardening *at my age*, and didn't I think it was a waste of time?'

'My God.'

'I know. I told her that I had no intention of popping off any time soon, and most certainly not before these tulips have come out. They cost a fortune from the garden centre.'

Lucy giggled. She stood up, arching her back, and looked up at the sky. It was grey again, and threatening rain.

'I think we've got these in just in time. Shall we go and have some lunch?'

'I think that's an excellent idea.'

In the kitchen, she busied herself making some cheese sandwiches and heating up a tin of soup for them to share. Bunty sat in the tall chair at the end of the dining table, leafing through the local paper. They ate lunch together in a peaceful silence, chatting occasionally about nothing in particular. It was nice, after all this time, that they'd reached a place where they could be quite comfortable in each other's company. It was hard to recall quite how cantankerous and difficult Bunty had been when they'd first met back in July.

Once they were finished Lucy cleared the table, and Bunty stood up. She hesitated for a moment, then went across to the dresser and took down the diary from the shelf.

'I've been thinking about this for a while. You know, I'm not going to be around forever, and it struck me that I'd rather like the right of reply. If I'm going to share my story, I'd prefer to be around while it's being read. If you'd like to read it, that is.' She placed it carefully on the table in front of Lucy. 'I think I can trust you with it. And then, afterwards, perhaps we can talk about what's inside.'

Lucy's heart thudded. She didn't dare reach out for the diary, because she was terrified that if she did, Bunty might snatch it up, saying she'd changed her mind. But after a moment, Bunty tutted disapprovingly.

'Don't you want to read it?'

'Of course I do!' She picked it up.

'Well, off you go, then.'

Chapter Twenty-one

Lucy read long into the night. The early entries made her laugh. She could hear Bunty's acid tongue and her sharp sense of humour, and her observations of life settling into a village that was far removed from the city she'd grown up in were all too familiar. Bunty had taken Lucy under her wing, and appreciated that living in Little Maudley was a shock to the system after living in Brighton.

She shifted on the sofa. She'd been sitting there for ages, and her leg had pins and needles. She got up and let Hamish out into the garden for a sniff and a wee. Then she poured herself a glass of red wine, put another log on the log burner – the evening was cold as well as damp – and curled up to carry on. Bunty had worked so very hard. But oh, the romance of meeting Harry at the telephone box! No wonder she hadn't wanted it to be taken down and replaced with a boring old bench.

Oh, dear diary. A note! "Meet me at the telephone box Friday 1800hrs."

Oh my goodness. You should have seen Mrs Brown's face. Her eyes were out on stalks and she crossed her arms very firmly and reminded me, young lady, that she was responsible for my good name, and that I shouldn't be doing anything my mother wouldn't approve of. But how could Mother have disapproved of something so lovely?

We walked all the way to Preston Bissett and back, chatting the whole way. He's so kind and thoughtful – he brought me toffee sweets, and told me all about his mother and sister back home in New Brunswick. He said they'd love me. He's promised that the next time he flies over the village he'll fly down low and wave. Oh, my heart. I have to go to sleep now, because Milly is fussing about the light again. I don't think I can possibly sleep. I'm too excited for words.

Lucy could imagine a young Bunty, lying wide awake, staring at the ceiling, feeling thrilled at the prospect of romance in the midst of all the drudgery of her daily life. Harry must have seemed like a breath of fresh air.

She read sweet stories of stolen kisses and brief meetings, dances at the aerodrome and even dinner with a reluctantly welcoming Mrs Brown, who apparently chuntered disapproval until she too was charmed by Harry's sunny, open nature. Lucy sighed happily at the romance of it all. Outside it was pitch dark now, and the log burner was almost out. She drew the curtains, called Hamish in and headed upstairs to carry on reading in bed. Oh poor, poor Bunty. It was unbearable to read.

The most terrible, unthinkable news. Bombs fell again and I've had word that both Mother and Father are gone. I can't believe that I will never see their faces again, or hear

Mother fussing on the telephone asking if I'm wearing warm underclothes and keeping myself nice. This wretched war is taking everything away. I can't bear it. I saw Harry tonight and he wrapped his arms around me. It didn't make anything better, but it was such a wonderful feeling to know that there was someone who was there who cared for me. It's such a blessing to know that amongst all of this, he's here safely with me for the next few months at least.

Lucy wiped away a tear as she turned the page. Bunty's writing was smaller and neater, as if it was taking everything she had to control how she felt.

Given leave, but I don't see much point in taking it. What would I do? There are no bodies to bury, and our little family is all but gone. Aunt Mabel is in Essex, my cousin Sarah in Edinburgh. We have a war to win, and people all over the country are losing people left, right and centre. It seems self-indulgent to take time off to grieve when the work still has to be done.

She sounded so alone. But time had a different quality in those dark days. The weeks passed, and she started to sound more like herself.

September 3rd, 1941
I was standing in the back garden yesterday, hanging out sheets for Mrs B, when two bombers approached, flying so low that I thought they must surely hit the oak tree at

299

the end of the garden. I looked up, out of fear, and realized that at the window, aviator cap and goggles pushed up off his face, was Harry. He gave a huge wave. It cheered me up no end. And then today there was a note pushed through the letterbox. Meet me at the telephone box, it said, and bring your gumboots in case of rain. Mrs B was most intrigued – despite the fact that she's given him the seal of approval, he still sneaks notes into the telephone box because it's our little secret – and Milly thinks it's unbearably romantic. I do too. Going to have to borrow her gumboots, though, because mine have a hole in. There has been such a rainstorm today, if I go out in shoes I'll be soaked through in moments and end up with trench foot. That wouldn't be unbearably romantic.

(still the 3rd but only just – it's ten to midnight, and I'm writing this by candlelight)

I arrived with Milly's gumboots in a kit bag I'd sewn years ago for school, and there he was waiting at the telephone box, looking absolutely dashing in his uniform. He asked how I was feeling and we chatted about everything under the sun, and when I cried he gave me his handkerchief and told me I could keep it. It smells of his cologne, and I've put it under my pillow. Oh, it was absolutely wonderful to spend time together, despite the drizzling rain. We walked miles, and eventually the sun came out and we spotted the most beautiful rainbow. Eventually we arrived at a tiny little stone hut in the middle of a clearing in the woods – 'I noticed it the other day when I was on training,' Harry told me, 'and I thought we could investigate.'

Inside it was full of dried leaves with grass growing around the spaces where the window had been, but it was dry and cosy. It felt like we were having an adventure and that we'd left real life far behind us. Harry had brought a picnic rug, rolled up in his pack, and a picnic of fruit cake, some cheese, apples and even some ham. It tasted absolutely wonderful, the way that food does when you have it outside, but even more wonderful was the feeling of being together and so, so comfortable in each other's company. He even had a little hipflask of brandy and we shared that, too – it burned my throat and made me feel quite giddy. And then – well, perhaps I'll keep that to myself. But oh, my. I don't know what came over me – afterwards I thought of Mother telling me to keep myself nice, but then I remembered that there was nobody there to make sure I did any more, and anyway – well, I'm glad I did it. I kept looking at the others over dinner, wondering if they could tell that I had. Harry walked me all the way home to the cottage and kissed me on the cheek outside the gate. Oh, and I almost forgot – we bumped into two of the Land Girls on the way back, Hilda and Eunice, and they gave us The Look and went off giggling after saying hello. It wasn't until I got back to Mrs B that I realized the collar of my dress was all crushed and sticking up at the back. I looked as if I'd been rolling in a hayfield, which made me blush absolutely scarlet, because, oh, dear diary – I suppose I had.

There were several more pages, filled with the outpourings of a young girl who had clearly fallen quite madly in love with her handsome Canadian airman. Lucy, sitting up in bed with the curtain not quite pulled to, found herself gazing across the lane at a light glowing upstairs in Sam's cottage, wondering what he was doing there.

She read on, yawning despite herself, desperate to know what happened next. And then she turned the page, and her heart dropped.

September 22nd, 1941

The most awful, awful day.

Harry is gone. I have sat for hours trying to pluck up the courage to write those words. I thought perhaps if I didn't that it might not be true. But no. I stood by the telephone box, waiting for him to arrive. I checked his note in case I'd got my days in a muddle – I even went home and laid out all the other notes he'd left for me in the telephone box, but no – it said very clearly 'I will see you here at six – your loving H.'

At first I was cross, and then I was worried. And yet somehow, deep inside, I had the most awful sinking feeling that something dreadful had happened – I don't know why.

In the end it was Len – dear, kind Len, my sweet friend – who told me. He'd seen me standing there, and walked past a couple of times before he asked if I was waiting for my Canadian chap. He bicycled off, and when he got back I was still there and he'd pulled some strings, asked what was going on at the airfield, and discovered there'd been a terrible crash during a training exercise. They'd been on a navigational flight, and something went wrong. Three Canadian airmen were killed outright. I'm weeping as I write that word. I can't think of my Harry – my lovely, funny Harry, so full of life and kindness – as being gone. I can't ever imagine getting over this.

Lucy had tears streaming down her cheeks. Poor, poor Bunty. She closed the diary and put it down on her bedside table. She'd read enough for one night.

The next morning she got up early and sat down on the sofa in pyjamas to carry on. She'd had a disturbed night, tossing and turning, her head full of confused dreams about Bunty and the man she'd loved and lost. And Sam seemed to be caught up in there, too. Lucy yawned and rubbed her eyes, stretching her arms out widely. She looked down at the diary again, imagining Bunty's heartbreak.

A knock at the door made her jump and she stood up, hushing a barking Hamish. She pushed back the curtain in front of the door and opened it, wiping tears from her eyes.

'Oh God, I'm sorry,' Sam said, looking at her with concern. 'Is this a bad time?'

Lucy rubbed another tear from her cheek, and Sam reached into his pocket, handing her a white handkerchief made of cotton. She looked at it, startled, then dabbed at her eyes.

'I'm so sorry.' She went to hand back the hanky, but Sam shook his head.

'You keep it.'

'It's just – oh God.' She collapsed back onto the chair, motioning for him to sit down. 'I've been reading Bunty's wartime diaries, and they're absolutely heartbreaking.'

He glanced across at the black diary, still open to the page that Lucy had just finished reading. He closed it, gently, and handed it over before Hamish tried to lie on it. He'd leapt onto the sofa beside Sam and was very insistently demanding that his tummy be rubbed.

'I came to ask if you'd like to come to the pub quiz this evening, but if you're feeling a bit –' he inclined his head towards the handkerchief, lying on the side of the chair – 'perhaps not?'

'Yes, please.'

He gave a half smile. 'I hoped you'd say that. Mel reckons you'll be the secret to us finally being in with a chance of winning.'

'I'm not sure about that. Does she know something I don't?'

'You're a history teacher. That's better than any of the rest of us.'

'No pressure, then?' She gave a self-deprecating smile.

'None at all.' Sam made a face. 'I'd better get off. I'll see you later.'

Lucy closed the door, made herself a coffee, and climbed back onto the sofa to finish reading Bunty's diary.

She went next door after lunch. She'd read all the way

to the end of the diary, which ended not long after Harry's death.

'Hello,' Bunty said, and the expression on her face said it all. 'You've read it, then.'

Lucy nodded. Bunty wasn't the hugging sort, but she reached out a hand and squeezed her gently on the arm. Bunty smiled sadly.

'I couldn't sleep at all well last night, thinking of you reading it.' She led Lucy through to the sitting room and sat down in her armchair. For a moment, neither of them spoke. The clock ticked the seconds away.

'I can't tell you how grateful I am that you shared it with me. There's so much – you lost so many people that you loved.'

'Oh, my dear. We all did. War is a terrible, terrible thing.'

'It's just – you all had to cope with so much. And working every day there, doing the same thing, crammed in that little building with the men.'

Bunty took a breath. She seemed to grow taller, as if she was preparing herself for something dreadful.

'I've not been – altogether honest with you. You know, before I gave it to you, I read back over the words I'd written, and since then I've been thinking about the past. Something I saw the other day made me think about mistakes we make because we believe we're doing the right thing.'

Lucy leaned forward slightly on the sofa, listening intently.

'It's not only because of my war work that I've been reluctant to talk to you. I mean, of course we all signed the Official Secrets Act, and for some of us that meant we kept our mouths shut, despite what people might want us to do. It's not that I think they're wrong to tell their story, but – well, keeping secrets – it's become something of a habit of mine.'

Lucy nodded.

'It's about Gordon.'

Lucy thought about Bunty's stolid, law-abiding son. He was a pillar of his local community, retired accountant, married to Margaret, who was a good fifteen years younger – which was, she thought, probably the raciest thing he'd done in his life.

'One of the reasons I don't really want to go over the past is because – like most of us who lived through the war – things were, well . . . they were complicated. War made one see very clearly, in some ways.'

Lucy had heard this before. She'd spoken to a woman the other day who'd run off to join the Land Army at seventeen because it didn't require permission from her parents, and fallen in love with the farmer where she worked, scandalizing the village – not to mention his wife.

'The thing is,' Bunty continued. 'I knew if I told you about my war, it would bring it all back. And I can't –' She faltered. A moment later she'd taken a handkerchief from her cardigan pocket and dabbed at her eyes, surprising Lucy.

'It's okay,' Lucy said, trying to smooth things over. 'I don't want you to get upset. You don't have to tell me anything you don't want to.'

'But I do.' Bunty blew her nose. 'I can't keep it to myself forever. I thought perhaps I could. But I think – somehow – if I don't tell someone, then it's as if it never happened.'

'Harry?'

Bunty nodded. 'After he died, I realized quite quickly that something was amiss. Of course in those days there wasn't much one could do, and luckily – well, I did something which might seem rather selfish.'

Pieces of the jigsaw were beginning to come together in Lucy's mind.

'Of course, Len had been sweet on me for a while. He was one of the ARP wardens in town, along with Henry. He was very kind. A stickler for the rules –' she gave a mischievous smile – 'which was clearly contagious, because my goodness, Gordon is a chip off the old block in that regard.'

'But his father?'

Bunty nodded again. 'Was Harry.'

'And nobody ever suspected?'

'Oh, I think there were probably a fair few who had their private thoughts. It's difficult to explain what it was like. All bets were off, in some ways. People were dying all over the place, or they were apart for years and years, marriages were falling apart. Nowadays there's this rose-tinted view of the war years as everyone pulling together for the greater good. There was plenty of that, but we had a lot of fun, too.'

'So you married Len and – did he know?'

'I think he worked it out. But he never breathed a word. And we were perfectly happily married. He was a very nice man.' Lucy turned and watched as Bunty eased herself up from the chair and made her way across to the window of the cottage. She looked across at the graveyard that sat behind the village green, and the telephone box where she'd met Harry, the man she'd adored – the father of her son.

'I still think about him often. Wonder what my life would have been like with him in it.'

'He sounded like a lovely man.'

'Oh, he was. I found out, years later, that when they found the plane – still smoking – they found a wristwatch near by, the strap broken, still ticking away.' Bunty put a hand to her heart.

'I wonder what Gordon would have made of him.'

'That's a question.' Bunty frowned. 'I often wonder if he'd have been more carefree if he'd been brought up by Harry instead. Len was so worried about everything, it rather rubbed off on Gordon.'

'But he's a nice man.' Lucy thought of Gordon, bumbling along, doing anything he could to keep Margaret happy.

'Yes, he is. A good man. But heavens, you can imagine how it would feel to discover the truth after all this time. Gordon's such a stick-in-the-mud that I think it would probably be the end of him. And goodness knows what Margaret would think. She's such a prude.' Bunty gave a sudden bark of laughter. 'The war did funny things to us – we took risks, did things that nice girls didn't do because we didn't know when the next bomb was going to drop, or even if we were going to survive.'

'I can understand that.' Lucy nodded.

It made sense. Everything she'd read, everyone she'd spoken to had said the same thing. It was a different time – as if the everyday rules were suspended for a while. It wasn't surprising that there were consequences to that.

After a long soak in the bath, and with Bunty's sad story still on her mind, Lucy made her way through the village to the pub. She was looking forward to the quiz. Mel and Sam were sitting at a table by the fireplace, and there was a wooden stool waiting for her. There was also another man sitting at the table who Lucy didn't recognize.

'This is Dave. He's our secret weapon.'

Dave, Sam's friend and head teacher at the local secondary school, was short and round. He was wearing a t-shirt with a rainbow-coloured dog on the front, and had more hair on his chin than he did on his head. He beamed at her.

'Hang on.' Lucy looked at Sam, narrowing her eyes jokingly. 'I thought you said I was your secret weapon?'

'He did?' Dave made to get up, laughing. 'I'll be off then.'

'With your encyclopaedic knowledge of music and Lucy's wisdom on all things historical, we're sorted.'

'And don't forget,' Mel added, getting up and taking her purse from the table, 'my specialist subject. We're sorted if there's anything on gossip from *Heat* magazine. Drink?' she said to Lucy, who nodded.

'I can't imagine they're going to be quizzing us on the latest reality TV stars, somehow.'

'You never know. Bob, the quizmaster, takes this stuff very seriously. He won't even let his wife Jane have a peek. Locks himself in the study to get it done, and prints off all the quiz sheets at work.' Sam passed Lucy a sheet of paper, printed with a collection of black-and-white photographs.

'D'you recognize any of those?'

Lucy peered at the photographs. 'That's whatshisname from *I'm a Celebrity*, isn't it?'

'Told you,' said Dave, triumphantly.

'But what's his name?'

'Whatshisname,' said Lucy and Dave in unison, catching each laughing.

'Watch out,' Mel said in a stage whisper an hour later. They'd failed in spectacular fashion at the first two rounds, and now Helen was approaching.

'*Hello*, you four,' she said, in her loud voice. 'So nice to see you so at home, Lucy. Any chance you might decide to stay on?' Without waiting to be invited, she pinched a stool from the table beside them and wedged herself in between Sam and Mel, beaming directly at Lucy, who fiddled with a beer mat and pulled a non-committal sort of face. She didn't want to think about leaving the village when she was right in the middle of a perfectly nice night out, thank you very much.

'Mel, Lucy – if you could have a look and see if you have anything you'd like to add to the collection for the library. We're planning to have a sort of rotating selection available.'

'I've got the full set of *Fifty Shades* books, if you want them?' Mel snorted with laughter.

'Good heavens, no,' Helen looked shocked. 'I think we'll keep it PG at best. Can't have children going in there and finding themselves faced with a lot of smut, can we?'

The woman whose chair Helen had stolen had returned and was standing beside the table holding two wine glasses with a boot-faced expression. Helen noticed – although not until Mel had cleared her throat several times and inclined her head with decreasing amounts of tact in the direction of the disgruntled woman – and removed her neat bottom from the chair.

'See you on Thursday, then,' she trilled, disappearing into the throng that surrounded the bar.

'Okay, well, you were rubbish as a secret weapon,' said Mel later, as they made their way down the hill and back towards home. She'd had several rum and cokes, and ricocheted gently off a green wheelie bin as they walked in single file down Lacemaker's Lane. Sam turned, making sure Lucy, who was bringing up the rear, was okay.

'I'm fine.'

'I'm pissed,' said Mel, unnecessarily. She took a flower from a stem of gladioli outside a cottage and put it behind her ear, twirling around and pretending to play the castanets. 'Who wants to come in for a nightcap?'

Sam shot Lucy a brief glance, raising an eyebrow in query. She wasn't quite sure what it meant, and yet somehow it made her stomach flip over.

'I wouldn't mind a coffee, actually,' Lucy said, thinking perhaps it'd help sober Mel up before she had to get up in the morning and deal with a houseful of doggy guests.

'Good idea.'

'You two are such boring old farts,' Mel said, pulling her keys out of her pocket. 'No wonder you make such a good match for each other.'

Luckily it was dark, so nobody could see the expression on Lucy's face. She looked down at her feet as Mel opened the door, avoiding Sam's gaze.

The moment Mel put the key in the lock, a cacophony of barking started. 'I'm coming, I'm coming,' said Mel, slurring slightly.

'Bloody hell,' came a shrill, outraged voice from the top of the stairs. 'Mum, couldn't you come in without setting off all the dogs in the village?'

'Sorry, lovey,' Mel said, dropping her keys in the fruit bowl on the dresser. 'Shh. Go back to bed.' She giggled. 'Right. Coffee for the old farts, and a brandy for me. You two sit down there. I'll put the kettle on.' She motioned to the sofa.

There was a huge, shaggy-haired lurcher curled up asleep on the armchair, so there was nowhere for them to sit but beside each other. Lucy felt alarmingly aware of the sensation of Sam's body close to hers. Mel reappeared a moment later with three mugs and plonked them on the table. She crashed down on the sofa, squashing them even closer together.

'No milk. So I thought we could drink a toast to something lovely.'

'I don't mind having it black,' Lucy began. Sam shot her a look and rolled his eyes.

'Don't be silly,' Mel said, heaving herself up. 'Forgot the brandy. Hang on.'

'Did she have much more to drink than we did?' Lucy whispered, watching as Mel made her way out the door, stopping to pat the lurcher on the head.

'She got talking at the bar before we arrived. Steve, the landlord, has a bit of a crush on her. Think he gave her a couple of free shots before, and then again after the quiz. Mel's always been the same – she's Mrs Wholesome Outdoor Living ninety-nine per cent of the time, and then once in a while she lets herself off the leash, gets plastered, wakes up with the hangover from hell and swears she's never drinking again.'

'Here we are.'

Mel sloshed a huge measure of brandy into each mug.

'So the big question is,' she said, sitting back with a sigh against the sofa cushions, 'what's going on with Freya? You figured it out yet?'

'She's been a bit less grouchy this week. Maybe it was hormones or something.'

Clearly Sam hadn't got to the bottom of it. Lucy perched on the edge of the sofa, not wanting to sit back because if she did she'd sink into the cushions and end up wedged between the arm and Sam, who was now sitting with a Jack Russell curled up on his knee.

'I tried to give Camille the third degree, see if I could get anything out of her. But nothing.'

'I'm sure it'll sort itself out,' Sam said, easily. He stroked the head of the Jack Russell. Lucy noticed that, like her, he wasn't touching his drink.

'Mmm,' said Mel.

A moment later, there was a faint sound of snoring from her end of the sofa.

'I'll get her a blanket,' Sam said, passing his mug to Lucy. 'She'll wake up covered with dogs.'

Ten minutes later they let themselves out of Mel's house and stood for a moment on the footpath. Sam pushed his hair back from his forehead in the gesture that had grown familiar, and smiled ruefully.

'See you at the phone box meeting, then?'

Lucy felt the sensation of her stomach dropping to her feet. God, it would be so easy to curl her hands up and around the back of his neck, lean her face up and kiss him. For a second, she wondered if she could – but then turned away, with a casual wave. She'd never been that sort of person. The kiss on the cheek she'd given him the night they'd drunk too much wine had been so out of character. Just because she could still feel the graze of his stubbled cheek on her lips and smell the faint, oaky smell of his aftershave, didn't mean –

'Lucy.'

Sam's voice was soft. She turned around, halfway across the lane, and looked at him. He was standing on the footpath, hands by his sides.

'Yes?'

'I'll see you on Thursday. Thanks for a lovely evening.'

Chapter Twenty-two

Oh, for God's sake. Sam woke up the next morning, remembering. If he'd – oh, why the hell didn't he just admit how he felt about Lucy? He gave a groan of frustration, and rolled over onto one of the dogs. Amber gave a woof and jumped onto the wooden floor of the bedroom, nails clattering on the wood, whining immediately to be let out.

He opened the curtains and looked across the road, as had become habit. He could see Lucy's sitting room curtains were open, and – he stepped back out of view, realizing she was coming out of the front door. This was ridiculous. He was turning into a peeping Tom.

Just then Freya emerged from her room.

'Morning, darling. You organized for school?'

She nodded, not looking up from her phone.

'I'm going to be late tonight. Got study stuff on.'

'Do you need me to pick you up?'

'Nah. Cam says she'll get the bus back with me.'

'Okay.' Sam tipped dog food into two bowls, flicking on the kettle. 'God, I didn't realize the time. I better get in the shower. See you later.' He put a hand on her shoulder and dropped a kiss on her head.

He stood in the shower, feeling the needles of hot

water pummelling his shoulders, running over the day's plans as he always did. They had a few last pieces to finish off on the treehouse, and then he was taking the lads to their weekly college course in Bletchley. After that, he had a quote to do, and bloody Annabel Bevan wanted him to come back again and double check something. And then it would be Thursday, and the WI meeting. He felt a buzz of excitement. What the hell was going on with his life, if he was getting excited at the prospect of a bloody WI meeting about a telephone box?

It was all down to Lucy. He'd gone to sleep last night with her on his mind, and then dreamed about her. It was ridiculous. She was a temporary visitor, and he had a responsibility to Freya to be the best parent he could be – the only parent she had. Maybe once she was grown up, he'd think again. But right now he needed to be there to make sure she stayed on the straight and narrow and didn't veer off like Stella had. That was one of the worries that niggled away at him in the middle of the night. Right now, though, she wasn't showing any signs of being like her mother. Freya was very much her own person, and he was proud of her for that.

He was in the midst of taking some measurements for a quote when his mobile rang.

'D'you need to get that?'

If it was Freya, she'd message – teens never actually used their phones to make a call. He shook his head at the owner of the big country house on the other side of Bletchingham, who was after a two-storey treehouse for his teenagers to escape to. If the weather held, he could get it done before winter really hit.

'It's fine, my voicemail will catch it. So when you say you want an apex roof, are you thinking something like this?' He pulled out some paper and started sketching. The phone started ringing again. He hit the mute button, silencing it.

'So sorry.'

'Not at all.'

It rang again twice, buzzing in his pocket like an irritating wasp. Shaking hands with the potential client, he headed back to the truck. Next stop was driving back to Brackley to collect the lads from college. He sat down and closed the door of the cab, pulling out his phone. *Bletchingham High School – four missed calls.*

Shit. He hit the return call button, worried sick.

'Hello? This is Freya Travis's dad. I've had a missed call – well, four of them.'

'One moment.'

'Mr Travis,' said a voice, smoothly. 'No need for alarm, I'm sure. I wanted to check with you as we hadn't had a call this morning to say Freya wasn't going to be in.'

'I'm sorry?' His stomach lurched.

'The automated text system. We didn't get a reply back from you to our message asking why she hadn't registered this morning.'

All his nightmares were coming true. Where the hell was she?

'She's not with me. I mean, she might be at home. I need to go. I need to find her.'

Hitting the phone buttons with shaking fingers, he tried her number.

'Hi there,' said Freya's chirpy voice. *'I can't come to the phone right now because I'm busy, or I'm asleep, or it's been confiscated. Please leave a message and I might call you back . . .'*

'Freya, darling. Where the hell are you?'

He tried calling the landline at home, but it rang out until he heard his own voice on the answer machine. Mel didn't pick up – probably in the middle of a dog training class. He dialled Bunty's home number.

'Little Maudley 823390,' she said, crisply.

'Bunty, it's Sam. Have you seen Freya?'

'I'm afraid not. Has she gone AWOL?'

'I think so. She didn't turn up at school today. Probably taken herself off to Milton Keynes shopping, or something like that.' It sounded plausible. He'd played truant enough as a teenager – maybe she was taking after him.

'I expect so. I'll keep an eye out, and let you know if I hear anything. Oh, here's Lucy. I'll let her know.'

'Thanks.'

He wished for an irrational second that Lucy was there with him, calm and kind and easy-going. She'd know what to do. And – he looked at the clock – God, he had to collect the boys from college. He turned on the truck and reversed out of the drive, feeling sick.

He tried Freya's number again, and this time it rang out.

'Hello?'

Keeping both eyes on the road, trying to be heard over the sound of traffic on his hopeless Bluetooth speaker, Sam could have wept with relief at the sound of her voice.

'Where the hell were you?'

'What d'you mean?'

'Where are you now?'

'I'm coming out of school.'

Oh, she was going to play it like that, was she? Right. He took a left turn and headed for the community college, parking up outside and waiting for the boys to appear. One by one they peeled themselves off the wall they'd been leaning against and slouched towards him.

'Okay, I'll see you at home then?'

'Yeah,' said Freya. 'I thought I'd make some cake. Might pop up to the shop and get some stuff so if I'm not there when you get back, that's where I'll be.'

No you will not, young lady – you'll stay exactly where you are, Sam thought. 'Okay, see you in half an hour,' is what he said.

He dropped the boys off in Bletchingham and spun round, heading back to the village at top speed. He pulled up outside the cottage and left the truck sitting on the road – there was no way he had the patience to carefully reverse it into the drive in his current state of mind.

Inside the house, Freya was sitting quite comfortably on the sofa, watching YouTube on the television screen while scrolling through Instagram on her phone. She looked up with an angelic smile that made him feel quite cold. For a second, she looked so like her mother that it threw him.

'Hi, Dad,' she said, blithely. 'Sorry, I haven't made cake yet. You don't fancy nipping to the shop to get me eggs and some more butter, do you?'

'I think I'm fine for cake,' he said, grimly. He sat down on the armchair, leaning forward, his elbows on his knees, and looked directly at her. 'How was school?'

'Fine.' She didn't look up from her phone.

'You sure?'

'Absolutely. I mean boring, but fine.'

He turned his phone to face her, showing the missed calls on the screen. For a second she looked at them uncomprehendingly, then the penny seemed to drop.

'You weren't at school.'

'All right.' She chewed her lip. 'I got the bus to MK. I went to the shops and wandered around and had a coffee. Then I came back in time to get the school bus home.'

He looked at her for a long moment. Freckles scattered across her nose, her hair in two long plaits tied together at the back. She had two silver hoop earrings in each ear – against school rules, but disregarded by her form tutor, who believed that there was no point in creating battles over minor indiscretions. And Freya was a model pupil – or she had been, until recently.

'You could have told me,' he said, feeling a bit hopeless.

'What? "Hey, Dad, I've decided to wag off school

today, see how it feels?"' She laughed. 'And you'd be okay with that?'

'No, of course not.' He felt completely out of his depth. Maybe someone else would ground her, or cut off her access to the internet or something, but he'd never really parented that way. 'Just please don't do it again, okay? I was worried sick when I didn't know where you were.'

'I won't,' she said, cheerfully. 'It was quite boring, actually. And I kept worrying people would be thinking I'd wagged off because I was in uniform.'

'You're supposed to take clothes in your bag and change,' he said, almost without thinking.

'Like you did?'

'Exactly. And you don't want to end up like me.' He smiled, despite himself. She knew exactly how to wind him round her little finger.

The next day, he got home from work early, showered, and stood trying to decide what shirt to wear.

'Have you got a hot date?' Freya appeared, flopping onto the bed and looking at him thoughtfully.

'No, it's the final meeting about the phone box library. Remember? Aren't you coming?'

'Oh God. Yeah. I forgot.' She looked up at him briefly. 'Actually, I think I might skip it.'

'But she's the one who came up with the idea.' Sam shook his head in despair.

'That's just teenagers,' Lucy said with a shrug. They were sitting with Mel on uncomfortable plastic chairs in the village hall, waiting for the meeting to begin. 'If you express the slightest interest in something, they usually drop it, because the fact you're interested automatically makes it supremely uncool.'

'Totally. Camille wouldn't be seen dead here. Or within about fifty metres of me, unless I've got my wallet open and I'm offering to buy her stuff.' Mel laughed. 'Even then she'd rather take my bank card, and leave me sitting outside in Nandos while she goes mad in H&M.'

'Freya wasn't like that, though,' he began, tailing off as Helen marched onto the wooden dais at the front of the village hall.

At the end of the meeting, Mel got chatting to a friend and insisted they go ahead without her.

'What happened to the bat walk?'

'Good question. I think all the village stuff has been so focused on the phone box library that it's somehow fallen by the wayside.'

'Shame,' Lucy murmured. 'I was looking forward to it.'

'I'll take you,' he said, realizing he sounded as keen as a schoolboy. But he didn't care. 'How about tomorrow? Freya's on a school residential, so I don't have to worry about getting back for her.' As soon as he said it he realized this sounded a bit presumptuous, so he followed it up quickly. 'In fact, I could really do with more of your professional advice.'

He explained what had happened with Freya truanting,

and how she'd seemed quite insouciant about it after-wards. 'I can't help worrying that she's going to end up like her mother,' he said, finally.

'She's her own person,' Lucy said, as they stopped outside the terraced row of cottages. Hamish's head popped up from underneath the curtain, making them laugh.

'That's what I worry about. So was Stella.'

'But she's been brought up by you. A bit of rebellion doesn't do them any harm. Honestly. Shows they've got a bit of spirit.'

He sighed. He had a feeling there was more to it than that. 'I suspect she's got that. I used to wag off school as much as I could.'

'That was because you were struggling, though, wasn't it?'

'Yeah.'

'And Freya's not struggling with schoolwork.'

'No. She definitely didn't get her brains from me.'

Having said goodbye, Lucy let Hamish out into the garden. Despite what she'd said to Sam, something niggled at her about Freya's absence this evening. She felt torn between telling Sam what she knew and not breaking a confidence – but for now, Freya seemed safe, which was the most important thing. She'd have to play it by ear.

It was all very complicated. She got into bed and pulled the covers up, laughing at Hamish as he did his usual routine of hopping in circles to make himself a nest in the blanket at the end of the bed. She thought about how much she was looking forward to seeing Sam tomorrow night. As a friend. Just a friend.

'Hi.'

'Hello.'

'D'you want to come in? I wasn't sure what the protocol was. Do I need a torch?' Lucy hadn't known what to wear for a bat-spotting walk. She'd settled on jeans and a blue-and-white striped jumper, her hair tied back in a loose ponytail.

Sam shook his head, smiling. 'No torch. Just yourself.' Hamish circled around his legs, his stumpy tail wagging. 'And no dogs, I'm afraid.' Sam leaned down, scratching him behind the ears.

'Do we need to wait until it's dark?'

'No – if you're ready, we can go now.' He opened the door, standing back to let her out. 'After you.'

It was strange how awkward she sometimes felt in his company. Lucy got the feeling that he was uncomfortable, too. Without Mel there to act as a foil, or the girls, or the dogs, the silence as they walked along the leafy path towards the allotments was deafening.

'How's Freya?'

'Good. Off on her school trip. And definitely on her trip,' he grinned, 'because I saw her off on the bus this time.'

'That's a relief.'

'I don't often get a night off. The trouble with being a single parent is you're pretty much on call 24/7.'

'I'm honoured you're spending it with me,' Lucy said, puffing slightly as they trudged up the hill to the woods.

'I can't think of anyone nicer to spend it with.' Sam swatted at a tiny bug on his forehead. 'You, me, several bats, and the entire mosquito population of Buckinghamshire.'

'You're not joking.' She scratched her head. 'I think I've been bitten.'

'Hopefully that means our little bat friends will be coming to join us soon.'

'*Our little bat friends*?' She looked at him sideways.

'I don't know,' he said, the corner of his mouth quirking in a half smile.

'Have you got me up here under false pretences?' She sidestepped to avoid a puddle, her shoulder brushing against his arm. It felt solid with muscle. She stepped away again, wishing for another puddle to avoid. The path was clear.

'No, I'm not in the habit of luring women to the woods after dark for anything dubious, I promise.'

Shame, thought Lucy, widening her eyes at her inner thoughts. She must get a grip. They were here to look at bats. It was a perfectly normal thing to do.

'Look!' Sam pointed upwards.

She peered into the sky. 'What am I looking at?'

'Pipistrelles. They're tiny. Look, little dots in the air, there –'

Lucy scrunched up her eyes. 'Nope, I can't see them.'

Sam laughed. 'That's because they've gone.'

'Right.' She shaded her eyes, despite the fact that the light was falling rapidly. The sun had dropped below the horizon, leaving a pale, luminescent orange-streaked sky.

'It's like looking for a shooting star. You've got to sort of look everywhere and nowhere at once.'

Lucy turned to look at Sam. He dropped his gaze from the sky and looked at her directly.

'You realize that what you're describing is physically impossible?'

'Yes. That's why it's so much fun.' He was teasing her. 'Look, I can show you.'

He took her shoulders and turned her gently so she was facing towards a gap in the trees at the mouth of the woods. His hands stayed there, weighting her shoulders.

'If you stand here . . .' She was alert to the sensation of his body behind hers, as if there was some sort of charge between them. Her heart was thudding as she stood completely still, hoping that he couldn't sense the fact that her legs were trembling, despite the unseasonable warmth of the evening. 'We'll both be looking exactly the same way. That way you'll see what I can see.'

Her heart was thumping so hard in her chest that she was certain he could hear it. She let out her breath slowly, wondering if it sounded as shaky as it felt.

'There,' he said, his voice low in her ear.

'I see them!'

'Gorgeous, aren't they?' He was still holding her shoulders.

Three bats swooped back and forth across the darkening sky. Another couple joined them then, and they stood together watching. And then in a second they were gone.

'Let's go in a bit – there'll be more. Harder to see as it gets dark, though.'

The trees were etched ink-black against the sky, and all around them was silence. Lucy hoped he'd offer to show her where to look again, and when he did, her insides melting, there was a part of her that wanted to simply lean back against him and close her eyes. Never mind the bats.

An owl hooted overhead. She pushed hair back from her face, tucking it behind her ear, brushing away another mosquito as it hummed close to her face. And then something brushed against her skin and she stepped backwards, bumping into Sam, and spun around in a second, gasping an apology.

'I'm sorry. I think it was a moth or something.'

'I'm not complaining.'

She could hardly see his face in the deepening dusk. Neither of them moved. If she was going to kiss him ever, this was it. She lifted a hand, tentatively first, and then touched the scruff of stubble on his cheek.

She felt him inhaling sharply. He took her hand, lacing his fingers between hers. For a moment they stood in silence, the only sound the owl hooting somewhere in the trees above them. And then he said, his mouth almost on hers –

'Can I –'

She gave the briefest of nods, and as they kissed for the first time she felt his fingers curling around hers, his other hand reaching to feel the curve of her waist. She snaked her hands around his neck as he brought his mouth down on hers. She pulled away for a second and looked at him, her breath uneven. His eyes locked on hers and he lifted a hand to her face, running a finger down her jawline for a moment. Lucy's breath caught as he leaned forward, kissing first her jaw and then the corner of her mouth so gently that all the hairs on her neck rose up. Her hands were still tangled in his hair and she pulled him closer in the shadowy winter evening.

'I think we might frighten the wildlife if we stay here much longer.' He gave a slow smile, some time later. 'Shall we head back?'

He rubbed gently on her palm with his thumb as they walked back in the darkness, which had fallen all at once. His hand was warm and he squeezed her fingers in a silent gesture. She felt as if someone had charged her with electricity.

Just before they reached the lane, he stopped, pulling her into his arms again.

'I've thought about that for a long time.'

She was leaning against a wall, looking up at him. His eyes were dark.

'Me too.'

Infinitely gently, as if they had all the time in the world, he leaned towards her, dropping a kiss first on her temple, then on her jawbone, and then – finally – on her mouth.

Lucy felt herself arching up towards him. She felt him catch his breath.

'Let's go.'

They went to his place. The dogs were half asleep in the kitchen. He took a bottle of red wine from the counter, and handed her two glasses. She followed him through to the sitting room where the log burner was slumbering. Opening the door, he tossed in a couple of logs and in seconds the fire blazed into life. Like me, Lucy thought, watching as he poured two glasses of wine and handed her one.

He sat down beside her on the sofa, taking a drink, looking at her over the top of his glass. She took the glass from his hand, placing it beside hers on the table in front of them, and leaned towards him.

'I don't want you to think I'm taking advantage of you because Freya is away,' she said, teasingly.

'Oh.' He cupped her face in one hand, looking at her wonderingly for a moment before kissing her. When they came up for air, he said, laughing, 'I rather hoped you might.'

Chapter Twenty-three

'I have to go.'

Sam rolled over. It wasn't his imagination. There, lying in his bed, under his covers, was Lucy. She reached out and touched his arm, as if she couldn't quite believe it either.

'You have to go where?' He glanced over her shoulder at the clock. It was half past five in the morning.

'Hamish. He's probably eaten half the furniture and peed on the remains.'

'D'you want me to come back with you?'

Lucy shook her head. 'Don't worry. If I go now, maybe we'll avoid activating the village gossip systems. But I'll see you later?'

He watched as she pulled on her clothes. Her hair was ruffled at the back and she had smudges of mascara under her eyes and she looked utterly beautiful.

'Okay.' He tried for a second to play it cool. 'When?' And failed. He'd been holding back for so long, and now that he'd actually spent the evening with Lucy in his arms – and in his bed – he couldn't stop himself. He wanted to pull her back into bed, and when she sat down on the edge of it, leaning over to kiss him goodbye, he curled an arm around her waist and murmured, his mouth almost on hers, 'Stay. We can buy new furniture.'

'Don't tempt me.' She wriggled out of his grasp and gave him a cheeky smile. 'I won't be far away.'

He groaned. 'I know. That's what makes it harder.'

Lucy raised an eyebrow. 'Really?'

He shook his head, laughing. 'Go. Now.'

Back in the cottage, Lucy was relieved to find that Hamish had – far from dismantling the place and weeing everywhere – been a paragon of virtue and was curled up, fast asleep, on the armchair. She opened the back door to let him out and gasped with surprise. Hamish stopped stock still, eyes popping. A hedgehog was bumbling across the gravel path, heading for the house Sam had built.

'Wait,' she said to Hamish, who was completely confounded by the sight of a walking, spiky pom-pom. It disappeared into the darkness of the little wooden house, and Hamish skittered up the garden to do his business.

Lucy leaned back against the cold stone of the house wall, listening to the silence of the night. Her chin was stinging with stubble rash from hours of kissing, and she felt – well, it had been a long time. Everything ached, but in a very good way. She called Hamish in, ran a hot shower, and climbed into bed and slept almost until lunchtime.

Waking, feeling smug and sated, she rolled over and stretched her limbs. Perhaps she could pop over later and see if Sam wanted to go for a walk with the dogs. A walk with plenty of opportunities for kissing breaks. And if there happened to be a chance afterwards to spend the evening together . . . she sighed, happily.

She popped in to see Bunty, who was grumbling about an unexpected visit from Gordon and Margaret.

'Honestly, I wish they'd give me some advance notice. I was quite happily minding my own business when they turned up.'

'Maybe they wanted to say hello.' Lucy was feeling amenable towards everyone.

'Humph.' Bunty made a face. 'More likely Margaret wanted to see if I'd croaked.'

Lucy gave a gasp of horrified laughter.

'You're in a good mood today. What have you been up to? Or –' Bunty peered at her through narrowed eyes – '*who*, perhaps I should say?'

'What do you mean?' Lucy took a step back, protesting innocence. She noticed Stanley coiled on the dresser beside her and took another hurried step sideways.

'I'm not as green as I'm cabbage-looking. I know that look.'

Lucy cleared her throat. 'I thought I'd pop in and see if you needed anything. Do you want me to put some washing on, or . . . anything?' she tailed off, lamely.

'I do hope you and Sam have stopped dancing around and realized you're made for each other.'

Lucy felt herself blushing. It was such an irritating habit. She couldn't hide a thing from anyone without her face giving her away.

'Heh.' Bunty slapped the table with a triumphant noise. 'About bloody time, too.'

'What do you mean?'

'Oh for goodness' sake. Anyone could see it.'

'But I'm only here for –' Lucy began.

'Nonsense. My goodness, when I showed you my diary I hoped it might make you realize that life is for living. I could have turned down the chance to walk out with Harry because he was Canadian, or because it was too risky, or because – oh, a million reasons. But I will never regret grabbing those moments of happiness.'

'Even though you ended up married to Len, and never had any more children?'

'Even though. Len was a nice man, and he treated me well. I loved him, and he loved me, in his own way. But I knew what it meant to be truly adored.'

'You still love him – Harry, I mean?'

Bunty nodded. 'After all this time. Yes.' She smiled wistfully. 'And that's precisely why I think you and Sam should blooming well get on with it. Mel and I have been placing bets on how long it would take for the two of you to realize what was right in front of your noses.'

Lucy put a hand to her mouth. 'Really?'

'Yes.' Bunty chuckled. 'Now get over there, and don't waste any more of your precious time worrying about me.'

Lucy ran a hand through her hair and swallowed hard before knocking on the door of Sam's cottage.

'I'll get it,' came Freya's voice from inside.

'Hi,' Lucy said, smiling. 'How was the school trip?'

'Amazing.' Freya looked almost feverish, her usually pale cheeks flaming and her eyes sparkling bright. Perhaps she hadn't slept.

'I thought I'd pop in and –' Lucy took a sharp intake of breath as Freya opened the door wider.

'Come in and meet my mum,' Freya said, beckoning her inside. 'Lucy, this is – Stella. My mum.' The colour in her cheeks rose further.

'Hi,' said a tall, slender woman with long, sleek, dark hair.

'Lucy,' said Sam, emerging from the kitchen. He hadn't shaved, and his cheeks were shadowed with stubble which was echoed in the shadows beneath his eyes.

'I think maybe . . . this isn't a good time?' Lucy took a step backwards, bumping into the sofa.

Stella didn't say anything more, but looked at her, steadily and calmly. The expression on her face suggested that she knew she had a role as Freya's mother, and that she felt Lucy was surplus to requirements. Lucy side-stepped, avoiding the sofa this time and, apologizing for her bad timing, hurtled out onto the street.

'Bloody hell,' Mel said, opening her door. A sea of dogs milled around her feet and she shooed them backwards, letting Lucy inside. 'You look like you've seen a ghost.'

'Not a ghost.'

Mel stood for a moment, hand hovering between the

bottle of sherry that was sitting on the kitchen worktop and the kettle. The sherry won.

'Won this in a raffle. I think you need it more than tea.'

'Thanks.' Lucy took a large gulp. It was disgusting, but it helped slightly.

'So what's happened?'

'Oh my God. Well.'

And it all poured out. Their night together ('I knew it,' Mel said triumphantly) and going home feeling like she was on cloud nine, and then knocking on Sam's door to discover –

'No way. In his house? Bold as brass?'

'She seemed perfectly normal.'

'What were you expecting? Horns?' Mel tipped more sherry into their glasses. 'What the bloody hell is she up to? She must be after something. She can't just turn up out of the blue after all this time.'

'It's not, though.' It must be all right to break Freya's confidence now, surely. 'Freya told me she'd found her. She searched for her online. I think she's been trying to track her down. I think she's hoping they'll get back together.'

Mel gave a bark of laughter. 'Not a chance in hell.'

'Not even for Freya?'

Mel shook her head again. But Lucy thought of Bunty, staying married all those years to a man who wasn't the one she loved, just for the sake of giving Gordon a stable background. Sam loved Freya fiercely.

Did he love her enough to forgive Stella's behaviour and take her back?

'I think you might be wrong.'

Mel's face clouded over. 'I think it's extremely unlikely.'

Sam was wrestling with his conscience. Freya had admitted that she'd been the one to get in contact with Stella, and Stella had admitted over lunch in the restaurant that she'd chickened out, leaving Freya stranded in the shopping centre. 'I thought you might have guessed then,' Freya said to him, picking up a piece of pizza thoughtfully, 'but you didn't have a clue.'

When Freya went to the bathroom, he seized his chance. 'So why now?'

He looked at Stella's sharp, foxy little face and thought how different she looked to Lucy. 'I've spent the last couple of years in therapy. When Freya got in touch, it felt like a sign.'

Sam raised a dubious eyebrow. 'Therapy?'

'Expensive therapy.' She lifted a long, slim hand. It took a second for him to register that she was wearing both an expensive-looking diamond and a wedding ring. 'I'm not coming back to claim what's mine, if that's what you're wondering.' She gave a catlike smile. 'Or hoping.'

He laughed drily. 'You're fine, thanks.'

'The girl who turned up earlier?' Stella looked at him.

'Lucy. She's called Lucy.'

'Seems nice. Very – wholesome.'

'Don't.' He could hear the warning in his tone.

'I wasn't.' She smirked slightly. 'Just, you used to be more – well, let's put it this way. You're far more settled than I ever expected you to be.'

'I didn't have much choice,' he said levelly, picking up a napkin and folding it. 'I was left holding the baby – literally.'

'You've done a good job.' Stella inclined her head in the direction of the restaurant loos. Freya was standing, head down, looking at something on her phone.

'She's a good kid.'

'You're a good dad.'

He felt a sick sensation rising inside him. 'You're not about to waltz in here and demand custody or something?'

Stella shook her head. 'Hardly. I think Gavin might have something to say about that.'

'Your husband?'

She looked at him, her voice quite steady. 'I promise you, I'm not planning to stage a coup.' This was a new Stella, he acknowledged, looking at her as she fished in her bag for a lipstick. She flipped open a mirror and applied a layer, looking at him for a moment. 'Don't worry. You – and your sweet-looking Lucy – are quite safe there.'

Not completely new, then. She lifted an eyebrow slightly. The sharp tongue he'd once found amusing just left him with a sour feeling in his mouth.

'Lucy?' Freya had appeared at the table without either of them noticing. She slid into her chair and looked from one parent to the other. 'What's Lucy got to do with this?'

'Nothing,' he and Stella said in unison.

That was one thing they both agreed on, at least. Stella sipped her drink and looked out of the window. He took the opportunity to size her up, slightly loathing himself for doing so. She looked good – hair perfectly styled, the sort of understated accessories that were inevitably expensive, and of course that ring. A diamond that size didn't come cheap. He felt a wave of something – relief, perhaps? He'd always wondered what he'd do if she reappeared, wanting to be part of their lives again.

'It would feel weird calling you Mum,' Freya said, chewing a lock of hair and looking at Stella, thoughtfully.

'You don't have to,' Stella said. 'Stella is fine.'

'Maybe.' Freya shrugged. 'It might just take some getting used to.'

'Whatever makes you happy,' Stella said, reaching across and touching Freya gently on the arm. He watched her face light up briefly, and an expression on Stella's face that he couldn't read. Regret, perhaps? It can't have been easy for her. He could hear Mel snorting with derision at that, telling him he was a soft touch. But the truth is that Stella was Freya's mother, and they were going to have to find a way to be a family of some sort – or to work together as one – despite what had happened in the past.

He splayed his hands, running them through his hair as he tried to think what was best. Freya looked at him from beneath her hair, which she'd allowed to drape over her face. She always did that when she was uncomfortable. And she was biting her thumbnail. Stella sat poised, back very straight, eyes wide. For a moment it felt as if the tension and their silence were ballooning out, filling the whole restaurant. But then a waiter dropped a knife on the floor with a clatter and apologized to them, and it was as if someone had broken the spell. He could hear chatter and laughter, the clattering of plates. Freya looked from him to Stella, still not speaking. Stella raised an eyebrow.

He'd have to take control of the situation.

'I think we need to sit down and work out the practicalities of all of this, don't you?'

'That sounds very wise,' Stella said. 'Maybe we should do it over pudding and coffee?'

'That sounds even better,' said Freya, with a slightly unsteady smile.

Sam reached out and encased his daughter's small hand in his own, squeezing it gently. 'We don't have to rush into anything. You call the shots, darling.'

Stella nodded agreement, and he allowed himself the tiniest flicker of hope that this might work out in the end.

'In that case –' Freya gave him a mischievous look – 'can we have the super double chocolate layer cake?'

'I think that would be a very good start.'

Chapter Twenty-four

It would have been easier if it hadn't been for Stella, Lucy reflected, standing back from the cottage window and looking out.

Stella's car was parked outside Sam's cottage again, as it had been the day before when Lucy had girded her loins to go and have the 'look, it was very lovely that we slept together but clearly it's not going to go anywhere' conversation. So that's another day when I can't do it, she thought, sighing and turning away. She pulled the covers up over her bed and left the bedroom, with Hamish scampering down the stairs behind her.

In the little sitting room there were stacks of papers and notepads from the work she'd been doing on the WI anniversary booklet. If nothing else, she could get that sorted and out of the way.

She'd been working hard for an hour when there was a knock at the door. Hamish leapt across her legs, scattering pieces of paper and barking with excitement. She pulled back the latch, heart thudding in the hope that it might be Sam, to find Susan standing there with a big leather satchel slung over her shoulder. She was holding a cardboard box from the village shop.

'Hoped you wouldn't mind the interruption, dear – but

RACHAEL LUCAS

I thought as we're almost there with the booklet, I'd pop round and see if we can just go through it together?'

Lucy cast a glance around the little sitting room, which was covered in books and papers. 'No, that's lovely,' she said, sounding more convincing than she felt. 'Let me just clear a space for you.'

'Oh good,' said Susan, brandishing the box. 'I hoped you'd be fine with it. I brought some chocolate brownies from the shop as brain fuel.' She beamed, setting them down on the little coffee table between the sofa and the log burner.

Lucy swooped in. 'I'll move them, or Hamish will snaffle them before we even sit down. He's already had to visit the vet once in Brighton after getting hold of a bar of chocolate and wolfing the lot. Now, shall I make us some tea?'

'Lovely.'

'This looks really quite wonderful,' Susan said a couple of hours later.

Lucy had popped into town and bought a cheap printer, so they'd run off a rough copy of the booklet.

'Eighty years of the WI here in Little Maudley. Just imagine.' Susan leaned over, looking at one of the photographs they'd been given by people from the village. 'I think that's my big brother Joseph in that one.' She picked it up, frowning. 'It is. How funny.'

'I thought we could do a display of all of these,' Lucy said, indicating the whole collection of photos.

'That's such a lovely idea. Yes. I don't remember the war, of course – I was only very young. But I do remember

342

we had a little fete to celebrate VE Day, over there on the green. They decorated the telephone box with bunting and hung it from the trees, and we all had cake and sweets.'

'The telephone box really does seem to have been a focal point here, doesn't it?'

'It has, dear, yes. I'm personally very glad that Helen didn't get her way about having it removed.'

'Not that you'd know it. She's taken over completely.'

They laughed.

'Not long now. Sam's got the shelving under control, I believe, and then we can get all the books in and have a grand opening.'

'I thought Bunty could be the one to cut the ribbon.'

Susan nodded. 'Well, yes – she's the oldest villager, so that would be rather nice.'

Lucy gathered up the papers. 'I think we've pretty much got this all sorted.'

'It's a shame we couldn't persuade Bunty to talk about her war, isn't it?'

'Mmm.' Knowing what she did now, Lucy could appreciate why Bunty wanted to keep her war story to herself. 'I've done a lot of reading about people from that time. For every one that wants to share their memories, there's another who would rather forget, or keep them close to their heart.'

'I think we have to respect that, don't you?' Susan looked thoughtful.

'Definitely.'

'Now, if you email those finished pages over to my

343

nephew Matthew, he'll get them printed up and then we can have our little celebration on the thirty-first.'

'Don't you mean the thirtieth?'

There had been signs around the village for the last couple of weeks, reminding everyone that Hallowe'en was coming.

'Gosh, yes. How could I forget?' Susan picked up her big bag and hefted it over her shoulder. 'Will you be taking part? The village does rather go to town for Hallowe'en. And then for bonfire night, too.'

Lucy shook her head. 'I'm going to see my brother in Brighton on the thirty-first, but I'll definitely be around for bonfire night. I love fireworks.'

'Well, you're in for a treat. The cricket club do a wonderful event every year – it's their fundraiser.'

'I'll look forward to it.'

As she was seeing Susan out, Sam opened the door of his cottage. He looked momentarily confused, as if he couldn't quite work out what to say. He rubbed his chin, glancing back over his shoulder, and then stepped out hesitantly. 'Lucy.'

'I'll let you young ones get on,' said Susan, cheerily. 'See you at the village hall for the meeting and the unveiling.'

'You've got all the photographs?' Lucy turned round to check inside the cottage.

'All here in my bag,' Susan patted it. 'The next time you see them, they'll be up in the hall for everyone to admire.'

With that, she beetled off up the road. Sam was standing, as if frozen to the spot, outside his door. After a moment he stepped forward, crossing the road. He pushed the sleeves of his flannel shirt up, rubbing his arm as he spoke.

'About the other night. I'm really sorry – I didn't want to just send you a message, but –'

'It's okay. I guess with everything that's happened, you've had enough to think about.'

'It's not that – I mean, there's nothing going on with me and Stella, if that's what you're thinking.'

Lucy felt a wave of relief, despite herself. She hadn't wanted to think that Sam's ex had suddenly sprung back into his life and they'd decided to play happy families, but when she'd been lying in bed at night, unable to sleep, wondering . . . well, the thought had crossed her mind once or twice. Or more.

'I didn't think you had.'

'But you've got – well, I mean you've got other stuff – and I need to make sure Freya's okay.'

She nodded. The truth, which Sam didn't know, was that she'd pretty much decided that the *other stuff* – by which he meant a life and a job back in Brighton – wasn't what she wanted. But that had nothing to do with Sam. This was about her future; it was a decision she'd made for herself.

'How is she?' She fiddled with the button on her shirt, twisting the fabric around her finger.

'Good. Surprisingly good. I mean, at the moment it's

the honeymoon period, isn't it? Stella's taken her out for lunch today, and they're going to the cinema.' He frowned slightly, biting his lip. 'I do feel a bit like I'm the one going on about making sure she doesn't forget her homework and tidies her room, and Stella gets to come in and do all the fun mum stuff.'

'That's teenagers for you. Right now she's focusing on what's in front of her. They can be incredibly perceptive and thoughtful one moment, and as self-absorbed and thoughtless as toddlers the next. That won't last.' Lucy thought for a moment. 'She's always going to know that you're the one who brought her up and kept her safe.' She reached out a hand and touched his arm lightly. 'That bit matters.'

He nodded. 'I guess you're right.'

'I usually am,' she said, with a note of amusement in her voice.

He smiled and shook his head. 'So what's the plan with Susan? What have you been up to?'

'Oh, you know; partying, hanging out with the stars, that sort of thing.'

'Yep. Definitely.'

'We were finishing off the booklet for the WI anniversary. They're having a little celebration on the thirtieth, if you fancy it?'

'I dunno – it sounds a bit rock and roll for me.' He gave a teasing smile.

Lucy shook her head, laughing. 'Yeah, all right. I admit it's not exactly a glamorous book launch.'

'I think it's lovely,' he said, sincerely. 'You didn't have to do any of this village stuff, and you've really thrown yourself into it. I heard Beth telling someone the other day that she thinks you've really settled in well. It's a shame you've got to –' He stopped himself.

A knot tightened in her stomach. 'I didn't mean to get so caught up in it all. It just sort of – happened.'

His eyes met hers and neither of them spoke for a moment.

'Anyway.' She cleared her throat.

'Yes.' Sam pulled his phone out of his back pocket. 'I better get going. I've got places to go . . .'

'Treehouses to build.'

'That sort of thing. Exactly.'

She watched him spin round on his heel and head to the Land Rover, climbing in and closing the door. As he drove off, he gave a wave. The knot in Lucy's stomach tightened a little bit more.

The WI anniversary celebration was a big event in the village calendar. Lucy arrived at the village hall to find it decked with floral bunting, and Helen and all the local worthies milling about in smart clothes. Music from the 1940s was playing through the speakers, and the photographs had been displayed on a brightly coloured wall chart which went from 1939 to the present day, dotted with various notices and ephemera that had been handed in, as well as some of the artwork and crafts made by the women of the village.

'Here we are,' said Susan, resplendent in a green suit and blouse which looked more suitable for a garden party at Buckingham Palace than a damp October evening in a village hall. 'The guest of honour!'

Lucy looked around to see who she was talking about.

'You, my dear.' Susan took her arm and led her to the top of the hall, where a stack of books was sitting on a table. They looked very smart – Susan had clearly turned on the charm with her nephew, because rather than the soft-covered booklets she'd been expecting, they were very handsome-looking green books with a pretty line drawing of the village printed on the front, and 'Little Maudley WI, 1939–2019' along the top. She opened one. Inside, there was a list of contributors – all the villagers she and Susan had spoken to – and underneath, her name was printed in black and white. Lucy Evans – editor. She turned to Susan, her heart soaring with happiness.

'They look amazing!'

Susan beamed. 'Don't they just? I think we've rather outdone ourselves.'

'Hello, my dear,' said Henry, the elderly man she'd interviewed about his time working as an ARP warden alongside Bunty's husband Len. 'I wondered if I might trouble you for your signature?'

Lucy looked at Susan.

'Go on, dear. Here you are – I brought a nice pen, just in case.'

She rifled in her green handbag and pulled out a lovely fountain pen. Lucy took off the lid and bent over the

348

table, signing her name on the flyleaf. She looked up at Henry, whose eyes were twinkling.

'You've done a wonderful job with this, my dear. It's a shame the village will be losing you.'

Lucy swallowed back a wave of sadness that threatened to wash over her. When she spoke, her voice wobbled slightly. 'Thank you.' She straightened up, and was surprised when Susan – not normally demonstrative – put an arm around her shoulders and spun her round to face the room.

'Ladies, gentlemen.' Her voice was loud and clear. 'A moment, please.'

Helen looked up from the side of the room where she'd been organizing teas. Lucy suspected that Susan had sneaked in with an announcement before Helen could take over. The WI power struggles were amusing to behold. Susan – seeing Helen mouthing something – carried on regardless.

'Now, I have someone here who has worked incredibly hard – and for no reward – to bring together this little book, this wonderful book. And I wanted to take a moment, before we all get stuck in to the tea and cakes, to say how much I have appreciated her help.'

Henry turned to look at Lucy, giving her a wide smile.

'Lucy only came to the village for a short time, and has been kind enough to spend a lot of that time helping us out. I'd like to raise a toast.'

Lucy looked across the room and spotted Bunty, who normally avoided anything to do with the WI like the plague ('I don't like jam, or "Jerusalem", or being organized'). She lifted a casual hand in greeting and gave a small smile. Lucy beamed and waved back.

'To Lucy, with huge thanks.'

'To Lucy!' The room echoed with voices toasting her name. Lucy felt a rush of warmth for this funny little village and all the people who lived there, and even for – well, perhaps not quite for Helen.

'*Susan!* I can't believe you've pre-empted my speech. I had it all written down on my iPad, look.' Helen hurtled across the room, her voice low but her eyes narrowed in disapproval.

'We don't need a ten-minute speech, Helen,' said Susan, squaring her shoulders as if preparing for a fight. 'I just wanted everyone to thank Lucy for her work, and then we can get on with enjoying a nice glass of bubbly and some cake.'

'Well,' said Helen, who'd been well and truly shut up. She opened and closed her mouth a couple of times like a furious guppy, then marched off to find her husband.

'He's going to get it in the neck now,' said Henry, sagely.

'Look at this,' said Bunty a while later, as they leafed through the booklet together. She pointed to a photograph. 'There's Milly, my schoolteacher friend. What a lovely surprise.'

'That was given in by one of the women from the village. She said it was on the wall in her aunt's house.'

Bunty peered forward. 'I remember the day that photograph was taken. Milly borrowed that dress from me.'

They turned a few more pages.

'Gosh, this all takes me back. I have to admit,' Bunty said, turning to Susan, 'it's been rather nice to have this little trip down Memory Lane.'

'Not too late to join us,' Susan said, hopefully.

'I think perhaps that ship has sailed,' said Bunty, laughing wheezily. 'But you've done a wonderful job. And so have you, Lucy.'

'Hello!'

Freya appeared from nowhere between them.

'Come to join, have you?' Bunty laughed.

'I don't think it's my sort of thing.' She shook her head. 'But I wanted to come and have a look at the photos, and see Lucy's book. Can we buy a copy?'

'I've got one already.' Sam's voice made Lucy turn, the hairs on the back of her neck prickling. He was holding a copy. 'It looks amazing.'

'Thanks.'

'Let me see.' Freya took it out of his hands, and a moment later somehow she and Bunty had disappeared together, leaving Sam and Lucy alone by the wall of photographs. Lucy fiddled with her hair, catching a strand in her fingers and twirling it.

'I didn't think the WI was your sort of thing. Are you even allowed to *be* here, with the whole *being male* thing?'

'It's not my sort of thing at all.' Sam indicated the group of elderly women to their left. 'I just thought I'd come and cheer you on.'

'That's really nice of you.'

'I *am* nice.' His eyes sparkled with amusement.

'Ah, Sam,' said Helen, who had no ability to read the room whatsoever. She was bearing her iPad, which was open on a list-making app. 'Just the man I wanted to see. Now, about the bonfire.'

Sam shot Lucy a look that spoke volumes.

'And you, Lucy – just checking you're still happy to help out with choosing the books for the library?'

'And me!' Freya reappeared. 'I want to help, too.'

'Excellent.' Helen typed *Books – Lucy and Freya* onto her iPad. 'Just let me know when. I've got a surprising number of boxes already, just from village donations.'

'I hope they're not all boring,' said Freya. 'I'm relying on the telephone box library to keep me in reading material.'

'I think you'll be quite happy with what we've got so far,' said Helen, briskly. 'Now, Sam, back to what we were talking about –'

'Lucy,' said Susan, tapping Lucy on the arm. 'There's a man here from the *Advertiser* who would like to take a photograph.'

By the time Lucy had finished having her photograph taken, sitting side by side with Susan behind a table with a pile of the books and posing with Henry by the photograph display on the wall, Freya had nipped across to tell her that they were going home. Mel, who had popped in briefly, gave her a kiss on the cheek and bought a copy of the commemorative book, then scarpered.

'Sorry, it's not you, it's me. I'm allergic to this sort of thing. Plus the dogs are at home.'

'The dogs are always at home.'

'I've left the kettle on.' Mel stuck out her tongue, laughing. 'Something like that. Come and see me tomorrow.'

'I can't. I'm going down to Brighton. Need to have a chat at the school and work out what I'm doing next.'

Mel looked at her thoughtfully. 'Don't talk about that. I don't want you to leave me to the tender mercies of Helen.'

'You've got Sam.'

'Yeah, and Stella's back on the scene.' She made a face. 'Everything's changing and I don't like it.'

'I'll come and see you when I get back,' said Lucy.

'Let's go to the bonfire? We can drink mulled wine and toast marshmallows.' Mel wrapped her scarf around her neck and fastened her coat. The weather wasn't messing around this autumn – there was a chill in the air, and the forecasters were even talking about a white Christmas.

'Now you're talking. It's a deal.'

Mel blew a theatrical kiss. 'See ya.'

Lucy walked home with Bunty, waiting at the gate until she'd gone safely inside. She turned, something inside her compelling her to look across at Sam's house, where a light glowed from the window upstairs. She shook her head, chiding herself for being ridiculous, and turned away, opening the door of the cottage to a

RACHAEL LUCAS

disapproving Hamish, who thought she'd been gone far too long.

She got up the next day and headed down to Brighton, leaving Hamish in the capable hands of Bunty. Tom was at the flat when she popped in, sprawled on the sofa doing work.

'Hello,' he said, climbing out of a mountain of scatter cushions and papers. 'I wasn't expecting you until later.'

'I know. Decided to get up early and drive down first thing.'

'That sounds very efficient. Is this the old workaholic Lucy coming back to life? Are you off to resume your duties?'

She shook her head. 'Not quite.' The flat looked different, somehow. Tidier. 'What's with all the cushions?'

'It's Kate. She bought them. Said I needed to make the place look less like a doctor's waiting room.'

Lucy laughed. She'd taken her colourful throw up to the cottage, and without it the room had looked a bit bare and beige. But she'd always been so busy with work that she hadn't had time to notice, or to do anything about it.

'She's got a point. But buying sofa cushions together? That's a big commitment, Tom.'

He laughed, throwing one at her head. 'Even your big brother has to grow up sometime.'

'She'll be moving in next.' She cocked her head, sizing up his response.

'Well, actually,' Tom began, 'about that . . .'

An hour later, after a long heart-to-heart, Lucy gathered up some of the bits and pieces she'd left in her room. It was strange, looking around, to realize how much stuff she'd left behind when she went – as if she'd made a conscious decision to walk out of one life and into another. It was as if one part of her had known she had no intention of coming back.

The head teacher's office hadn't changed. Someone had hung up a colourful poster on the wall that said 'Just Smile – and Remember Why You Wanted to Teach'. Nick glanced at it and then gave Lucy a knowing look.

'The new school secretary. She's very fond of a motivational poster.'

'I bet that helps no end when you've got school inspectors breathing down your neck.'

'Oh, it makes all the difference.' Nick shook his head and sat down at the desk, motioning for her to take a seat. 'So – you've come to see me about starting back in January, right?'

'Not exactly.' Lucy looked out of the window at the streams of children heading back into their classrooms after lunch break. She couldn't help narrowing her eyes, trying to focus and pick out the ones she'd taught last year. There was Jack, about six inches taller and with his dark curls tied back in a ponytail. And Naima, talking animatedly to a blonde girl who was showing her something on her – off limits in school hours – phone.

'And there's nothing I can do to persuade you?' Nick

looked at her directly. When she'd been signed off work with stress and they'd agreed she would take a sabbatical, he'd made it very clear that the door was always open for her return.

'Nothing.' Lucy had made her mind up.

'What are you going to do?'

She shrugged. 'My brother's going to buy me out of my half of the house, so I'll have a decent nest egg behind me. I'm not giving up teaching – it's in my blood. But I'm not rushing into anything. I might do some supply, then hopefully work part-time. Somewhere smaller – less pressure.'

He raised his eyes in slight acknowledgement. The school had been a pressure cooker for years, and it wasn't likely to change.

'You're a bloody good teacher, Luce. Our loss.' He reached out, putting a hand on her arm. 'I can't make you change your mind?'

She shook her head. There was no way she was going back to everything she'd had in the past – working ridiculous hours, lying in bed worrying about staffing policies, her health suffering – that wasn't what she wanted.

He looked at her for a moment, sizing her up.

'You look different. Happier.'

'I am.' She gave a nod of acknowledgement.

He narrowed his eyes. 'And all this glowing health is just the side-effect of escaping the chalk face?'

'Mm-hmm.'

He raised a sceptical eyebrow. 'Come on, Luce. You've

been married to the job as long as I've known you. There's more to it than that. Have you –' He frowned slightly, scrutinizing her face. 'Have you – met someone?'

'Not really.' She'd been notoriously single the whole time she'd worked there, claiming she was too busy to worry about relationships.

'Not really?' He gave a brief chuckle. 'That sounds like code for something interesting.'

Lucy shrugged and laughed. Whatever was going to happen in the future, she was making this decision for herself, and for her own happiness. That was the thing that mattered most – and coming back here, to the place where she'd worked herself to breaking point, just proved it.

'So you're heading back to the village today?'

She nodded. The back seat of the car was packed with cardboard boxes of stuff she wanted to keep. Whatever she was doing, wherever she was going, she'd sort it back at the cottage. That way, Tom and Kate could get on with making the flat into a home.

'And what's happening in the village this week? I have visions of it being like *Midsomer Murders*.'

Lucy laughed. 'It's not that far off – without the murders, so far, anyway. I need to get back because we've got a mountain of discarded paperbacks to sort out for the telephone box library, and then there's the cricket club bonfire this weekend.'

'Well, I can see how Brighton would struggle to compete. It sounds like it's a complete riot.'

'It's one of those you-had-to-be-there things.'

'Clearly.'

He stood up, and so did she. Surprising her, he went to shake her hand but instead enveloped her in a bear hug. 'Take care, Luce. Don't forget you're a bloody good teacher.'

'Thanks, Nick.'

Tears were stinging her eyes as she turned to leave his office. His phone rang as she put a hand to the door and he raised a hand in a silent goodbye, picking it up as she left.

Bunty's words popped into her head as she drove for the last time out of the school gates. She was right. If you only have one chance to live life, you should choose to be happy.

Chapter Twenty-five

Freya was out with Stella again. Sam was feeling a bit redundant, and trying hard not to show it. Apart from the brief chat they'd had that day on her doorstep, he hadn't had a moment to speak to Lucy alone, and it was nagging at him. Everything was changing. Lucy's car had reappeared earlier, its back seat covered in cardboard boxes. His heart had thudded to his feet when he'd seen that. It was as if someone had knocked all the air out of him, and he didn't want to admit to himself exactly why. The car was gone again now, and he felt utterly miserable.

He had decided to head over to Mel's, and she was now giving him a talking to.

'You need to tell her how you feel.'

'I can't.'

'Don't be so bloody ridiculous.'

'It's not the right time. I've got all this stuff going on with Freya and Stella. Lucy's about to leave –'

'What makes you think that?' Mel looked up sharply.

'Car full of boxes is a bit of a giveaway, don't you think?'

Mel's gaze drifted out of the window towards Lucy's cottage. He followed it, not speaking. They watched as Lucy's battered little Corsa pulled up outside, and

Lucy – dressed smartly in a green patterned dress and knee-length boots – climbed out.

'Looks like she's been somewhere nice,' commented Mel, looking at him pointedly.

'And?'

'I suspect she thinks you're avoiding her.'

'I thought she was avoiding me.'

'You're a pair of adults behaving more like Freya and Camille. You need your heads banging together. Why don't you nip over and see her, clear the air?'

'Maybe she thinks what happened was a mistake.'

Mel shook her head. 'I think she thinks *you* think that. Which means that unless you want to throw away one of the best things that's ever happened to you, you might need to get a grip and start acting like an adult.'

'Thanks, oh wise one.'

'Welcome.' She gave him a shove. 'No time like the present.'

He shook his head. He'd need an hour to shower, find something decent to wear, work out what he was going to say. He couldn't screw this up.

Later that evening, he gathered the courage to cross the road and knock on Lucy's door. Hamish leapt up at the window, barking in greeting, but she was nowhere to be seen.

'If you're looking for Lucy,' Bunty said, looking over at him from the rosebush in her garden with two milk bottles in hand, 'she's up at Helen's place, sorting books with Freya. Didn't she tell you?'

'It's okay,' he said. 'I forgot about that.'

He couldn't face going up to Helen's. He'd been finishing off the shelving for the telephone box library in recent days, and she'd been hassling him incessantly about the tiniest details.

'Haruumph,' said Bunty disapprovingly. 'You're going to miss the boat, Sam, if you're not careful. And you've only got one life to live. Why not make it a happy one?'

He nodded, and left. On his way back to his house he took a detour to check on the phone box. Opening the door, he was assailed by the smell of the hanging air freshener Helen had insisted on putting inside. It mingled with the scent of freshly cut wood. He ran a hand along the shelves, feeling for any missed rough patches. It looked very smart now.

Meanwhile, up at Helen's house, Lucy and Freya were surveying a pile of books that they'd chosen.

'I can't understand why we've been given six copies of this *Riders* one.' Freya lifted up a copy and raised her eyebrows at the image on the front.

'It was very popular at the time, I understand,' said Helen, disapprovingly. 'I don't think it's the sort of thing we want in the library.'

'I think it's *exactly* the sort of thing.' Lucy giggled. 'That's for the yes pile. I bet Susan would appreciate it.'

Freya flicked open a page and gave a snort of surprise. 'Oh my God.' She put it back down again, eyes wide in astonishment.

'Jilly Cooper is an absolute genius,' said Lucy. 'It's a

complete classic. I like the next one, *Rivals*, best, I think – you should read it.'

By the end of the day, they'd boxed up a selection of books for Helen's husband David to drop off at the weekend. The library would be operational for the whole month of November, but the official celebratory opening was taking place on the first of December.

'Why do we have to wait so long?' grumbled Freya as they walked down through the village later that evening.

'Because Helen's going on holiday to the Maldives for a fortnight, and as chair of the parish council it was agreed –'

'You mean she overruled everyone?'

'Well, yes – that's what an agreement means, in Helen's world – that the first weekend in December was a lovely time to do it.'

'She's unbelievable.' Freya shook her head.

'She is, but she also gets stuff done. Every village needs someone like her.' Lucy echoed Sam's comment, unthinkingly.

'That's a terrifying prospect.'

They walked along the lane in darkness. Left over Hallowe'en decorations still hung from the porch of one cottage. The streetlights gave off a pale orange glow, and residents could be seen pottering about inside houses where the curtains were still to be drawn. A little girl peered out of the window of her bedroom, thumb in her mouth. Freya looked up at her and waved.

A firework squeal made them jump. They both looked up, but couldn't see a thing – the sky was dark and heavy with clouds.

'I hope it doesn't rain for the bonfire night tomorrow.'

'Me too.'

Lucy said goodbye and crossed the road, not looking back as Freya headed inside.

Chapter Twenty-six

They hadn't been joking when they said bonfire night was a big event in Little Maudley. Lucy crunched across the gravel car park of the cricket club, past a pavilion strung with fairy lights and warm with the scent of spiced mulled wine. The bonfire was stacked up and ready to go on the rough ground beyond the cricket pitch. Crowds of people jostled around, holding sticky toffee apples, long scarves wrapped around their necks against the sharp early winter cold.

'You wait here.'

Mel rushed off to get them both a drink, leaving Lucy taking it all in.

She couldn't see anyone she recognized in the darkness. Everyone was wrapped up and disguised with hats and warm coats. She stood by the wooden railings and waited.

Bunty had been happy to stay at home with Hamish, grumbling that Guy Fawkes had been far nicer when they were young and there weren't all these loud crashes and bangs which disturbed the animals. Hamish, who agreed, had curled up on the mat beside the fire in Bunty's sitting room. Mr Darcy, her cat, gave him a beady look through one half-opened eye, but carried on snoozing on the armchair.

'Lovely to see you, Lucy,' said one of the WI committee members, tapping her on the shoulder. She spun round and smiled hello, but they disappeared into the throng. A little girl looked up at her, smiling a gap-toothed smile.

'I like fireworks. Do you?'

'I do, very much.'

'What's your favourite?'

'I like the ones that go *wheee*, then BOOM and make a big explosion of colours in the sky.'

The little girl nodded solemnly. 'Me too. And the circle ones that go round and round.'

'Mattie, Daddy says we all have to stick together.' An older girl, clearly her big sister – they looked almost identical – took her by the hand and pulled her towards a group of children who were standing together with their parents. It was only a second later that Lucy realized Sam – dark curls escaping from underneath a woolly hat – was chatting to the father. The little girl was tugging at his leg. She watched him for a moment, unnoticed. That must be Harvey that he talked about – his friend from school with the hordes of children.

'Harv! If I'd known you two were here I'd have got you a drink as well.'

Mel appeared behind the two men, shouting hello. Sam bent over to kiss her on the cheek.

'Is that one for me?' Sam said, reaching out for the mulled wine she was holding.

'It is not.' Mel pulled her hand away. 'It's for Lucy. Who is . . .' she screwed her eyes against the darkness.

The light was shining in her face, so Lucy was silhouetted in the darkness.

'Who is here.' Lucy stepped out of the shadows.

'Lucy, hi.' Sam stepped forward instinctively. For a second she thought he was going to kiss her, too. But he seemed to stop himself and stood awkwardly for a moment. 'Harvey, this is Lucy, who I mentioned? She's been staying in Bunty's little cottage.'

'Lovely to meet you.' Harvey put out a hand and shook hers. It was harder than you'd think with gloves on.

'Are you friends with my uncle Sam?' The little girl – Mattie – looked up at her again.

'Yes,' said Lucy, shooting him a brief look. 'I am.'

'She is.' Sam reached down, picking her up. 'Do you want a carry, little pickle, so you can see the fireworks?'

'Yes please!'

Sam hoisted her onto his shoulders. She beamed down from her vantage point.

'You can see all the fireworks first,' Lucy said.

'All of them,' Mattie nodded. 'Suspecially our favourite ones.'

Sam looked at Lucy and mouthed, 'She is *adorable*.'

Lucy nodded.

People surged forward in a last-minute rush as the first fireworks began. Lucy found herself pressed up against the bars of the wooden fence, with Sam close beside her. Her heart was banging hard against her ribcage and she felt acutely conscious of every movement she made.

'You used to carry me like that.'

Sam turned, hearing Freya's voice. She was with Cammie and another couple of girls from the village, and somehow she'd squeezed her way through the crowds to find them. She smiled up at Mattie, who was thoroughly overexcited and who'd pulled off Sam's hat and was waving it around in the air. His hair was probably sticking up all over the place and making him look ridiculous in front of Lucy, but he couldn't exactly let go of Mattie's legs to check it. He'd just have to hope the darkness disguised whatever was going on.

The fireworks were almost over, and he didn't want them to end. He stood in the crowd, aware of Lucy's body pressed up against his side; in a moment everyone would step back, take a breath, get another mulled wine and prepare for the lighting of the bonfire and the burning of the guy. He stole a look at her. Underneath her red woollen hat, dark strands of hair had come loose and curled against her high, freckled cheekbones. Her mouth was parted slightly – he exhaled – the mouth he'd kissed before and desperately wanted to kiss again. She sensed him looking at her and turned to him, lips curling into a smile.

'It's like a school reunion.'

The last firework shot into the air with a squeal and then fizzled out. Sam and Lucy turned at the same time, just as the family behind them moved away to reveal Stella standing there. His heart sank through the floor.

'Mum!' Freya sounded as delighted as he was dismayed.

'Hi, Stella.' He tried to keep his true feelings out of his

voice. It was all very well Stella coming back into Freya's life, but she was bloody everywhere all of a sudden.

'Well, this is nice,' said Mel, somehow managing to simultaneously give Stella a smile of welcome and him a look that spoke volumes. 'Harvey, did you know Stella was back?'

He turned. 'Bloody hell.'

'Daddy! Language,' Mattie said crossly from somewhere over Sam's head. He'd almost forgotten she was there.

'Can I let you down, sweetie?'

'Here, I'll take you,' said Mel, reaching up and helping her down. Sam rolled his shoulders and stretched his neck back until it gave a slightly alarming crack.

'Mum said she might come and say hello.' Freya looked delighted.

'For old times' sake,' said Stella, giving Lucy a slightly thin smile. Mel had already handed Mattie back to Harvey, who was holding his daughter by the hand. His wife was tucking a sleepy toddler into a pushchair. Sam bent down to give her a padded mitten which had fallen onto the damp grass.

There was a lull in the proceedings and Mel and Lucy headed off to get another drink, leaving Sam there with Stella. Freya and her friends disappeared off to look at the boys from the next village who'd arrived in a gang and who were lurking in the shadows. He hoped they wouldn't get up to anything.

Stella looked out of place in a long, expensive-looking

coat and a shawl, with high-heeled boots that were sinking into the grass. She looked around, taking in the world that had once been hers. It made him feel uncomfortable. He needed to get over that – just because she was back in Freya's life, it didn't mean she had to be *there* all the time whenever he went anywhere.

'So what's going on in your world, Stell?' Harvey gave her a brief one-armed hug of welcome. Sam took the opportunity to step back and out of the conversation.

'Oh, you know,' she said, airily. 'The usual.'

Harvey looked at her and raised his eyebrows.

'You disappear for ten years, and that's all you've got to say?'

She shook her head and smiled. 'It's a long story.'

Sam decided to take the bull by the horns. He tipped his head, indicating to Stella that he wanted to have a chat. They moved slightly apart from the others. Lucy, queuing with Mel at the wine stall, caught his eye briefly and gave him a fleeting half-smile of encouragement.

'Look.' He shoved a hand through his hair. 'We need to talk. Without Freya.'

'Of course.' Stella lifted her chin slightly, pushing a strand of hair behind her ear. 'What's up?'

'I'll support Freya in whatever she wants – and she wants you to be a part of her life.' It still made something in his stomach churn anxiously when he said that. Sharing parenting after all these years of doing it solo just wasn't as easy as all that. He swallowed. 'But you don't get an all-access pass to every part of our lives.

We need to have plans, and invitations, and there has to be compromise.'

Stella looked at him for a moment, her mouth open. No words came out. And then she seemed to gather herself, and nodded firmly. 'You're right. I'm sorry.'

He was taken aback. This calm, measured response wasn't what he had expected. He almost wanted to reach out and shake her firmly by the hand.

'Hey.' Lucy appeared with a cup of mulled wine for him. She handed it over and Stella gave a brief smile and moved away, checking her phone. Mel, following behind, was carrying a basket of chocolate brownies she'd won in the tombola. Harvey's horde of children – with noses like bloodhounds – circled her almost instantly.

'Oh yum,' said Mattie. 'Are they for us?'

They watched the fire burning – Lucy still standing close to hand, Stella hovering. Sam's face was hot from the fire and he unfastened his coat, unwinding the scarf he'd been wearing.

Lucy and Mel left while Stella was talking to him about arrangements to collect Freya for a shopping trip to Oxford. He watched them heading back, giving a wave goodbye across the cricket field, and wanted to scream in frustration. He'd tried to speak to Lucy but Stella was wedged in between them and the moment was lost. Time was running out. The telephone box library was almost complete, Lucy's book was finished, and her time living in Bunty's cottage was coming to an end. Would he ever find a way to tell her how he felt?

Chapter Twenty-seven

It didn't get any easier the following week. Bunty headed off somewhat reluctantly for a week in Wales with Gordon and Margaret, and Lucy took the opportunity to go to Paris for a week to visit an old university friend. Sam had caught her, bag in hand, coming out of the cottage. She'd looked glowing and excited, and explained that her friend had suggested the trip and as part of her new decision to live life in the moment, she'd decided to go for it.

'I think I need some of Lucy's all-new *life is for living* approach.' Sam said ruefully, sitting in Mel's kitchen with a beer.

Mel, who was Hamish-sitting, shook her head in amusement. 'You need to make a move, man. It's going to be too late if you're not careful.'

'It's not that easy. And she's leaving, anyway.'

'Or is she?' Mel said, waggling her eyebrows in what she clearly thought was an enigmatic manner. She finished doling out dog biscuits and set all five down on the kitchen floor, calling them one by one. He marvelled as her older two dogs waited obediently, then went straight to their own bowls.

Hamish beetled in from the sitting room and helped

himself to a mouthful from the three remaining bowls before settling down at his own. He looked quite at home in Mel's untidy but comfortable kitchen. The spaniels shifted over, making space for him. Like they had for Lucy, he thought.

'What d'you mean, *or is she*?' he said, a moment later.

'I dunno.' Mel shugged. 'I think she's become quite attached to the village, and –' she gave a knowing look – 'some of the people in it.'

Sam didn't say anything.

Freya went to Oxford with Stella, where they apparently had their first disagreement, and she came home in a mood and flopped angrily onto the sofa, saying that she could see why he'd left her (Sam didn't point out that she had in fact left him) and that she couldn't see why her mum was such a bloody old cow. He'd found himself sticking up for Stella, who'd actually been quite reasonable and had put her foot down when Freya wanted to buy a pair of shoes in a vintage shop that were not only completely impractical but two sizes two small.

When Lucy returned home she popped in to say hello, and found an overexcited Freya up to her eyes in slightly premature Christmas decorations. She hadn't messaged Sam when she was away, so he hadn't messaged her – although he'd composed several funny little texts about things that were going on in the village, and the excitement over the unofficial opening of the library. Lucy pulled a box of beautifully wrapped truffles from her bag and handed them to Freya.

'How was Paris?'

Freya ripped off the ribbon and opened the box, offering them round. Sam took one and watched Lucy shake her head no and smile at Freya, who gave a groan of pleasure as she popped one in her mouth.

'These are gorgeous,' said Freya, rolling her eyes. 'Oi!' She slapped his hand away as he reached for another. 'These are mine.'

'I got you some too,' said Lucy, handing Sam a grey bag tied with a chic burgundy ribbon. 'Even gift-wrapping is beautifully done in Paris. Have you been?'

He shook his head. 'I'd love to go,' he said, adding mentally, 'with you'. God, he really needed to get a grip. 'Do you want a drink?'

'No, I just popped in for a moment.' She looked at Freya, who was rummaging in a huge plastic box in the hall. 'What's she doing?'

'Don't ask.'

There was a hoot of triumph. 'Found it!' A moment later, she reappeared in the kitchen with her arms full of tinsel.

Lucy frowned in confusion. 'Isn't it a bit early for decorations? It's not even December.'

Freya looped tinsel around the beams in the sitting room, humming a Christmas tune. For a fleeting moment Sam wished he could just freeze time, make this little scene his new normality.

'It's not December for long enough,' Freya said indignantly. 'I want maximum Christmas.'

'You sure you can't stay?' He turned to look at Lucy, hopefully.

'Oh, go on then.' She smiled.

'I've got a bottle of red lurking in the cupboard some-where, but I can't guarantee it'll be up to fancy French standards.'

Lucy bent down to ruffle the ears of both spaniels, who were weaving around her legs, hopeful of treats. She looked up at him. 'I don't mind.'

Half an hour later, there was a brief knock on the door and then Mel burst in, swearing furiously about bloody printers. Cammie followed behind, hair tied in a knot, wearing a jumper and a pair of brightly checked pyjama trousers.

'Can I just borrow yours?' She caught a glimpse of the open bottle. 'Ooh, and I'll have a glass if we're cele-brating. What are we celebrating?'

'Christmas,' crowed Freya, dancing into the room with a tinsel halo wrapped around her hair. She hooked an arm through Cammie's and they disappeared out of the sitting room. Moments later the sounds of music came thumping through the house.

'She seems cheerful,' Mel said.

'Yeah.' Sam tipped some more wine into Lucy's glass, and his own. 'We had a good chat the other day – talked about the whole Stella situation. I think she had a bit of a wobble, wondering what would happen if she just disappeared out of her life again.'

Lucy curled her legs up on the armchair and shifted

slightly to accommodate Bee, who tucked herself in beside her. 'I've been wondering about that too – I was thinking about it on the train to Paris.'

'She's not exactly known for her reliability, is she?' Mel made a face.

'I dunno.' He looked into his glass as if searching for the answer. 'I think she's changed, actually.'

'Stella?' Mel's tone was sharp.

He nodded. 'They had a falling out, and she dealt with it pretty well. She's seeing a counsellor, which I think helps a bit.'

Lucy looked across at him, her expression thoughtful. 'I think that sounds pretty positive.'

'I hope so.'

The wine finished, Lucy and Mel stood on the pavement outside Sam's cottage after they'd left. Cammie ran ahead, saying she'd put the kettle on for hot water bottles. It was amazingly cold – far colder than it ever seemed to get in Brighton – and Lucy shivered, wrapping her arms round herself to get warm.

'Are you all set for the grand opening of the library?' Mel asked.

'I am.' She nodded. 'It's a bit weird, given that it's been all ready to go for two weeks now.'

'Yes, but – Helen. We must do things *just so*.' Mel did a passable attempt at her clipped accent.

Helen had been appalled that nobody had yet borrowed the clearly unread copy of *War and Peace* she'd donated ('an absolute favourite of mine'), and Lucy had spotted

her on more than one occasion hovering around the telephone box, waiting to see the library in action.

'Just checking everything is going to plan,' she'd
explained, when Lucy had come out of the cottage and
unloaded some of the boxes she'd brought back from
Brighton.

'Of course,' Lucy had smiled, and disappeared back
inside.

She'd taken the opportunity to go through the stuff
she'd brought back – most of it was either papers for
recycling, or old stuff she didn't want – and had filled
up the boxes with it all, ready to take them to the tip.
Sam had been coming out of the house early one morning
when she'd seen him and waved hello. It was, she
decided, just one of those things. She'd never been the
sort of person for a one-night stand, but then she'd never
been the sort of person who gave up a perfectly good
career as head of department in a school before, either.
Maybe it was all part of the same thing.

Tell yourself that often enough, she thought, and you
might believe it. She bit her lip and looked in the rear-
view mirror of her little car, watching as Sam drove off
in his Land Rover.

Later that afternoon she set off for Bletchingham with
Bunty, who had decided she wanted a new cardigan.
They drove through the village. The Christmas tree was
already in place on the green, ready for the official
switching on of the lights the following weekend. Some
houses – Sam and Freya's, of course, and several with

small children – had already put their decorations up, and the lights sparkled brightly from windows that glowed in the dim midwinter light. Despite the cold, the warm glow of the stone seemed to make the village light up against the dull grey sky.

They stopped at the junction – where once they'd taken a detour – and waited for a tractor and trailer to rattle past.

'You don't want to stop at Signal Hill again?' Lucy smiled.

Sitting in the car, wrapped up warmly in a thick woollen coat, Bunty gave a look of surprise.

'Do you know what? I think I do.'

And so they bumped up the track and got out of the car. The rosebay willowherb that had skirted the edges of the worn-out path up to the building was faded and dried now and the field beside it was scored deep by the plough, ready for a new year's crops to be planted the following spring. It was so cold that the frost that rimed the windowsill hadn't melted.

'Does it bring it all back?'

Lucy turned to look at Bunty. She seemed lost in thought. For a moment, Lucy could imagine her as a young girl cycling up here in the freezing winter, wrapped up against the cold, spending long shifts inside this building with only a temperamental little stove to keep it warm. From this unprepossessing place, black propaganda was broadcast across Occupied Europe. Fifteen miles away stood Bletchley Park, where so many other young people worked – never knowing precisely what they were doing, or questioning it – to do their bit. She looked at Bunty and felt a surge of admiration for the girl she'd been, and the woman she now was.

'It brings it all back.' Bunty nodded. 'But actually, it's rather nice.'

She gave the building a gentle pat, as if to acknowledge it, and turned back towards the car.

As they drove towards Bletchingham, Lucy ventured a question she'd been dying to ask. It hadn't been clear in Bunty's diaries, and the answer had been nagging at her.

'So –' she began, carefully. 'Afterwards – I mean, after Harry had been killed . . .'

Bunty looked straight ahead at the road. 'How did I end up married to Len?'

Lucy nodded. 'I mean, when you had been madly in love with Harry.'

'I loved Len. He was a good, kind, gentle man. I adored Harry, of course. But Len picked me up, took me out to the cinema and for tea on my days off. And when I realized I was pregnant, he said that he loved me and that he was sure I'd love him, too, given time.'

'And you did?' It seemed a huge leap – and a huge sacrifice for Len to make.

'Oh, yes.' Bunty paused for a moment. 'I had to be practical, too. I couldn't have raised a baby alone and supported us both in those days. And the scandal –' She shook her head. 'Luckily it all turned out well, in the end.'

Lucy indicated left and pulled into the car park behind the old library building. It had a planning sign attached to metal grilles outside. The car engine stopped and Lucy took the key out of the ignition.

'Len wasn't second best, you know. That's why I would never want Gordon to know that his father – well, that his biological father wasn't who he thought. And why I wouldn't ever want anyone to know – no matter what rumours there might have been back then, they've been long forgotten.'

Lucy thought back to Henry's comment that Bunty had had an interesting war. He hadn't said another word, besides that.

'Well, I'm very grateful that you shared it with me. And I promise that I will never breathe a word.'

'I'm very glad to hear it.' Bunty smiled slightly. 'But there is one thing I'd like you to consider, not in return, but just because I've become very fond of you.'

'Of course.'

Chapter Twenty-eight

'Are you ready?'

Lucy stood shivering on the front step of Bunty's cottage, waiting for her to emerge. She couldn't find any gloves, and her hands were freezing. They'd woken to a thick frost, the first of the winter, and over the last hour tiny bright flakes of snow had started to spin down from a pale sky.

'Here I am.' Bunty came out of the formal sitting room, the one that was never used. She'd put on a slick of red lipstick and was wearing a very smart brown felt hat, along with a woollen coat and scarf. Outside the snow was still falling, dusting the top of the stone wall that enclosed the cottage garden. It iced the dried brown flower heads of the hydrangea bush and was just starting to settle on the grass.

Beth from the shop had come down to the village green, and was standing with a thick puffa jacket over the blue-and-white pinny she wore to protect her clothes.

'Hello, you two,' she said, lifting her chin and smiling at them. 'Haven't seen you around for a while, Lucy. What have you been up to?'

'Oh, this and that,' Lucy said. She wasn't giving anything away to Beth. Bunty gave Lucy a tiny sideways smile.

There was a little crowd gathering around the telephone box library, and a photographer from the local paper, his camera around his neck, shooing people out of the way to get some pictures. Someone had crocheted a garland of colourful flowers, which had been hung around the phone box like bunting. Freya ran over to them, grinning.

'Doesn't it look amazing?'

Bunty took her arm. 'It looks splendid. Your dad has done a lovely job with the fittings.'

'He's over there,' Freya said, excited.

'Hi.' Sam looked up, his hand still on the door of the phone box.

Lucy felt her stomach give a disobedient swoop of excitement.

'Hello, stranger.' He let go of the door and leaned over, kissing her on the cheek, surprising her. Her stomach flipped over, sending a fizz of excitement through her body.

'Oh for goodness' sake,' grumbled Bunty. 'I do wish they'd hurry up with all this preamble. My toes are freezing.'

'Ladies and gentlemen,' began Helen, loudly. Having had her thunder stolen at the WI meeting, she was clearly determined to get in first. Susan looked across at Lucy and gave her the tiniest wink of complicity. Everyone carried on talking.

'I heard there was mulled wine afterwards,' said Henry loudly to nobody in particular. Susan put a hand on his arm and shushed him, smiling broadly.

Helen cleared her throat, and one of the WI women offered her a microphone from a box on a trestle table behind them. She shook her head.

'It's fine. I just need everyone to stop chattering.' Helen clapped her hands loudly. That did the trick.

'She doesn't need a microphone,' whispered Freya, 'She's like a foghorn.' It made them all giggle. Helen launched into her speech.

'Ladies and gentlemen,' she began again. Everyone stopped talking. 'As chair of the Little Maudley WI, it gives me enormous pleasure to celebrate the opening of our very own telephone box library. When we discovered that with the decommissioning of the phone box there was a possibility for us to take it over, we talked for a long time about the different options open to us.'

'I thought you wanted it knocked down,' said Henry, loudly.

Helen shot him a disapproving look.

'D'you want a drink?' Mel handed Lucy a silver hip flask. 'Knowing Helen, this could go on for some time.' Lucy took a sip and passed it on to Sam. He was standing close by her side again, just like the bonfire night, clad in a thick flannel shirt. He had a black woollen hat pulled down over his dark hair, and his collar turned up. Lucy, who had dressed more for the event than the weather in a navy wrap dress and a pair of tights and boots, shivered in her thin coat.

'Do you want my jacket?' Sam turned to her, his voice low.

'Better not,' she whispered. 'I don't think I'd be very popular if I helped Bunty cut the ribbon wearing a lumberjack shirt. Can't let the side down,' she added, imitating Helen's plummy tones.

He gave a snort of laughter, earning them a glare from one of Helen's minions.

Lucy realized that she'd better be standing by Bunty just in case she needed a hand, so squeezed through the little crowd of villagers. Bunty turned to her and gave her a brief smile of welcome.

'. . . and so, as the oldest resident of the village . . .'

Bunty gave a look of such horrified disgust that Lucy had to cover her mouth with her hand to stop herself from snorting with laughter.

' . . . we thought it only appropriate that Bunty, who has seen the telephone box every day from her cottage window, and who – like all of us – has her own memories of meeting friends and making calls from it . . .'

Bunty slid a glance at Lucy that made her smile. Only they knew the secret of what the phone box meant to her, and the memories it held.

'Oh, get on with it, I'm blooming freezing,' shouted a voice from the crowd, and everyone started to laugh.

The snow was getting heavier now, swirling through the air, covering the top of the wooden bench Sam had made to sit outside the phone box.

Bunty took the scissors, and Lucy held the ribbon firmly. With one swish, she cut it in half.

'I now declare our telephone box library open,' she

said loudly. 'And rather than droning on, I'd like to say just a few words of thanks. First of all, to Lucy. She's been an absolute gem, and I'm sure that everyone will agree she's been a wonderful addition to the village. So I'm delighted to say that she's decided to stay with us permanently.'

Lucy looked at her feet, almost afraid to see what the reactions from the people she cared about would be. It took a split second for Bunty's words to sink in, and then both Mel and Freya gave a whoop of delight. Lucy looked over at them. Mel was doing a vigorous fist-pump and Freya was beaming from ear to ear. She couldn't see Sam – she craned her neck discreetly, trying to spot him.

'Watching everyone pull together to turn the telephone box from an eyesore into a place where the community can gather and share something that means so much – the love of books – means a great deal to me, especially at a time when we're losing libraries all over the country,' Bunty continued.

Helen shot Lucy a look of alarm. The local reporter's ears pricked up as he scented an angle for his story.

'While free libraries like this are a wonderful boon to little villages like ours,' she carried on, 'it is a terrible shame that we are losing them in towns like Bletchingham. They are not just a place to borrow books, but a hub of the community, and somewhere people can get together and meet.'

'Hear, hear,' said a man in a flat cap and a long over-coat.

'I'd like to end this little speech by saying thank you to Freya here . . .'

Mel gave Freya a shove forward so that she was visible to everyone in the crowd, absolutely scarlet with teenage embarrassment. Bunty reached out her hand, and Freya took it and stood beside her, smiling shyly.

'She was the person who had the idea in the first place, and I think we can all agree that it's been a very good one.'

There was a cheer, and the photographer insisted on including Lucy and Freya in the pictures, taking several snaps of them with Bunty, standing beside the local worthies.

'What Bunty said earlier – are you *staying* staying?' Freya asked Lucy.

'Yes, she is.' Bunty beamed. 'Not only do we get to keep Lucy permanently, but I get to put Margaret's nose out of joint. She was absolutely desperate to get the cottage let out for holidaymakers.'

'Dad will be pleased.' Freya gave Lucy an arch look. Lucy ignored it.

'You might not be. I'm going to be teaching you history next term.'

'You what?' Her eyes widened in surprise.

Lucy nodded, smiling.

Over the lunch in town, when Bunty had invited her to stay in the cottage for as long as she wanted, she'd talked about what she was hoping to do. As if the universe was working in her favour, a quick internet search had shown that the local school was looking for a history supply teacher to cover maternity leave for the following two terms.

'Does that mean I have to call you Miss instead of Lucy?'

'At school, it does, yes.'

'I can cope with that if you'll help me with my history homework.' Freya grinned.

'What about you? We haven't had a chance to talk about it much. Are you glad to have your mum back in your life?' Lucy looked at Freya. Her long eyelashes were sparkling with tiny flakes of snow. She nodded.

'Yes. Well, she's never going to be a mum sort of mum, but at least she's not just a mystery any more.'

'Are you going to be seeing her regularly?'

She nodded. 'No stress. I don't want to feel like I'm being forced into some sort of new family thing, but she seems to understand that. Right now, we're just doing days out. Maybe I'll stay over sometime, but not until I want to. She and Dad had a chat with me about it.'

'I'm glad for you.' Lucy put an arm around her shoulders and squeezed. 'And for your dad.'

'Oh, I don't think he's quite as happy as I am,' said Freya, airily. 'Look.'

Sam was standing alone, looking thoughtful.

'I'll go and say hello.'

'I'm going to see if I can nick some mulled wine from the cafe without anyone noticing,' said Freya, disappearing before Lucy had a chance to reply.

Taking a deep breath, she headed over to Sam. 'Hi.'

'Is it true? You're staying?' he said, in a low voice. Snow was dusting his shoulders and clinging to the black wool of his hat. His eyes met hers and she nodded.

'It's weird. I spent all those years focusing on the job, and I didn't take the time to actually look around and work out what it was I wanted. And I love it here.'

He took a step towards her. Their breath was clouding in the freezing air. 'It's funny, isn't it? You wanted that, and I wanted –' He looked over at Freya, stopping mid-sentence.

'You wanted Stella back?'

'No!' He shook his head emphatically. 'I don't think I realized that I was holding my breath, hoping maybe she'd come back and I could make everything okay.'

'It doesn't work like that,' she said, gently.

'I'm glad it doesn't. Otherwise . . .' He picked up her hand, taking it in his. 'Your hands are freezing.'

'All of me is freezing.'

There was a commotion behind her and they both peered over, seeing Freya gathering the first scrapings of snow into a snowball. She looked at them with a mischievous grin and pelted it directly at Sam, hitting him on the shoulder.

Bunty, who had been cornered by Helen, appeared, laughing, her arm tucked inside Mel's. She took one look at them and linked her other arm in Freya's.

'Would you two hurry up and get on with it, please. I'm absolutely ice cold, and there's going to be none of that mulled wine left.'

'Yeah, get on with it, you two.' Mel grinned.

'What are you talking about?' Sam looked at Lucy, laughing.

'You love her,' Freya said, as if it was the simplest thing in the world. 'Now will you bloody well kiss her and then we can go inside?'

Sam looked down at her. 'I don't think we'd better cross those three.'

'I think you're right.' Lucy curled her freezing hands inside his thick coat, feeling the warmth of his body and the solid muscles of his back. His hand cupped her face, and she didn't mind one bit the feeling of his cold fingers tangling in her hair. He brought his mouth down on hers, and Lucy knew that right here in this village she'd found home.

By the time they looked up, the village green was empty.

Acknowledgements

I would like to start by thanking both the Royal Literary Fund and the Society of Authors for their kind and generous support in the form of grants, which allowed me time to write, and for which I am enormously grateful.

This book is set in a fictional village. I have taken the liberty of moving Gawcott, the village in Buckinghamshire where I lived for many years with my children, and shifting it slightly south so that it sits just on the edge of the Cotswolds. But if you know the village, you might recognize the telephone box library, which stands on the green beside the old water pump, opposite a beautiful white thatched cottage. You might also have heard tales of the buildings at Signal Hill that were used during the war. What I didn't expect when I started to do research into a book set around Bletchley Park was the true story of what went on in a sleepy little village near Buckingham.

I'd like to thank Judith Harper for being the inspiration for Janet – and Ellie, who was inspiration for Fiona. When I first moved to the village of Gawcott, Judith – who has fostered over one hundred children – welcomed me and the children to the village. She's an absolute star, and I'm so happy that she was recently awarded a very well-deserved MBE for services to fostering.

A book is a huge team effort, which is why my thank-you list is always so long. My name might be on the cover (which was created by the brilliant Sarah McMenemy), but it takes a lot of work behind the scenes.

I'd like to thank my agent Amanda Preston, who has cheered me on and who always believes in me, even when I don't – I am so grateful to you. You are bloody amazing.

To Alison and everyone else at LBA – thank you for everything you do, and for making me laugh with funny tweets.

To Louise, Caroline, Jayne and all the brilliant people at Pan Macmillan who work so hard chasing authors (sorry) and making everything come together behind the scenes – thank you so much. You are all absolutely amazing!

Thanks to everyone at Bletchley Park for the work you do in keeping these important stories alive for future generations. Thank you also to Gladstone's Library – not just for a space to write, but also for incredibly valuable research material from the archives.

Thanks to the bloggers who work so hard to share their enthusiasm for books and reading with the world, and to everyone online who cheers me on and sends little messages to say hello when I'm writing – I really do appreciate it!

To The Prime Writers and the Book Camp gang – thank you for cheering me on, making me laugh and for being bloody brilliant friends, as well as the talented writers of books that I love.

Huge thanks to my writing twin Miranda – your love and support this year have meant so much. And to Alice, Keris and Hayley – thank you for holding me up. To Elise, Jax and Rhiannon – thank you for being there, always.

This year I have spent a lot of time gadding about doing bookish things and travelling as well as writing. It's been amazing, but it wouldn't be possible if there weren't someone at home keeping things together – thank you to my lovely husband Ross for that bit and for lots of other bits as well, and to the children for being generally wonderful (but please don't put your clean washing back in the laundry basket because you can't be bothered to put it away, thank you very much, love Mummy xoxo, etc.).

Finally, thank you to you for reading this book – there are lots of them out there, and it means a lot to me that you chose this one.

Finding Hope at Hillside Farm

Sometimes first love needs a second chance

Hillside Farm, nestled in the rolling hills of the Welsh countryside, is a safe haven for Ella. Working with her aunt Bron, she runs her own business, sharing her love of horses to help transform the lives of those in emotional need. Living on the remote farm, and with just the horses and Bron for company, Ella thinks she has finally found a place where she can forget her own past and find peace.

But the arrival of a small girl called Hope and her father Harry changes everything. As Ella helps the pair come to terms with their loss, she realizes that she too deserves happiness. But is it too late to find it?

Finding Hope at Hillside Farm is a heart-warming tale of loss, love and new beginnings.